A DECEPTION MOST DEADLY

CHAPTER ONE

Fall 1883. Fernandina Centre Street Wharf –
Amelia Island, Florida

"Harold. Harold. You smell that?"

Cassie Gwynne's eye twitched as a brassy voice clanged through the busy dockside clamor and into her consciousness. A few feet from the bench where she was sitting, a fleshy woman in a fur-lined pelisse stood at attention in front of the wharf's ticket shelter, snuffling the air with Shakespearean import. She wore tinted spectacles with gold-and-diamond frames and a hat topped by an implausible mass of flowers and feathers; from there, a length of mosquito netting hung over her face like a bizarre sort of bridal veil.

"Seems they call it the Land of Flowers for a reason, eh?" The woman snuffled again.

Her companion, a monocled gentleman with an umbrella hooked on his elbow, lowered the tourist pamphlet he was reading and took a sniff. "Indeed. That's a sweet perfume on the wind there, Iphie."

"Lilies, perhaps."

A sneeze erupted from the reed-paneled pet case at their feet.

"Or hydrangeas."

Another sneeze.

"Maybe some sort of exotic—"

"It's bird crap." Having settled that, the sour-faced woman behind the ticket desk yanked her sou'wester down over her ears and returned her glare to her book, leaving the couple blinking at the top of her hat.

Cassie coughed. "I think she's referring to guano, which is made from seabird, uh, ordure. For fertilizer. A great number of shipments come through this port, so…"

When that only seemed to cause more blinking, Cassie bit her lip and dug a piece of chewing gum out of the pouch hanging from the silver chatelaine at her waist. She shouldn't be involving herself in other people's business, anyway. As it was, she was so full of nerves that, in the short time since her steamship had arrived that morning, she'd already dropped a bracelet in the commode, stabbed her finger with a hatpin, and been forced into temporary hiding after letting a puff of digestive air escape next to the captain. Not to mention that one of the buttons of her complicated new traveling dress had suffered an unidentified trauma between the breakfast room and the porters' stand and was now dangling down the front of her bodice, marring the tidy column of mother-of-pearl circles like a drunk cadet at inspection. She wondered what would happen if she just reboarded the ship and waited for it to turn back for New York.

Above, dawn had given way to day, and over a palm-tree-lined harbor dotted with paddle steamers, fishing vessels, and multi-masted sailing ships, orange and pink swirled together to make blue. The calls of seabirds crowded together on the wharf's weather-beaten pilings mingled with the shouts of dockside vendors, the resulting cacophony layering over the chatter of disembarking passengers like notes in a chord. The dock thrummed along beneath her feet, alive with footsteps and the rumbling of cart wheels, and as Cassie hugged her satchel to her chest, a breeze swelled through, leaving wet kisses on her cheeks and an unexpected smile on her lips. Perhaps she had been making too much of things, as usual.

The woman in the pelisse tittered. "Well, aren't we foolish! To think we were going on like that about bird—Eee!" She clapped a hand to her hat as the wind tried to carry it off.

Roused by his mistress's cry, the creature in the pet case, a pocket-sized terrier of some sort, leapt to its feet but was immediately beset by another round of sneezes, each detonating on top of the other like a string of firecrackers.

"For cookies' sake, Oscar!" The man stared at the case as if the animal might explode. "Don't you go making a fuss now. As we discussed, you'll stay in there until we're safely inside the hotel. We don't want an alligator or some other such beast snapping you up."

Cassie cocked her head. "I wouldn't think there's much danger of—"

"Oh, the guidebooks are quite clear on that." The woman nodded in agreement with herself as she tugged her hat strings into a bow. "The Florida wildlife can be very dangerous to precious little pets. Did you know there're rattlesnakes swimming around in these waters?"

Cassie stuffed another piece of gum in her mouth.

"But what you said about the 'guano'… That *is* something. Are you from here? I remember seeing you when we boarded the steamer. The detailing on your lace parasol caught my eye. But these days one never knows where anyone—Forgive me. I'm Iphigenia Huddleston, and this is my husband, Harold Huddleston. And Oscar Huddleston, of course. We've come to spend the season 'amongst the gentle zephyrs of the Island City.' A 'trio of weary winter pilgrims fleeing the arctic tundra,' you might say."

Someone's spent a bit of time with the travel literature. Cassie extended a gloved hand. "Cassie Gwynne. And no, I live in New York. But my father is—was an attorney, and one of his clients was a guano importation company. I walked the warehouse with him many times."

Her last word broke as she fought back the familiar lump rising in her throat. It was like swallowing a block of wood, but she had never, not once this entire wretched year, allowed it to turn to tears in front of anyone, and she certainly wasn't about to now.

She flicked her gaze back toward the ship, where porters were hurrying trunks and parcels down a network of planks like ants who'd found a piece of crumb cake.

"A lawyer's daughter, huh?" said Mrs. Huddleston. "Say, Harold, now we'll know who to call on the next time that partner of yours gets himself caught up in a gaming raid!" She snorted and slapped him on the back.

Mr. Huddleston chortled as he grabbed onto the bench to steady himself. "Right, 'my partner'! So what brings you to Fernandina then, Miss Gwynne?"

"I've come to see my aunt." It still felt strange saying that. "She owns a perfume and scented goods store in town. She should be along any time to collect me."

At least she hoped so. In their last telegram exchange, her aunt had said she would meet her at the wharf, but there was still no sign of her among the people bustling about. Not that Cassie knew what she looked like. Or very much else about her, for that matter.

Her nerves began to crackle again.

Mrs. Huddleston seized her husband's arm. "Your aunt isn't Flora Hale, by any chance, is she?"

"Yes, actually—"

"How delightful! I've read all about her work. They say her orange blossom scents are particularly spectacular because she makes the—what was it, Harold, 'neroli'?—from her own orange groves. Ooo! Can you believe it? Now we practically know her. Say, will you two be attending the season's opening ball at the Egmont Hotel this weekend? It promises to be a most exciting affair. String orchestra, Chinese lanterns, fireworks—Oh." She slapped a hand to her waist. "Oh. Oh, dear."

"What is it, Iphie?"

"My pocket. The one where I keep my money. It was tied to my belt, but now it's gone."

As the couple clucked and tugged at Mrs. Huddleston's dress, Cassie glanced down the dock. Then jumped to her feet. While most passersby were focused on the commotion surrounding the Huddlestons and their increasingly frantic dog, one was slinking off in the other direction, a man with a ratty green derby tipped over his face. And a lady's pocket under his arm.

Cassie watched him slip past the coffee stall and disappear behind a dray piled with luggage. She looked around. No one else seemed to have noticed.

Then her gaze fell on Mrs. Huddleston, who had scooped up her dog and was blubbering into him like he was a furry handkerchief.

This doesn't involve you, Cassie. She glanced at the dray again and back at Mrs. Huddleston. *But what am I supposed to do? Stand by and watch?*

She stepped out from the bench, craning her neck. She hadn't seen the man re-emerge from behind the dray, so he was probably still hiding back there. If she got a better look, she might—

Someone slammed into her from behind, and the next thing she knew, she was sprawled on her stomach, her arms and legs stretched out like a mounted starfish. Letting out a small whimper, she lifted her head. There was no sign of the thief, or his ugly green hat.

As she dropped her face back onto the dock, however, a groan issued from the space next to her—a man with reddish-blond hair, crawling to his feet. His upper lip, which was framed by a long, drooping mustache, had a petulant turn to it, and the state of his simple gray sack suit suggested its usual storage place was a heap on the floor. But, with his strong shoulders and searing blue eyes, Cassie noticed, he was far from unhandsome.

"Why in blazes did you jump out like that?" he fumed, sending her thoughts skittering like insects exposed under a piece of wood. He shoved his hat onto his head. "Now he's gotten away."

Cassie sat up fiercely but found she could only manage an indignant grunt in response.

"Yes, you did. I was running after a thief when you jumped right into my path."

"I do apologize, *sir*." Breath being in short supply, sass won out over affrontery. "For failing to consider how having the wind knocked out of me would inconvenience you."

Unfortunately, the man, who had pressed his hands to his temples and launched into what sounded like a growl being shaken inside a bottle, no longer appeared to be listening. Cassie sighed and made a show of getting to her feet.

"For the record—" She stumbled on a bit of petticoat that had wrapped itself around her boot heel. "I didn't 'jump' anywhere. I saw the man who took that woman's pocket run behind a cart, so I thought I would—"

The man snickered. "Would what? Go after him yourself?"

"No. But what would be so funny about that?"

"What would you have done once you caught up to him? Stood on a crate and beat him with your twenty-dollar hat?"

Cassie controlled her breathing as her hands balled into fists at her sides. There were few things she disliked more than not being taken seriously. Sure, people's tendency to underestimate her occasionally worked to her advantage. She had utilized it often when her father needed an uncooperative witness to let information slip. But mostly it made her want to break things.

And her hat had cost ten dollars, not twenty. She realized it was still far too much to spend on a hat—ordinarily, she would have found two dollars the limit of reasonableness—but she did have the money for it, and these were special circumstances.

"I'm twenty-three. I can handle myself."

"Don't tell me... You have a pretty little knife strapped to your boot."

"I do not. But I'm not helpless."

She hovered a hand over the items on her chatelaine, wishing she had something on there more intimidating than travel-sized sewing scissors. In an attempt to manage the paranoia that had settled in alongside her grief over the previous several months—"perfectly normal," the doctors had assured her, irritatingly, "given what she'd been through"—she had recently taken to studying a book she'd found about ancient Chinese combat. But it hadn't exactly been an instructional volume, and she hadn't had any opportunities to practice the movements on an actual person. Nor had she been able to bring herself to wield a real weapon of any sort yet. Especially not a knife.

Her neck throbbed under the collar of her dress, where an ugly scar stretched from her ear to the hollow of her throat.

"Sure, sure," the man said. "Still, I'd leave catching criminals to those who know what they're doing."

Cassie fixed her hat. "And where would I find someone like that?"

"What's that supposed to mean?"

"Well, you did let a helpless little girl spoil your heroic capture."

"A little girl with a dress so big it could house a small zoo in the rear."

Cassie saw red. *Again with the clothing commentary?* While it was true the dressmaker had been a touch overzealous with her bustle (apparently, that unfortunate bit of seventies fashion was back and he hadn't wanted to fall behind), she didn't need this rumple-trousered lout pointing it out.

"At least I don't have a mustache that looks like a lady's hair switch."

"A lady's hair switch! Just because I condition—"

"Excuse me!" Mr. Huddleston pushed toward them through the crowd. "Officer!"

Officer?

With some amount of difficulty (as they were now standing forehead-to-chin, the difference in height making nose-to-nose impractical), Cassie dropped her gaze to the man's vest. Sure enough, there was a shiny policeman's badge pinned by his right hip, a few inches above a rugged leather holster.

He stepped around her. "Officer Austin Hughes here."

"Officer Hughes, my wife's pocket has been stolen."

"Right. I saw the whole thing and will have the thief apprehended before the day's out. I would have taken him just now, in fact, if this—small woman hadn't gotten in my—"

"Yes, that was certainly a tumble, wasn't it!" Mr. Huddleston appraised Cassie with concern. "Are you sure you aren't injured, my dear? You look a state."

Cassie inspected herself. One of her sleeves had acquired a brownish-green smear from its encounter with the dock, and she'd lost another button, but she didn't appear to be hurt.

"I'm fine, Mr. Huddleston. But *thank you for asking.*" She threw Officer Hughes an accusatory glare, which he ignored.

"Sir, I need you to come to the sheriff's office with me," Officer Hughes said. "I have to collect a witness statement in order to write up the theft."

"I'd be happy to, except that would mean leaving my poor wife on her own." Mr. Huddleston turned back to Cassie. "Perhaps you could go instead, Miss Gwynne. You saw everything as well as I, maybe even better. I'd bet you take after your father."

"Oh, I—" Cassie shifted her satchel on her shoulder. "I'm flattered, but I ought to wait here for my aunt. She'll worry if she can't find me when she arrives."

"Mrs. Huddleston and I would consider it a great personal favor."

"But—"

"And I'm sure it wouldn't take very long, would it, Officer?"

"No, not long," Officer Hughes answered begrudgingly. "But it'd be best if—"

"Wonderful. Thank you both." Mr. Huddleston squeezed their hands and hurried off.

Since the matter had apparently been decided, Cassie left a message for Flora with one of the wharf clerks and hurried after the police officer as he stomped across the wharf past the train depot and onto a dusty footpath that ran alongside the railroad tracks lining the waterfront. As promised, however, after only a short walk, they arrived at a red-brick structure framed by hickory trees and flowering wax myrtle, which might have been pleasant if it hadn't been for the iron bars in the windows.

Cassie read the sign above the entrance. "Nassau County Jail?"

"My desk's in the back."

Stepping in turn over a hairy clump of weeds sprouting through the threshold, they continued on into a dim, creaky intake area that stank of sweat and stale pipe smoke, then into a dim, creaky hallway beyond that. When they turned the corner, however, Cassie's thoughts were flooded by a blinding sea of golden dust, conjured by the sun pouring through a row of skylights in the ceiling, and she let out a sneeze so loud Officer Hughes tripped.

A woman's voice, deep and melodious, drifted toward them as though in a dream. "Ah, see? I'll bet that's the sheriff now, coming back to let me out early."

"I wouldn't count on it, my friend," a kindly voice boomed in response. "He said you have to stay 'til the end of the day. You can't disturb the peace at breakfast and expect to have your debt to society paid in time for luncheon."

"Again, I wasn't the one disturbing the peace. Anyone who beats an animal like that should be locked up. In either case, I have something especially important to attend to, so I must insist…"

The voice trailed off as Cassie and Officer Hughes entered the musty chamber at the end of the hall. Opposite them, a stunning, dark-haired woman of about forty, dressed in a terracotta tunic embroidered with sunflowers, stood behind the bars of a holding cell. A man in a dirty slouch hat occupied the cell next to her, and at the center of the room, sitting with his boots propped up on a table, was a white-bearded jailor whose pink cheeks and mirthful belly were, in Cassie's opinion, uncomfortably juxtaposed with the mean-looking rifle slung across the back of his chair.

"Ooo, lookee here!" The disheveled man, an inebriate by all appearances, tried to whistle but belched instead, then choked on whatever came up with it.

"Major," said Scary Santa. "You're not exactly convincing me your sobriety is imminent."

"Aw, you're no fun."

The woman, however, was gazing intently at Cassie. "Cassie? Cassie Gwynne?"

After casting a glance over her shoulder for some reason, Cassie nodded and tucked a loose curl behind her ear.

"You look just like her. With that delicate little nose. And those eyes, dark and gray as a storm gathering over the harbor… *Mon Dieu*. It's as though she's standing right in front of me."

Cassie's breath caught.

"Who?" The jailor looked back and forth between them and bit into a cookie.

No. This can't be—

"Why, my sister, Emma, of course." The woman smiled. "I'm your Aunt Flora, Cassie. And I'm so very pleased to meet you."

CHAPTER TWO

Cassie felt as though her head might drift into the rafters if her hat weren't weighing it down. This was her Aunt Flora? Here? In *jail*?

Flora stretched a hand through the bars. "Come closer, dear girl."

Cassie obeyed, and, as Flora folded Cassie's gloved hands between her bare ones, she was enveloped by the delicate scent of orange blossoms, tuberose, and nutmeg.

"I can't believe you're really here," Flora said. "After all this time."

Still without words, Cassie simply stared back at her. She often looked at her parents' wedding-day daguerreotype, which her father had gotten reproduced and set into a locket as a gift for her last year, so she knew that her mother, who'd died when she was very young, had been beautiful. But she hadn't expected Flora to be quite so remarkable. She was beautiful, too, certainly, but it was more than that. There was a brightness about her, and not a shallow kind like the shine on the surface of a penny. Rather, it seemed to come from a simultaneous vibrancy and earnestness in the way she moved and spoke, as though she wore her soul on the outside.

Flora's smile, warm as a hug, deepened. "How was your trip? I hope the weather was reasonably calm for you?"

"Oh, it was—" Cassie's voice cracked. "No complaints. We had a little rain as we were pulling out of port, but it was clear skies the rest of the way."

They nodded about that for a while.

"Uh, here." Cassie fumbled with the buckle on her satchel—actually, her father's satchel, which he used to bring to his office every day and Cassie was now carrying as her travel bag—and pulled out a small, shiny parcel tied with an unreasonably large bow. "I brought you some chocolates from Henri Maillard's."

Flora inhaled. "What a treat! Thank you. I would eat chocolates for every meal if I could. That or cheese."

"Me, too!" Cassie clapped a hand to her mouth. She sounded like an empty-headed schoolgirl.

It was true, though. She loved all food, but there was nothing better in the world than good chocolate or good cheese.

"That proves it," Flora said, laughing. "We are related! But I do hope you didn't spend too much. The packaging is so lovely, I almost hate to disturb it—"

When Flora reached for the box, however, the jailor sat up. "I'm sorry, Miss Hale. I can't let anything pass through those bars without inspection."

Cassie fell back. She'd almost forgotten Flora was a prisoner.

"Mr. Kriegel is right," Officer Hughes said. "And as fascinating, and enlightening, as all this is, I need to get—"

"You must be wondering why I'm in here." Flora was studying Cassie's expression. "I'm sorry, I should have started with that. Well, early this morning, I was out by the cow pen on Ash Street delivering a speech against the animal-handling practices at the Meeks-Shaw cattle operation—it's shameful, you know, the way they treat those cows. I'll admit it's probably natural for humans to kill to eat, even if I personally find eating meat both unnecessary and unhealthy, but one can at least treat the animals humanely while they're alive. After all, the only part of existence, for humans and animals alike, we actually know anything about is what we experience here on Earth. Why should we let cruelty have any part in it?"

Behind Flora, the inebriate mimed hanging himself with his beard.

"If you ask me," Flora continued, "how a person chooses to treat others, animal or human, tells you a great deal about him. Did you know—" She stopped. "Oh, dear. I've gotten off track. What was I... Oh, yes. I was delivering my speech when Mr. Meeks, one of the owners of the cattle yard, arrived to chastise me. And, true to form, he promptly proved his barbarity by striking his horse for halting short of the hitching post. Anyone could see the poor creature had an injured foot and was balking because it hurt to step on the gravel."

"Miss Hale," Officer Hughes started again, "If I could—"

"It was heartbreaking, Cassie, seeing her stumble and cry out as he beat her, over and over. I couldn't just stand by and watch. And, well, when the man hit himself in the nose with his own stick—a complete accident on my part, I promise you, if I did have any part in it—he threw a fit and insisted the sheriff take me into custody."

I couldn't just stand by and watch.

"That's... quite a story." Being arrested was no small matter, but Cassie couldn't honestly say she disapproved of Flora's actions. After all, her own behavior, especially of late, was at times only scarcely more decorous, and she usually had far less gallant reasons for behaving as she did.

But, still. She looked around. Flora, her aunt, was in actual jail.

"I hope I haven't scared you off," Flora said.

Officer Hughes snorted, startling the inebriate off his cot. "Scare *her* off? You really must not have met before."

Cassie shook her head, a little too emphatically. "Oh, no. No. Of course not."

What else was she supposed to say?

"Okay, good."

Flora grew quiet. "Cassie—" She seemed almost shy all of sudden. "It's a bit strange to ask, but did you bring them? The letters?"

Cassie mouthed the words back, then straightened as her brain snapped back into focus. Right, the letters. Of course Flora would want to see the letters.

"Uh, yes. Just a moment." She was reaching back into her satchel when the door slammed open and another man dashed into the room. Several years older than Officer Hughes, this man had wavy brown hair and a short beard and was dressed in an unusual mix of fashions, dusty breeches and paddock boots with a formal frock coat, crisp black derby, and emerald-green ascot tie. Cassie caught a flash at his hip. Another badge.

"Flora," he said, breathless. "I went to the passenger wharf, but I didn't see your niece, only her luggage. I don't know if something has—"

Flora lifted her hand. "Don't you worry yourself now, Jake. She's right here. Cassie, this is my dear friend Jake Gordon. Not only is he a strapping police officer who protects our town, but he can hire you the best carriages around, since he's also the manager of the Egmont Hotel's excellent livery stable."

The man bowed modestly and removed his hat. "Uh, yes. Good to meet you, Miss Gwynne. You can call me Jake."

Dear friend? Cassie had noted the color that flooded the man's cheeks when Flora spoke about him. *I wonder whether he sees her the same way.*

"Pleased to meet you, too, Jake. And it's Cassie."

Officer Hughes threw up his arms. "All right, this is getting ridiculous. I can see you all are busy combing each other's hair and whatnot, but some of us have a job to do. I need to take Miss Gwynne's statement about the incident on the wharf so I can get on with my day."

"What incident on the wharf?" asked Flora. "Cassie, what happened?"

"Oh, nothing to worry about. A thief took a lady's pocket, and I saw him run off with it. I was only a bystander."

"A bystander who obstructed justice," muttered Officer Hughes.

"Only if being bowled over by a hotheaded police officer while you're standing still qualifies as obstructing justice," Cassie retorted.

"You weren't standing still. You jumped out in front of me."

"I took one step away from a bench. Maybe you should try watching where you're going."

"Maybe *you* should try watching where *you're* going."

"Good one."

Jake's lips twitched. "Cassie, what did the thief look like?"

Cassie smoothed her dress. "Short and thick. And he had an old green derby pulled over his eyes."

"Ah. That would be Tommy McDuffy, our resident moll-buzzer. Got away from you again, eh, Hughes?"

"No. I mean, he wouldn't have if—Well, she's the one who—"

"I must apologize for my colleague's appalling manners," Jake said. "He doesn't handle it well when things don't go his way. You won't hold him against the rest of us, will you?"

Hughes huffed and threw himself in a chair. When Cassie saw Flora had turned away, too, however, her face grew hot.

There you go again, Cassie. One contrary word and all pretensions of refinement sail out the window. She hadn't started it, but she shouldn't have let her temper get the better of her.

And she had so wanted this trip to be a fresh start. New people, new place, new Cassie. She'd styled her hair, shined all her boots, and, after a long internal debate, allowed herself to dip into the sizable inheritance her father had left her and purchased an entirely new and fashionable (or at least fashionably priced) wardrobe on Ladies' Mile. She'd even created a page in her diary listing all the things she should do to be more "ladylike."

1) Mind my skirts in muddy areas, even if I'm in a rush.
2) Chew with my mouth closed, even if the food is really good.
3) Resist adjusting my drawers in public, even if it feels as though there's more inside than out...

It was unlikely "engage in a petty battle of wills with a policeman, even if he's acting like a constipated toddler" qualified.

Finally, Flora looked up, her eyes wet with laughter. "Oh, Cassie. I'm not trying to make light of things, but now I really know you're family." She wiped her cheek. "We Hales are passionate people. We feel more, and more deeply, than other people do most of the time, both the good and the bad. And we're downright miserable at hiding it either way. Why, if anyone could tell me of one time my father, your Grandpa Maro, received a slight or witnessed some injustice and didn't immediately let everyone within earshot know exactly what he thought about it, I'd stand on my head and whistle 'Goober Peas' backwards."

Cassie let go of a breath she hadn't realized she was holding.

The jailor, who had disappeared into the hall at some point, waddled back into the room with a slip of paper. "Good news. The sheriff had to leave town—the legislature's refusing to pay his fees again, so he went off to Tallahassee to let 'em have it—and he says Miss Hale can go, long as she covers the arrest and jailing costs. And promises she'll mind her behavior in the future."

Flora winked at Cassie. "I can always try."

"He also says—Hold on, I want to get this part right." He perched a pair of small, round spectacles on the tip of his nose and held the paper out in front of him. "As he has not yet appointed a deputy, Officer Gordon is to be in charge until he returns. However, *however*—"

He directed his voice at Jake, who had broken into a celebratory jig in front of Hughes and received a retaliatory ear flick in return.

"*However*, Officers Gordon and Hughes are specifically admonished that they are to 'play nice' and not to do anything that is 'going to make a mess for him to clean up' when he returns. Or else neither will be considered further for the permanent position."

The two men, who had been poised to punch each other in the arm, put up their hands.

"What about me? Am I excused?" asked the inebriate, hanging from the bars. He paused to empty his stomach contents onto the floor then leaned back with watery-eyed relief.

The jailor sighed and headed toward the mop leaning against the wall. "This is why I don't wear my good suit to work."

Cassie, Flora, and Jake had just turned onto the road outside the jail when Jake stopped so abruptly Cassie nearly stepped on him.

"Sakes alive," he said. "What's he doing with that?"

A pretty little barouchet drawn by a pair of marsh tackies was bouncing along the street toward them, driven by a boy in an oversized sailor suit and a floppy boater hat made from woven palmetto leaves instead of straw.

"Greetings, Mr. Jake, sir!" The boy, who was perched next to a bundle of newspapers almost as big as he was, raised a hand in salute. "Good morning, Miss Flora, good morning, Miss Cassie Gwynne from New York. Say, you okay? That was some wallop you took back there on the wharf!"

Cassie winced.

"Whoa, Castor, whoa, Pollux!" Jake brought the horses to a halt and flashed his eyes up at the boy. "Paddy, I told the dock porter to wait with this."

"He had to go help at the freight dock, so he asked me to watch it. Then, I'm sittin' there and I say to myself, 'It's all loaded up. I know where they all are. Why don't I save 'em the trouble of coming back for it?' So I brought it over."

"You knew where Miss Gwynne was? Why didn't you say something when I was searching for her on the dock, all in a panic?"

"A bunch of ladies getting off the steamship bought all my newspapers, so I had to run and get more. Besides, I figured the wharf clerk would give you the message Miss Cassie left."

"Well, he didn't."

Cassie frowned. *That was fifty cents well spent.*

"And you went to the right place anyway—"

"Okay, never mind." Jake adjusted his grip on the carriage traces. "The real issue, Paddy, is this is a two-horse team. Far too big for you to drive. You could've hurt yourself, or damaged the vehicle even, which would have been my neck since it belongs to the Egmont. Now get down from there. And don't think you're getting a tip for this."

"Aw. How 'bout a newspaper then?"

"Not funny."

While Jake checked the horses' fittings and turned the carriage around, Cassie and Flora continued up the road, and Paddy traipsed along behind them, dragging an old palmetto branch around in the dirt. Birds of a dozen varieties whistled and chirped in the brilliant sunshine, and every so often a gust of wind rushed through, rustling the surrounding trees' branches so loudly that, for a few seconds, it drowned out the enthusiastic sawing of the cicadas in the canopy above.

When they drew close to Centre Street, however—which, Cassie remembered from the map she'd purchased before she left, ran east from the passenger wharf as the city's main street—it was Cassie who stopped short.

To their left was a charred expanse of dirt and debris. Much of it was covered in unidentifiable rubble, but here and there part of a building remained, dark and haggard, waiting to be torn down and put out of its misery. A large-eyed façade with nothing behind it, streaked half-black like a Venetian mask. A two-story store cut into a dollhouse cross-section. A set of stairs leading to nothing.

Cassie peeled off a glove and picked up what appeared to be a piece of a sign.

"Chilling, isn't it," Flora said. "We had a severe fire here a few weeks ago. It started very late on a Saturday night, but, thankfully, Paddy saw it and sounded the alarm bell. If he hadn't done that so quickly, things would have been far worse."

Paddy nodded. "I was only up for a glass of water, but when I looked outside, I saw smoke and flames shooting straight up from behind Weil's barroom like the horns of Jesse himself!"

Colorful.

"So, I went right for the alarm. Mr. Banks even mentioned me in the *Mirror* Special." He pulled a newspaper from his stack and thrust it into Cassie's hands.

Cassie read the headline out loud. "'Paddy Hu? A Young Hero, That's Who.' Very impressive."

Paddy grinned. "You can keep it, if you want." His rich brown eyes, just visible beneath the brim of his hat, had something different about them she couldn't quite place.

"Sure. Thanks."

"That'll be a nickel, please."

"Pardon?"

"Paddy." Jake had caught up to them, horses and carriage in tow. "That paper's three weeks old."

"Okay, three cents."

"Paddy!"

"Just a joke. Welcome to Fernandina!" Letting out a puckish laugh, Paddy scampered off to join a group of shoeless boys who were tossing a baseball around in the street, ducking in and out of the dust clouds stirred up by passing buggies.

Flora shrugged apologetically. "Anyway, the fire destroyed pretty much everything this side of Centre between Second and Third." She gestured out over the burned area. "Most of the structures were old and made all out of wood, a tinderbox waiting for a strike, really, but that didn't make the losses any less devastating. Whole buildings and, for some, entire life savings went up in flames overnight. Even I didn't escape without a scrape. Whoa!"

She threw an arm in front of Cassie as the boys who had been playing with the baseball flew past them, one on a velocipede and the others on foot, hotly pursued by a red-faced man holding a hand to his head. A few seconds later, Paddy popped up from behind a rain barrel and peered out after them.

He noticed Cassie and Flora looking at him. "What? Some people don't know how to catch."

"Oh! Wait here, Cassie. I'll be right back." Holding onto her hat, Flora dodged through traffic toward a slim Chinese man in a silk cap and queue who was pushing a cart heaped with oysters on ice. "Mr. Green, *ni hao*! How are you today?"

"Mr. Green owns an excellent dining establishment in town," Jake said. "Sun's Parlor Restaurant, up on North Second, between Centre and Alachua."

"Bless you." Cassie cracked a smile.

"Thank you." Jake cracked one in return.

As one of the horses warmed her cheek with its muzzle, Cassie looked back at Paddy, who had pulled off his hat and scampered over to where a street performer was mimicking the sound of sawing lumber for a crowd of well-dressed ladies. Maybe that was what had caught her attention before: Paddy was Chinese. Or was he? His hair was rather light-colored, with a reddish tinge, and his nose and forehead were distinctly Western to her eye.

"He's half," Jake answered, before she could formulate the question. "His mother was Irish."

"Oh! So Mr. Green—"

"No relation."

Cassie bit her lip. Nothing good ever came from assuming too much.

"But Mr. Green does look after him often. We all do. Paddy's mother has passed, and his father works aboard one of the merchant ships based out of here so is away at sea for long stretches, unfortunately. Paddy stays in Mr. Green's apartment above the restaurant whenever his father's on assignment."

Cassie recalled the day she'd gone into the Chinese area of the Five Points immigrant slums with her father for a case. He'd made her stay in the carriage while he took his meeting, so she hadn't been able to explore, but she remembered thinking that, between the musical clamor of strange dialects, the fluttering red-and-gold ornaments over the doorways, and the smell of incense swirled together with that of cooking food, it had felt like an entirely different place and time.

"It must be lonely, straddling two worlds," she said, "belonging fully to neither."

"Oh, I don't know about that. When I see Paddy flit about the way he does, I tend to think both rather than neither."

With that, they fell quiet and watched life trundle by on Centre Street. Steady streams of skirts and derbies flowed along the sidewalks in front of vendor stalls, red-bricked stores, and taverns shaded by broad-leafed trees. Merchants smoked and argued politics as they laid out their stock. Laborers whistled and pounded hammers into nails. By the waterfront, the local artillery barked and marched along the railroad tracks, practicing formations for an upcoming parade.

Paddy giggled, and when Cassie saw what he was looking at, she couldn't help joining in. In a building across the way, a baker stood in the window fanning himself with his apron, his eyes closed in ecstasy as his bare belly, which steadfastly refused to be contained by his shirt, rippled in the breeze. Cassie almost wished she could do the same. Unlike the air she was used to in the crowded streets of New York, thick with the odor of garbage and sweat, the air here was cool and fresh and tinged instead with the scent of jasmine, salt, and fresh-cut wood.

At the same time, despite the town's abundant charm and the glamor of the well-heeled tourists who had flocked to the island for the season (it seemed someone whose opinion mattered had declared it "the thing" for people of taste to do nowadays), there was a certain edge to it all. Something unfinished, wild even. It reminded her of a traveler's account she'd read once describing Florida as the "frontier of the South," with "alligators and marshes instead of wolves and deserts." It was as subtle and fleeting as a glint of sunlight in the window of a passing carriage—a splash of tobacco on a shiny leather boot. Sandspurs embedded in lace. Gold paint peeling from the wheel of a fringe-topped Victoria, ravaged by the heat.

Certainly, anything could happen in a place like this.

Cassie's thoughts turned back to the letters. All written from Flora to Cassie's father, Tom Gwynne, they spanned nearly two decades and bore postmarks from all over the world, and once Cassie had begun reading them, she hadn't been able to stop. From weather events and local news to philosophical ramblings about fruits and flowers, Cassie devoured it all. Flora had attended a women's college and traveled to three continents all on her own. She collected books for schools and advocated against the cruel treatment of animals. She even owned her own business. She was educated, worldly, and independent, everything Cassie aspired to be. But, above all, though all she had to go on were a few written words, Cassie could see there was a distinct sensitivity in her, a sense of care and connectedness to the world, the likes of which she had never encountered before.

What she couldn't see was why her father hadn't ever mentioned Flora. Flora seemed to be someone she would have very much enjoyed spending time with growing up, especially since she hadn't had the chance to truly know her mother. And he hadn't simply failed to mention her. He'd kept her letters hidden. Cassie had found them only by happenstance earlier that summer, tucked away inside an old spice tin in the scullery.

There was another odd thing, too. While letters normally read as one side of a conversation, asking and answering questions, reacting to stories and news, Flora's seemed more akin to monologues. They didn't refer to anything Cassie's father might have said in a letter of his own, or ask anything, or otherwise seem to reflect or expect a response.

It was the way Cassie spoke to her father now, at his place in the churchyard.

Had he not written her back? Why not? If he hadn't, why had Flora continued to write him? And why would he have kept the letters?

"Mr. Green has pledged one of his lucky dragon carvings!" Flora called as she wended her way back toward them, slowing twice to exchange a greeting with someone passing by. "He's also going to make a batch of his steamed white buns for the buffet tables." She beamed at Cassie. "It's all for the season's opening ball at the Egmont Hotel this weekend. I don't often get involved in these sorts of things, but I was promised that if I joined the planning committee, I could include an auction to raise money for the victims of the recent yellow fever outbreak in Pensacola."

"I've heard it's to be quite the event." Cassie tried not to let her attention drift. A few yards away, the grumpy ticket agent from the wharf had just slipped out from between two buildings, checked over her shoulder, then hurried across the street and down an alleyway. Immediately afterward, a man in a long canvas duster turned from the tea vendor's stall and took the exact same route.

A coincidence. That's all. What was wrong with her? It was like she was *looking* for things to stick her nose in.

Flora pressed her hands together. "Well, we should get going. And we might as well drive, since Jake has the carriage." She waved Paddy over as Jake climbed onto the driver's bench. "Paddy, why don't you come with us? You can earn that tip and a slice of rosewater cream cake besides if you help Jake with Miss Cassie's luggage."

Tossing Jake a triumphant grin, Paddy clambered up and wedged himself next to him. Flora hopped in behind them and reached down to help Cassie up.

"All right, boys." Jake batted Paddy's hand away as he picked up the reins. "On to Flora's."

CHAPTER THREE

Flora's house was a lilac cottage with a pitched roof and white gingerbread trim surrounded by cabbage palms, flowering shrubs, and citrus trees. It was a full two and a half stories, raised off the ground by brick columns fronted with vine-covered latticework, and had a broad porch that wrapped all the way around, making it appear wider than it was tall and heavier at the bottom than at the top. Coupled with the way the house was nestled at the bottom of a broad dip in the road, it gave the impression of a lady settled in an armchair among friends.

They had almost reached the gate when Jake jerked the reins. "Oh, for the living—Duck!"

Flora pulled Cassie down just as something round and pink sailed over their heads and landed on the floor of the carriage with a wet *plop*.

"That was just for spite!" Jake sputtered. "We were nearly stopped."

Cassie picked up the unusual missile. "A grapefruit?"

It had split in the middle and was dripping sticky, fragrant juice onto her glove.

"Courtesy of my charming neighbor Peanut," Flora said, hopping to the ground. "He owns the house across the street and the open parcel next to me, so, through some kind of cockeyed logic, he's decided he has the right to control the road in between. His latest efforts consist of hurling fruit at passersby he thinks are driving too fast. Thankfully, he has miserable aim."

On a scraggly strip of grass on the other side of the road, a wiry little man with a ten-gallon hat and a coal-black beard was scowling at them from what appeared to be a dining chair. A basket of grapefruits sat between his feet, and, on either side of him, rising out of the ground like tombstones, were a half a dozen crudely constructed signs, each painted with such pleasantries as "Private Property," "No Trespassing," and "Intruders Will Be Shot." As if to emphasize the last, he cradled a long-barreled shotgun in his lap.

Beyond the fence behind him loomed a shadowy netherworld of gnarled trees which, judging by their contortions, were either being strangled by the vines hanging from their branches or suffering from dyspepsia. The ground was thick with spiky palmettos strewn with cobwebs and Spanish moss, and, at the center of it all, beneath an ancient oak shaped like an ogre trying to cast a spell, stood a house with bare paneling and unframed windows. It was large and sturdily constructed, but when it came to anything outside of functional, it was clear every expense had been spared.

Cassie wondered what hordes were trying to storm *that* castle.

Leaving Jake and Paddy to manage the luggage under Peanut's baleful gaze, Flora and Cassie passed through a fence covered with purple flowers shaped like trumpets and onto the stone-paver path that wound through Flora's garden to her porch.

"Voila." Flora threw the door open with a flourish. "Welcome to *Chez* Hale."

As she did so, an intoxicating medley of scents—rose, jasmine, citrus, and a dozen others—rushed forth to greet them, followed immediately by a pair of barking dogs.

"Danger! Down!"

Cassie was about to drop to the floor again when she realized Flora was addressing the three-legged mastiff pawing at her dress. Pawing at the mastiff was a puppy with bangs so long there was no way it could see what it was barking at.

"You, too, Luna! Settle down."

"Settle darh!" A small bird, mostly white and gray but yellow from the neck up, with doll-like orange circles on its cheeks, flew in repeating the command and perched on Flora's hat. It had a crest on its head that flared toward the back, giving it a mildly deranged appearance.

"I hope you don't mind animals, by the way," Flora said, bending to check on the puppy, which, likely owing to the curtain of hair over its face, had clocked itself on a chair leg. The bird did a little buck-and-wing dance to maintain its position. "I should have warned you before you arrived. This house is not only my home and store but also a menagerie of sorts."

"Certainly not. It's delightful."

"All my animals were rescued from various dire situations, you see, since, as you might have guessed, I am utterly incapable of turning my back on any of God's creatures in need. Kleio, the cheeky cockatiel here, was left homeless when a widower over on Calhoun passed away. I found Danger wounded at the beach, and—Ow."

The dogs, who were now grappling noisily in front of them, had tumbled into her shins. Cassie couldn't tell for sure, but the bird appeared to be egging them on.

"The puppy joined us a week ago when a boy dropped her in the harbor, apparently with the object of teaching her to swim. Thankfully, Danger jumped right in and hauled the poor thing back to shore... Needless to say, when the boy's horrified mother asked me to take her, I gladly did so." She transferred the bird to the coat rack and untied her hat. "And, finally... ah, there he is!" Letting her hat fall, she dropped down and held out her arms to a bright-eyed pig trotting toward them, each of his footfalls accompanied by a joyful *urmff*. "This is my sweet Roger, whom I rescued as a piglet from the butcher a couple of years ago. The smartest of the lot, if you ask me. And the best dressed."

Cassie looked again. The pig was wearing an ascot around his neck.

"Here, Roger. Pigpigpigpigpigpigpig," sang Kleio, skittering back and forth on her perch.

Flora stood. "It's a bit quiet in here, human-wise, don't you think? My assistant, Esme Cole, should be around. She lives in the house with me." She lifted the curtain separating the foyer from the parlor, but it was pitch black inside. "And we never close the drapes—"

"Surprise!"

A chorus of voices sang out, and orange flashes filled the room as their owners struck matches all at once to light the candles they were holding up to their faces. Jake and Paddy, who must have run around the back instead of unloading the luggage, were among them, grinning like jack-o'-lanterns along with the rest.

"Surprarh!" Kleio squawked from the foyer.

A young girl about Paddy's age ran up to Flora, her arms outstretched. "It's a 'Welcome Cassie to Fernandina' and 'Welcome Flora Home from Jail' surprise party!" Her shiny sausage curls bounced with excitement. "We've been planning the first part for a while, but we added the second part this morning after you beat up mean old Mr. Meeks."

"We're going to have to talk about that last bit later, but thank you, Miss Metta!" Flora scooped the girl up in her arms. "I'm fantastically, amaze-tastically, ecstat-tastically stunned!"

"Those aren't real words, Miss Flora," Metta giggled.

The dogs scrambled in circles around them, their paws slipping and sliding on the floorboards, while the pig did his best to keep up, *urmff*-ing all the way.

Smiling to herself, Cassie surveyed the room as the party guests tied back the drapes and began bringing up the regular lights. She was curious to see what Flora's store was like. Flora had mentioned on the drive that it was modeled after the perfumery where she had apprenticed in Paris, but, unlike many of the other girls Cassie knew, who took a trip to Worth's every year to have new dresses made, Cassie had only been to Paris once. And on that occasion she and her father had filled most of their time with visits to museums and cheesemongers, as well as the dozens of patisseries whose colorful window displays had caught their eye along the way.

Along one side of the room stood a glass-fronted counter filled with delicate bottles of all shapes and colors, behind which white shelves framed by arches and columns and lined with silver-spigoted vessels climbed all the way to the ceiling. The other walls, papered in a soft pink and decorated with botanical drawings of flowers and herbs, were lined with tables draped in pearly fabric displaying scented fans, handkerchiefs, gloves, and sachets. Cassie's favorite part, however, was the set of Wardian cases—small, birdhouse-shaped greenhouses containing tiny bursts of ferns and orchids—that hung by the window.

The little girl fell in next to her. "Good day, Miss Cassie." She slipped her hand into Cassie's. "I'm Metta Gordon, Officer Jake Gordon's daughter. My name comes from the Far East practice of Buddhism and means 'loving-kindness.'"

"Um, good day, Metta."

The girl waited.

"Oh. My name comes from a story about an ancient princess who could see the future, but no one believed her and lots of terrible things happened." Cassie punctuated her report with a nod and gave the girl's hand, which was very warm, and a bit sticky for some reason, a sort of sideways shake. She hadn't had much occasion to interact with children before, so she wasn't sure what the etiquette was.

"Now, that was only one Cassandra, Miss Gwynne." A statuesque Black man with a gray-speckled beard nodded to her from one of the pink settees by the window. "The name itself can actually be taken to mean 'shining upon man,' or 'helper of man.' So, I'd say, look on the bright side. So to speak." He chuckled and reached down to rub Roger's upturned belly.

As the man murmured to the pig and it grunted happily in return, Cassie noticed that, while he wore a dark patch over one of his eyes, there was something different about the other one as well. It seemed perpetually focused somewhere far away. Recalling a man she'd met once with the same quality, she realized he must be blind.

She selected a berry hand pie from one of the many plates of miniature sandwiches, cakes, and cookies stationed about the room and sat next to him. "Thank you. I suppose I should take that advice, Mister…"

"Sergeant Robert Denham. At your service."

"A pleasure to meet you, Sergeant Denham." Cassie balanced the tiny pie on her knees and picked up his hand, squeezing it in greeting. "You can call me Cassie."

He squeezed back. "Glad to meet you as well, Cassie. And glad to see you've inherited your father's perceptiveness. My deepest condolences on his passing, by the way. It's tragic what happened to him. To the both of you. A most terrible case of being in the wrong place at the wrong time."

Cassie stared back down at her pie, her throat so tight she could barely move her head. *But we wouldn't have been in that place, at that time, if it hadn't been for me. If I hadn't gone off like that, trying to prove I don't know what, Father wouldn't have come looking for me—*

"I didn't know your father well," Sergeant Denham continued, "but I owe him my life. Early in the war, I caught the edge of an explosion, and your father found me in the woods, left for dead. I couldn't have been a pretty sight, nearly blown to bits like that, but he picked me up, gentle as could be, and carried me into town on his own back. Yes, I'd have lost a whole lot more than my sight if it hadn't been for him. And these days I owe my life to your aunt, too, in a way. Here in this store of hers, among all the perfumes and things, is the closest I get to seeing color again."

Flora gave him an appreciative smile as she re-pinned her brooch, a bronze orange blossom with white enameled petals and a cluster of orange gems at the center, but there was something sad about it, too.

A young woman in a gray dress and matching lady's turban stepped out from behind the perfume counter. "Miss Gwynne, a light celebratory supper will be served later, but there are Cajun-spiced stuffed eggs in the kitchen if you're hungry for something more substantial than finger sandwiches and sweets. I made them for Flora, since she doesn't eat meat, but there are plenty."

Flora's assistant, Esme, Cassie deduced. She had been working so quietly, writing out labels and pasting them on the small ceramic vessels lined up in front of her, Cassie had almost forgotten she was there.

Cassie took a bite of pie. "That's very kind. But what you've already put out is more than adequate." She pushed the rest of the pie into her mouth and lifted a pitcher of punch from the tea table, where it had been perilously within range of Danger's wagging hindquarters, and placed it on the mantel. "Your necklace is fascinating, by the way—" Seeing a crumb fly off her lip, she covered her mouth as she finished chewing and indicated the diamond-shaped flacon hanging from a chain around Esme's neck. It was made of a periwinkle-blue glass that sparkled brilliantly against her otherwise plain bodice.

Esme brightened. "It's a travel perfume bottle, filled with the first *eau de toilette*, which means a low-concentration perfume, that I made as Flora's apprentice. It didn't turn out exactly as I'd hoped, but the memory it represents is a precious one." She uncorked the bottle and held it out for Cassie to smell, which Cassie regretted almost immediately. It seemed to be some combination of ginger and camphor. And old seaweed.

"Come to think of it, the concentration of aromatic elements is probably higher than an *eau de toilette*," Esme went on. "More like an *eau de parfum*."

"Or maybe a straight *parfum*." Sergeant Denham wiped a tear from his eye.

Several nearby guests wiped their eyes in agreement.

Flora laughed and patted Esme's arm. "Don't worry. Practice and dedication will get you a long way. To think, when we first met, I thought I was only hiring a housemaid. But here I am, two years later, with an eager apprentice. And a most wonderfully loyal friend."

Paddy, who had been hard at work maintaining an uninterrupted flow of apple dumpling from a serving platter into his mouth, emitted a barely concealed belch that made the puppy jump out of Metta's lap.

"Paddy!" Metta stuck out her bottom lip. "You'll send our new friend running all the way back to New York!"

"Oh, I think it would take more than that to send any daughter of Tom Gwynne running," said Sergeant Denham.

Paddy performed a minor encore and patted his stomach. "Sorry. But I needed the space for supper. When are we going to eat?"

Perhaps Paddy was on to something, because what Esme had referred to as a "light celebratory supper" turned out to be a hearty spread of pan-fried snapper with bitter orange sauce, mashed potatoes, and buttered asparagus, followed by an incredibly moist and fragrant orange Madeira cake. Everything was excellent, and as Cassie waddled outside with the others to watch the sunset from the side porch, she almost felt content.

Carefully balancing her coffee, she settled into a rocking chair and watched the lamplighter weave from post to post with his brass-tipped staff, leaving a trail of glowing lights in his wake. In front of him, what was left of the sun sank sleepily into the harbor, swaddled in color.

"I'll wager you don't get many evenings like this up north, Cassie," Jake said.

He snuck a look at Flora as she leaned on the railing, casting a graceful silhouette against the glowing sky.

"No, I don't suppose we do."

"How long do you think you'll stay?"

"Well, I haven't entirely decided yet, but—"

A scream pierced the air.

Dropping their mugs in unison, the entire party raced around the corner to the front porch, where they found Metta at the top of the steps, recoiling as if she'd been struck. Then it hit the rest of them.

Jake gagged into the back of his hand. "What's that smell?"

"My bet would be on rotten fish," coughed Sergeant Denham.

He was right. At Metta's feet, half-hidden by the shadows, lay a great, stinking fish, gutted as for market, with a floppy ascot tucked around where its neck would have been if it had one. A card scrawled in sloppy script lay on top.

"That's Roger's tie," Flora whispered. Holding onto the railing for support, she bent to pick up the card. "'*Not so nice when people don't respect your property, is it.*'"

The note fluttered to the ground.

"No." Flora stared at her empty hand. "I know Roger got out and rooted up his vegetable patch a bit the other day, but—Even he couldn't be that cruel. No. No! Roger? Where is he?"

She tore around the side of the house, calling for her pet. By the time she circled back to the front, her despair had ripened into rage.

"Peanut, that horrible, heartless man! I'll kill him! You hear that, Peanut? I'll kill you!" She grabbed a shovel that was leaning against the wall and tore down the path. The dogs broke into an agitated chorus of barks, yips, and growls, and Sergeant Denham had to straddle Danger to keep him from lunging after her.

"Flora!" Jake tripped down the steps as Flora charged across the street. "Wait!"

The rest of the group, human and otherwise, crowded into the yard to watch.

"Now, I wonder what's crawled up your skirts today, Miss Hale," said Peanut, sauntering onto his stoop.

"This is low, Peanut, even for you!" Flora's voice was forceful enough to make the trees quiver. "I won't let you get away with this."

"Finally got my little note, I see. Aw, don't tell me you're crying. Why are women always crying?"

Jake, who had just caught up, ducked as Flora swung her shovel in response. Halfway through the arc, the shovel slipped from her grasp, landing with a clatter at Peanut's feet.

Peanut laughed. It was an ugly, raspy laugh, mean enough to bring an involuntary frown to Cassie's lips.

"That's better. But still tiresome. I think you'd better get off my property now... before I get grumpy. We've got a ship coming in, and I have to be on lookout duty at two in the godforsaken morning."

Jake stepped between them, his back to Peanut as he murmured to Flora in earnest. After a moment, Flora's shoulders began to lower, and finally she turned back toward the house.

Peanut laughed again as he lit his pipe. "That's right. Be a good girl and listen to your man."

Flora spun back around. "How dare you!"

Jake, however, on his guard, caught her and pointed her back the other way. When they reached Flora's gate, the group scrambled back onto the porch and awaited their approach in nervous silence.

Flora's gaze fell back on the fish. "Esme, hand me the other shovel."

"Flora," said Jake. "What're you—"

"I'm going to put this poor creature to rest. Such a waste of life." Taking the shovel from Esme, she scooped up the carcass and carried it down the steps.

Metta buried her face in her father's hip. "I want Roger."

"I know, sweet girl."

Paddy, who had been taking everything in quietly, picked up Luna and placed her in Metta's arms. Hugging the little dog to her chest, Metta blinked gratefully and allowed herself to be led back inside.

One by one, the others followed, but Cassie remained on the porch, watching Flora mutter to herself as she dug a grave for the fish, not even slowing to wipe off her face when fat drops began to fall from the sky. Cassie tugged her wrap tighter around her. It was a warm, mild evening, despite the rain, but she was beginning to feel chilled.

And to wonder, once again, whether she should have come after all.

CHAPTER FOUR

Before even the sun had roused itself the next morning, all the birds on Amelia Island gathered outside Cassie's window and launched a boisterous debate over their plans for the day. Or at any rate that was what it sounded like to Cassie when their voices chattered their way into her sleep. She muttered an oath involving wild game pie and clapped her hands over her ears.

"Gracious. Was something wrong with the bed?" Flora stood in the doorway with a breakfast tray, her eyebrows so high they had disappeared into her frizzled bangs.

Raising her eyebrows in return, Cassie sat up and realized that she was, as Flora had suggested, not in bed but rather on the floor in front of her clothing trunk. Her arms and shoulders were tangled in a green petticoat, a portion of which was tucked into the front of her nightdress like a dinner napkin, and her toes were buried under one of the charred logs in the fireplace.

Not again.

"Oh, uh, no. It was perfectly comfortable." Cassie struggled to her feet. "I just sometimes… change locations while I'm asleep. An old childhood habit that resurfaces from time to time." Truth be told, as of late, "time to time" had become almost daily, but she had hoped the change of location would improve things. No such luck, it seemed. "On previous occasions, I've woken on the landing, under the dining table, or even sitting up against a bookshelf with a fruitcake in my hand, so the fact I'm still in the bedroom is arguably a minor victory." She chuckled awkwardly then mentally kicked herself in the shins. No one wanted to hear that sort of thing from a houseguest.

Flora closed the door, nudging Danger's inquisitive nose back with her knee. "Ah, a migratory sleeper." She said that as casually as one might say, "Ah, an avid reader." "Well, as long as you keep your feet out of any *lit* fireplaces, you're welcome to sleep wherever you like. Anyway..." She smiled and lifted the tray, which was loaded with cheesy eggs, berries, and some kind of beautifully fragrant baked goods. "I come bearing a hot breakfast, an amends of sorts for yesterday. I can only imagine what you must think of me, given what you've seen so far."

Cassie sighed as the aromas did a tantalizing dance under her nose. She was still paying the price for her overindulgence the evening before, but she had never been one to turn away food. "Thank you, but there's no need for amends."

She reached for the tray, but Flora, not seeming to notice, set off busily across the room with it.

"I always try to live my life in an accepting, loving way." Flora put the tray on the desk and leaned over it to tie back the curtains. "But there are certain things I simply cannot tolerate. Though, I know I should also consider how I'm viewed by others... There are already plenty who find me—unconventional."

"Unconventional?" Cassie craned her neck toward the food.

"Oh, nothing shocking. Well, depending on your perspective. I think the crux of it is I don't need or want the things other people seem to think one should, and I *do* want, and need, things that other people don't think one should... If that makes any sense."

Cassie flicked her eyes back to Flora. Oddly enough, it did. She wasn't sure the specifics were the same in her case, but she had often felt a hazy discomfort around other girls her own age, particularly in groups, due to her inability to care about the things they cared about. She never bore them any ill will about it, nor they her (as far as she knew), but it did make her feel rather lonely at times.

"But never mind all that right now," Flora said. "I'll be the first to admit that I've been more excitable than usual recently. My business has gotten so busy, and then there's everything that happened with the fire... I'm not sure if I mentioned?"

"All you said was you didn't escape the fire without a scrape. But I thought perhaps I'd misheard, since your store appears intact. And well out of the fire zone, as I understand."

Cassie's hopes toward the breakfast tray rallied when Flora finished with the curtains, then retreated when she turned around and sank onto the chair in front of it.

"Yes, right. I was talking about my rented annex space inside Mr. Adler's fine-goods store, which is—was on South Second, a couple doors down from Centre, directly on the burned block. I had a portion of the display counter for my perfumes, as well as use of the back room, where I mostly conducted auxiliary distilling and enfleurage operations. I'd recently started offering orders by catalog, and the demand was more than I was set up for here.

"Make no mistake. Money-wise, I wasn't damaged anywhere nearly as badly as some others. My friend Mrs. Keene's son-in-law, Charles Hiller, is the local insurance agent, so the equipment I lost was well covered. But it was a real blow losing my notebook."

"Losing a notebook was worse than losing your equipment?"

"It wasn't just any notebook. It was the one I used to record all the compositions and techniques I'd come up with for making my perfumes. I'd had the same one for years. But, as Jake keeps reminding me, I should be grateful it was burned up, as opposed to taken or something. If it were to fall into the wrong hands, my livelihood could be irreversibly damaged."

Cassie dredged a legal term from the recesses of her brain. "It contained your trade secrets."

"Exactly." Flora twisted the corner of her apron. "It was so foolish of me. I knew I was going to be at Mr. Adler's for the day, so, as I often did, I'd brought my notebook so I could work out some ideas while the distillers ran. But when Esme came in and told me about the emergency at the depot—one of the delivery vehicles from my citrus groves had had an accident and someone was badly hurt—I simply threw it in a drawer and ran off. I was in such a hurry I didn't even write down what I'd just worked out. It was a real breakthrough, too, for a custom perfume I'd made for the Egmont auction. And I still can't remember what it was, for the life of me.

"Anyway, I usually keep the notebook in a safe here in the house, but I suppose I figured it would be all right where it was for a short time. No one but us even knew it was there. Even Mr. Adler was away on his annual fishing retreat with his brothers. But the possibility of fire never occurred to me."

"Most people don't go about assuming a fire will break out at any time."

"True. But it certainly has been wearying work trying to reconstruct what now only exists as bits and pieces flying around in my head. And I've had the projects for the ball as well, along with my usual commitments, and your visit to prepare for..." She tugged at a bit of fabric around her wrist—Roger's tie. "Now my heart goes and gets broken like this."

Cassie's own battered heart squeezed in sympathy. "I'm so sorry. Still no sign of Roger?"

Flora shook her head, her gaze fixed on the ascot.

"I wouldn't lose hope yet. You don't actually know he's been harmed. And are you even sure Peanut is responsible? The note wasn't signed, was it?"

Flora sighed and looked out the window. Even in the warm, pink light now filling the room, there was a weariness about her Cassie hadn't noticed before.

"It had to be Peanut. Remember how I said Roger had gotten out a few days ago and rooted up Peanut's vegetable patch? Well, I fixed the gate he'd slipped through right away and promised to repair the damage, but Peanut said it wasn't good enough. He told me, 'That animal needs to be put down for what it did to my property. Get rid of it, or I will'... And Peanut is entirely capable of such evil. He's a bully, through and through. So, when I think of Roger, that sweet, defenseless creature, in his hands, I—" Her voice broke. "He was supposed to be safe with me."

Cassie passed her a handkerchief.

"Thank you. Goodness." Flora dabbed her eyes. "Look at me. Tears won't bring him back, will they?" She rose to her feet. "Come, you haven't even touched your food. I insist that you try one of my scones. I made them with candied orange peels and orange blossom water from my distiller. And once you've dressed, we'll walk up to Old Town. I have something I want to show you."

Cassie dutifully complied, and several scones later, she was walking with Flora up a white dirt road sprinkled with gray and pink shells, her stomach almost as full as it had been the night before. Based on her experience thus far, it was probably a feeling she was going to have to get used to around here.

She gave her corset, which she had laced extra loosely this morning, a discreet jiggle. Nothing she couldn't handle.

"I know I asked this already, but are you sure you want to be in those clothes?" Flora asked. "This walk is closer to a tramp in the woods than a walk about town."

Cassie shifted her parasol so she could lift the front of her (also new) visiting dress, which was made from pale green silk and had four tiers of ruffles around the bottom, to step over a root. The close fit around the hips and knees made it a challenge to get her foot high enough, but she managed to clear it with about a millimeter to spare. "Yes, I'm fine, thank you. I'd rather be overdressed than underdressed."

That was a complete lie and therefore something she had never said to anyone before, but she'd heard it uttered by enough society women back in New York to give it a try.

"Okay." Flora looked at her dubiously but continued on with what she had been saying. "So, Old Town, which is about twenty minutes north of here by foot, is the original site of Fernandina, where most people lived until the fifties, when the FT&P Railroad came in. The railroad people wanted to make Fernandina the terminus for their new line, but they realized if they started the tracks in Old Town, they'd have to cross the salt marsh with them. So, they bought up the land below the marsh instead, where the old Yellow Bluff Plantation used to be, put in the tracks and depot, and parceled the rest for sale to individuals."

"Where Fernandina is now."

"That's right. Or New Fernandina, as us older folks call it. It wasn't a perfectly peaceful process, but eventually most everyone moved to the new area. The only people still up in Old Town these days are waterfront folks. Fishermen, sawmill workers, harbor pilots. And speaking of the marsh—"

Cassie let out a thunderous sneeze.

"Oh, my. That was you I heard at the jail yesterday. I'd assumed it was Officer Hughes."

Cassie sneezed again, this time sending her fresh gum flying into the bushes. "Excuse me. It's the sunlight that does it. Or really any sudden bright light."

They weren't facing directly into the sun, but its rays were reflecting off the light-colored ground with such intensity they might as well have been.

"Yes, of course," Flora said, handing Cassie a pair of tinted spectacles from somewhere in her colorful, loose-fitting robes. "It must run in the family. Once, your father's sneeze startled a woman so badly she fell off the sidewalk." She started to laugh but stopped when a tear spilled onto her cheek.

Cassie struggled to keep a hold of a rogue tear of her own. It was the first time they had spoken of her father together. She had been close to bringing him up many times since she arrived, but she still didn't know how to ask what she wanted to know.

"Are you sure I'm not keeping you from your store?" she asked instead.

"It's no problem. Esme prefers backroom tasks, but she'll run the store counter when needed. Mind you, she's been waking later and later these last several weeks. I just hate to say anything because I know she has such a time sleeping—Hold on. You'll want to watch your step here. This is the marsh I was talking about."

Directly ahead, the road fell off into a brown and green expanse of cordgrass growing tall, straight, and dense like giant hairbrush fibers, interrupted only where a few narrow stretches of water, smooth and shiny as a new looking glass, had cut a path through. Cassie looked around. The only way forward she could see was a wooden plank walk, narrow, rough-hewn, with no railings of any kind, that was snaking through the vegetation toward a scraggly tree line in the distance.

She tightened her grip on her parasol. "Are we to walk on that?"

The moisture of the previous night's rain hung heavy in the air here, steeping their clothes and skin in a heady perfume of decaying plant matter and wet dirt and, Cassie had to assume, coating the planks with a good old layer of slippery slime.

"There's also a carriage road that goes around the marsh, but it's much longer. Don't worry, it isn't as bad as it looks." With that, Flora marched ahead, the dull crunch of her boots turning into echoing *thunks* that caused a nearby flock of snowy egrets, who were perched about a southern magnolia tree like dozens of white, feathery Christmas ornaments, to take off all at once, filling the pale blue sky with their wings.

Cassie watched the birds shrink into specks and tried to decide whether whatever Flora had planned was worth a potential dunk in the swamp. She could say one thing about the woman: she didn't fear much. Perhaps she should take a lesson.

Pushing a new piece of gum into her mouth, Cassie shoved her shoulders down and plunged forward. Besides, she'd come too far to be left behind.

Soon, having managed to make it across with only a few bouts of floundering like a newborn deer and cursing like an old sailor, Cassie joined Flora at the foot of a pebbly forest road on the other side. After a quick rest to catch their breath, they continued on, and in a few yards, the trees opened up on the left to reveal a grassy, bench-lined square overlooking the water—an old parade ground, Flora explained, remaining from the Spanish occupation at the turn of the century. Past that, the trees fell in again around a collection of small, colorful houses decorated in nautical themes, over which the grand old oaks stretched their branches like hens sheltering their chicks.

Behind a yellow house with sailor-gnome statuary and a fence fashioned from dock pilings and rigging rope, a second, smaller clearing opened up on the right. It was covered by a sea of knee-high grass, and at its center a latticed wooden tower stretched into the sky.

"That's the harbor pilots' lookout tower," Flora said as Cassie slowed. At the top of the tower, there was a covered platform with a flagpole.

"Harbor pilots?"

"Sea captains who are experts at navigating the local harbor. Here, the sandbar between the ocean and the Amelia River can be treacherous, so large ships need the pilots to guide them in and out. Essentially, how it works is a customer messages ahead an expected arrival time, and the pilots use the tower to watch for the ship to come around the tip of the island. Once it's spotted, a crew rows one of the pilots out, and he takes over command of the ship until it's safely berthed. The reverse is done when the ship departs."

Catching a gentle fragrance in the air, Cassie saw that a rose garden had been planted all around the base of the tower. Her mouth tugged into a smile. There was a note of guano along with the rose.

"The transfer of a pilot between vessels is actually a pretty exciting thing to watch," Flora continued, "though you were probably asleep when your own steamer came in. Once the pilot boat is in position, the pilot makes a death-defying leap onto a ladder hanging down the side of the target ship, which he then has to climb to the top, thrown about by the wind all the way."

Cassie slapped at a bug on her arm. "I think I do remember something… I had been—" She paused. The rest of that phrase was "asleep in a coil of spare rigging rope on the deck" (her "sleep migrating," as Flora had dubbed it, had been in full operation during the voyage). "I was awakened in the early morning by shouts and whistles from the deck crew, and when I went to see what was happening, there was a group of sailors pulling a man onto the deck by the captain's bridge… I'd assumed they were helping someone who'd nearly fallen. And it was so far down to the water level!"

"Yes, you'd really have to be fearless of heights for that task," Flora said.

Cassie gazed back up at the tower. "And for the lookout task as well, I'd think. Say, are others permitted up there? Do you think we could go see the view?"

"I don't—I mean, I'm sure it's possible. But it's Peanut's turn up there this morning, and I don't think I could face him right now."

"Ah." *So that's what Peanut had meant by "lookout duty" last night.* "I didn't realize Peanut was a harbor pilot."

"Yes. A skilled one. Though that doesn't make him any more tolerable a human. I honestly don't understand how the others put up with him. That Captain Beale, the head pilot, must have the patience of a saint."

"I thought the harbor pilots lived here in Old Town."

"Most do. But Peanut's property was inherited. His wife's family are heirs of the old Yellow Bluff Plantation and used to own the whole area where our neighborhood is. Most sold all of their property to the railroad, which, in turn, sold it to the rest of us, but Peanut's wife's parents held onto a couple of their parcels. Those eventually went to Peanut's wife, well, actually Peanut, since they were married. It's probably why he acts like he's entitled to control the whole neighborhood. And everyone in it."

Cassie watched her pull a long pine needle off her skirt and throw it on the ground. It must be difficult to be on such terrible terms with one's neighbor—When there are problems in the place where you live, there's nowhere to go to get away from them.

"Um, Aunt Flora?" Cassie squinted at an area to one side of the rose garden, where something small and black lay in the grass. "What's that?" The stillness of it, conspicuous against the undulation of the surrounding vegetation, had caught her eye.

"What's what?"

Cassie lifted her skirt and moved toward the object, her heeled boots making little sucking sounds in the mud. Whatever it was, it was partially obscured, so she wasn't able to identify it until she was almost on top of it. A man's shoe. What was that doing here?

She stepped forward to pick it up. But, instead of the squish of soft earth, her boot encountered a spongy resistance. She looked down… and swallowed her gum.

She was standing on a hand.

A hand connected to a body.

A body as still as the shoe.

Flora hurried toward her. "Cassie, what is it? Is something the—Oh, good Lord in Heaven." She drew back, a hand over her mouth. "Peanut."

Cassie lifted her foot and placed it back next to the other.

What was the saying? "Speak of the devil and he shall appear"?

CHAPTER FIVE

Peanut lay on his back among the rose bushes in a white, gold-buttoned shirt and a vest made from green silk, both crisp and neatly pressed, aside from a spray of mud along either side. He was hatless, though, so as Cassie pulled her skirts up as high as they would go and lowered herself beside him, following Flora's lead since she didn't quite know the right thing to do in this situation (running off screaming and throwing herself into the marsh seemed incorrect), she could see he was completely bald, a fact emphasized by the bushy black eyebrows perched on his forehead like miniature fruit bats. Fortunately, his eyes were closed, so she tried to think of him as asleep, but that was hard to do given the blood spilling out of his mouth. And the arm facing the entirely wrong direction.

"Peanut, you old fool. What's happened to you?" Flora said under her breath, making an obligatory, but obviously futile, search about his neck and wrists for a pulse. She placed her hands on her knees with a sigh. "Stay here while I go get help, okay?"

Leaving Cassie's protest fluttering on her lips, Flora ran back into the road and waved down a man passing by on a horse. After a short exchange, she climbed up behind him and they thundered away.

Cassie wanted to stand, but her knees were as soft as pudding. She wanted to stretch her arms, but they were too heavy to lift. She wanted to close her eyes, but her head was spinning so much she worried she would become ill.

And, if Peanut's lifeless face no longer filled her vision, she knew whose would take its place.

So, she remained as she was, staring at Peanut's hard, lined features. Would anyone miss him? He had lived alone, and, by all accounts, had been mean-spirited and shared a mutual dislike with nearly everyone he met. Even she had wanted to set fire to his lawn after only a minute or two in his presence. But, seeing him lying there, broken, vulnerable, made it difficult to think about him that way. Death, the great equalizer, had stripped him bare and exposed him for the mere human he was.

To distract herself, she decided to examine the shoe that had first drawn her attention. In keeping with the rest of Peanut's clothing, it was elegant, made from smooth black leather, and was in fairly new condition, aside from a splash or two of mud. There was some kind of shiny debris in the grooves of the sole as well. But more interesting was the scuffing at the back of the shoe, about an inch above the heel. She checked Peanut's other shoe. It had the same mark. How had he managed that?

A strangled cry sounded behind her. She spun around with the shoe raised to strike, electricity sparking in her joints.

"Metta!"

The girl, dressed in a blue-and-white pinafore with a red sash that matched the sunbonnet dangling down her back, stood motionless in front of her, her usually shining face as pale as Peanut's. In a surge of unexpected maternal instinct, Cassie lunged toward her, almost knocking her to the ground, and drew her close, trying to use her own body as a shield against a sight she knew nothing would ever erase.

"I'm so sorry," she murmured as she rocked the sparrow-like frame trembling in her arms.

Metta's tiny heart beat against hers, fast and frightened.

"You're not meant to see such things. Not yet."

Finally, after what felt like several lifetimes, Cassie heard the fall of hooves. Flora was riding toward them on a wiry Texas pony with a chestnut coat, followed by Jake and two other men. One of the men was dressed in a top hat and a pin-striped jacket with a yellow carnation tucked into the lapel. The other wore a tent-sized overcoat and carried a black doctor's case.

Beyond them, people were starting to trickle in from several directions.

"Cassie! What the dickens is Metta doing here?" Jake jumped off his horse and took the girl into his arms.

"I—She just appeared."

"No, no, it's my fault. I promised her we would go searching for Roger this morning, but I got called away to deal with something at the stables first thing. She must have figured she would start without me."

"Metta," Flora called, "I need your help with something very important. Sage here is feeling pretty scared right now and could use your braveness. How about giving her a good, strong hug?"

Metta perked, seeming to rise to the responsibility, and the color began to return to her face as her father led her over to the animal.

Flora slid to the ground and strode over to address the others. "Gentlemen, this is my niece, Cassie Gwynne. Cassie, this is Dr. Timothy Ames—" She gestured toward the man with the case, who was already lumbering toward Peanut, a sleek briar pipe clamped between his teeth. "And this is the coroner, Richard Shaw. They've come to examine the body." The other man gave a stiff nod but remained on his horse.

Dr. Ames hunkered down next to Peanut with a grunt and removed his hat. After placing an ear to Peanut's chest for several seconds, he pulled a stethoscope from his bag and listened again (what one method could tell him at this point that the other could not, Cassie couldn't say) then prodded his chest and neck and peered into each eye with a magnifying glass, hmming importantly.

"Right. Well, he sure is gone, Mr. Shaw." Dr. Ames sat back on his heels and considered the tower as he puffed. "Devil of a fall. Wonder how he managed that."

"There are those next to him," Flora offered. A few inches away, next to one of Peanut's hands, lay an expensive-looking pair of binoculars.

"What? Oh, yes, of course." Dr. Ames picked them up. "He must have been looking out at the water for a ship to come in and slipped over the edge. It was good and wet out last night." He aimed the binoculars into the trees and let out a low whistle. "Say what you might about the man, but that Peanut certainly didn't abide inferior products. Pristine condition, too."

Feeling a twitch in her brain, Cassie opened her mouth then shut it. She couldn't help having discovered the body, but she could help blurting out whatever she was thinking at any given moment. She reached into her pouch for a piece of gum.

As she pulled it out, however, a woman with a baby jostled her and she dropped it in the mud. The crowd of murmuring onlookers was growing quickly, and Cassie had to throw out her elbows to maintain her position.

"How awful."

"Look at his arm."

"Did he fall from all the way up there?"

"I didn't know the bastard could look so peaceful."

"Mr. Weil." Mr. Shaw turned to address the last speaker, an older man with a thick German accent. "Peanut may not have been the town's most beloved citizen, but we must be respectful. This was a terrible accident."

Cassie pressed her lips together as Mr. Shaw climbed down from his horse, parted the crowd, and joined Dr. Ames at Peanut's side. Ordinarily, the man's choice of clothing would have suggested a festive persona to her, but his manner reminded her more of those businessmen down on Wall Street who wore a harried expression everywhere they went, just so others would know how busy and important they were.

"Lord knows we wouldn't want *that* ghost haunting us."

Cassie turned around. It was the inebriate who had been in the holding cell next to Flora yesterday. He smelled like someone who'd washed his laundry in whiskey.

"Aw, don't start with the ghost talk, Major Drury," said the man next to him, waving the stink away from his face.

Major Drury crossed himself and spat over his shoulder. "They're out there, I tell you. I've seen one with mine own two eyes, not but a few weeks ago. On the night of the fire. It was right there on the roof of Weil's barroom, real as you and me, wearing a cloak billowing with smoke, and holding two glowing orbs above its head—"

Mr. Shaw cleared his throat. "Someone'll need to check the safety of the platform railings and the stairs." He pulled a handkerchief from his coat and laid it over Peanut's face. "We don't want this happening to anyone else."

A man wearing a bright white Panama hat with a feather in it stepped forward. "I'll take care of that, Mr. Shaw." His skin was brown and tough, beaten into living leather by the elements, but his suit, like Peanut's, was well tailored and made from high-quality fabric.

It seemed the harbor pilots were a dapper lot.

"Good. Thank you, Captain Beale."

Beale. That was the head pilot Flora had mentioned.

"It's no problem. I have to go up anyway. The ship we're expecting hasn't come yet, thankfully, but we need to get eyes back on the water as soon as possible." He took off his hat, revealing a thick mass of hair that had been carefully divided down the middle and oiled flat, and scratched his head. "But I must say, I don't understand how Peanut could've fallen like that. When you're on lookout, you're mostly sitting, watching the water. Matter of fact, the only time you need to move is when the ship arrives and you have to signal the ground crew to go and meet it. And Peanut was surefooted as any of us. Mean as spit, but surefooted."

"Well, that's what makes an accident an accident, isn't it, Captain?" Mr. Shaw said. "If we expected it to happen, it wouldn't be an accident. But I don't need to tell *you* that."

Someone gasped, but Cassie barely noticed because her lips were hurting from squeezing them together so hard. She had to say something or she might injure herself.

"Excuse me," she said, a little more bumptiously than she intended. She gave the donkey-toothed man who had been trying to slide in front of her a check with her hip.

Mr. Shaw looked up from his paperwork. "Did someone say something?"

Realizing he probably couldn't see her over the others, Cassie wedged a shoulder and a boot against someone and pushed, popping out of the crowd so forcefully she had to hop to avoid stepping on Peanut (again).

"Uh, yes, that was me."

"All right, girl in the fancy dress." Mr. Shaw gave her a skeptical once-over, and the rest of the crowd seemed to follow suit. "What is it?"

Cassie tugged her skirts back into place. She wasn't used to having so many people looking at her at once. "What if it wasn't an accident?"

"Not an accident? Why would you say that?"

"Well, for one thing, the harbor is on the other side of the tower."

"Correct."

"So why would he have fallen on this side if he was looking out over the water?"

Mr. Shaw was silent for a moment. "Maybe he was looking at something else."

"What about the binoculars? One would expect some kind of damage if they fell from the same place Peanut did, but Dr. Ames said they were in perfect condition."

"She's right." Jake had surrendered Metta to Flora and was now standing next to Dr. Ames, turning the binoculars over in his hands. "Not even a scratch."

Mr. Shaw huffed. "The ground has obviously been softened by the rain. Their fall was cushioned."

"Hardly even a splash of mud, in fact," Jake said.

"Fine. What's your point, girl?"

Cassie rubbed her arm. "My point is it's a possibility the binoculars didn't fall but rather were placed. Staged. To make you come to the exact conclusion you have, that Peanut was looking out at something and fell over the edge by accident. There's also the matter of his shoes—"

"Tell me your name again."

"Cassie Gwynne." Though, the way things were going, perhaps Cassandra (the ignored prophetess one) would have been more appropriate.

"And you're Flora Hale's niece. That would make you Tom Gwynne's daughter."

"Yes, sir."

His eyes grew harder. "Right. I see it now. What about the shoes?"

"There's, uh, scuffing on the back of them." Cassie scratched her nose uncomfortably. "Above the heel. An odd place for a scuff, I'd think, especially for otherwise new-seeming shoes. Which makes me wonder how it happened. I could hypothesize a scenario or two, but someone should really go up on the tower platform and take a look at things."

Mr. Shaw gave a dismissive wave. "Too much conjecture. If you're suggesting there are circumstances here warranting an inquest, I'm going to need more than your 'wondering.' I've an election coming up. I can't be wasting the public's time. And inquests cost money, you know."

"If the cost is the issue, I'd be happy to cover it in the interest of—"

"The issue is that in my experience, most things, most of the time, are exactly as they appear." He adjusted his carnation. "And, in my opinion as coroner, which is the opinion that matters when it comes to deaths in this county, this death appears to be an accident. Dr. Ames, we're done here."

Dr. Ames pulled a bedsheet from his bag, shook it out, and laid it over Peanut's body.

"Mr. Cranstock—" Mr. Shaw gestured to a man in work clothes smeared with blood and smelling strongly of the ocean. "We'll need your fishmonger's cart to move the body. Mr. Ambler—" He turned to a dull-eyed man who was peering down the barrel of his gun, trying to clear something out with a stick. "Go up the tower and collect Peanut's personal effects. They'll need to be managed along with the rest of his things once we identify a next-of-kin. Take these, too." He snatched the binoculars from Jake and held them out.

"Me?" Mr. Ambler looked around him.

"Yes, you." Mr. Shaw shook the binoculars at him. "Who else could I possibly mean?"

"But I—I don't—"

Mr. Shaw scoffed. "Go on, now, be a man. We all have to do our part. And it'll be good for you. You can see what it's like to be useful."

While Mr. Ambler pondered that, Jake spoke up. "I'll do it. Sheriff Alderman's put me in charge while he's away. And while I'm up there, I could—"

Mr. Shaw cut him off with a click of the tongue. "Sudden deaths, Officer Gordon, as you know, are the coroner's jurisdiction, not the sheriff's. Let's review. If a body appears, the *coroner* determines how, when, and where the individual came unto his death. If the death was sudden with unknown cause, violent, or unnatural, the *coroner* decides whether to hold an inquest. If there is an inquest, the *coroner* appoints a jury and conducts an inquiry. If the jury returns a verdict involving culpability, the *coroner* names a suspect, arrests him, and commits him for trial. Do you see the pattern here?"

"Yes. But the sheriff still ought to be involved—"

"Perhaps I was unclear. *Stay out of this.* Or I'm going to have to lodge another complaint about you boys interfering with my matters." He smoothed his jacket. "But don't fret. I promise to send for you immediately if I find a vagrant sleeping on my porch or someone rifles Mrs. Raleigh's sweetmeats jar again. In the meantime, perhaps you should mind that daughter of yours, instead of letting her run around in the streets like a Dickens urchin boy. The same goes for you, Miss Gwynne."

Cassie started. "Pardon?"

Not thinking anyone was still paying attention to her, she had turned around to examine the back of her dress. She'd heard a small ripping sound when she lowered down next to Peanut earlier but was hoping it sounded worse than it was—As it turned out, it was worse than it sounded. She had a distinct split right over her rump.

"It's very simple," Mr. Shaw hissed. "I don't care who your family is or how much money you have—" He smoothed his own jacket self-consciously. "You stay out of this, too. I don't need your 'what ifs' and 'wonderings' stirring people up. Your father may have indulged in that sort of arrogance and reckless-ness when he was around, but I'm in charge now, elected to this office by the people three times in a row. And I say this matter is closed. Understand?"

Without waiting for a response, he spun on his heel and stalked away, barking at the crowd to stop gawking and go on home.

*

"Miss Gwynne!" Esme called as Cassie stomped toward the road. "Where are you going?" She was standing next to a mule buggy a few yards away, along with Flora, Metta, and a handful of the other bystanders. "Hey, your dress is split!"

Cassie shrugged without slowing her pace. At this precise moment, she didn't care a whit about the tuft of petticoat fluttering in the breeze through the gaping hole over her bottom. Nor did she know where she was going. For now, she just needed to stomp.

Esme jogged to catch up to her. "Mr. Shaw had no right to speak to you like that. Well, I couldn't hear everything he said, but I'm sure he was being a pompous ass, as usual."

"He dismissed and reprimanded me, even when all I was trying to do was help. And then he insulted my father. I think."

"Wait. Miss Gw—Cassie, please." Esme caught Cassie's arm. "Don't you pay him any heed. From what I understand, he has quite the chip on his shoulder, and it has nothing to do with you. He and your father used to serve on the Town Watch together, back when that was how most law and order was kept—no small job at a time when sheriffs rarely lasted more than a year—but they didn't get along. Seems your father had a habit of showing Mr. Shaw up in front of the others. At times with a bit of theatrical flair."

"'Theatrical flair'? What does that even—How do you know that?"

"Flora told me."

Cassie chewed on a fingernail. That didn't sound like her father. None of this did. Even Sergeant Denham's amazing story about the war had felt a little surprising. Her father was as brilliant as they came, of course, and cared deeply about others, but the person she knew was a stoic, bookish man who was careful with money and preferred quiet projects at home to anything else. At times she'd even had to pry him from his chair to ensure he attended a social commitment.

She tried to envision him as frontier law enforcement, tall and tough atop a sturdy quarter horse, with spurred boots and a ten-gallon hat, and a .36 Colt Navy at his hip... but it was just plain strange. She knew he had spent time in other, less patrician, occupations in his youth, but the way people here were describing him couldn't be right. Arriving at the train station less than an hour before departure had been too much excitement for him, for Heaven's sake.

Then again, she'd never forget the way he looked that last night, when he saw her in trouble, or the ferocity with which he came to her defense. If he hadn't been so outnumbered, things surely would have gone differently.

"Mr. Shaw's not so fond of Flora, either," Esme went on. "Dear Flora. Especially recently. She's been a right thorn in his side about that stockyard he runs with Carlton Meeks."

"Mr. Meeks from yesterday morning?"

"Yes. Mr. Shaw is his partner. And brother-in-law."

"Right. Meeks-Shaw. Flora did mention she took issue with that business."

"She's gone after them pretty intensely, with monographs, signs, notes in the Town Talk column of the newspaper, that sort of thing, trying to get them to close down. Or at least change how they run things. And I have to say she's been successful in getting people's attention. The stockyard's business has slowed, and many are starting to reconsider their support for Mr. Shaw's re-election as coroner."

Cassie flicked a leaf from her elbow. "I suppose that would explain it. But it doesn't excuse it."

"Here." Tossing a furtive glance over her shoulder, Esme reached into her skirts and pulled out a jelly jar containing a brownish liquid with lemon peel floating in it. "This will help you forget all this ugliness."

Suddenly realizing how thirsty she'd become, Cassie gratefully unscrewed the cap and took a big gulp. Then promptly realized the drink wasn't intended for hydration.

She spat on the ground and pressed a hand to her mouth, her nostrils and throat on fire.

"What *is* that?"

"Rye whiskey, bitters, sugar. A couple of other things. It's a recipe from someone I used to know, may he rest in peace. It'd be better with cognac, if one could ever get their hands on any these days."

"It's liquor? I thought it was tea." Cassie bent over, her eyes watering.

"Oh, my. I should have told you to sip."

"Is something the matter over there?" Flora called.

Keeping her back to the group, Esme raised a finger to her lips with a conspiratorial smile.

"Uh, no need to worry, Aunt Flora," Cassie answered. "I'm just a little overwhelmed, I think."

"Atta girl." Esme put her arm around Cassie's shoulders. "I think you and I are going get along just fine, Cassie Gwynne."

Coughing in return, Cassie was handing the jar back when she saw Mr. Ambler shifting from foot to foot by the tower steps, his eyes darting about like a bank robber's lookout. What was going on over there?

"You know what?" Cassie's tonsils were still burning, but the drink had actually made her feel a little better. Or braver at least. "Mr. Shaw can go suck a lemon. I'll be back."

CHAPTER SIX

Leaving Esme and her bottle of fire behind her, Cassie strode back over to the pilots' tower. She never let anyone tell her what to do—Why should this Shaw character get that privilege?

Mr. Ambler tipped his hat as she drew close. "Oh, hello, Miss Gwynne."

Cassie pursed her lips. He was addressing her as if they'd chanced into each other about town, even though she had just watched him notice her approach, cast about for a hiding place, then, finding none, pull out a newspaper and assume a casual stance against the rail.

"Hello, Mr. Ambler. I thought you were going up the tower to collect Peanut's belongings."

He eyed the stairs, which, in all fairness, were little more than a series of slanted wooden ladders with handrails nailed to the sides, and tugged his collar. "Uh, yes. I was about to. But, before I do, I need to check the, uh…"

He dropped the newspaper and grabbed her hands. "Please don't tell Mr. Shaw, Miss. The man scares me."

"Tell him what?" She supposed it was a little cruel, poking at him like this, but she'd had a rough day.

"I couldn't do it, all right? Me and heights, we don't get along. I have what they call a sensibility to high places. Can't move a danged muscle if I get above a certain distance off the ground. So, Jake Gordon went for me."

"I see." Cassie took back her hands. "How about this. I don't tell Mr. Shaw about your arrangement with Officer Gordon, and you don't tell him about this?"

Mr. Ambler bent to pick up his newspaper. "Don't tell him about what?"

But Cassie had already started up the tower.

It took her longer than she'd anticipated, owing to the fact that the whole tower seemed to sway every time a breeze came through, requiring that she hug a handrail with both arms until it passed, but eventually she reached a sub-landing at the top of the steps where a rope ladder dangled from a hatch overhead. Bracing against the wind once more, she grabbed hold of the rungs and climbed through the opening onto the platform.

"Cassie! How did you get up here?" Jake was standing in front of her, one hand on Captain Beale's shoulder and the other on the back of a bolted-down chair. Evidently, he was feeling less confident about the ascent now that he'd done it.

"Used the stairs, same as you." No need to go into any more detail than that.

"That was a dangerous thing to do," Jake said. "This whole tower is a death trap, in more ways than one."

Cassie surveyed her surroundings. The platform area, most of which was shaded by a sloped sheet of canvas tied to a frame, was small and furnished with little more than a portable flat-wick lamp and the chair holding Jake up. She pulled off her glove and touched a hand to the floor. The covering had kept the boards fairly dry.

There's another point against the slipping and falling theory.

"Aw, it's not as bad as all that." Captain Beale spat on his thumb and used it to clean a smudge from one of his cufflinks. "I've checked all the railings and steps, and I assure you everything is perfectly in order."

"And didn't Mr. Shaw tell you to stay away?"

Cassie put a hand on her hip. "Yes. Which was an excellent way to ensure I would not. Besides, I seem to recall him telling you the same."

"You think I'm going to take orders from that windbag? He's always chasing us off 'his' cases, but we're law enforcement, too. And we're the ones who deal with crime every day." He fought the wind for his hat. "Anyway, what you said down there was smart, so I felt the responsible thing to do was to come and have a look around. Though, I'll admit, I don't rightly know what I'm looking for."

"Oh." Cassie wasn't prepared for the compliment folded into that rant. "I don't specifically know, either."

Out on the water, the grand ships that had loomed over the passenger wharf the day before bobbed and swayed like a child's bathtub toys, so small she was tempted to try to pick one up. She could also see where the railroad tracks began their run along the waterfront beyond the marsh, connecting a string of wharves that jutted out into the water. Directly inland from there, the town of "New" Fernandina, with its tidy blocks of homes, steeples, and broccoli-shaped trees, sprawled across the island like a Dean & Son pop-out panorama.

She inhaled deeply, and her eyes watered again, pleasantly this time, as the salty air struck the back of her nose and throat.

"I don't know what you all are looking for either," Captain Beale said, "but I'll say this again. I still don't see Peanut falling over by any accident. Do you think he might have wanted to harm himself? Nah, that's not right. He's actually been in a better mood than usual for some months now."

"A better mood?" Cassie recalled the spiteful little man she'd seen only the day before, throwing grapefruits and berating Flora.

"Relatively speaking, of course. It's not as if he was walking around ruffling babies' hair or anything. But I can tell you he hadn't been harping on the apprentices or pilot boat crews as much. Matter of fact, one day, when one of them said something to him that would earn a knock upside the head from most anyone, Peanut simply lit his pipe as if he hadn't heard it. Last week he even nodded to a group of pilots when they walked into Three Star."

"What's Three Star?" Cassie asked.

"Three Star Saloon. It's over on Centre, across from the burned-out block. Peanut drank there a lot and took his supper there most days, too. Though that second bit's always been a mystery to me. Mrs. Marsden, the proprietor's wife, is by all conceivable measures a frightful cook. One whiff of her pot cheese is enough to scare the nose hairs right off."

"What caused the change?"

Captain Beale smirked. "The men think it's a woman who was softening him up. What else could it be? 'Specially since he started wearing so much cologne you could smell him before you saw him. Now, I enjoy a spritz of Florida Water on occasion, maybe on a hot day, or after a shave, but it was like he'd bathed in the stuff. We all figured he was trying to impress someone. Or maybe"—his smirk widened into a dirty grin—"it was perfume he had on him, which someone had 'impressed' all over him, eh?"

Cassie and Jake took turns coughing and studying the canvas above their heads.

Peanut was courting a woman? Reverse that. A woman was letting Peanut court her? Cassie had a hard time picturing it. Especially since she didn't want to. "Captain Beale, was Peanut having problems with any of the pilots in particular? Causing any special grief?"

Captain Beale moved Jake's hand off his shoulder and onto the chair. "Oh, no, no, no. I don't think so. No more than usual, anyway, but who can really say. Officer Gordon, how about I give you a hand collecting Peanut's things?"

Cassie blinked after him as he bustled to the edge of the covered area and lifted a navy-blue frock coat and a walking umbrella from the hook beneath the lamp. Then he picked up the hat by his feet, which, by some miracle, hadn't been blown away, and pushed the pile into Jake's arms.

"Uh, thanks." Jake teetered slightly. "Well, we should probably go through these things now. I doubt Mr. Shaw will let anyone near them later." Once he had settled himself firmly in the chair, he put down the hat and umbrella and began emptying the coat's pockets. He passed the items as he went to Captain Beale, who, in turn, passed them to Cassie: pipe, box of tobacco, matches, coins, loose pocket watch. Cassie fiddled with the watch's winding stem as she turned it over in her hands. It carried no inscription other than the name of the maker, Patek Philippe & Co.

While Jake returned the items to the coat, Cassie moved to the edge of the platform closest to where Peanut had been found. From this vantage point, she could see that his body had broken the branches on several of the rose bushes on the way down, throwing off their careful symmetry.

Captain Beale joined her at the railing. "This is a terrible thing to say, but my wife is going to have a fit when she sees the state of those roses, dead man or no." His smile seemed out of place on his face, like an Easter tie at a funeral. "She led the committee that planted them. They wanted to make the clearing feel less 'lonely.'"

"They're certainly beautiful. So many blooms, even with winter approaching."

"This variety, Louis Phillipe, is known for its love of cooler weather. But my wife'll tell you it's the fertilizer that's the key: guano, the high-purity kind. She dresses the soil with it and also makes it into a sort of a 'tea' that she sprays right on the leaves and branches. She wants to do the same with our garden at home, but I don't know if I can afford that. And you do know what it's made from, don't you? It'd make me think twice about cutting a bloom for my lapel, if you know what I mean."

Cassie's eye caught movement below. Someone was rounding the side of the tower, headed for the disturbed bushes. Some member of the community with too little to do, probably, drawn by morbid curiosity.

A passing gull called overhead and the person looked up.

"Is something the matter?" Jake asked as Cassie, having dropped into an abrupt squat (for which her dress was already primed, thankfully), sidled away from the railing like a fiddler crab. The person below was that angry policeman from the day before, Hughes.

Cassie paused mid-sidle and considered the possibility that she was in the midst of an overreaction. But if Hughes were to see her, she'd no doubt be in for another tirade about what she should and shouldn't be doing, and she certainly wasn't in the mood for that right now.

"Oh no. I was just checking the, uh—Hey."

There was a black mark on the wood next to her knee. It was about three inches long, and there was another one parallel to it. Continuing her sidle along the floor, she found several more of the same marks between the chair and the edge of the platform.

Jake sat up. "What is it? You find something?"

"Maybe." Cassie stood. "This is going to sound strange, but could you come around behind me and hook your arms under mine? Right here, under the shoulders."

Looking as if he'd been asked to play the violin in his underthings, Jake released his grip from the chair and shuffled around behind her.

"Your, uh, dress—"

"Don't worry about it."

He stuck out his arms.

"Okay," Cassie said, tucking him into position and kicking out her feet. "Now, without loosening your hold, take two or three steps back."

"What?"

"Trust me."

Jake complied, and when he was done, Cassie twisted to examine her boots. As she'd expected, there was a scuff on the back of each heel, in nearly the same place as on Peanut's shoes. There was also a pair of marks on the portion of the floor they had crossed, in the same color as her boot polish.

"Well," Jake said. "I'll be."

"Me, too."

Captain Beale itched his knee. "What?"

"It seems Peanut was dragged," said Cassie. "Unconscious, most likely, all the way to the edge there. Or over it, rather."

Captain Beale stared at her for a moment. Then he crossed himself.

"Well," Jake said again. "Looks like Mr. Shaw is going to have to hold that inquest after all."

CHAPTER SEVEN

Back on the ground, Jake and Cassie decided they would talk Mr. Ambler through what they had found, since Mr. Shaw had made it abundantly clear he was finished hearing from either of them on the matter. It took a while, as they had to dictate what to say word-by-word and have Mr. Ambler recite it back, but, finally, after giving him strict instructions to leave them out of it, they sent him off to find Mr. Shaw. When they returned to where the buggy had been parked, however, they found that everyone had left other than Flora and Esme, who were waiting with two of the horses.

"Where did you go, Jake?" Flora asked. "Metta was still a bit shaken, so I sent her home with the whist-club ladies. Mrs. Grayson said she would stay with her in your room at the Florida House until you return."

"I'm sorry about that, Flora. I didn't mean to run off, but, as Cassie said, something didn't seem right, so I wanted to go up and see the platform while I had the chance. Cassie did, too. And, after finding what we did, I think foul play may have been involved. More than think."

"Foul play?"

"Yes. Maybe even murder."

Esme dropped her reins and hurried to gather them back up. "But I thought he slipped and fell."

"It's still a possibility. But someone else was probably up there with him."

"How do you know that?"

"Cassie found streaks on the platform, black like Peanut's shoes, leading to the edge. So, we conducted, well, an experiment of sorts, which suggests Peanut was dragged. It explains both the marks on the platform and the marks on his shoes."

Esme's hand brushed the area of her skirt where she kept her drink jar. "This is too much. Do you think there'll be an inquest?"

"I'd say so." Jake wiped his forehead with a handkerchief. "Mr. Ambler's gone to tell Mr. Shaw about what we found, and if Mr. Shaw cares at all about being re-elected next month, he'll call one. There's no way people will be satisfied with an accidental death finding once they hear about this."

Cassie thought about the blood on Peanut's face, and his wrong-facing limbs, and her head began to spin again.

Flora caught her arm. "I think we'd better get you back to the house."

"I should be getting on back, too," said Esme. "We left in such a rush to get here I didn't close up the store."

Flora handed her reins to Esme. "In that case, take Sage and go on ahead with Jake. Once you get home, Jake can bring her the rest of the way to the stables. Right, Jake?"

"Yes, ma'am." Taking his own reins from Esme, Jake swung onto his horse and gave it a strong pat on the neck. "Devil of a way to start the day, eh, Pollux?"

At the edge of the old Spanish parade grounds, Flora stopped Cassie with her hand. "Shhhh, look. Isn't that a sight for sore eyes?" She nodded across the road, where a small gray kitten was cavorting among the wildflowers, leaping, twisting, and pouncing at a feather caught in the breeze. Every few swats, it tumbled over its own feet, only to roll over and spring once more. "Animals do remind us joy can be found in the simplest of things, don't they?

They give us a glimpse of life in a purer form, unburdened by so many of the ugly things that plague us humans. Shame, doubt, regret. Duplicity, manipulation. Evil."

"Evil?"

"Yes. I believe evil is something uniquely human, because only we have the ability to make truly self-aware choices. Evil is done when one knows he has a choice and still chooses to do harm. Animals know no such thing. Therefore, they're incapable of evil. But that doesn't mean they can't love. Choice isn't required to love. In fact, it's often irrelevant."

Cassie tilted her head. She hadn't encountered that particular philosophy before, but she was beginning to realize there were a lot of things about Flora she hadn't encountered before. And she was fairly sure she liked that. In any case, she was glad for the peaceful scene. It was a welcome distraction from the grisly one they'd just left behind.

Their reverie was shattered, however, when a distant rumble of hooves swelled to a roar.

"Oh, oh! Oh, no!" Cassie cried.

A pair of mounted men were tearing around the bend, and the kitten, chasing after the feather with single-minded gusto, had tumbled into the street. Right into the path of the charging horses.

Without a word between them, Cassie and Flora dashed forward, Flora shouting to the riders and waving her arms, and Cassie running at the kitten with her hands outstretched. Seeing Cassie hurtling toward it, whooping like a demented screech owl, the kitten shrieked and shot into the bushes. Cassie, on the other hand, somersaulted into a ditch.

The riders came to a halt a short distance away.

"Miss Hale!" one of the men said, turning around in his saddle. "What were you thinking, running out into the street like that?"

"One might ask what *you* were thinking, Mr. Brooks, riding down the street like that," Flora responded.

"Now, now, first things first," said the other man. "Is anyone hurt?"

Cassie, who had been floundering among her skirts, trying to figure out how to stand without falling back into the mud, bolted straight. It had been years since she'd heard that voice, but she'd know it anywhere.

Sam Townsend.

Handsome, perfect Sam Townsend.

What was *he* doing *here*?

"Cassie?" Flora called. "Are you all right?"

"Nononononono," Cassie whispered as she looked down at herself in a panic, fizzling all over like a warm glass of soda. In addition to her split bottom, her dress was filthy from her roll in the mud, and, as the distorted reflection in the puddle next to her showed, her hair was sticking out at odd angles from under her hat, taking her typical windblown-on-a-still-day appearance to a new height. Of all the people who could be coming down the road at that exact moment, why did it have to be him?

Her thoughts fled, and, following their lead, she dove behind a tree, smacking her head on a low-hanging branch as she tumbled into the brush. Hot blood rushed to the point of collision, but she pushed up and crawled soldier-style along the bed of pine needles, hardly reacting as twigs jabbed her skin and spiderwebs caught in her mouth.

"Where is she going?" came Sam's voice once more, closer than expected.

Cassie didn't know the answer to that. Nor did she know what to do now that she'd been spotted. So, with no better idea forthcoming from her crackling brain, she simply froze, like a chameleon waiting for a predator to pass by.

She had almost convinced herself it was working when two strong hands slid around her waist and propped her against a tree trunk, as easily as if she were a doll. She swiveled her head and found herself gazing into a pair of hazel-green eyes which, even set into a fully grown man's face, complete with square jaw and sculpted beard, were as familiar as her own... and still capable of sending waves of heat crashing through her body. Her lips parted at the sensation.

Sam's laugh shocked her back to her senses. "It *is* you! Cassie Gwynne. My word. I was starting to worry you had knocked something loose when you hit your head over there. Are you hurt?" He touched a finger to the lump on her forehead.

"Yes, I do. I mean, I don't think so." She wished to Heaven she'd been born with some measure of grace.

"Good. Now I can apologize." He helped her to her feet. "We're expected for a hunting excursion this morning on an island nearby—one of the Du Pont boys is in town, and he's impossible to amuse any other way—and this one" —he jerked a thumb at the other rider—"was supposed to meet me at the Egmont with the horses so we could take them over with us on the ferry. But he was late, and we missed the ferry, so now we're rushing up to the Old Town Wharf to bribe some crusty old sea captain into taking us across. We still shouldn't have been riding like that, though."

"Oh, uh, it's no harm. Done." *Blast it all.*

"I'm glad. And Lily will be so delighted to hear I've seen you. I'll tell her straight away when I return to the hotel."

So, Sam's little sister, Lily, was in town as well.

Sam slapped his knee. "I can't believe it. What are the chances of us encountering one another like this? After ten years, is it, since we saw each other last?"

"Nearly. I was thirteen when your family moved back to Savannah."

"Do you still live in New York? We're still at Belle Pierre, but we come down here for the occasional holiday. It's murder on the old wallet—well, going anywhere with that sister of mine in tow is—but we've both taken a liking to the island's ocean beach, and we have friends who bring their sporting yachts around from time to time."

"And there's me, of course." The other man, who was, if such a thing were possible, even more dashing than Sam, had walked over to join them. He was long and lean and fashionably dressed, almost to the point of being foppish, and wore a mischievous grin that compelled one in return.

Annoyance flickered on Sam's face but was quickly masked by a practiced politeness.

"Yes, and there's you. Cassie, this is Atherton Brooks. He owns a gentlemen's clothing business in town. And is Lily's, uh, friend."

"Special friend," corrected Mr. Brooks. "With the intention of soon becoming even more special."

Sam folded his arms. "Atherton, this is Cassie Gwynne. You'll remember Lily telling you we lived in New York for a few years while we were children. Cassie's father, who's a prominent lawyer up there, worked for our father, and we all used to play together. Mr. Gwynne works with all the best families."

Cassie shifted. *He doesn't know.*

Mr. Brooks bowed. "An extreme pleasure, Miss Gwynne. And, as Mr. Townsend mentioned, I overslept this morning due to a small problem with a run-down pocket watch, so this entire affair is my fault. Tie me up, take me away." His eyes twinkled and his dimples deepened. "Tell me, how long have you been on our fair island? If it's been any length of time, I shall never forgive myself for having failed to notice such an enchanting creature."

Cassie made a feeble attempt to tuck her hair back into place. "Not long. I came down yesterday morning on the *City of San Antonio*. Miss Hale here is my aunt."

Flora extended her hand to Sam. "Flora Hale, Mr. Townsend. It's lovely to meet you."

"Likewise, Miss Hale, despite the circumstances."

Cassie hopped. "Oh, yes. Uh, Sam, this is my aunt. Flora Hale. Aunt Flora, this is my old friend Sam Townsend. But you already knew—Did that." Cassie wondered where she could get a fork to stick in her eye. A twig might have to do.

Flora turned to Mr. Brooks, who was somehow still flashing his dimples at Cassie. "Mr. Brooks, I should tell you, since you were Peanut's colleague—"

"No, no. You'll remember I only spent a short time with the harbor pilots, and that was ages ago. I hardly know the man."

"Well, you may still be interested to know Peanut has died. We found him at the foot of the pilots' tower this morning. It seems he suffered a fall."

Mr. Brooks took off his hat and lowered his head. "How awful. I knew that monstrosity was an accident waiting to happen."

"Actually," Cassie said, struggling to scrape some of her dignity off the ground, "there's a fair chance it wasn't an accident."

"Oh?" Mr. Brooks ran a hand over his blond hair, which was, as everything else about him, assiduously styled. The well-oiled strands gleamed like gold tinsel in the sun.

"My niece here has made some very clever observations about the matter," said Flora. "So I believe we will see a murder inquest take place in the very near future."

Sam snapped to attention. "A murder inquest? Why, a town embroiled in such a thing is no place for a lady!" He turned and strode toward his horse. "Forget hunting. I need to take Lily home immediately. Brooks, get to it, man."

Giving a distracted tip of his hat, Mr. Brooks followed, and in another moment they were gone.

Cassie's stomach folded over on itself. That was it? No promise to write or hope to meet again, or even a goodbye? She didn't mean to be selfish, but the interaction had left her off-balance, as though she'd reached the top of the stairs without realizing it and taken an extra stride through the air. Or begun to sit down, only to find there was no chair.

"So, this Mr. Townsend… Did you mean old friend or old flame?" Flora gave Cassie a sidelong glance as she re-tied her hat.

"What? Oh, no. Hardly either, actually. We've not seen or spoken to each other since his family moved away all those years ago."

"Ah. I noticed he doesn't seem to have heard the news about your father."

"Well, he lives far away in Georgia, so I wouldn't expect him to have, necessarily. I mean, I sent our condolences to his family when his father passed, but—It doesn't matter. Well, it does matter, but it seemed—I'm not sure how one is supposed to bring that up in casual conversation."

"Your reaction to seeing him didn't seem casual to me."

Cassie flushed. "My reaction? I don't know what you're—"

"Old flame it is, then."

"I—"

"Come. No one nearly knocks herself out over someone she doesn't care for."

Cassie dropped her shoulders. "All right." It was hard not to smile at the ridiculous "knowing look" Flora was giving her. "Just stop wiggling your eyebrows at me like that."

Flora laughed and did it again.

"If you must know, I might have admired him years ago, but that was when we were children. And I assure you, he never took any notice of me in that way."

"He may see you differently now you're both grown."

"Oh, I wouldn't expect so, especially after that little performance of mine in the brush." She lifted her chin. "Besides, I'm not the kind of woman who harbors absurd notions of romance, believing what happens in novels holds any resemblance to real life."

Flora caught Cassie's eye on its way up from her empty ring finger. "That I've never married doesn't mean I'm ignorant of such matters, Cassie."

"I wasn't—" Cassie dropped her gaze. "Of course. I wouldn't— Oh, the kitten!"

She fell to her knees and crawled toward the gap in the bushes where she'd seen the kitten disappear. When she turned an ear, she heard a faint mewling in the shadows. The poor thing was terrified. She thought for a moment then opened her pouch and pulled out a square of cheddar wrapped in a handkerchief, which she had tucked away at breakfast on the ship the morning before.

She broke off a piece and placed it on the ground. Soon, a nose emerged from the shadows, searching for the source of the savory odor, followed by a progression of whiskers, eyes, and ears. In another blink, the cheese had disappeared, and the kitten was climbing into Cassie's lap, casting about for more. Cassie broke off another piece. She could see now not only how matted and filthy the animal's fur was but how skinny its little body was.

It took three more pieces but finally the tiny creature, belly full, gave its paw a token lick and nestled into the folds of Cassie's dress. Then, as though feeling Cassie's gaze, it looked up with sleepy eyes and let out a mew.

Cassie's heart took a long-awaited breath.

"See?" Flora said. "Love."

Back at the cottage, Cassie carried the kitten up to her room and, despite her vocal protests and attempts to climb over Cassie's shoulder, gave her a thorough bath in the washbasin. Once she was clean and dry, Cassie discovered that, while she had gray markings at the points—nose, ears, paws, and tail—most of her fur was not gray, after all, but rather a bright, lovely white, from which her blue eyes shone out like splashes of summer sky breaking through a cloud.

"You're as soft as a rabbit." Cassie ran her hand along the kitten's back and up her tail. The kitten purred and butted her arm in response.

Leaving the kitten to her inspection of her new home, Cassie stripped down to her shift, dragged the dressing table chair over to the washstand, and, letting out a forceful exhale, began the task of cleaning herself up.

She worked at every inch of herself with a washcloth, trying to remove not only the mud but also the stench of death sticking to her skin. The latter, of course, she knew was entirely in her mind. She'd read enough of her father's scientific books to know that. But she couldn't help feeling a bit like Lady Macbeth as she scrubbed herself raw with soap and water.

Maybe it was because that wasn't all she was trying to wash away. She had told Flora she was too practical to think life was anything like the romance stories she used to squeeze in between the technical texts her father gave her to read, but that wasn't true. Since the day Sam and Lily moved away, she had secretly hoped she would have such a story of her own. That one day she would meet Sam again unexpectedly, at a ball or at the opera perhaps, and she would no longer be the scrappy girl who climbed and ran and dug in the mud. She would be a real lady, refined and sophisticated, and, with a single look, Sam would fall for her hopelessly.

Well, part of that had come true. She and Sam had met again. But, even with all her efforts to remake herself prior to coming to the island, in almost the most literal way possible, she had been the same disheveled girl, covered in dirt.

She scoffed at herself. When Sam had said this was "no place for a lady," he hadn't even hinted a glance in her direction. Perhaps Lady Macbeth was as close to a lady as she was going to get.

As she reached for one of the jasmine-scented hand towels stacked in front of her, she caught her reflection in the mirror. And there was that. Chin still dripping, she tilted her head to examine her scar. It started at the base of her earlobe and ran across her throat on a diagonal, cross-hatched at intervals where the stitches had been like a train track missing a rail. For months it had been an angry red, but now it was white, lighter than the surrounding skin, and had a sort of a sheen. She ran her finger along it, feeling the rise and fall of each globular lump. It probably wasn't going to get much better than this—The doctors said it would fade but never completely disappear. Like her memories of that horrific day, it would be with her for the rest of her life.

She shoved back from the table, ashamed of her vanity.

She'd been the lucky one.

"Mreow." The kitten was staring up at her from between her feet, her eyes large, round, and black.

Cassie smiled in spite of herself. She had never had any pets of her own, but she knew enough to understand that when a kitten's eyes were dark and wild like that, all pupil as though possessed, it was up to something.

Sure enough, when Cassie tried to stand, the kitten sprang off the floor, paws splayed, and wrapped herself around her leg. Hugging Cassie's ankle in what was probably intended as a death grip, the kitten swung around onto her back and, all the while keeping her eyes locked with Cassie's, furiously pedaled her back legs, eviscerating her imaginary prey. Cassie laughed so hard she almost fell over the chair.

"How did you know exactly what I needed right now?" She reached down to tickle the kitten's belly, and the kitten transferred her battle hug from ankle to wrist.

"I should give you a name. But it has to be something that truly suits you—"

There was a knock at the door.

"It's me," Flora called as Cassie threw on a robe. "I just wanted to let you know that Esme's pulled some hot water down in the kitchen, in case you'd like a bath."

Cassie opened the door, hopping as the kitten darted through her legs. Danger, who was panting next to Flora, hopped as well when the kitten jumped up to bat the tag on his collar.

"Thank you. A bath sounds wonderful. But I don't want you to go to any trouble—"

Flora seized Cassie's face between her hands and brought it in line with hers. "Now, Cassie, listen to me carefully because I'm only going to say this once. You are *family*. And doing things for family is not trouble. Understand?"

Cassie nodded slowly, her lips puckered between Flora's palms.

"Good." Flora released her. "I've waited far too long to have my family, what's left of it, back, and I'm not going to waste time standing on ceremony. If you're thinking something, say it. If you need something, ask. And I'll do the same."

Cassie rubbed her cheek. *She doesn't have anyone else, either.*

"Understood." She picked up the kitten, who had just received another bath from Danger's tongue, and dried her with her sleeve. "So, what's for lunch?"

Flora beamed in approval.

"Ah! There she is!" Flora jumped out of her rocking chair as Cassie stepped onto the front porch the next morning. She threw her arms around her. "Good morning, my sweet niece!"

Reeling from Flora's easy intimacy, Cassie squinted at the sun, then sneezed. "Excuse me. Uh, good morning. What time is it?"

"Nearly ten. You'd been up there so long I thought maybe I should check whether you were still in your room. You know, in case you'd wandered into the marsh in your sleep..." She sobered. "But I'm sure you needed the rest. Yesterday was—a tough one."

"Yes, it was." Cassie massaged her temples. "Goodness. I don't even remember falling asleep. How did I—"

"You nodded off right in the middle of a game of Hearts with Esme, Sergeant Denham, and me. We had a terrible time pulling your cards from your grip so we could get you upstairs."

Cassie bit her lip. As Flora was speaking, bits and pieces were coming back. "You tucked me into bed."

"Just like I did when you were very small." Not giving Cassie any time to be embarrassed about that, Flora took her hand and led her to a table at the end of the porch loaded with baked goods. "And another thing I used to do when you were small was feed you breakfast. I remembered how much you used to love bananas, which are still in season right now, so this morning Esme and I took it as a theme. We have banana loaf, of course, banana muffins, banana pancakes, and, there, to the left of the kitten, banana doughnuts. It is possible we got carried away."

The sweet scent of the fruit coming off the baked goods was so thick and luscious Cassie could feel it on her skin. "I disagree. Heartily."

She was reaching for one of the doughnuts, which were decorated with a layer of fresh banana slices, when two girls, perhaps around fourteen or fifteen, walked up to the gate. They whispered and jostled each other, as though daring one other to go in, then ran off.

Flora turned to Esme, who'd come onto the porch with a coffee tray. "It just happened again, Esme."

Close to where the girls had been standing, there were a number of other people wandering by in the street, some staring up at Flora's house and others staring up at Peanut's. Peanut's yard, as dreary and foreboding as always, was full of people, too.

"It has to have something to do with whatever's going on at Peanut's house," Esme said.

Flora looked out over the railing. "Yes. I don't believe I've ever seen so many people on that property at once."

"Hey! Miss Hale!" A dirty-haired boy punted the gate open and sauntered up the path.

Esme slammed down her tray. "Neily Cranstock, it is incredibly rude to yell at people like that. If you have something to say to Miss Hale, you come closer first and address her in a respectful way."

"I'm closer now," the boy mumbled as he reached the steps. Given the way he was glaring at the ground with his hands shoved in his trouser pockets, it was clear he wasn't here for a social visit.

Flora waved at Esme to stand down. "What is it, Neily?"

"I'm supposed to tell you and Miss Gwynne to come to Peanut's house."

"Come to Peanut's house? Why?"

"You're wanted at the inquest for an interview with the coroner's jury."

Flora glanced at Cassie. "So Mr. Shaw has called an inquest, after all."

"That's what I said."

Cassie's stomach rumbled. She had only gotten to take one bite of doughnut before they were interrupted. "What do they want with us?"

"Lady, all I know is I'm supposed to tell you to come to Peanut's house."

"But didn't anyone say—"

"We'll be right over," Flora said. "Just give us a moment to get ourselves together."

Rather than waiting, however, the boy turned and trotted away, pausing only to kick over a watering can before disappearing through the gate.

Esme crossed her arms. "So much for reminding that boy of his manners."

*

As they passed through the gate to Peanut's house, Cassie marveled again at the house's gloominess, though the effect was tempered at present by the motley assortment of people milling about the property. Some were weaving around the yard, pausing every few feet to turn over a rock or pick through a bush; others were skulking around the porch doing inane things like peeking under mats or digging through Peanut's basket of grapefruits, which he had left on one of the steps. One man had even taken it upon himself to climb the ogre-tree and was now peering nervously at the ground, possibly having failed to consider the old adage that what goes up must come down.

And people call me *nosy.*

What was merely off-putting became unsettling, however, when they were about halfway across the yard and people started noticing them. One by one, in a quickening progression, heads turned, and Cassie felt Flora's arm slide into hers. What exactly were they looking at?

Neily, who was waiting impatiently by the grapefruit basket, hopped up the last few steps when they drew close and opened the door with a key. When they reached the porch, however, he threw up a nail-bitten hand.

"Only Miss Hale can come in right now. Miss Gwynne has to wait outside until it's her turn."

"Oh? All right." Flora disengaged her arm from Cassie's and smoothed her dress. Her voice was steady, but Cassie noticed a slight tremble in her hands. "Well, my niece, see you on the other side." She entered the foyer, and Neily, after giving Cassie an authoritative glare, followed her in and closed the door behind them.

"*Psst.* Cassie. Over here." Jake was beckoning to Cassie from around the side of the house.

When she walked over to where he was indicating, she found him squeezed in with several women beneath an open window.

One of the women, who was dressed in a blue Mother Hubbard with a lace collar and crab-shaped buttons and was almost perfectly round, bounced as she approached. "Look, Alice, there she is!"

"Yes, I have eyes, too, Lottie." The woman next to her, a near geometric opposite to her friend, had a long, curveless figure, made even more so by the man's vest and linen trousers she wore. "Now shut it, or they'll hear us."

Jake shushed them both. "Cassie, this is Miss Charlotte Porter, owner of the new Lottie Cottage boarding house on Sixth Street, and Mrs. Alice Keene, who runs a Florida Collectibles and Curiosities Store on Centre with her husband, Captain Keene. They're good friends of Flora's but were late coming back from a supply run upriver so missed the party."

"We've been so very excited to meet you, dear," said Miss Porter, attempting a whisper but achieving almost no reduction in volume. "Your aunt has hardly been able to speak of anything else since she received your letter."

Mrs. Keene spat a sunflower seed husk. "We weren't late. *Someone* had the wrong danged date for when we were supposed to be back."

"Alice, language!"

"Made us miss the only not-cussedly-boring night around here in months."

"Maybe if I didn't have to cover my ears half the time you talked, I'd have known what I was being asked." Miss Porter took up Cassie's hand and patted it. "You are very welcome, is the point. My, you're lovely. Just like your mother."

"Um, thank you." She suffered Miss Porter's adoring stare and Mrs. Keene's appraising one for another moment then cleared her throat. "What exactly are all of you doing here again?"

"Listening to the proceedings," said Jake.

Cassie wriggled her way in and hunched down next to him. "You do realize you're squatting with a bunch of people under a dead man's window, right?"

"Mr. Shaw made it a closed inquest. Won't let anyone in. He said he didn't want the town to get overexcited, but it's only making the clamor worse, if you ask me. Look at all the souvenir seekers and gossip gatherers prowling around."

"Aren't you one of them?"

"Doesn't make me wrong. There're even a few still poking around the pilots' tower. Good thing Mr. Shaw's asked for a policeman to go over and deter the more foolhardy individuals from trying to climb the thing, or else we might have some real accidents on our hands."

Cassie grimaced. "What's happening, then? I've been asked to come in and speak with the jury."

"I know. I would have come by to warn you, but I didn't want to miss anything over here. As expected, when Mr. Shaw heard about the marks on the platform yesterday morning, he gave in and had Dr. Ames conduct a postmortem. As soon as he got the report, he couldn't assemble a jury and start conducting interviews fast enough."

"My word. What was in that report?"

"From what we could overhear, even though Peanut had all the 'usual' injuries for a fall from a high place—fractured ribs, punctured lungs, burst spleen, that sort of thing—Dr. Ames couldn't say for certain the fall was the actual cause of death."

"Why?"

"He found a terrible stab wound!" cried Miss Porter.

Cassie grabbed onto the wall as a voice—a doctor's voice—echoed in her head.

That cut on your neck will heal, Miss Gwynne, as bad as it seems now. But I'm afraid your father wasn't so fortunate. He received several very serious stab wounds.

"Yes, under the left arm," said Jake. "One that could have, or would have, killed him, all on its own, even if he hadn't gone over. Dr. Ames said the entry point was small, but, on the inside, there was a whole mess of damage. Like someone had inserted something sharp and twisted it all around."

There was extensive internal bleeding and damage to his internal organs. I'm afraid there was nothing we could do.

Mrs. Keene took a bite of an apple. "Like scrambling an egg." She shrugged at the green faces around her. "Doc's words, not mine."

Cassie tried to keep her voice even. "But we didn't notice any blood on the platform."

"Dr. Ames said there probably wouldn't have been much, if any," said Jake. "Something to do with the shape of the wound. There was so little bleeding even around the wound itself, he almost missed it. Oh, and there were also some scratches on the palms of Peanut's hands. But no one knows what to make of those. Apparently, they didn't seem like something the rose bushes would have done because they were clean. No debris."

Cassie pondered the possibilities, finding a reprieve in the mental effort. "Maybe they were from something being pulled from his grasp."

"Clever girl!" Miss Porter clapped her hands.

The group shushed.

"Come to think of it," Cassie said, "Peanut's hat was also lying on the floor up on the platform. It could have fallen off in a struggle. That would mean we were right. Pushing Peanut over the edge, putting the binoculars on the ground, that was all to make his death seem like an accident. So people wouldn't look too closely. And it nearly worked. Did Dr. Ames say what kind of knife was used?"

Mrs. Keene threw her apple core over her shoulder and licked her fingers. "He said he didn't know. He could only tell it wasn't a normal one. Not a pocketknife or Bowie knife or anything. Something long and thin, with a small, sharp point."

Cassie looked at Jake, who'd fallen silent. His eyebrows were pinched together tightly enough to hold a nickel between them. "What is it, Jake?"

"There's another thing. Mr. Shaw's put Mr. Meeks on the jury."

"Arrogant, good-for-nothing slugs, the both of them," said Mrs. Keene. The others murmured in agreement.

"What does that mean?"

"Given the damage their business has suffered from Flora's demonstrations against the stockyard," said Jake, "and with the coroner's election around the corner, they must be thinking of the publicity to be had by identifying and committing the offender for trial as quickly as possible. They'll want to be heroes."

"That's not surprising. People often take advantage of situations like this for political gain."

Jake tugged at his sleeve. "That may be so, but, and I'm no expert, after listening to the interviews they conducted this morning—they've made their way through most of the neighbors already—I wonder whether personal… motivations are affecting their search for the villain."

Cassie's stomach turned cold. "Are you saying… you think they're saying they think Flora might have had something to do with Peanut's death?"

The looks and whispers were starting to make sense.

"I think they may be saying, thinking—that, yes." Jake let go of his sleeve and pushed his hand down. "Or, maybe worse, wanting to think that. Either way, Cassie, your aunt may be in some real trouble here."

CHAPTER EIGHT

Jake had hardly finished speaking when Officer Hughes pushed through the bushes behind them, his mustache twitching.

"So, things aren't looking too good for your special lady friend, eh, Gordo?" One of his hands was wrapped in a bandage.

"For the thousandth time," Jake said, "she's not my—You have no right to—" He huffed. "Anyway, that isn't funny. None of this is. And don't you have boots to sell?"

"Don't you have buggies to polish? Besides, while you've been sitting here wallowing in gossip, I've been conducting my own investigation into Peanut's death. And once I get the culprit in custody, Uncle—I mean, the sheriff will realize I should be his deputy. It's in my blood, after all."

"We're cousins, so it's in both of our blood," Jake muttered. He stood and straightened his coat. "I'm investigating, too. Who's to say I won't get him first?"

"Investigate away. But don't feel bad when you lose."

"You seem to be forgetting which of us the sheriff put in charge while he's away."

"He just hasn't seen what I can do yet."

"He saw plenty of what you can do when your mistake got the Earl of Something-ton stripped down to his socks and searched for stolen jewels."

Hughes's ears turned pink. "It wasn't a mistake. I had bad information."

"Maybe if you asked politely once in a while rather than demanding, you'd find your sources more cooperative."

"It's called having a firm hand, something you wouldn't know much about. Now, if you biddies will get out of my way, I have work to do. Cluck-cluck."

Giving his derby a haughty pat, Hughes elbowed his way toward the backyard. As he passed Jake, however, he said something under his breath. Jake responded by throwing his arm around Hughes's neck, and in a flash the two men were locked in a mutual headlock, jerking about like a beast with four legs.

Cassie had once read a description of how bull elk lock horns while vying for dominance. She suspected it looked something like this.

Jake released his grip to swing a fist at Hughes but missed. Taking advantage of the shift in weight, Hughes drove his shoulder into Jake's ribs and sent him tumbling into a pile of chopped wood. When he turned to revel in his success, however, he slipped on a loose rock and fell on top of Jake.

"Crap in a bag." Mrs. Keene ducked as Mr. Shaw thrust his head out of the window above them.

He scorched the crowd with his glare. "Pardon me, but if you all could take your roughhousing and idle chatter somewhere else, the coroner's jury would be much obliged. We are attending to important matters in here, in case you haven't noticed." His gaze fell on Cassie. "Hm. I suppose I shouldn't be surprised you're a part of this foolishness as well, Miss Gwynne. Well, don't go anywhere. We'll be calling you just as soon as we've finished with Miss Hale." Throwing out another general look of disdain, he pulled his head in and slammed the window shut.

"Now you've done it, you dunces," said Mrs. Keene. "We won't be able to hear any more of the inquest with the window closed."

Miss Porter puffed. "We're missing Flora's interview because of you!"

Jake and Hughes, meek as scolded schoolboys, dipped their heads, and the window crowd began to disperse. Hughes skulked out from under Mrs. Keene's wrathful eye and around the back of the house.

Cassie turned toward the front yard, which was still full of trespassing "souvenir seekers and gossip gatherers," as Jake had put it. Unfortunately, such behavior was not uncommon where a lurid crime was involved—she'd seen it before while shadowing her father—but that didn't make it any less uncomfortable or confusing to her. Who were these people? Why were they compelled to hang on every sordid detail of other people's misfortunes? She supposed she was as susceptible to a titillating story as anyone else, but didn't they have anything better to do than kick dirt around in a dead man's yard? Surely some of them had children to attend to, or occupations of some kind.

What was more disturbing was the way they had looked at Flora. Given the size of the city, some were bound to be friends and neighbors, or customers, of hers. They clearly knew who she was. But they had stared at her as if she had grown an extra set of eyeballs on top of her head. And those girls jostling each other at the gate had seemed afraid of her. Could Jake be right? Did the coroner's jury truly consider Flora a potential murderer? And, perhaps just as bad, did the rest of Flora's own community suspect her as well?

After about twenty minutes, the door opened, and Flora came out. Jake jumped up from where their group had settled at the foot of the stairs.

"Flora, what happened? What did they ask?"

"I—I'm not entirely sure." She held onto the railing and stepped down slowly, unsteadily, like she was feeling her way through a fog. "But they don't seem very pleased with me. And, apparently, they're not the only ones."

She faltered, and Mrs. Keene and Miss Porter rushed to her side.

"Hush now, dearie," Miss Porter said. "Let's get you home so you can take a little rest. We can talk about it later."

Mrs. Keene stuck her chin out at Jake. "That's right. What were you thinking, hounding her with more questions when she's just sat through so many?"

"Where's Cassie?" Flora leaned against Mrs. Keene.

"Right here, Aunt Flora."

"Don't let them upset you, okay? Just answer what they ask, and everything will be all right."

"Of course. Don't worry about me."

After another short wait, Neily Cranstock opened the door and led Cassie down a shadowy hall adorned by a garish parade of mounted hunting trophies and into a small dining room, where Dr. Ames and Mr. Shaw stood by the window, smoking pipes. Beyond them, four other men sat lined up on one side of a long table.

She recognized two of them, Mr. Ambler, who pretended he didn't know her, even after Mr. Shaw recounted how they'd met earlier, and Mr. Cranstock, the fishmonger who had helped transport Peanut's body away from the tower (and, if logic served, the father of the boy who had summoned her to the inquest). The others, she was informed, were Mr. Newell, a pear-shaped man with an uncanny resemblance to a turtle, and Mr. Shaw's brother-in-law, Mr. Meeks, who had beady eyes and a fat bandage over his nose.

Peanut's coat, hat, umbrella, and binoculars were lined up in front of them on the table, along with his shoes and the contents of his coat pockets, and as Cassie lowered herself onto the chair opposite them, she shuddered as though sitting down to an unappetizing meal.

"I hope our little conversation yesterday didn't offend." Mr. Shaw's expression brought to mind a snake regarding a mouse. "I was only trying to perform my duties, you understand. And we do appreciate your coming in to speak with us, don't we, gentlemen?"

They all nodded, other than Mr. Newell, who seemed to have fallen asleep.

"Right. Let's begin. Mrs. Newell has brought us a basket of walnut chicken salad sandwiches and molasses cookies, and I know we're all eager to get to it." Mr. Shaw prepared his pen. "Miss Gwynne, I'm going to ask you some questions now. Bear in mind the coroner's court is a court of law, so you are to answer truthfully, under the penalty of perjury. First, how and when did you discover the body of Captain Theodore H. Runkles, the man known as Peanut?"

Theodore Runkles? No wonder Peanut hadn't objected to his nickname.

"Yesterday morning my aunt, Flora Hale, took me on a walk up to Old Town. When we came upon the clearing by the harbor pilots' lookout tower, I saw something on the ground and went over to investigate. That was when I stepped—found... Captain Runkles. It was about eight."

Mr. Shaw mm-hmmed. "You've known your aunt for, what is it, two days?"

"Well, yes. I met her for the first time, at least that I can remember, after I arrived on the island Tuesday morning."

"And when you met her, that first time, she was in jail for striking a man."

Cassie frowned. Neither of those were exactly questions. "Disturbing the peace, actually. And she maintains that what happened was an accident."

"What was on the ground? In the clearing?"

"Peanut's shoe. It had been dislodged from his foot."

"Where was the body, more specifically?"

"Among the rose bushes on the east side of the tower. There were binoculars on the ground nearby. There was also some strange scuffing on his shoes."

Mr. Ambler perked up.

"Which I connected to certain markings up on the platform, suggesting the victim was dragged, unconscious, to the edge, a hypother-sis later supported by the postmortem, which identified a stab wound." He spoke slowly and deliberately, as a child does when adding numbers in his head, and beamed proudly when he'd finished.

"So it was your aunt's idea to go up to Old Town," said Mr. Meeks.

Cassie noticed the canvas duster draped over the back of his chair. She knew he seemed familiar. He was the man she'd seen that first morning, creeping after the ticket-agent woman on Centre Street.

"That's right. She wanted to show me something."

"Interesting. And what was that?"

"I don't know, actually. I think it was meant to be a surprise, but we never got there. And after we found the body, we—"

"How did Miss Hale seem when you found the body?"

"How did she seem?"

"Did she have a normal reaction? Was she shocked, horrified, unable to speak?"

"I don't—She didn't fall into hysterics, if that's what you mean."

"Ah, so she was nonchalant. Maybe even glad." Mr. Meeks leaned forward as he spoke, his high-pitched voice working an unsettling harmony with the whistle emanating from his bandage.

Mr. Cranstock shifted uncomfortably in the chair next to him.

"She was neither of those things. She was simply trying to figure out what to do."

Mr. Shaw gave his piece of paper an authoritative shake in Mr. Meeks's direction. "Next question. Miss Gwynne, are you able to vouch for your aunt's whereabouts Tuesday night after she threatened Captain Runkles's life?"

"She didn't threaten his life. She was just upset because she'd received a frightening message."

"And what was this 'frightening message'?"

Cassie inhaled slowly. "There was a note on her doorstep suggesting she was being punished for not respecting someone's property. It had been placed on top of a dead fish. Which was wearing a tie. Belonging to Flora's pet pig."

Mr. Meeks sniggered, though he couldn't be hearing this story for the first time.

"I still don't think a pig wearing a tie is that odd." Mr. Ambler stroked his chin thoughtfully. "Mrs. Palmer knits sweaters for her dog. And Mr. Livingston once put a hat on his horse. Cut holes for the ears and everything."

"As you informed us earlier, Mr. Ambler," said Mr. Shaw. "Now, what—"

"No, before I was talking about Mrs. Swann's goat, which has an evening gown—"

"What did Miss Hale think the message meant, Miss Gwynne?" continued Mr. Shaw.

"—and long gloves and everything."

"She believed her pet pig had been harmed," said Cassie.

"And how did she feel about that?"

"Terrible, of course. Devastated, furious. She cares deeply for her animals."

"And who did she believe left that message?"

"Peanut. Captain Runkles."

"And why was that?"

"Because Roger had gotten out and rooted up Peanut's vegetable patch a few days before, and Peanut had threatened to destroy the animal if she didn't do so herself."

"And did she or did she not then, referring to Captain Runkles—"

"—say the words 'I'll kill him'?" Mr. Meeks cut in. "Loudly enough for the neighbors to overhear from their porches? Mind, several of those neighbors have already given their accounts of the incident." He was sneering, which was an impressive feat, given the bandage on his face.

"It was only a figure of speech." Cassie blew out a breath. A hot, sticky sweat had started to gather under her arms.

She briefly dipped her head to the side. It didn't smell very good, either.

Mr. Meeks scoffed. "Now, how can we be sure of that? Everyone knows Miss Hale and Peanut have hated each other for years." He pulled something out from under the table: the shovel Flora had thrown on Peanut's step the night before. "And she attacked him with this very weapon directly afterward, correct?"

Cassie's breaths grew shorter and fiercer. "That's a gardening tool, not a weapon. And she was fifteen feet away when she swung it. You can't think she was actually trying to strike him."

"Right. That would come later, when Officer Gordon wasn't around to control her. Sheriff Alderman ought to have left her in jail. She's clearly dangerous. You can see what she did to me."

"*Point is,*" Mr. Shaw said, "you cannot deny Miss Hale uttered words that, by their very meaning, were a threat on Captain Runkles's life, only hours before that life was in fact taken."

"But that's absurd!" said Cassie.

Mr. Newell cracked an eye open briefly before sinking back into his stupor.

"She backed down. And when she came back inside later that evening, she was perfectly in control!"

"Like you are right now?"

"Yes!" Cassie bit her lip.

"Let's set that aside for now and return to the original question," said Mr. Shaw. "Which is, can you vouch for your aunt's whereabouts the night Captain Runkles was killed?"

"She was at home in her bedroom," Cassie answered. "I spoke with her briefly as she was turning in, and I didn't see her after that until the morning."

"But it's possible she left after you went to bed, without your noticing, correct?"

"I was in a room separate from hers, so, of course, it's possible."

"Meaning you can't say for certain she didn't."

"You can't say for certain she did."

Mr. Shaw gave her a long look then put down his pen. "Thank you, Miss Gwynne. That's all we have for you. Mr. Ambler, please see her out."

"No. I have something else to say." Cassie gripped the table, her bottom cemented to the chair.

"We're very busy, Miss Gwynne."

"I know some of you in here would like to see Flora suffer. But this isn't a game."

Mr. Meeks lifted out of his seat. "What exactly are you suggesting?"

"An actual woman's life is at stake, and you're sitting here throwing around accusations without the least—"

"That's enough!" said Mr. Shaw. "Miss Gwynne, please go."

Pulling away from Mr. Ambler's outstretched hand, Cassie pushed through the doorway and stormed into the hall.

After a pause in the parlor to collect herself, Cassie was turning to leave when a face popped up in the window, startling her into an end table crowded with stuffed squirrels.

"Sakes alive, Jake."

He gestured for her to open the window. "How was the jury interview?"

"Wait there. I'll come outside."

"No, the door'll lock and we won't be able to get back in."

"'Back in'?"

"I want to take a look around the house. No way I'm letting Hughes get ahead of me on this. Especially where Flora's involved."

"All right. Hold on." Flinching at the groan the window gave as she pulled it closed, Cassie went to the front door and let Jake in. "I don't know where that Neily Cranstock boy is, though. I don't think he would appreciate my usurping his gatekeeping duties."

"No need to worry about him," Jake said as he strode into the parlor. "He went back up to Old Town on an errand for his father. We have plenty of time." He started walking around the room, pausing every so often to scribble a note in the pink child's notebook he'd pulled from his coat.

Cassie took out a piece of gum and chewed it agitatedly. "You were right, by the way. Mr. Shaw and Mr. Meeks were the only ones who spoke during my interview, and it was abundantly clear what assumption they were laboring under." She stepped aside to let Jake crawl past with a magnifying glass hovered over the floor. "The whole thing was a farce. Mr. Meeks even asked about Flora's 'reaction' to seeing the body, as if he could discern anything useful from that. What kind of a way is that to conduct an investigation? Even if Flora were guilty, this would be infuriating."

Jake sat up under the squirrel table, nearly banging his head. "You do know she's incapable of something like this, right?"

"Of course. I wasn't suggesting—"

"Good. I—She needs you to be sure."

Cassie studied him as he returned to his search of the floor.

"You really care for her, don't you."

She bit her tongue. It had just slipped out.

Jake slowed. "Sure I care about her. I've known her for a very long time. When my father was injured and couldn't work anymore, your grandfather gave me a job maintaining the garden around their house so we'd have money to live. Flora would come out and help me in the afternoons, so I wouldn't have to be alone. Since I was only a boy, really. And later, when my wife… left us, there she was again, taking care of Metta and me every day until I could bear to get out of bed. That's the kind of person she is."

"I see. But—I meant you *care for* her. As in, Keats care for her." Cassie chided her mouth for its continued disobedience.

Jake picked up one of the squirrels. "It doesn't matter whether I do or not. She doesn't feel that way about me."

"Why not?"

"She—Her heart is otherwise occupied. And, believe me, there's no competing with it."

"'Otherwise occupied'?" Cassie was confused. She hadn't met anyone so far who had anywhere near the intimacy with Flora that Jake seemed to have.

Jake put down the squirrel and wrote something in his notebook. "Never mind. I shouldn't be talking about her like this."

"But I—"

"And we ought to focus on what we're doing here. What you were saying about the jury, it's all the more reason for us to do everything we can to make sure they don't get carried away." Jake tucked his notebook back into his coat. "Remember, even aside from whatever personal agendas they may have, they're just ordinary people, not trained for this sort of thing. Mr. Shaw and Mr. Meeks are stockyard owners. The others—a fishmonger, a baker, a log driver—they were assembled from whomever happened to be around when the inquest was called."

Cassie followed him to the fireplace, her mind trailing behind slightly.

"And if I'm to be entirely honest"—Jake pulled off a shoe and used it to sift through the ashes—"we policemen, hard as we might try, aren't either. We're primarily watchmen, peacekeepers. We don't have any instruction in crime solving, not like they do up there in New York or in Chicago or Boston. We're barely even paid for our efforts. Which is why we all have to mind our other occupations, too. For me it's the livery, for Hughes it's the boot store. Even Sheriff Alderman relies on the income from his wood yard.

"In other words, a lot of the time what we accomplish is as much luck as it is skill. In fact, I'll bet what you learned from your father about talking to people, figuring out what they're about, already makes you more qualified than the rest of us combined."

"I don't know about that. So far I only seem to be making things worse around here."

"You've sought out the truth. We could all take a lesson from you there." Jake put his shoe back on. "Now, we'd better keep moving. Who knows how long we'll have before someone finds us and throws us out."

CHAPTER NINE

Cassie and Jake finished in the parlor and quietly moved on to the rest of the floor. As they worked, however, an unexpected mix of sadness and apprehension crept over Cassie. Oddly enough, it wasn't the ghastly animal heads haunting the halls that affected her the most, though those were certainly disturbing enough. It was all the normal things scattered about the house, remnants of the life that had been conducted there day after day, until one day it wasn't. Reminders of all the little tasks people do thousands of times with hardly a thought, never considering that any one time might be the last. A dish left to dry. A basket of linens set out to be laundered. A shopping list written out in small, neat capitals: potatoes, bacon, flour, fruit.

Cassie was drawn back, against her will, to the first time she had gone into her father's study after his passing. She'd spent hundreds of hours in that cozy, wood-paneled room, first as a girl, curled in her father's lap as he read her articles from *Scientific American* magazine, then later as an adult, taking notes on client interviews or helping research legal briefs. But on that day, as she stood in the stinging darkness, her gaze wandering over the stacks of treatises and case digests, the socks on the fireplace grate, the teacup on the window ledge, stained from a last sip dried at the bottom… it had felt wrong to be there. As if she were the one who was dead, a ghost haunting a place she no longer belonged.

Hearing voices in the kitchen, they stopped to peek through the cracked door. Evidently, this was where Dr. Ames had conducted the postmortem. Peanut was lying on the table, covered to the waist by a sheet, above which a large, stitched "Y" stretched across his chest. Behind him, a sturdy-looking woman was washing strips of surgical fabric in a basin by the window. Another woman, very thin and fully gray, despite otherwise appearing little older than Flora, sat next to him with her back to the hall, her hand on his as she gently, almost tenderly, wiped his face and neck with a cloth.

Cassie noticed a doe head above the stove, and it occurred to her that the poor creature now had the privilege of looking down on the corpse of her own killer.

"Yowch!" hissed Jake.

Taken aback by her own thoughts, Cassie had unconsciously stepped backward, bringing the heel of her boot down on his toe.

The woman attending to Peanut spun around on her stool, and Jake pulled Cassie against the wall. It was that ticket-agent woman again. Only now, her face, instead of being pinched in an expression of perpetual annoyance, was slack and pale, its only color the red rims around her puffy eyes.

She stood.

"Sarah!" Mr. Meeks appeared through an internal door from the dining room. "What in Sam's satchel are you doing here?"

The woman's mouth opened and closed soundlessly before her voice came. "I came to help Mrs. Meeks. She has pain in her back, so she can't properly lift—"

"I am well aware of my wife's 'back pain.'" Mr. Meeks turned on the other woman, who looked as though she would have climbed into the washbasin and submerged herself among the bloody rags if she could only fit. "Mrs. Meeks, if it wouldn't tax you too terribly, we're trying to eat our lunch in there and could use some settings."

Mrs. Meeks scooped up an armful of cutlery from one of the drawers and escaped into the other room.

As soon as the door closed, Mr. Meeks grabbed the first woman's arm, his grip so tight his fingers sank into her flesh.

"You listen here," he said, his voice hushed but his nose whistle just as resonant as before. "Your being here is sheer foolishness. People will talk."

"Carlton, stop."

"Not to mention beyond disrespectful to your husband. What if he finds out what you've done?" He released her and pressed his hands to his face. "What if he's already found out?" He looked over at Peanut and shuddered.

The woman glared at him, rubbing her arm.

"Go home," said Mr. Meeks. "Go home and speak to no one. Understand?"

"Don't tell me what to do."

"Just listen to me, dammit. Please. For once in your entire life!" Seeming to notice how loud his voice had become, Mr. Meeks lowered his shoulders and gave his nose bandage a delicate pat. "Now, if you'll excuse me."

The woman glared after him as the door swung shut, then, as if remembering something, turned back toward the hallway.

Cassie and Jake backed over each other and fled soundlessly toward the rear staircase.

"Who is that woman?" Cassie whispered as they climbed, trying to keep her footsteps from thudding. "Do you think she's in danger?"

"Sarah Meeks. I mean Shaw. Mr. Shaw's wife, Mr. Meeks's sister. And I don't think you need worry for her. She's tough. She was one of the few people stubborn enough to stay when the town evacuated during the war. Made a living selling food to the soldiers who'd occupied the place."

"What could they have been talking about?"

"Your guess is as good as mine. Some kind of family dispute, sounds like."

They continued their search on the second floor but found little of note until, at the very end of the hall, past a series of closets and eerily empty rooms, they arrived in Peanut's bedroom. Much to Cassie's surprise, it was bright, airy, and pleasantly decorated. The pinewood bed, which was made up with coordinating bedspread and pillow covers, stood beside a window hung with colorful drapes. There was an elegantly carved steamer trunk at its foot, and across from that a pair of wardrobes had been positioned side by side to give the impression of one larger one.

The contents of the toilet area were unexpected as well. Next to the washstand was a table displaying an elaborate collection of beard oils, perfumes, and aromatic waters, all carefully arranged by size and color. Most of the bottles were of a relatively simple design and labeled for use by men, but, among them, there was also a blown-glass perfume dispenser shaped like a swallow holding a miniature anchor in its beak.

The wind rustled a tree branch outside the window, sending a ripple through the dapples of sunlight on the floor, and a glint of something caught Cassie's eye. She dropped to the floor and reached under the bed.

"You know, Captain Beale may have been right about Peanut having a lady friend." She held up the item she'd retrieved, a teardrop-shaped pendant. It was made up of tiny, glittering gemstones, and when she moved it in the light, miniature rainbows danced on the wall.

"What is it?" asked Jake.

"It's a woman's necklace, or a part of one. The chain doesn't appear to be here anywhere. It must have broken off."

"Well, I'll be." Jake slapped his knee. "There *is* a woman in this world who can stand being around Peanut."

"Other than his late wife, you mean."

"Right. Sorry."

On the other side of the room, next to a tapestry depicting a hunting party in off-putting detail, there was another doorway. It opened into a small but similarly well-appointed study, complete with fireplace, floor-to-ceiling bookshelves, and, beneath a circular window roughly the size of a dinner plate, a heavy oak desk and a reading chair upholstered in blue-and-gray checks.

Jake lifted the top from a box on the floor next to the desk.

"What's all this? *Harper's Bazaar. Godey's Lady Book. Peterson's. New York World.* Why does Peanut have a collection of ladies' magazines?"

Cassie flipped through the box. "They all seem to be pretty recent. And look, some of them have pages marked." She pulled out the *Harper's Bazaar* and opened it to a dog-eared page. "The description for this fashion plate mentions Flora and recommends one of her perfumes to go with the dress. It calls her products the 'work of a pure artistic genius.' I didn't realize they even wrote about that kind of thing in here."

Jake put the box lid down and picked out an issue of *Peterson's.*

"This one is a comparison of sorts, evaluating several different perfumes, including one of Flora's. It describes hers as being 'akin to something you might find in the finest stores in Paris.' Sakes alive. Flora mentioned she had gotten attention from beyond the island, which is why she started selling by catalog, but I didn't know it was anything like this." He lowered the magazine. "But Peanut hated Flora. None of the perfumes or oils in his collection are even from her store. Why was he collecting news about her?"

A quick search through the other materials revealed more of the same, but no explanation as to their presence. Cassie moved to the bookshelf and ran her finger along a few of the spines. Most addressed topics she might have expected: fishing, woodworking, the anatomy of common game animals. Others, however, ventured into more far-flung territory, such as floriography and ladies' garment-making.

"Peanut certainly had diverse interests." She opened a volume called *The Book of Perfumes* by Eugene Rimmel. There was a nameplate inside the cover. "'Property of G. Runkles.' But Peanut's name is Theodore."

"Peanut's wife's name was Gilda. That must be her book."

"Ah." Cassie thought about the perfume dispenser in the bedroom. That had probably been Gilda's as well. She doubted that explained the pendant under the bed, though.

She tried a different line of thought. "Jake, did Peanut do anything other than piloting? As you said, a lot of people have more than one line of work around here. Maybe a business of some sort? Perhaps with a partner?"

"None that I know of. But some of the other pilots certainly do. Captain Strough owns a furniture store near the depot, and Captain Jones and Captain Hills went in together on a haberdashery on Second Street, which is run by their wives." He sunk onto the armchair. "Peanut didn't strike me as the type of man to go into business with anyone else. At least, not unless he was in control. He was a real miser—I'm sure he would never trust another man as far as he could throw him when it came to money."

"Actually, I don't blame him for that," Cassie said. "My father saw a lot of awful things in his practice when it came to business partnerships. You wouldn't believe what people will do to each other, even to those who are supposedly closest to them. He used to say there's a special place in Hell for those who betray their friends for the sake of money."

"That certainly sounds like Tom."

Cassie put the book back on the shelf. "I take it you knew my parents when they lived here?"

Jake took a small pipe out of his jacket and gave it a thoughtful puff—not that this accomplished much, since he hadn't lit it. "I was rather younger than they were, being even younger than Flora. But, yes, I knew them. Of course."

"What were they like? My father spoke very little of their life here."

Jake puffed the unlit pipe again. "Well, whenever I think about your father, I envision a sort of a whirlwind. He had an unusually sharp wit and was strong and generous, but what was most striking about him was how he was always moving, always doing, always talking. Mr. Hale used to describe him as having two speeds, galloping and asleep. And if you got close to him, you couldn't help but get swept up, which meant he pretty much always got whatever he wanted." He shifted. "I'm sorry. I didn't mean that."

Here, once again, was this Tom Gwynne who bore so little resemblance to the father she'd known, she almost wondered whether she had accidentally asked about someone else.

"What about my mother?"

Jake drummed his fingers on his knees. "Yes, sweet, kind Emma. She was, in many ways, very similar to the rest of the Hales. She felt everything that happened to her and to those around her, both the good and the bad, deeply. But, unlike the others, for her, all of those feelings seemed to stay inside. Never a raised voice, never an excited word. She was always reserved, gentle, and polite."

Cassie picked at her glove. "Sounds like she and my father were an unlikely pair."

"One could say so."

"How did they meet, then?"

"As the story goes, soon after Tom moved to town to work for Mr. Hale's shipping company, he was invited to join the family for dinner. At the end of the meal, Emma went to the piano to sing for everyone, and Tom sat right down next to her and made it a duet."

It was a lovely picture, her father and mother sitting together at the piano. Encouraged, Cassie pushed on. "I was also wondering, seeing how Flora wrote to my father so many times over the years… One would think they were close, right?"

Something in Jake's eyes flickered, like a candle flame when someone passes by too closely. "Yes."

Cassie waited for him to go on, but he simply tucked his pipe into his coat and folded his hands. Was that really all he had to say on the matter? Or had she upset him somehow?

"I'm sorry," she said. "Have I said something—Wait!" She grabbed Jake's shoulder to stop him from leaning back. There was an oily, head-shaped stain on the antimacassar draped over the back of the chair.

"Curious." She leaned closer but quickly stood back up. She had always hated the smell of Macassar oil, which some men found necessary to apply to their hair by the tinful, unfortunately, and this particular vintage was uncommonly potent.

As she straightened, she spotted a small Grecian clock lying on the floor by the bookcase. The face was cracked, and the hands had stopped. "Unless… Has the jury been in here yet, do you think?"

"No, not yet," said Jake. "They've been too busy interrogating every last person in the neighborhood. But I heard Mr. Shaw say they planned to walk through the house before they leave today."

"And the house has otherwise been sealed up like a bank vault since yesterday morning. In that case, I believe there's been an intruder in here. Other than us."

"An intruder? Why do you say that?"

"To start with, like its master, I doubt this timekeeping device fell to the ground of its own accord."

Jake let a grin slip out. Whatever Cassie had seen in his expression a few seconds before had disappeared. Had she simply imagined it?

"And I would assume if Peanut had been here when it fell, he would have picked it up. Look, it's stopped at two thirty-two. That must mean it stopped at two thirty-two in the morning the day of the murder. After Peanut left for his post."

"That's right. Peanut said he had to be there at two, which means he would have left here by around one thirty, one forty, at the latest. So it had to be someone else. Maybe the owner of the pendant we found?"

"That's a thought. But there's also the soiled antimacassar. Which, since most women I know don't make a habit of styling their hair with gobs of Macassar oil, would suggest to me our intruder was a man."

"But Peanut was a man. Who's to say it was an intruder who left the stain?"

"Peanut was a *bald* man. He didn't use hair oil. Also, there's a basket of dirty linens downstairs, ready for the laundry. If the antimacassar had been soiled by an actual visitor before Peanut left for the night, Peanut most likely would have put it in the basket with the rest of the dirty linens and replaced it with a fresh one."

Jake glanced back at the oily spot. "Okay. But why would an intruder have sat down?"

"You're an intruder. You sat down."

"Good point."

"Did Dr. Ames have an estimate of what time Peanut died?" Cassie peered under the armchair to see if there was anything else out of place.

"Between three and five in the morning, give or take."

"And it's about twenty minutes from here to the tower, by way of the plank walk?"

"Depends on how fast you're walking, but yes, about that."

"I suppose even if it took quite a bit longer, that would still leave plenty of time for our intruder to have been our murderer as well. Perhaps he couldn't find what he was looking for, so he went after Peanut up in the lookout tower."

"What makes you think he was looking for something?"

Cassie found the wastebasket and spat out her gum, which had gotten so tough it was hurting her jaw. "Most of the books on the shelf are lined up with an unusual degree of care. He even pulled each one to the edge of the shelf so the spines are lined up. But here you have several thrown slapdash on top. And there—" She pointed behind the desk. "The edge of the rug is folded over, and one of the desk drawers is ajar. Once again, if the exceptional tidiness of the overall house is any indication, Peanut wasn't one to neglect such details."

"All right. Then what do you suppose he was looking *for*?"

"That would be the question, wouldn't it." Cassie kneeled by the rug and gently examined the exposed floorboards, expecting to find a loose one disguising a secret hiding area, but there was nothing but solid wood. A search of the bookshelf was similarly disappointing.

But right as she was beginning to think she had taken too much inspiration from certain stories by Edgar Allen Poe, she realized something was off about the desk. Either her eyes were misperceiving depth or the size of the bottom drawer wasn't matching up with that of the desk frame. Sure enough, when she felt around inside the drawer, she found a panel disguising an extra compartment, inside of which was a sort of ledger book. It was longer than it was wide and had a cover made from light-colored olive wood.

Jake examined the writing on the spine. "'Accounts.' Ordinarily that would sound painfully boring to me, but since we found it hidden away… Maybe this is what—"

"Well, well. What do we have here?" Officer Hughes was standing in the entrance to the study, his legs spread and his thumbs hooked on his holster like a character from a Buntline dime novel.

"How does he keep doing that?" Jake said under his breath. He turned around and positioned himself in front of the desk, allowing Cassie to hide the ledger behind her back. "How did you get in here?"

"Easy," said Hughes. "I climbed the trellis on the back side of the house and walked the roof from there to the bedroom window. I had to use my mustache comb to lever the window up enough to get my fingers under it, but that didn't take but a moment. Say, does Flora know the two of you are whispering together alone in here? Tsk. Tsk."

"Don't be crass," Jake said. "I've half a mind to—"

They were interrupted by voices on the stairs. It seemed the jury had finished their lunch and decided to take that walk through the house.

Throwing the tapestry aside, Hughes darted back into the bedroom but caught his leg on the corner of a decorative side table.

"Fuh—*nicular.*"

"Hurry!" Cassie pushed Jake over the windowsill and turned to Hughes. "Come on. I'm the only one who has any reason to be inside the house. If Mr. Shaw finds you here, the sheriff won't hear the end of it, and I don't think that's what you want."

Hughes paused. "You mean you're not going to tell—"

"Of course not! Now go."

But Hughes lingered another moment, looking at her.

Her stomach fluttered. *What—*

By the end of her blink, however, he'd gone. Shaking herself, she pulled up her rear skirts and shoved the ledger upward until it was wedged between the edge of her corset and one of the steel rings of her bustle frame. Then she closed the window, straightened the side table Hughes had run into, and headed for the hall.

She had just pulled the bedroom door shut when Mr. Shaw reached the top of the stairs, followed closely by Mr. Meeks, Dr. Ames, and the rest of the jurymen.

"Miss Gwynne." Mr. Shaw staggered as the others domino-piled into his back. "What are you doing here? I told you to go home." He sniffed suspiciously.

Cassie pretended to turn with a start. "Dear me. How do I say this? I was looking for… a place to address a need."

When that was met with blank faces, she adjusted her subtlety level and tried again.

"I was trying to locate the—" She daintily cupped her hand to her mouth. *"Commode."*

The men took a collective step backward on the stairs.

"Oh, uh, Peanut was not one for such luxuries as indoor plumbing," Mr. Shaw answered, carefully avoiding eye contact. "I believe you'll find what you're looking for out back."

Cassie let out the slightest of breaths (she had worried Mr. Shaw might be lacking in normal sensibilities) and started down the hall toward them, her back arched so sharply to accommodate her contraband she had to waddle like a duck with a bum leg.

"Why didn't you just go back to Miss Hale's?" Mr. Ambler asked, evidently experiencing a rare, if inconveniently timed, flutter of coherent thought. "It would have been faster."

Mr. Shaw paused.

Pretending not to hear, Cassie quickened her waddle and squeezed past them down the stairs. Once she was outside, she dipped behind the bushes to dislodge the ledger from her vertebrae then, hugging the book to her chest, broke into a run to Flora's house.

CHAPTER TEN

"Aunt Flora?" Cassie slammed the door shut behind her. "Hello?"

"Hello!" Kleio responded from the coat rack.

"Quiet, quiet, the both of you." Esme shushed the bird with her hand and hurried down the stairs. She slipped a small bottle into her apron. "I've just given Flora something to help her fall asleep."

"Quiet!" Kleio bellowed enthusiastically.

Esme checked her turban in the hallway mirror and sighed. From what Flora had told her, Cassie understood Esme to be close to Cassie in age, but her sallow complexion and the worry lines around her eyes and mouth made her appear at least a few years older.

"Come." Esme took Cassie's hat and hung it on the rack. "Let's go on into the kitchen. Everyone's been waiting for you."

For several long moments after Cassie recounted what had happened at Peanut's house, the only sound was the pounding of Miss Porter's fists beating a mass of green-speckled dough into the kitchen table. Mrs. Keene, who was sitting next to her peeling potatoes, watched her warily.

"This is Un-Ac-Ceptable," Miss Porter said finally, punctuating each syllable with a blow to the hapless lump.

Sergeant Denham turned from the sink, where he was shucking oysters. "Miss Porter, my friend, I think that dough has suffered enough."

"Frankly," Mrs. Keene agreed, "it's for stewed dumplings, so I don't know why she's kneading it in the first place."

Cassie put the ledger down next to a basket of fruit and walked around the table. "Try not to worry, Miss Porter." She gave the woman's shoulder a tentative pat.

"Oh, you *are* a dear!" Miss Porter threw out her flour-dusted arms and pulled Cassie to her with remarkable strength, submerging her face in her ample motherly bosom. "It's all so awful, isn't it?"

"Yeph ih is."

"It's absolutely shameful how they're treating Flora. Attacking her with all those questions… where were you, what did you say, prove this, prove that… like she's some kind of criminal. And with no lawyer or anyone there to defend her, either. Just hearing her tell us about it was infuriating."

"Technically"—Cassie sucked in a grateful lung of air after somehow extracting herself from Miss Porter's grasp—"inquests are *ex parte*, not adversarial, proceedings. There's no sort of legal defense allowed. Not until there's a trial." She smoothed her dress. "*Unless* there's a trial. Hypothetically."

Miss Porter clicked her tongue. "Oh, no, none of that talk. It's bad enough they've told Flora she's 'not to go anywhere.' What's that supposed to mean? Where would she go? It makes no sense whatever. As though that sweet woman could ever cause harm to another living thing." She threw the dough to the side and pulled out a tub of peas, dropping it on the table so hard several pods leapt out like sailors from a burning ship.

"If you ask me—" Mrs. Keene grabbed air as one of her peeled potatoes also hopped off the table. "Those jurymen aren't worth a fart in a whirlwind. This town is rife with more-likely culprits. Including me, if the measure is not being torn up over Peanut's getting what was coming to him. Why, last summer, when I complained about him shooting squirrels in Central Park, he—"

"Where?" Cassie must have misheard.

"Central Park, the public park over on Eleventh. Not as fancy as the one you have up there in New York City, but it's got a fountain." Mrs. Keene examined the dropped potato then wiped it on her sleeve with a shrug. "When Peanut heard I'd said something to the sheriff, he came over and put a dozen holes in my shed with his shotgun. Lucky the captain was home to calm me down, or else I would have put a dozen holes in him with my knitting needle."

"You shouldn't joke about such things, Mrs. Keene," said Jake, who had come in through the back door.

The dogs tumbled in behind him, followed by Metta and Paddy. "Who says I was joking?"

"Alice is right." Miss Porter began to shell the peas vigorously, throwing each husk into a pail with a resonant *ping*. "Peanut has made himself more enemies than friends in this town. You remember when old Widow Abernathy first got the council to try out that new electric streetlamp across the street, how he went right up to her house in the middle of the night and berated her about it shining on his house. She doesn't have any family left to defend her, so Big James had to go scare him straight about raising his voice at little old ladies."

Ping.

Sergeant Denham wiped off his shucker. "And the time the Starkeys hosted that bonfire party next door and Peanut stayed up until dawn banging pots and pans in the street to protest the noise."

Ping.

"Don't forget his endearing way of policing vehicles in the street," added Mrs. Keene.

Ping. Ping.

Miss Porter wiped her face with her sleeve. "Actually, there's a point. They should be questioning Ambrose Smalls."

"Who's that?" Cassie tried not to stare as Paddy settled onto a stool next to Metta with a dwindling plate of banana doughnuts.

"A local merchant," answered Sergeant Denham. "He sells fine articles, imported dishes, that sort of thing." He leaned to the side as Esme reached over him with the drip pan from the refrigerator and poured the meltwater out of the window. "One night a couple of weeks ago, Peanut got the idea to dig a pit in the street and fill it with rocks so people would have to slow down and—"

"Isn't that dangerous?"

"Terribly. And, what would you know, Mr. Smalls drove over the pit first thing the next morning and capsized. He made it through intact himself, but the load of Chinese porcelain in his cart didn't fare as well."

"That's right, I was here having breakfast with Flora and Esme at the time," Mrs. Keene said. "Mr. Smalls was hopping mad. Literally! When he realized who was responsible, he bounded right up to Peanut's door like a danged marsh rabbit being chased by a bee." She guffawed and picked up another potato. "Then he started stomping on his hat and ranting about how Peanut's 'little stunt' was going to ruin him."

Cassie set down the loaf of sourdough Esme had handed her and began to cut it into thick slices, shoving the warm, crusty end piece in her mouth as payment for services rendered. "Do you think Mr. Smalls could be out for revenge?"

"He was pretty thundering furious. Mr. Starkey had to run over half-shaved and half-clothed to keep him from kicking in the door. And Peanut wasn't even home. Everyone knew he had watch duty that morning. But Mr. Smalls kept demanding he 'stop hiding' and face him. Must have been out of his blazing mind."

Sergeant Denham swept a pile of oyster shells into the bin by his feet. "I heard from Mrs. Rydell that Mrs. Hand told Mrs. Harper that Mr. Lucas heard Mr. Smalls say he was 'leveraged to the hilt' on that shipment and that Peanut 'had better pay for the damage, or else.'"

"Or else what?" Cassie asked.

Sergeant Denham shrugged.

Jake took a doughnut off of Paddy's plate. "I think it's a threat worth looking into. I'll stop by Mr. Smalls's on my way to the stables later this evening."

"At least there's nothing actually placing Flora near the tower at the time of the murder," Cassie said. "I can't imagine the coroner would try advancing a verdict against her without that."

Sergeant Denham lowered his head. "As much as it pains me to say it, I've seen people hung on less."

"But that wouldn't happen to Flora, certainly." The spoon jangled in the butter dish as Esme placed it back on the table. "Public opinion wouldn't stand for it."

Mrs. Keene scoffed. "I wouldn't put your trust in public opinion. When we were walking back here with Flora, we passed Mrs. Handel, one of Flora's most frequent customers, and she couldn't even be bothered to return a wave. And that after Flora spent a month last summer helping her find those herbs she needed when her son was sick."

"I don't understand it." Miss Porter took on two pea pods at once. "If supposed friends can turn on her so fast, based on a whole lot of nothing, how can we expect anything better from the rest?"

Jake tossed the remainder of his doughnut to Danger, who snapped it out of the air with a deep woof and licked his chops noisily. "Well, *real* friends don't abandon faith in each other so easily, nor do family. And Flora has both. Right, Cassie?"

"Uh, yes. Yes, of course." She thought about how her father had thrown himself into danger to protect her, without the slightest hesitation. "But we won't let it come to that." No matter what, she certainly wasn't going to leave Flora's fate in the hands of mindless town gossips or that lot in the jury room.

"What in the devil's armpit?" said Mrs. Keene.

Miss Porter had fallen back against the stove, her hands in the air, and was wiggling her legs and hips like a marionette caught in the wind.

"Something… furry is scaling my—*unmentionables!*"

Knocking over a pyramid of peeled carrots, Mrs. Keene dove in and started slapping at Miss Porter's skirts while Miss Porter wailed.

"Wait!" Cassie had a suspect in mind. One with blue eyes, four legs, and hair all over. "Mrs. Keene, try giving her petticoats a good shake."

As Miss Porter let out one last wail, Mrs. Keene followed her instructions, and, sure enough, a melon-sized ball of white fur and kitten tumbled onto the floor. Unfazed, the kitten rolled to her feet and, uttering her most ferocious mew-roar, pounced on Miss Porter's bow-lined hem with all four paws.

Cassie lifted the kitten, paws still swinging, and cuddled her to her chest. "I was wondering where you'd gotten off to." As she stood, however, she knocked a large chopping knife off the table with her elbow. Fortunately, Esme reached out and caught it before it landed, blade down, right in the middle of her foot.

"Good catch," Jake said.

Esme put the knife back in its place. "Well, Jake, and Cassie, be sure to let me know if there's any way I can help. Flora means a great deal to me, and I would be devastated if anything were to happen to her. Truly."

"So would we all," Sergeant Denham said.

Miss Porter, a hand on her chest, puffed as she returned to her peas. "Yes, she has such a big heart, a quality which those with smaller hearts can't appreciate, and she shares it with all of us every day. That's why we, her real friends, are going to be here for her until this is all over. Starting with cooking her favorite meal, stewed parsley dumplings in lentil and root vegetable stew. I may not be able to do much else, but at least no one's going hungry on my watch."

Ping.

*

As it turned out, Flora was still asleep when the food was ready and not readily roused, but Miss Porter insisted that everyone stay and eat together anyway, on the theory that the voices and the friendly clink of dishes would sound through Flora's dreams and bring her a little cheer. They dutifully complied, and, as promised, Miss Porter turned out an impressive feast. In addition to the stew, there were roasted oysters, cold cabbage slaw, and freshly baked bread, with a chocolate and strawberry charlotte russe for dessert.

By the time they had finished eating, the lamplighter was making his rounds, and everyone dispersed to attend to their various other responsibilities: Jake and Metta to the stables, Miss Porter to her boarders, Mrs. Keene to her inventory. Sergeant Denham mentioned something about a project for church, and Esme had to run out on an errand. Relieved to have some time to herself at last, Cassie headed toward her room to examine the ledger from Peanut's study.

While she was passing Flora's room at the top of the stairs, however, she noticed the door was cracked, and a little light was coming through. She poked her head inside and saw that Esme was in there, sitting in a chair next to the bed. The dogs were there, too—Luna curled up under one of Flora's arms, and Danger on the floor with his head leaned against the side of the bed, directly below Flora's.

"I thought you had to run an errand," Cassie whispered.

"I wanted to check on Flora first." Esme beckoned to her. "You can come in. I don't think anything is going to wake her right now."

Flora stirred.

"Are you sure?"

Flora inhaled deeply and her eyes fluttered but didn't open. "Tell him I'm sorry. I didn't mean to—Tell him I—I'm…" Her words trailed off, and her breathing slowed again.

Esme straightened the blanket and re-tucked it around her. "Oh, she's just dreaming. She'll sleep through the night."

"I'm sure she needs it."

"Yes. Today certainly… took a turn."

"And we thought yesterday was tough."

"Indeed."

Cassie watched Esme fill Flora's water glass and turn down the lamp, then check the blankets once more. She certainly went above and beyond what would normally be expected of a store assistant.

"She's lucky to have you," Cassie said. "From what I can gather, Flora is always busy doing things for other people, so it's good to see she has someone she can count on when she needs something. And that she's not alone in this big old house." She knew what that was like.

Esme nodded, almost to herself, as she moved her chair back against the wall. Then she looked up at Cassie with a smile. "And now we both have you."

Back in her room, Cassie set herself up at the desk with pen and paper, a bright table lamp, and the ledger from Peanut's study.

"Finished with that fish I gave you already?" she said to the kitten, who had perched herself regally on the ledger as though captaining a ship. The kitten gave an affirmative mew and purred as she bent to lick a paw.

"Okay, good." Cassie lifted her onto the bed. "Now, let's see what this book has to tell us."

The title page read simply, "Project Golden Bluff."

Interesting. Cassie remembered Flora telling her "Yellow Bluff" had been the name of a plantation once located where the town was now, but she hadn't heard of any "Golden Bluff."

The next page, however, didn't shed any more light. Rather, it confused her more. This didn't seem like any ledger she'd ever seen. She turned page after page, on to the end, but there were no bookkeeping-type entries at all. Instead, there were a series of pasted-in drawings consisting of intersecting lines and notations about acreage and degrees. Property surveys, possibly. For some, there were also legal descriptions and transcriptions of associated deed records, but she didn't know enough about the town to recognize exactly what properties and structures they described. She would have to ask Jake.

Inside the back cover, she found a sleeve containing more loose documents, but those items were even more perplexing. Some had to do with property, like the drawings: letters, maps, tax certificates, more transcriptions of deed records. But the rest—obituaries, ship and train schedules, newspaper articles about house fires, loose-leaf pages covered in tidy notes ranging from arithmetic calculations to observations about Peanuts' neighbors' comings and goings—seemed random, even downright strange.

Cassie tried arranging the documents into some kind of an order on the bedspread, and the kitten dutifully sniffed and sat on each item as she placed it down. But after half an hour of debating whether to go chronologically or alphabetically, or perhaps by keyword, she needed to regroup.

She pressed a hand to her abdomen, letting out a sigh that slid into a groan. Her dress felt like a sausage casing.

"The way I've been eating, you'd think I'd never seen food before," she told the kitten, who was sprawled on the coverlet on her back, all four legs splayed out in the most unladylike manner. Feeling a sheet of paper brush her paw, the kitten flipped over and started chewing on it, punching a neat set of kitten-tooth-sized holes in the corner.

"No, no, don't do that," Cassie said. "That might be impor— Whoa." She wedged a finger between the kitten's jaws to disengage them and lifted the sheet. It was a promissory note, executed only three weeks before, for a loan Peanut had provided to someone named Matthew Downing. The loan was significant, and listed a whole house as collateral. And when Cassie scanned the rest of the agreement, she was shocked by what she saw: extraordinarily high interest rates, onerous repayment terms, and a sweeping acceleration clause giving Peanut the right to make the entire debt due in the event of default, as determined in his sole discretion, at which point he could take ownership of the house if the debtor couldn't pay.

"Who would be desperate enough agree to this?" she murmured, turning the sheet over. There was a printed letterhead on the back, and, in a different hand, a few lines that had been scribbled out. The sheet had probably been taken from a waste bin. The letterhead read:

William Marsden
Centre Street, Fernandina

Marsden. Where had she heard that name before?

She slapped her leg, startling the kitten. That was it. Mr. Marsden ran the Three Star Saloon, where Captain Beale had said Peanut used to take his supper. The place with the horrendous cook.

She checked the mantel clock. The night was progressing, but a place like the Three Star Saloon was probably only getting going.

"If you'll excuse me, miss," she said to the kitten, giving her a rub on the forehead and starting toward the door, "it's time for my evening constitutional."

With only a few wrong turns and one step in a mud puddle, Cassie found her way back to Centre Street. It was different at night, as most things are, but just as alive. Many of the same characters inhabited the street: Fashionably dressed ladies strolled arm in arm, eating fresh orange wedges as they swept the streets with their skirts. Nodding gentlemen puffed on cigars. Merchants and laborers sat together on the sidewalk, washing down the crumbs of the day's exertions with bottles of beer.

But the flow of movement along the sidewalks was eddied now, swirling here, around a group of men throwing and catching a die across a makeshift table, and there, around a man playing old plantation songs on a banjo, and here again, around a woman selling newspaper cones filled with roasted nuts. The air had a crisp, piney smell to it, courtesy of one of the local sawmills perhaps, and the light from the streetlamps lent a storybook glow to the displays in the darkened store windows.

Cassie shivered, partly in excitement at being in a new place, and partly in relief. For several blocks after leaving Flora's, she had hurried from streetlamp to streetlamp, trying to stay ahead of the faceless assailants her imagination had convinced her were lurking in the shadows. It wasn't like her to be so skittish, but some feelings were hard to shake. She touched a hand to her neck.

Half a block past Third, one façade shone out brightly from among several dim ones, and a jumble of music and voices spilled into the street through its weathered batwing doors. Cassie's gaze drifted upward. Across the top, three star-shaped windows flickered red and orange.

"Look out!" cried a voice. Not knowing precisely what to "look out" for (that particular admonition had always struck her as too vague to be useful), Cassie pressed herself against the side of the building between a broken table and a barrel of pungent food waste.

Almost immediately afterward, however, she realized the shout hadn't been meant for her. A few feet ahead, by the entrance to the saloon, a deliveryman had just careened his sack truck off the sidewalk to avoid running into someone.

The deliveryman flung up his arms.

"I almost hit you, you lout," he said as the would-be victim, a man dressed in an elegant evening suit, belched and stepped-fell off the sidewalk. "Have you no regard for—Bah!"

He dismissed him and turned on the aproned man by the saloon doors, who was polishing a glass with the towel slung over his shoulder. "You could have turned him out before he reached this state, Marsden."

Marsden. Cassie had found the man she was looking for.

"So what if he's got a brick in his hat?" Mr. Marsden said. "The Three Star Saloon… is a *saloon*. Not a *nursery*." The way he chortled at his own cleverness, it was clear he wasn't unaffected by drink himself. "Besides, who am I to turn away good money? If I send him off, he'll simply go somewhere else. So, long as he's paying, I'm pouring." He blew his nose on a corner of his apron and used the other side to rub the glass.

Over in the street, having achieved a wide, deer-legged stance, the man in the evening suit began the process of bending over to pick up his top hat.

"I'm with you, Marsden," chimed in another man, buttoning his trousers as he rounded the corner. Major Drury, once again. Though, Cassie supposed, she should be less surprised to see him here. "Long as he's buying, I'm drinking. And is he ever buying tonight. Even more than last night."

"At least until the current coffers run dry," said Mr. Marsden.

Major Drury slapped his hat at something on his boot. "He says this time's different. But I dunno. Alls I know is tonight he's already bought enough rounds to get me locked up for public intoxtication again!"

The men guffawed and pounded each other on the back so hard they almost fell over, and Cassie was waiting for it to be safe to approach when the man in the evening suit, having finally secured his hat, faced into the light. It was Atherton Brooks, the man who had been riding with Sam Townsend the previous morning, Sam's sister Lily's apparent suitor.

How could Lily be interested in this man? Lily had always hated those who over-imbibed. At least she had when Cassie had known her. The elder Mr. Townsend had been a prime offender in that respect. In fact, that was one of the reasons Sam and Lily had spent so much time with Cassie while they were living in New York, even though their families might otherwise have moved in different circles. According to the neighborhood chatter, the only reason the Townsends were in New York at all was because Mr. Townsend had caused the family some kind of embarrassment back home in Savannah and been sent away to work at a trade for a time, as a penance.

"Sakes alive!" said the deliveryman.

Mr. Brooks, evidently drawn toward a group of young nuns coming out of the undertaker's office, had wandered back in front of him just as he started to move his load again.

Major Drury followed Cassie's gaze. "That Mr. Brooks is a handsome devil, I'll grant you, but I got other qualities. Come in and have a smile with old Major Drury. And then we can have a go on the billiards table. Maybe even shoot a game or two after." He gave her a suggestive wink, in case she had managed to miss his meaning.

Mr. Marsden rubbed his glass. "Better lay off it, Major. Or the wife'll make you sleep on the porch with the dogs for the third night in a row."

"Aw, I was only being friendly, a young lady standing out in front of this doggery all by herself. What if some degenerate comes along and tries to harass her?"

Cassie was about to inform him it was too late for that when a lavish brougham streaked by. It jerked to a halt next to the bench where the deliveryman had finally managed to settle Mr. Brooks.

The door flew open, and a woman's voice, high and agitated, rang out from the mass of pink ruffles spilling out of the compartment. The only other thing Cassie could see was the woman's feet, daintily clad in high-heeled kid slippers and kicking, but she had a distinct feeling she knew who it was.

"Just you wait until I… get my hands on—Quincy!"

The driver leapt from his seat and ran around to grab a hold of the woman's ankles. After a brief struggle, sure enough, Lily Townsend popped out of the carriage. She took a moment to organize herself then, hobbling as quickly as her knee-hugging dress would allow, made a beeline toward Mr. Brooks.

What was Lily doing here? Not only at the saloon but in town at all? The morning before, Sam had said they were going to leave for home immediately.

"Where have you been?" Lily swatted at the bottlebrush branch swaying overhead, sending several of the fuzzy red blossoms sailing through the air. "Everyone will be waiting."

Mr. Brooks leaned forward and tapped her nose with his forefinger. "Don't fret, my treasure. I was only having a little refreshment before the parlor concert. Which I am very much looking forward to, as it will be exceeding…ingly stimulating. And your brother and I enjoy each other's company, oh so very much."

"I am not in the mood, Atherton." Lily hoisted him to his feet. "You know how important this is. For the both of us." Throwing his arm over her back, she dragged him to the carriage and performed a startlingly adept shoulder-to-backside maneuver to load him in. Then, with an aristocratic pat to her hair, she climbed in after him, and the carriage took off.

Cassie stared after them. So that was Lily Townsend, all grown up. She wasn't quite as prim and collected as Cassie would have expected (granted, the present circumstances probably had something to do with that), but she certainly had the sophistication and glamor the child version of herself had suggested.

"Betcha I don't seem such bad company now, do I?" Major Drury had somehow sidled closer to her without her noticing. "Practically a teetotaler next to that feller." He cracked his dry lips into a grin, and the sour stench of tobacco, bourbon, and garlic flooded her nostrils.

"I don't…" Raising her handkerchief, Cassie turned to Mr. Marsden. "You're Mr. Marsden, the proprietor, right?"

"Depends on who's asking and why," he answered with a wink (which was only a mild improvement over the Major's).

"I'm visiting from New York and was told one could get a decent meal here." She tried not to wince as she accidentally made eye contact with something small and furry scurrying over the threshold.

Mr. Marsden considered her. "If it's a drink you're really after, we don't pass judgment here."

"Oh." Cassie became aware of the Major smelling her hair. "A drink it is, then."

CHAPTER ELEVEN

Cassie pushed through the doors into a haze of cigar smoke and waited by the bar counter while Mr. Marsden crawled underneath and took up his position on the other side. A group of scantily toothed men in faded blue kepi caps hunched over a card game behind her, occasionally trading gibes with the woman who was sitting on a nearby table, crossing and uncrossing her legs at passersby. Beyond them, next to a billiards table littered with gouges and cigar burns, a man in suspenders was playing a tune on the piano, accompanied by Paddy on the fiddle. Relieved to see a familiar face, Cassie went over to drop a coin in Paddy's cup and received a joyful grin in return.

"I was gonna tell you we don't keep any champagne around here," Mr. Marsden said when she returned. "But then I figured you're probably wanting something a touch stronger." He filled two cloudy tumblers with something that smelled like it belonged inside a lamp reservoir and pushed one toward her, taking the other for himself.

"Why is that?" Cassie eyed her glass.

"You're Flora Hale's niece, aren't you? Tom and Emma Gwynne's girl? I heard you're the one found Peanut's body."

A few heads turned down the bar.

"Yes."

"And that your aunt is the coroner's number-one suspect for it. Basically a done deal, if you listen to what people are saying. Next stop, state prison, and then—" He drew his thumb across his neck.

Cassie clasped her hands in her lap, trying to ignore the whispering that had started behind her. "I'm quite confident my aunt had nothing to do with it."

"Aw, I find it kinda hard to believe, too, even if she is an unusual one."

"'Unusual'?"

"She's always been decent to me, but, you know. Women like that, they're funny. They get an education, see some of the world, and they think they can do anything. That they don't need a husband or children, that maybe they'd rather own property or a business instead. What's next? Voting?" He snorted. "What I'm saying is, they're unpredictable."

Cassie fumed inwardly. What right did he have to pass such judgments?

"Besides, we all have our secrets. And how can you be so sure, anyway, throwing yourself behind someone you hardly know? Haven't you just met? Far as I remember, old Tom took off up north with you right after the war and never looked back. Guess you can't blame the man, after what he been through."

"I know enough to say she's not capable of such a thing."

"You'd be surprised what people are capable of, given the right situation."

Cassie looked at him, then, deciding she needed a show of strength, picked up her glass and poured the contents down her throat. It was far worse than the concoction she'd gulped that morning, and it exploded in her stomach like a hand grenade, but she gritted her teeth into a smile-like grimace.

Mr. Marsden raised his eyebrows in approval and poured her another.

Cassie pulled out the promissory note she'd found. "I have a question for you." She held it up and pointed to the letterhead. "I'm assuming this is your stationery?"

He took the sheet from her and squinted at it. "Sure is. Why?"

"Do you know anything about what's on the other side?"

He turned it over, then threw it on the counter like it was covered in fire ants. "Put that away. And keep your voice down, will you? My old lady'll have my manhood with a cleaver if she sees that. Usury's a cardinal sin in her book, and she wouldn't much like it to know I had anything to do with it." He downed his drink.

Cassie re-surveyed the scene around them. *That was the vice she had a problem with?*

The piano player finished his piece with Paddy. After a long pull from a bottle, he pressed his hat to his chest and, in a rough, twangy voice that made Cassie think of a threadbare blanket drying by the fire, began to sing, accompanied only by the rhythmic thumping of his foot against the wooden floor.

> *"In England some years ago*
> *the sun was pleasant fair and gay.*
> *John Love on board of a ship he entered*
> *and sailed in to A-merica."*

Cassie recognized the song as "The Murder of John Love," one of the folk songs her father's partner used to perform while entertaining clients. "Murder ballads," he'd called them, sung poems about famous crimes from the past. They were often requested over coffee and dessert, though the apparent appeal of pairing gore with sweets had always baffled her.

> *"Love was a man very persevering*
> *in making trades with all he see.*
> *He soon engaged to be a sailor*
> *to sail up and down Lake Erie."*

"Please, Mr. Marsden." Cassie pushed the promissory note back toward him. "I think it could help clear my aunt."

Mr. Marsden studied her as he took another sip of his drink.

> *"He then went into the Southern countries,*
> *to trade for furs and other skins,*
> *but the cruel French and savage Indians*
> *came very near of killing him."*

"All right. I don't know what it'll do, but I'll tell you what I know. As long as you put that away."

Once Cassie had folded the note and slipped it back into her pouch, Mr. Marsden leaned in with his head low, taking cover under the music. "One night, the man on that paper there, Downing, comes in for a drink, looking down on his luck. He sits at the end of the counter, sips on something for a while. Doesn't say much."

> *"But God did spare him a little longer.*
> *He got his lodging and come down the lake.*
> *He went into the town of Lockport*
> *where he made the great mistake."*

"Then old Grumblepuss comes in. And—"

"William Marsden, I told you not to call Peanut that," said a frizzy-haired woman standing in the kitchen doorway behind him—Mrs. Marsden, Cassie presumed, based on Mr. Marsden's reaction to her voice. She strode over and reached around her husband to collect some dirty glasses. "Especially not now. It's a damn shame about him passing. And so violent, too. I know he was a ripe old bastard, but I had a soft spot for him. Ate particular amounts of my liver pie."

"A wonder he didn't kick off sooner, then." Major Drury, who had popped back up next to Cassie, snorted and elbowed her in the ribs. "Am I right?"

Lifting her glass to her lips, mostly to defend against Major Drury's proximity, Cassie tipped the liquid in and blinked back the ensuing tears.

"Don't make me rather it'd been you, Major." Mrs. Marsden raised her eyes upward and placed a hand over her heart. "He said he liked my cooking because it reminded him of his late wife's. Especially my bone jelly and gristle soup." Sniffing wistfully, she returned to her task of dunking glasses in a tub of murky water and placing them back on the counter to be dried.

Over by the piano, Paddy lifted his fiddle, adding a wistful harmony as the piano player continued his story-song.

> "*With Nelson Thayer he made his station*
> *through the summer for to stay.*
> *Nelson had two brothers Isaac and Israel,*
> *Love lent them money for their debts to pay.*"

"Mrs. Marsden, if I may." Cassie tried unsuccessfully to wave Mr. Marsden off as he descended on her glass with the bottle again. "The harbor pilots think Peanut might have been keeping company with a woman. Did you ever see him come around with anyone? Maybe wearing this?" She held out the pendant from Peanut's bedroom.

Mrs. Marsden grabbed Cassie's hand and pulled it to her face. "Lord, that's pretty." She let go. "But I haven't seen it before. And I can't say I ever saw Peanut in here with a woman. Or much anyone else, neither. Mr. Brooks took up the stool next to him sometimes, but I couldn't say whether that was conversin' or Mr. Brooks letting his mind slop out through his mouth, as usual, and Peanut not bothering to move."

"Love lent them quite a sum of money,
He did befriend them every way—"

"They did know each other, though, didn't they?" Cassie remembered Flora's exchange with Mr. Brooks earlier.

Mr. Marsden, who was clearly growing desperate to be rid of Mrs. Marsden, gave her a plaintive look.

"But the cruel creatures they couldn't be quiet
till they had taken his sweet life away."

Major Drury bobbled his head. "Yeah, that's right. Mr. Brooks tried to apprentice as a pilot a ways back, and they set him up under Peanut. But he dropped out pretty quick. Who knows why."

"Maybe he didn't like the wind disturbing his hair." Mr. Marsden picked up his drink but, catching a withering stare from his wife, placed it back on the counter.

"Hey, what about—Whoopsie!" Major Drury grabbed onto the bar as he started to slide off his stool. "Wasn't there that one fellow, with the nostrils? Big enough to fit a fat thumb, each of 'em. Peanut and him seemed to get on, that time he came in, Saturday before last. I even saw 'em out by the outhouse, heads bent together over something, while I was, uh, making space for more beer."

"I remember him." Mrs. Marsden slopped another glass on the counter. "You could set a pair of upright nickels in those. But he must've been from out of town—never seen him before and never seen him since."

"Sure it's not the food keeping him away, Eleanor?" asked Mr. Marsden.

Mrs. Marsden shrieked and hurled a rag at his head, causing several patrons to slosh their drinks onto their laps. "Some people like it!"

She expelled an audible huff and stormed back into the kitchen.

"You look beautiful!" Mr. Marsden called after her. As soon as she was gone, he hunched back over the bar and slurped his drink. "Finally."

Cassie shook her head, trying to clear both the ringing in her ears and the fog sticking to her brain. Her eyes rolled toward her glass. Somehow, she'd emptied another one. Or was it two?

It was strange. The first one had been traumatic, but she'd hardly felt anything after that.

"Actually, Marsden"—Major Drury wiped his mouth—"that feller with the clam-sized nostrils did come back. Earlier tonight."

"When? I didn't see him."

"No idea. Watch's run down—lost my danged winder key for the hundredth time—and I was already too corned to read it anyhow. It was while you and the missus were in the scullery arguing about something or 'nother. Guess that doesn't narrow it much, tho'." He sniggered and sucked on his beer. "Anyhoo, soon as he heard someone talking about how Peanut was dead and murdered and there was an inquest and such, he flew out the door so fast he almost flattened Mr. Klaus coming in the other way."

Mr. Marsden shrugged. "Anyways, Downing's sitting there when Peanut comes in and heads straight towards him. That's when I realize Downing's on Peanut's stool, and I think, dad-blame it, there's going to be a row. But Peanut simply sets himself on the next stool over, calm as can be. Then, and this is when I really think I've got something comin' loose upstairs, since I never met a man who clings to his pennies like Peanut, he buys Downing a drink. Next thing I know, they're talking and, several pours later, Peanut's calling me over to give 'em some paper.

"But, believe me, when I saw what they were up to, I wasn't happy. At least the wife wasn't around to see. She was 'too shaken up by that awful fire' to work, she'd said." He snorted. "More like she thought she'd take a little holiday since we'd finally hired a girl to help in the kitchen. The fire didn't even touch us. Tell you what, though, I wish it had. I'd take the insurance money over this stinking pile any day. Start over, buy me some of those orange groves..."

"Did you see them together any other time after that?" asked Cassie. "Peanut and Mr. Downing?"

"Nah. Downing stuck his head in here night before last looking for him, but that's all. Peanut wasn't even here. Hey, that was the night he died, wasn't it? Let's not remind the missus he took his last meal somewhere else."

The saloon doors flapped open, and Officer Hughes strode in. He had a swagger in his step, more than usual, even, but he stopped when he saw Cassie.

He was giving her that look again, like he had earlier at Peanut's. No, not a look. A stare? Whichever it was, it was confusing. His overall expression was inscrutable, almost unsettlingly so, but his eyes fixed her to the spot, their unabashed directness boring into her and traveling all the way down to her toes.

She raised a hand to her chest, feeling slightly undressed.

"Officer Hughes," Mr. Marsden called. "The usual? Half beer, half water?"

Giving him a sharp nod, Hughes pulled off his hat and made his way toward Cassie.

"I wasn't sure you'd actually come in here, Miss Gwynne," Hughes said as he pushed a now-dozing Major Drury off his stool.

"And why is that?" Cassie gulped her drink. Hughes's shoulder had brushed hers as he sat down, and the spot was on fire.

"I didn't think someone like you would deign to patronize a hole like this. No offense, Marsden, though I did just spend part of my evening sorting drunkards who were trying to ride a goat through the door."

Cassie took another gulp. "Shows how much you know about me."

"I know that your shoes alone probably cost more than my suit, though why a woman who looks like you thinks she needs to spend money on fancy clothes is beyond me. And that, even though with that wit and those eyes you could have anyone you wanted, you think men like Atherton Brooks are worthy of your attention."

"You're—That's not true. Except maybe the bit about the suit."

What did he just say about me?

"Please." Hughes waved away a puff of smoke drifting past his face. "I saw you watching him out there. So he dresses well and has pretty manners. All he knows how to do is drink and chase women, and maybe sail a boat. Yet you all still flock about him as if he were a fairy-tale prince. Now, a *real* man—"

An uncharacteristically girlish giggle escaped from Cassie's lips, surprising her as much as Hughes.

"What?"

Cassie clapped her hand to her mouth but another giggle squeezed out. In the midst of Hughes's tirade about manliness, she'd noticed a cluster of delicate white blossoms clinging to the end of his mustache. It bounced gaily up and down each time he jerked his head to emphasize a point.

"I say, what on earth is so funny?"

"Nothing. You just have... some flowers—there." Hardly believing what she was doing, Cassie reached out and plucked the blossoms. She held them up. "*Aloysia virgata*, sweet almond. One of my favorites."

Hughes drew back and brushed off his face. "Must have gotten in there when I tackled those goat-riding idiots into the bushes. But see? I execute a feat of valor, and I get laughed at. Mr. Brooks nearly causes an accident, then falls off a sidewalk because he's too inebriated to lift his own feet, and you swoon. You know it's all a façade, right? That genteel and expensive appearance? There's nothing behind it. At least not anymore. I heard he used the last of his inheritance to buy that clothing store of his, and whereas it was perfectly profitable when he acquired it, he managed to send it into a downward spiral in a matter of months."

"I didn't swoon." Cassie had finally mustered up an appropriate amount of irritation. "I was simply getting out of the way when—Did you say Mr. Brooks's business was failing? Because I heard Major Drury say he had plenty of—"

A roar erupted from a large, rough-looking man at the card table. He kicked out his chair and glowered at the man across from him, who was even larger and rougher-looking.

"You callin' me a cheater?"

"If you're not, empty your sleeves and make me a liar." The second man wobbled to his feet and took a swig from his beer bottle, keeping his gaze locked with the other man's as blood dripped into his beard. Apparently, he'd found operating the swing stopper to be too much trouble and had instead broken the bottle off at the neck.

"Don't you try and intiminnate me."

"Gentlemen, why don't we—" A third man reached out to mediate but slipped and head-butted one of them, who swung back at him but missed, landing the blow on his original opponent's jaw.

Before the hit had even registered, the other card players were swinging and kicking, and, in an instant, the rest of the bar had joined the melee. Including Mr. Marsden, who picked up a chair with a wild cackle and broke it over someone's back in front of the door, blocking the exit.

"Everyone calm the blazes down!" Hughes shouted. He shot his gun into the ceiling, but neither the sound nor the ensuing shower of plaster had any effect on the chaos. The latter did, however, get in a man's eyes, causing him to trip onto Cassie and pin her to the ground under his bear-like mass of flesh.

A soft voice brushed her ear. "Hold on, Cassie."

Cassie felt the man roll off her chest, and she gasped as air rushed back into her lungs.

Then Esme's face appeared above her, perfectly framed by two fiery auburn curls that looked alive in the flickering light from the lamps lining the wall.

"Hello." The word stuck to Cassie's teeth. "Your hair is pretty."

Esme tucked the escaped curls back under her turban and pulled Cassie to her feet. "Come with me. Quickly, before you really get hurt."

CHAPTER TWELVE

Ducking past Major Drury as he whooped and twirled a billiards stick over his head like a battle staff, Esme walked to the back and disappeared through a curtain. Cassie staggered after her, and, after a minor altercation with the clingy fabric, she found herself in a storage area crowded with chairs, old newspapers, and sacks of cabbage and potatoes.

"Where are we going?"

"Out." Esme opened a door, revealing a steep set of stairs.

"But that goes up."

"We'll come down the next building over. You can get a lot of places here by rooftop, if you know where you're going."

Abandoning a shrug, Cassie fell onto the steps with an undignified grunt and began hauling herself up by the handrail. Finally, a sliver of light appeared above their heads, and Esme pushed on the ceiling. Moonlight shot to the base of the stairs, landing on an old shoe filled with cigar butts.

Cassie followed Esme's boots through the opening.

"Isn't it lovely?" Esme leapt over a chimney pipe and onto the next level of the building, her arms flowing behind her like fairy wings. "Being up here, above everything?"

Cassie murmured amicably, bemused by Esme's sudden gaiety after her earlier reservedness. When she got to her feet, however, she gaped with astonishment. A grand, unobstructed view across the island stretched out in front of them, and, above it all, the moon hung from the velvety, jet-black sky like a silver dollar in a numismatist's case.

"It's incredible." Cassie had always been drawn to high places. There was something fascinating, powerful, about how one could shrink the world by climbing up above it. And pretend for a time that all of one's problems went along to scale. "I used to sit on the roof at home sometimes, when I wanted to be alone with my thoughts."

Esme adjusted her turban. "Oh, I try not to be alone with my thoughts. I don't trust them." She followed that with a wink, but Cassie could appreciate the sentiment. Especially these days, when all her trains of thought seemed to end up at the same destination. "But, in all honesty, I mostly like how up here no one's looking at you. You can be yourself. Whatever that might be."

Cassie tried to nod but tripped, though she could have sworn she was standing still.

Esme peered over the edge. "Not to mention the opportunities to have a little fun."

Major Drury, who had found his way out of the saloon somehow, had taken up a stance in the grassy area below… and was relieving himself on the wall next to the outhouse. As Cassie screwed up her face in disgust, Esme scooped some sludge from the gutter, lobbed it over the side, and ducked. From the string of curses that followed, it appeared she had hit her mark.

Cassie laughed so hard she snorted.

"Let me try." Holding onto Esme for balance, Cassie slopped together her own sludge-grenade and tossed it. Astonishingly, she scored as well, and, letting their laughter go, the two women scampered backward and collapsed into a merry heap.

"I'm not even sorry," Cassie said between laughs. "I mean, he's already at the outhouse. Why not go in?"

She crawled back to the edge and, seeing the Major had fled, pushed herself into a sitting position. "Thanks for helping me back there, by the way. I don't know when I would have found my way out on my own." She swung her legs over the side.

"No thanks required. Anyone who's family to Flora is family to me... 'And doing things for family is not trouble. Understand?'" Esme chuckled and lowered herself next to her. "Flora thinks very highly of you, you know. And Jake does, too. Are you really as smart as they say?"

"I'm not sure how to answer that."

"You did figure out from little more than a clock and a basket of laundry that someone had searched Peanut's study the other night."

"Oh, I—"

"And the way you snuck that ledger book out using your bustle? Brilliant!"

Cassie grinned. "Thank you, but 'desperate' was more like it. I knew if Mr. Shaw saw it, he'd never let me get a look at it, so I had to think of something. Though I can't say I really understood what it was when I did look at it. But it did lead me to some interesting information. Someone borrowed a large sum of money from Peanut recently, and I'm wondering whether it had something to do with Peanut's death."

"Oh? Who?"

"A man named Matthew Downing."

"He lives next door to Peanut. Did something bad happen between them?"

"I'm not sure yet. All I know is one, Mr. Downing put his entire house up as collateral for the loan, and two, he was out looking for Peanut shortly before Peanut was killed." Cassie frowned and flicked a pebble off the ledge.

"You're thinking about your father."

Cassie flicked another pebble. "I wish he were here right now. I wish it so much it makes me sick." She looked at Esme. "Now he was the brilliant one. He'd know exactly what to do."

"Flora said his intelligence was truly something to be admired. Among many other things. She was very fond of him, I think."

"So was I." Cassie still felt a tingle of unreality whenever she spoke of him in the past tense like that. "He was my best friend. The one I went to when things were great and when things were bad. So, when he was gone, and my whole world was falling apart around me, I... Well, I couldn't go to him about it, could I?"

Esme drew her knees to her chest. "If you don't mind my asking, what exactly happened? With your father."

"Oh."

"You don't have to talk about it if you don't want to."

"No, it's okay." Cassie coughed and tried to pull herself up straighter. Her speech had slowed, and her eyelids felt as if they were tied to fishing weights. Even the lump in her throat, the one that always crept up, or sometimes leapt up and punched her in the tonsils, when she spoke about her father was sluggish.

"There's not really too much to tell. I had found this invitation of sorts on our doorstep, an announcement about a special book market taking place for one night only in Madison Square Park. It was being held at a fairly late hour, but the information promised an entire booth dedicated to Asia travelogues, a particular fascination of mine, and Father was going to be busy at the office, so I—decided to go." She scratched her arm. "I knew I shouldn't have—It was far too late and dark for anyone to be wandering the city alone. But, well—Father and I had argued that morning before he left for work, see... He'd wanted me to start taking the housekeeper, Mrs. Wagner, to the market with me, though I'd been doing the shopping on my own for ages, and while he'd said it was just good sense given the rise in crime in the city, I accused him of not recognizing me as an adult, of doubting my independence and competence... I suppose I was trying to prove something. Or maybe I was just being defiant, like a child. Either way, it was foolish."

Cassie stared into her lap, watching the pattern on her skirt ripple as a breeze brushed by. "And, what do you know, I mistook the details somehow—I'd dropped the handbill somewhere along the way so couldn't even check it—and when I arrived where I thought the event was being held, there was nothing there but an empty piazza fraught with shadows. I started home immediately, but then these men, these masked robbers, jumped out and, without saying a thing, they…" She tugged at her glove, searching for the words. "They pinned me to the ground with a knife to my throat and I got cut when I tried to get away."

Esme touched her arm. "I didn't mean to make you—"

"No, no. It's okay. I—Well, before anything else happened, my father appeared from out of nowhere and threw himself at them, even though there must have been half a dozen to his one. He saved me. Gave his life for me." Cassie swallowed. "And I couldn't do a thing about it."

They sat in silence for a long while, listening to the night.

"It's confusing, don't you think," Cassie said finally, "what they say. That your heart is light when you're happy and heavy when you're sad. Because when you lose someone you love, it feels like part of your heart has fallen away. Shouldn't a full heart be heavier than one that's missing a part of it?"

Esme studied her boots. "I'm not the right person to ask, really. Because, I'd think, to know how it feels to lose someone you love, you'd have to love someone first. Pretty much everyone I've ever gotten close to has been, at best, a disappointment. Other than Flora, that is."

"I'm sorry."

"Don't be. It just is. The best thing I ever did was learn how to put, and keep, the past behind me. The way I see it, life is one long exercise in forgetting. From all the terrible things that happen to us and around us, to the fact that nothing we do really matters in the end. Dust to dust and all that. Otherwise, we couldn't go on."

"That's dark."

"No. Realistic. It's what lets us continue our lives. Dull the pain, clean the slate. There's only so much one can carry."

"I suppose that's true." Cassie tucked her skirts in around her knees. "But, for what it's worth, Flora does seem to care a great deal about you, too. Making you her apprentice? That's no small gesture."

Esme gave a soft laugh. "I still can't believe she did that, even after smelling what I was capable of!"

"Aw, it can't be as bad as we're making it out to be. Here, come here." Cassie reached toward her. "I want to smell that flacon again. The one you wear around your neck."

"No, you don't." Esme pulled away with another laugh.

Cassie sat back. "You're right. I don't." She squinted at the front of Esme's dress. "Where is it, anyway? What are those, pearls?"

"Thought I'd try something different today. Drink?" She dug out her jar.

Cassie declined with a shake of her head, which proceeded to loll onto her shoulder.

"You're right. It's evil stuff, isn't it." Esme held the jar over the edge as if to pour it out, but then seemed to change her mind and tucked it back into her skirt.

"Wow. Lookatthat." Cassie lifted her eyebrows to get her eyes to open wider.

A broad arch, soft and white through the main belt but outlined by a glow of color along the edges, had appeared above the swaying palm tree silhouettes on the horizon. It shimmered, almost shyly, as though it had noticed her watching it.

"That's a moonbow," Esme said. "Or lunar rainbow. Only visible when the moon is low and full and the sky is very dark at the same time, with the right amount of mist in the air. They're rare, much rarer than a regular rainbow, but this is actually our second in a month."

"I've never seen anything so beaut—" The world slipped upward, and Cassie felt Esme's arm catch against her chest.

"And it's time to get you home," came Esme's voice, swathed in cotton.

Cassie tried to itch her nose but missed. There was a scraping of shoes, a pressure under her arms, and she felt herself slide backward and up, her legs jangling below her before her feet found the floor.

"Only a few more steps and we can climb down through Mr. MacVittye's tailor shop. He leaves a door propped for his cats."

Cassie smiled faintly as a basket of kittens bobbed through her consciousness. Then she closed her eyes, letting the wave of darkness that had been cresting overhead finally crash down around her.

When Cassie woke up, she was back in her bed at Flora's house. Or, rather, sprawled on top of it, still in her clothes. Somehow Esme had managed to get her home without her involvement.

She pressed a palm to her temple, trying to quiet the throbbing bruise on her head, which was engaged in a percussive duet with one of her eyeballs.

Water.

She stood with shaky knees and felt her way toward the door, cursing as her foot collided with a chair. Every sound was an assault, the jingle of her chatelaine, the rustle of her skirts, the squeal of hinges as she opened the door. When she reached the bottom of the stairs, however, she heard a different set of sounds coming from Esme's room, a small offshoot of the kitchen at the end of the hall: voices, a man's and a woman's, soft murmurs punctuated by the occasional laugh and an urgent *shush*.

There was a chirp by her feet. It was the kitten, who had dutifully roused herself and followed her down.

"No need to make that face," Cassie told the sleepy creature blinking up at her. "Esme can do what she wants."

Cassie was, however, still thirsty, and she was trying to decide how she was going to work the water pump in the kitchen without making her presence known when she caught sight of a light bobbing in the street. Someone was out there with a lamp.

Tucking the kitten back with her toe, she slipped through the front door onto the porch and made her way down the steps. By the time she reached the gate, the light was hovering by the side of Peanut's house.

There was a tinkle of glass breaking, and the light disappeared.

Reacting almost automatically, Cassie ran into the street, bearing down against the sloshing in her stomach and the deafening crunch of gravel and shells below her feet. She pushed past Peanut's no-trespassing signs and through the gate, and, in a couple more strides, she reached the place where she'd last seen the light. The kitchen door was swinging in the breeze, its window glittering in shards on the ground.

Not sure what she would find, or what she would do when she found it, Cassie held her breath and passed into the darkness inside. Immediately, she heard footsteps creaking overhead. The intruder was upstairs.

She skirted the kitchen table, which, she was relieved to find, was no longer occupied by Peanut, and crept into the hall, pausing at the foot of the main staircase to listen. Then, gathering her skirts with one hand and unhooking the scissors from her chatelaine with the other, she started upward.

She gasped and fell against the railing. She'd stepped on one of her petticoats (it was impossible to hold all of that fabric out of the way with only one hand) and sent the basket of dirty linens she had seen earlier skittering across the floor. Fortunately, whoever was upstairs didn't seem to have heard; the footsteps continued uninterrupted.

Hiking her dress up around her hips, she resumed her ascent. The footsteps grew louder as she approached the top and were joined by the clatter of objects being shoved and drawers being slammed. The noise appeared to be coming from a room opposite the staircase—a taxidermy workshop of some sort, if she remembered correctly.

She darted across the landing and pressed her back against the wall, craning her neck to see around the doorframe. Inside, a portable lamp gleamed from a workbench, casting an eerie glow over an array of scalpels, paintbrushes, and needles, as well as a bowl of glass eyes and a collection of preserving jars containing items she didn't care to identify. On the shelf above it, more stuffed squirrels stared blankly into the darkness like soldiers awaiting orders.

The room darkened as the silhouette of a man passed in front of the lamp.

Cassie jumped into the doorway, her scissors lifted. "Who's there?"

The man froze like a field rabbit suddenly aware of a shadow overhead, and for several seconds neither of them moved, the silence broken only by the rustle of leaves outside.

Then the lamp flashed.

The man was hurtling across the room, straight toward her.

CHAPTER THIRTEEN

Cassie braced herself for impact. Then, right as the man was about to reach her, she changed her mind and stuck out her foot instead.

The man somersaulted past and landed on his back in the hallway.

As she had suspected, or hoped, he hadn't been trying to attack her. He'd been trying to make a run for it.

Cassie picked up the lamp and held it up to his face. "Who are you?"

The man, who appeared to be in his nightclothes, flicked his eyes toward the stairs, then down at his bare feet, which were pinned together between Cassie's boots.

"A neighbor." There were several spots of blood soaking through the forearm of his right sleeve.

"What are you doing here in the middle of the night?"

"One might ask you the same. Whoever you are."

"I'm Cassie Gwynne, Flora Hale's niece. But I'm not the one with cuts on my arm in a house with a broken window."

The man's mouth tightened.

"Well?"

He dropped his head back. "My name is Matthew Downing."

Cassie sucked in a breath and pointed her tiny scissors in his face.

"Whoa!" Mr. Downing threw up an arm. "What was that for?"

Cassie forced herself to lower her hand. He hadn't actually threatened her, not yet at least, so there was no reason to escalate things. "As I'm sure you can appreciate, given what's been going on around here, I'm interested to know why you've broken into a murdered man's house. And in your nightclothes, no less."

Mr. Downing struggled to sit up. He was about Cassie's father's age but slighter in frame and, judging by the sideburns extending below his nightcap, considerably grayer. He had the same lines on his forehead, too, the kind worn deep by nights spent squinting over books in candlelight.

Keeping him fixed with her gaze, Cassie dragged a chair over from the taxidermy room.

"Thanks." He climbed onto the seat, his joints crackling like lit kindling. He took a couple of breaths then considered her with tired eyes. "If I tell you why I'm here, will you promise not to tell anyone else?"

"I'll think about it."

"I guess that's the best I'm going to get." He rubbed his neck. "You've heard about the fire on Centre last month."

"Yes."

"That fire destroyed the entire three-story commercial brick block I own, along with most of the stock inside. A total loss. And, as luck would have it, my insurance ran out last April, and I failed to renew it, stupidly trying to save a few dollars on premiums. I was wiped out. Everything I had worked for, swept away in a matter of hours."

He removed his ring and rolled it between his thumb and forefinger.

"I married late in life, you see, and have a young family to care for. So, when Peanut approached me a couple of days after the fire, saying he'd read about my losses in the paper and could lend me the money I needed to get back on my feet, well, it felt like an opportunity I couldn't pass up.

"The price was steep, though I expected that. I've never known Peanut to do anything out of the goodness of his heart—certainly not since Gilda died. And he wanted my house as collateral. That part felt a little odd, since he'd tried to buy it from me last year and I declined, but I needed the money to rebuild. Some of the brickwork on the commercial plot was still viable, so I figured I could pay him back quickly and put it all behind me. Only, it didn't work out that way."

"Oh?"

"Almost immediately, we ran into issues with the foundation that made the construction more complicated than anticipated. Even with the temporary job I'd taken to tide us over, I realized I wasn't going to have enough even to make the first payment, so I—"

"Went looking for Peanut at the Three Star Saloon, to convince him to give you more time. Only, he wasn't there."

Mr. Downing jerked. "How'd you know that?"

"What happened when you found him? Was there an altercation? Did you try to get the agreement back?" Cassie thought of the cuts on Peanut's hands.

"What? No, I—"

"Mr. Downing, where were you the night Peanut was killed?"

"Now wait just an ever-loving minute!" Mr. Downing pulled off his nightcap and gestured at her with it. "I swear to you, I didn't have anything to do with that. I'll admit I broke in here so I could destroy the promissory note for the loan, but I only thought of that after I heard he was dead."

Cassie's shoulders fell. Despite his copious amounts of sideburn hair, Mr. Downing was, like Peanut, emphatically bald. He wasn't the man who had rifled through Peanut's study the night before.

"I never even got to speak to him," Mr. Downing continued. "I did go to Three Star that night looking for him, but he wasn't there and after that I had to report to that other job I mentioned, overnight patrolman at Mr. Bock's icehouse on the Broome Street Wharf. I was on duty from midnight until eight in the morning."

"Can anyone confirm that?"

"Confirm it? Well… Oh! Austin Hughes saw me a little later in my shift. It was right after the rain let up, by one of the old warehouses. I'd seen a light and come to check it out, but it was only him chasing out some vagrants who were squatting there. I helped him chain the place up, and after that we circled back every quarter of an hour or so until the end of my shift, in case they tried to come back."

Cassie leaned back against the wall. That was the end of that. Dr. Ames estimated Peanut had been killed sometime between three and five in the morning, and the rain had ended before three. She knew that because when the rain stopped, the sudden silence had woken her, and she'd looked at the clock, convinced she'd overslept. So, assuming what Mr. Downing was saying was true—she'd have to confirm his story with Hughes, of course—not only was he not the intruder from the night before, he was nowhere near the lookout tower when Peanut was attacked.

"I know where your note is," she said.

Mr. Downing dropped his nightcap. "You do?"

"I found it in Peanut's study down the hall earlier this afternoon."

"You mean you already knew about—Did you say 'down the hall'? I thought this was his—Then where is—Can I have it?"

Cassie hooked her scissors back onto her chatelaine while Mr. Downing's brain and words sorted themselves out. "I don't know."

"Please, Miss Gwynne." Mr. Downing stood. "My family doesn't know what I've done, the loan, the other job… Even at this very moment my wife thinks I'm in the outhouse suffering from the aftereffects of a questionable piece of meat. And, if that note's called in, we'll have nowhere to live."

"Destroying the note won't solve this," said Cassie. "Peanut will have filed a lien with the county. It's attached to the deed for your house now."

"That's not a problem. My nephew is a county clerk."

Cassie suspected she knew what he meant by "not a problem," but even so she couldn't help being moved by his plea. Peanut had taken advantage of a desperate man and hadn't cared that his actions could destroy a family.

"I'll tell you what. Once I confirm your story with Officer Hughes, I'll give you back the note. But if a will or a next-of-kin entitled to inherit Peanut's interests is found, you have to promise to pay the heir back at least the amount you borrowed. You can make it anonymous, whatever you have to do, but anything less would be stealing in my book."

Mr. Downing dipped his head. "I understand. You have principles, like your aunt. Who, for what it's worth, I don't believe is a murderer, either. She's outspoken, for sure, and a touch eccentric. Unusual, you know—"

"Why does everyone keep saying that? Maybe she's simply more honest about who she is than anyone else."

"Oh." Mr. Downing wiped the perspiration from his face. "I only meant—despite the Bohemian clothes and the loony-do moral crusades and all that, I've always known her to be kind and generous, as her parents were, and I'm sure she wouldn't hurt anyone." He put his nightcap back on. "But on that note, might I ask, I heard Peanut was stabbed by something... unique. Do you happen to recall any details about the weapon?"

Cassie paused, now both confused and irritated.

"I know it's macabre," Mr. Downing said, "but growing up I enjoyed reading about unusual weaponry, the way other children read adventure stories. I've always wanted to have a collection of my own."

"I see." And this man had called *Flora* eccentric? "All Dr. Ames said was he didn't think it was a normal knife, like one might use for hunting and such. It was long and thin, with a small, sharp point. Which created a specific sort of wound. There was little to no external bleeding, but a great deal of internal damage."

"Hm." Mr. Downing tapped a finger against his knee. "That actually does stir the mind. If I had to wager, I'd say it was the work of a stiletto knife. Fascinating weapon. Originated in Italy a long time ago, medieval times I think, where it was a favorite of assassins."

Cassie shifted.

"It's all about the shape," he went on, rubbing his hands together, "slim with a narrow point. Makes it able to penetrate heavy fabric and reach far inside the victim, where it can be twisted and thrusted for maximum effect before being withdrawn, yet easy to conceal, even up a sleeve.

"They're still used for that purpose sometimes, you know. My brother once told me about a friend up in Natchez, Mississippi, who went into hiding because he'd run afoul of an Italian named Mascio in New Orleans. Any time a person passed too close to him, he'd recoil, fearing a stiletto was about to be thrust in his side. That's one thing Mascio's men were known for, secret attacks with the stiletto. You'd never see it coming. The city tried outlawing such weapons in seventy-nine, but I doubt it's accomplished much."

The next morning, a low-pitched rumble close to her face stirred Cassie from her sleep, and she slowly became aware of a pressure on her chest. She wrinkled her forehead, her eyes still closed, and tried to breathe.

A grip seized her throat.

Sitting up in a panic, she threw out her fists. A thud sounded next to her and she twisted toward it with a sharp inhale—only to find the kitten looking up at her, apparently as confused as she was.

"Oh, bless it all." She released her breath. "I'd almost forgotten. It is a truth universally acknowledged that cats cannot abide people who are sleeping." She started to flop back down when she realized she was on the floor again. This time, however, she was next to the washstand, lying in a partial nest constructed from scented finger towels.

She sighed and lay back more carefully, tucking a handful of the towels behind her head. As soon as she was horizontal, however, the kitten, seeming to decide they had reached an understanding, climbed back onto her chest and resumed kneading her neck and chin with her furry little paws.

"Okay, okay. Hello." Cassie collected the kitten's front legs in one hand and held them away from her face as the kitten continued to purr and flex. Her paws were soft, but the tips of her claws were not. "I suppose I should thank you for waking me. I was having the dream again."

"The dream," which had been coming to her every couple of weeks over the past year, was less a specific dream than a dream setting, in which she would find herself incorporated into a series of stereoview cards. The number of cards varied, as did their exact content. But in each scene, she and everything around her were, as in images viewed through a stereoscope, three-dimensional, black and white—aside, perhaps, from the odd painted-in detail—and deathly still. She could see well enough, and she could hear, smell, taste, and feel everything as acutely as in life, yet she was frozen in place like one of Peanut's taxidermy projects, unable even to blink an eyelid over a glass eye.

Last night there had been three.

In the first, she sat on a rug. She must have been young because her feet were bare and the roses in the pattern below her, with their layers of softly curved petals, seemed large enough to nestle her face into. She didn't recognize the room around her, though. It wasn't in the brownstone, or any other place she remembered living in New York, but it was clean and cozy and lovingly decorated with wildflower drawings and hand-carved figurines of sea turtles at play, and it smelled of citrus and smoky pine. On one side of her, a black-bricked fireplace burned so fiercely the heat pressed into her cheek; on the other, Father sat in a rocking chair with armrests like fiddlehead ferns. He wasn't looking at her, though. He was looking out the window, past the snowing orange trees, at something far away.

Next, she was in her father's old bedroom, in the New York boarding house where they'd lived until she was eight. It was early afternoon, but the curtains were still drawn, letting in only a sliver of white sunlight. Empty vials, tipped onto their sides, littered the bedside table, and the air had a medicinal bite that mixed uneasily with the smell of roasted meat drifting up from below. She had called out several times, but still Father just lay there, his hair, uncut and unwashed, draped across the pillow like seaweed on the beach. She couldn't see him breathe.

In the last, she was fully grown. It was nighttime in New York, and she sat on the ground at the edge of Madison Square Park's glamorous cobblestone piazza. The nearby electric sun towers were bright enough to burn her eyes, but she was beyond the reach of their circle of light, cloaked in the shadow of that enormous statue of a torch-bearing arm, "Liberty Enlightening the World," which rose taller than the trees. Something warm and sticky dripped down her neck. A metallic taste coated her tongue. And Father, bruised and smeared with dirt and red, was heavy in her arms.

Her throat was raw because she'd been screaming. Screaming that they'd been attacked, that they'd been robbed and beaten. Screaming that her father was dying and someone had to help. Then just screaming. But now there were uniformed men about. They were trying to take Father away from her, and she'd had to stop screaming because she needed all of her strength to hold on to him. Because once she let go, he'd be gone forever.

The kitten squeaked and squirmed in her arms, and Cassie released her with a gasp. She hadn't realized she was holding on so tightly.

When Cassie finally went downstairs, she found Flora and Esme hunched excitedly over an array of vials and droppers on the counter. The dogs were pacing the floor in front of them, trying to determine whether food was involved, and Kleio was delivering a nonsensical speech from the head of the Athena bust above the doorway.

"Good morning." Cassie hadn't been expecting to see Flora out of her room. Or Esme, for that matter. And neither of them had a trace of the previous day's troubles about them. That should have been a relief, but it was actually a little disconcerting.

Flora waved a fistful of testing strips in the air. "Why, yes, it has been a good morning. For weeks, my efforts to recover the compositions in my destroyed notebook have been moving at a snail's pace, but there must be something in the air today because we've reconstructed two fairly complicated ones already since coming down." She turned a page in the notebook in front of her and scribbled something. "I have to give most of the credit to Esme, though. Each time I reach a mental wall, she helps me right over it."

"Here, Flora." Esme added a drop of something to a tiny dish. "This will do it. I can feel it."

Flora inhaled a couple of times through a piece of wool then bent over the mixture, waving her hand toward her nose.

"Yes, that's it! I'm almost afraid to stop now." She brushed a strand of hair out of her face, her eyes gleaming. "Maybe we'll even be able to reconstruct that scent I came up with for the auction this weekend. The one bottle I made got destroyed in the fire. Such a shame. I'd been tinkering with it for days and finally gotten it right."

Esme picked up a rag and rubbed at a black smudge on the cuff of her blouse. "I remember you working on it. What was the name of it again?"

"Dream's Edge. Because it made me think of the state you're in shortly after waking, when the details of your dream have gone, leaving you only with impressions and feelings, maybe the hazy outlines of things. Like you're right outside of a window but can only barely see through. A little ironic, given the circumstances."

There was a knock at the door, and Flora clapped her hands together. "Oh, I hope that's a customer! We haven't had any since that one man came in on Wednesday afternoon, and for all the time he spent wandering around the store, all he bought was a single scented bookmark."

Esme went to answer, and when she returned, she was holding a card bearing the Egmont Hotel insignia.

"No customer. Just a message for Cassie from Miss Lily Townsend requesting that Cassie join her, along with Mr. Samuel Townsend and Mr. Atherton Brooks, for breakfast at the hotel at ten."

"My," Flora said. "This is a pleasant surprise."

Cassie accepted the card from Esme. "Yes. I saw Lily drive by last night, so I knew they hadn't left yet, but I wonder why—"

"Cassie!" Flora slapped her notebook closed. "There's no time for that. You're expected within the hour."

"But are you sure I should be making social calls right now? Given what's going on with the coroner's jury—"

"The very last thing I want to discuss at this moment is the coroner's jury. Besides, I haven't heard a word from them since our interviews yesterday morning, so that has to be a good sign. Now, is that what you're going to wear?"

CHAPTER FOURTEEN

Shortly before ten, Cassie sneezed her way toward the Egmont Hotel in the blinding mid-morning sun, fighting the urge to abandon what remained of her ladylike pretensions and break into a full-out trot. After the fuss that had been made over her dress, her hair, and, of course, which of Flora's *eaux de toilette* to mist over it all, she had taken a detour by the Egmont's livery stable to drop Peanut's "ledger" off for Jake, so she was now very short on time, and she hated being late. Especially given who was waiting.

As she hovered on Sixth Street, waiting to cross, she performed a last-minute check of her dress, a multi-layered visiting gown of sapphire-blue faille and ivory damask that she hoped was worth the money. Even with Flora's discerning eye on the task, she wouldn't put it past herself at a time like this to misalign her buttons or tuck one of her skirts into her stockings.

Then, remembering one last item, she smoothed her fingers over the wide choker necklace around her neck. It was fairly constricting, but the dense web of black Spanish lace did a good job of covering up what lay beneath.

In a few steps, the Egmont Hotel soared into view. Four stories and gleaming white, the sparkling structure was swathed in wraparound verandas on each level and crowned by a squadron of pennants. Elegant equipages, including an omnibus set on tracks, awaited passengers by a hedge of plantered orange trees, and a tropical garden with a fountain swayed across the street. According to Flora, the hotel's inside features were similarly impressive.

In addition to all the newest modern amenities such as running hot- and cold-water baths and Creighton oral annunciators in every room, the hotel had billiards tables, lawn tennis and croquet courts, a bowling alley, and a shooting gallery.

Cassie climbed the front steps and, after passing through an airy piazza sprinkled with men in palmetto-weave chairs puffing cigars and reading newspapers, entered the lobby.

A clerk who appeared equal parts rabbit and nutcracker soldier stepped forward to greet her.

"Greetings, Miss. My name is George Littell, and I am the proprietor and head clerk here. How may I direct you?" His nose tipped upward as if testing the wind.

"Yes, I have an appointment in the breakfast hall. My name is—"

"Miss Cassie Gwynne! My word, how fine you look!" Mrs. Huddleston, the woman Cassie had met on the wharf that first morning, was waving to her from the telephone and telegraph exchange desk. Though they were indoors, she was again wearing tinted spectacles and a hat draped in mosquito netting, and as she barreled toward Cassie across the rich Brussels carpeting, an attendant pushing a cart of valises dove to get out of her way. Her dog, who was dressed in a pink sweater trimmed with lace today, panted along by her side, managing by some miracle to avoid being trampled to death.

"Good morning, Mrs. Huddleston," Cassie said. "Are you enjoying your visit?"

"I am very much indeed! Considering, of course. I did hear what happened to you and your aunt, finding that harbor pilot... you know. And the ugly business with the coroner's jury, you poor dears. But don't you worry. Everything will turn out just fine. I'm sure of it."

She clicked her tongue in a manner suggesting she was, to her great disappointment, sure of the opposite.

"Anyway, we did take the most fascinating supper last night at Sun's Parlor Restaurant. With no offense to the Egmont's 'chef doo cuisine,' it was the best meal I've had in a long time. Now, the oysters are excellent, but the secret is to ask the proprietor to prepare a specialty from his homeland in the Far East. And while I was nervous to try something so exotic, I always say one should never miss an opportunity to—"

"Tell her about your pocket, dear." Mr. Huddleston poked his head out from behind his wife.

Cassie jumped. She hadn't realized he was there.

Mrs. Huddleston clapped her hands. "Oh, yes! They've caught the thief, can you believe it? That policeman from the wharf—Officer Hughes, was it?—who wasn't even on duty at the time, spotted the rogue trying to remove a lady's bracelet during a tightrope exhibition yesterday afternoon. Apparently, he took him down with a flying leap that almost made the performer slip off his rope."

"How wonderful." Cassie was sincerely glad. And astounded Hughes had managed not to brag about it when he saw her at the Three Star Saloon. "Did you recover what was taken from you?"

Mrs. Huddleston picked up Oscar and tucked him under her arm like a football. "Unfortunately, no, though they did find a number of other 'borrowed' items on the thief's person. He claimed he lost all my coins a couple of nights before in a dice game behind Mr. DaCosta's grocery up in Old Town. And he threw the pocket in the river, which is the real shame. That pocket lent a touch of class, don't you think? Now, if you'll excuse me... Mr. Littell! Where has that clerk gone off to? Mr. Littell!"

"I am here, Mrs. Huddleston!" The clerk hurried back toward them, a muddy pair of men's dress shoes laid across his forearm like a serving towel.

Mrs. Huddleston harrumphed. "Mr. Littell, I need to have another word with the chef about Oscar's breakfast. He didn't care for what he had yesterday, so we really need to rethink the menu and—"

Oscar, who had been nosing at the shoes Mr. Littell was carrying, sneezed so hard he almost shot out from under Mrs. Huddleston's arm.

"Harold!" Mrs. Huddleston scrambled to hold on to the dog as he sneezed over and over. "He's going off again!"

Mr. Huddleston ran back behind his wife and crouched like a halfback waiting for a handoff. "Good London Weather! What is he doing with his face in those dirty shoes?"

Mr. Littell hopped. "Dear, dear me. I had forgotten I was holding these. Mr. Williams!"

Another clerk, a close copy of the first, appeared from around the corner, and Mr. Littell handed him the shoes. "Have these cleaned and delivered to the Florida House. Charge to the Townsend account." He lowered his voice. "And have it rushed. They were dropped at the desk the day before yesterday, but somehow we managed to overlook them."

He turned back to Mrs. Huddleston, who was rocking the spent dog in her arms.

"A thousand apologies, Mrs. Huddleston. If you would be so kind as to wait here, I will fetch Monsieur Ludwig immediately. Miss Gwynne, please come with me. The breakfast hall is *en route*."

His nose leading the way, the clerk marched Cassie through a series of handsomely appointed parlors and reception rooms. At the end of a long, carpeted hallway, he opened a set of doors into a sea of finely dressed ladies and gentlemen, who filled the air with the tinkle of spoons and teacups as they chatted around tables set with white linen and sparkling china. Behind them, sunlight poured through a wall of floor-to-ceiling windows, each framed by an arch and fluted columns with palm-frond capitals.

Mr. Littell halted in front of a grand fireplace and performed a brisk about-face. "And whom are you meeting this morning?"

"Samuel and Lily Townsend." Cassie forcibly relaxed her right arm, which had tensed in anticipation of a return salute.

"Ah. I do not believe they have come down yet. You are welcome to wait for them here, unless you would prefer I show you to a table."

"I'll wait. Thank you."

"Very good. Mr. Ford!"

A waiter glided over with a tray of champagne flutes, but Cassie declined. The smell of alcohol rising from the bubbling liquid, faint as it was, had instantly made her stomach churn in an alarming way. Instead, she turned to consider the painting hanging above the massive mantel, a portrait of a woman holding an infant child. The woman's neck was long and graceful, and her hair was so dark it nearly blended into the shadowed background. She wore a gown and matching mantle of deep red velvet trimmed with pearls and lace, and her son, who had on cherry red shoes, played with a crown.

Cassie removed her hat and gloves, wondering what kind of relationship the two had had in life. Whether they had played together. Whether he had gone to her when he was sad or lonely. Whether she had lived to see him grow into a man.

"Cassie?"

Sam.

Steadying herself, Cassie unhooked her fan from her chatelaine and turned with a smile.

"Why, good morning, Sam." She gave herself a languid wave with her fan, as Esme had taught her while she was dressing that morning, and tried to picture herself as a swan. A swan princess surveying her subjects.

She felt ridiculous.

To her surprise and delight, however, Sam's mouth fell slightly agape.

"You look radiant. That dress, those shoes—The quality New York has to offer continues to astound me."

"Thank you." Hardly daring to breathe, in case it ruined whatever she had accidentally done right, Cassie inclined her head toward the painting. "I was just admiring this touching portrait here." Esme had also told her commenting on art was a good way to spur conversation with a gentleman.

"Ah, yes. Catherine Perceval, Countess of Egmont, with her son, Charles. The picture of womanly and motherly virtue. The Countess and her husband, John Perceval, 1st Earl of Egmont, owned an indigo plantation on the island before the Spanish took it back from the English in the seventeen-eighties. In fact, the vats and works were located right where this hotel is standing."

"Fascinating. Was that Yellow Bluff Plantation?"

"No, Egmont Plantation. Yellow Bluff came later, after the Spanish government issued a land grant to a gunboat captain named Domingo Fernandez, one of the early harbor pilots here. There's a bit of an exciting story there, actually. I could tell it to you sometime, if you'd like. I remember your enjoying such things when we were children."

"I'd love you. That. To do that. Yes." *Jesus, Mary, and Joseph. On a donkey.*

Sam stopped a waiter who was passing by with tumblers of fresh-squeezed orange juice.

"Speaking of when we were children…" He regarded her as he handed her a glass. "If you'll forgive me, you seem, well, different."

Cassie pressed her fan to her chest with what she hoped came across as cool, feminine confidence. "It's been years, Sam. I'm a grown woman now."

"I've noticed."

An involuntary squeeze of Cassie's hands snapped her fan shut, and she cast about for another topic of conversation. "I have to say, I wasn't expecting Lily's invitation this morning. I thought you were going to depart on Wednesday."

"That was my intention, but Lily insisted we stay as planned. She said she's been looking forward to the ball that's taking place at the Egmont this weekend 'far too long to be denied the opportunity to show off her latest wardrobial acquisitions.' Whatever that means."

"From what I remember of Lily, that sounds about right. If you'll forgive my saying so."

"No forgiveness is necessary for speaking the truth."

Cassie sauntered to the mantel, glossing over a mild trip on the rug, and traced the carved detailing with her finger. "I imagine Mr. Brooks is glad you're staying. Do I sense an engagement on the horizon?"

"I would prefer not to hear that word right now."

"Engagement or horizon?"

She had meant to be clever, but when she saw Sam's expression, she realized she had touched a nerve.

"Lily's been hinting at such things since the moment she suggested this trip," Sam said, "and, to be honest, I couldn't be less thrilled."

Cassie dropped her voice. "Is it the drinking? Because I've... heard Mr. Brooks—"

Sam gave an unexpectedly rough laugh. "No, no. Despite growing up with my father, I'm no temperance zealot. Many men of importance imbibe. Though I do worry about Lily adopting Atherton's bad habits. A glass or two of champagne or wine in a properly decorous environment is acceptable, but no man wants to associate with a woman who would sully herself with liquor or the filth of a saloon or tavern."

Cassie nodded, wishing for a bath.

"Quite frankly, I don't understand it," Sam continued. "While I realize Atherton holds a certain fascination for women, more than charm and good hair are necessary for a proper match. Lily knows that. A man must have something behind him. Wealth, position, power... though nowadays, where wealth leads, everything else follows. A rich family is a good family, right?" He laughed. "But, in all seriousness, what does Atherton have to offer? Even that mercantile establishment of his is nothing but a pile of ashes now."

Cassie lowered her juice. "Mr. Brooks's store was damaged by the recent fire?"

"Yes. The entire building, and all the stock inside, burned right up."

"That's curious. Because I heard a rumor he's recently come into some money. Despite the loss of his store, apparently."

"Is that so?" Sam traded his empty juice glass for a flute of champagne. "I'd like to know how he managed that. His father passed some time ago, and, as far as I know, he's had no association with his family since. And he didn't even complete his university—My apologies. I keep going on, and we're only just getting reacquainted."

"Lily should be grateful to have such a concerned older brother."

Sam smiled. "You're rather special, aren't you, Cassie Gwynne. Intelligent *and* gracious. And beautiful, of course. I never would have—What I mean is, one doesn't come across such a woman every day, even in my set."

Cassie's thoughts fell away. She had been called intelligent, well, mostly smart-mouthed, before, but those other compliments were rarer, even if due in part to the infrequency with which she made an effort, and they shone like gold on Sam's lips.

"And please accept my condolences regarding your father. I would have offered them before, but I only learned of his passing last evening, while speaking to a friend in New York on the telephone exchange. He was an admirable man. And what a fortune he amassed for himself. You always lived so modestly I hadn't realized the extent. Quite well-deserved, of course."

Cassie was touched. "Sam, I'd like to help you."

"Help me?"

"I could find out where Mr. Brooks's newfound prosperity has come from. And his circumstances, generally. So you can make a fully informed decision about the potential match with Lily."

"You know how to do that?"

"I worked with my father for years. I know how to find information."

"Okay, then," Sam said, evidently impressed. "But only if I may treat you to a day at the ocean beach in return. We could ride the hotel's omnibus line over and collect shells from among the dunes."

"That sounds—Certainly. That is, if Lily has time."

"I meant you and me."

Cassie fumbled her fan. "I—"

Then she thought of Flora. How could she indulge in trivial pleasures when a terrible danger was hanging over her own aunt? She had made a promise. If not in words, with her heart.

"I'd love to, Sam, but I'm afraid this isn't a good time, with everything that's been happening with my aunt and the inquest."

"But what does that have to do with you? From what I understand, you're hardly even acquainted. If I were you, I would already be taking steps to tuck that association away. Lucky you don't share a name. In fact, if you need somewhere else to stay, I could inquire with Mr. Littell."

"Why would I do that?" Cassie set down her glass. "She's innocent."

"Suspicion is damaging enough. And easily spreads to those around it… Which is a good point. We can take things slowly if you wish, so you can tidy up your affairs. But it makes sense, doesn't it? You and me? Your father may only have been a lawyer, but he was well-respected and moved among an enviable set, even if mostly due to his professional role. And he certainly left you with more than enough resources to recommend you. Oh, there I go again. I haven't let you get a word in."

It was perhaps just as well. Cassie, who was rarely without something to say, was speechless for the second time in three days.

Sam Townsend was suggesting actual courtship. But he was also suggesting she distance herself from Flora, her own family. And what had he meant about her father being "only" a lawyer? He'd called him well-respected, though. And her beautiful.

She put one hand on her chest and the other on her stomach. She didn't trust what was going on in either of those places.

"Sam, dear!" Lily called from a table near the windows. Mr. Brooks was sitting next to her, unfolding a newspaper. "Are you two coming over here, or are you simply going to stand there making eyes at one another?"

"Yes, of course, Lily. We're coming." Sam took Cassie's elbow, and an intoxication resembling the alcohol-induced one the night before flooded her brain, flushing out whatever thoughts were in there. "Unfortunately, Cassie, my assignment was to find and retrieve you, not keep you all to myself."

Cassie walked with Sam over to the table, where Lily received her with outstretched hands. Mr. Brooks put down his paper and stood.

"My dear Cassie Gwynne." Lily delivered a kiss to each of her cheeks. "I can hardly believe it. It's wonderful to see you looking so well. Glowing, in fact."

Blushing, glowing. Same thing.

"Especially after hearing about your father. To think such a thing could happen in a civilized city in this day and age… You must be devastated. I know how close you were. Though, I see you've found a passable dressmaker for yourself. Wearing all that black for the full time was simply too much, I suppose."

And there it was, one of Lily's famous double-edged compliments. It seemed she hadn't changed much.

"Thank you for your sympathies, Lily." It was no use explaining to a person like Lily that her father had hated black clothing so she hadn't felt it appropriate to wear it in his memory. "And you, of course, are breathtaking as always."

Never one to be underdressed, Lily was a vision in a full promenade costume of pale rose silk, high-waisted and draped with an overdress of cream-and-white stripes trimmed with bows and lace. The fichu around her shoulders closed in front under a corsage of real pink roses, and her sleeves fluttered with a delicate fringe.

"Mr. Worth never disappoints."

No, she hadn't changed much at all.

"And Lily never disappoints Mr. Worth," Sam said.

Mr. Brooks reached out his hand. "We've already met, but it's still a pleasure, Miss Gwynne."

It was confusing to see him sober. After what she had witnessed the evening before, Cassie half expected him to tip forward onto the table. And as if that weren't bad enough, while they were shaking hands, he held her gaze and let his fingertips linger against hers for a little bit too long. Right in front of his soon-to-be betrothed.

They all settled into their seats.

"Did you see the moonbow last night, Cassie?" Lily asked. "After Atherton told me about the one he saw here a few weeks ago, I was so hoping to have the chance to see one for myself. I was thrilled to get my wish."

"Yes, I did. It was mesmerizing."

"That's exactly the word I used!" Lily tittered. "Look at us, still thinking alike after all these years. Croquette?"

Cassie doubted they had ever "thought alike" about anything, but she smiled back and examined the plate of food Lily was holding out. Whatever a croquette was, it smelled of cheese and meat and appeared to be battered and fried in oil, so she helped herself to two and was reaching for a third for good luck when she noticed the others' amused eyes on her. She placed the serving spoon back on the platter and took a pull of coffee.

"I always did admire that about you," Lily said. "It must be so freeing not to worry about your figure." Another gem. "Now, tell me what you've been doing with yourself all these years. I'm dying to know how you've been."

"Aside from my college years at Vassar, I've spent most of my time working with my father." Cassie was ravenous, but she didn't dare touch her food now. "Helped him research, conduct interviews. He even let me assist with court proceedings sometimes."

Lily cupped her hands under her chin. "That's all very interesting. But what I'd really like to know is whether any strapping young men have been calling around."

Cassie considered her response. As a matter of fact, though she had thought being in mourning would have discouraged that sort of attention, or, failing that, her curmudgeonly behavior would have, she'd been approached a number of times over the past several months. But not only had she been uninterested in those men, she'd realized most of the inquiries had come on the heels of a newspaper article speculating about the size of her inheritance—which, while not quite so large as the paper would have one believe, had turned out to be magnitudes greater than she or anyone else had expected.

Sam's friend in New York, since he'd known about her father's passing, had likely seen the article and told Sam about it. But Sam was different from those other men. Why else would she still melt at the mere thought of him, the way she had as a girl, after all these years?

"No one worth mentioning. But tell me about you. How did you and Mr. Brooks meet?"

"Oh, yes!" Lily shook out her napkin and placed it in her lap. "It was this past summer at a roller-skating masquerade Mrs. Carnegie put on with the local club. She'd come down to check on the progress of her winter retreat at Dungeness, I believe, and wanted something for the children to do. Anyway, I was terribly nervous about skating for the first time and, wouldn't you know, I hadn't been out on the floor for but a minute when a passing brute knocked into me. Fortunately, before I fell and ruined my costume, this dashing man skated up and caught me in his arms. It was love at once, just like in the books, wasn't it? Darling?"

Mr. Brooks looked up from his newspaper. "Uh, yes. Books."

Sam gave an exaggerated cough.

"Sam, please." Lily tipped a spoonful of sugar into her tea, a tiny blue vein pulsing on her temple. "Cassie, did you know Atherton owns his own business?"

"Yes, Sam mentioned that. Gentlemen's clothing, right, Mr. Brooks? I understand you suffered heavy losses in the recent fire."

"I did indeed." Mr. Brooks leaned back to pluck a glass of champagne from a passing tray. "Unfortunately, I was away at the time, or else I might have been able to run in and save some of my stock at least. Assuming I heard the alarm bell, that is!" He laughed, loudly, and took a swallow that emptied half his glass. "I sleep a little too well, you see. Always have. Once, at a boarding house I used to stay in up north, a branch broke through my ceiling during the night, and I didn't even notice until it began to rain."

Sam drained his own drink. "He still lives in a boarding house, by the way."

Lily added another spoonful of sugar to her tea.

"My accommodations at the Florida House Inn are perfectly respectable. And it's not as if I have a wife and children to shelter. Yet."

Lily dumped in another spoonful.

"That's rather presumptuous."

And another.

"Presumptuous, huh? Is that any worse than being an entitled son of a—"

Lily threw her spoon against her saucer.

"Atherton, darling." She picked up the spoon and gave her tea a delicate stir. "Would you please find Mr. Littell and have him change out the hand towels in my room? The ones in there are the wrong color for the walls, and it's driving me absolutely mad."

Inhaling stiffly, Mr. Brooks grabbed his glass and stalked toward the lobby.

Lily lifted her cup and blew across the top. "Sam, you are being arrogant and obstinate."

"And you're being immature and foolish." Sam watched her take a sip. "Why are you fighting me like this? It's unlike you."

"I know what's best for me."

"It's my job to decide what's best for you."

"You're deciding wrong."

"Perhaps—" The word was scarcely out before Cassie wished she could inhale it back in. "Perhaps, Lily, you should take your time with Mr. Brooks. There's a lot to consider."

Lily's eyes flashed. "I may be younger than you, Cassie, but that's no reason for you to patronize me."

"I'm not—"

"And I really don't see why it's any of your business."

"That's enough, Lily," Sam said. "We'll discuss this later. In private."

"I want to discuss it now."

"I said later."

"But—"

Sam slammed his hand on the table so hard the centerpiece toppled over, shooting mums and English marigolds across the tablecloth like fireworks from a tube. The vase water rolled to the edge and dripped onto the floor.

Lily folded her napkin, placed it next to her plate, and stood.

"If you will excuse me," she said, "I believe I'll go for my walk now."

When she reached the side door, however, she stopped and looked back at Sam. Her jaw was stiff, but her bottom lip was quivering.

"Even Father wouldn't have been so cruel." Lifting her chin, she turned and vanished into the white glare outside.

The people at the neighboring tables had all paused their conversations to stare at them, but Sam's gaze was still fixed on the door where Lily had gone out.

"Shall I go after her?" Cassie placed her own napkin over the growing puddle on the floor. "Sam?"

Sam remained still for a few more moments, then, as though suddenly aware of where he was, he smoothed his face and nodded to the onlookers with a smile sculpted from glass.

That unsettling smile stayed in place as he met Cassie's inquiring glance. "If you can find her, you're welcome to try to talk some sense into her. But I wouldn't get your hopes up. I honestly don't know what to do anymore."

CHAPTER FIFTEEN

Having had no luck elsewhere on the Egmont grounds, Cassie was in the hotel garden across the street, a colorful oasis planted with orange and lemon trees, cabbage palms, and roses, as well as a whole host of exotic tropical plants she had never seen before, staring up into the knotty branches of an old juniper tree, when a twig snapped behind her.

"Dad-blame it. Right in the eye." Jake stepped into the clearing with a hand over his face.

"Gracious," Cassie said. "Are you injured?"

"No. I'll be fine. As soon as I have a word with the groundskeeper about keeping this path trimmed back properly. Anyway, Mr. Littell told me I'd find you out here."

"Sam and Lily had an argument, and Lily ran out. I thought she might have come over here, but I don't see her."

"Those are your friends from New York?"

"Used to be."

Cassie trudged over to the stone fountain burbling next to the footpath and sank onto the edge of the reservoir. She'd forgotten how tired she was.

"How're you holding up?" Jake sat next to her, Peanut's ledger book in his lap.

"Oh, me? I'm fine, I think. It was good to see that Flora was in better spirits when I left this morning. More than better. Though, if I'm being entirely honest… I wouldn't say it was inauthentic, but it felt a little—"

"Emphatic?"

"Yes, actually."

Jake picked at the cover of the ledger book. "She gets that way sometimes, when something has really upset her. I think it's a way of coping, forcing herself to feel better. It may have something to do with the—incident that happened this morning at the house. Before you woke up."

"Something happened at the house? I had no idea."

"Someone nailed a placard to her store sign that covered up the word "perfumer" and replaced it with the word "murderer." I went over as soon as I heard and took it down, but the damage was done. Flora was very shaken by it. Less by the specific act, I think, than the fact that someone had thought of her that way, if that makes sense."

Cassie sighed. "I understand. I'm sure it made everything seem all the more real, too."

Jake nodded and opened the ledger. "So I took a look at this ledger book you left for me."

"Any idea what it's about?"

"I wouldn't go that far, but I've at least recognized a common thread. Most of it seems to relate to various properties in Flora's neighborhood."

Cassie picked one of the purple wildflowers growing in the grass by their feet. "Including Mr. Downing's?"

"Peanut's next-door neighbor? Probably, but I'm not sure. I'm not experienced enough at reading these kinds of documents to tell specifically what relates to what." Jake opened the book and started flipping through it. "I especially haven't a clue what these notations at the top of some of the pages are about." He pointed. "Like this, a dollar sign circled together with a percentage symbol. And here, an hourglass next to a skull and crossbones. And this one looks to be, what, a flame?"

Cassie chewed on her lip. "I don't know if this is relevant, but the reason I asked about Mr. Downing is there was a promissory note in the sleeve of loose papers at the back of that book, relating to a loan Peanut gave Mr. Downing. It lists Mr. Downing's house as collateral."

"I didn't see that."

"Oh, here."

Pulling the document out of her pouch, Cassie told Jake about everything that had happened the night before (aside from her passing out like a drunken sailor and being carried home over someone's back, which didn't seem important).

"But don't tell anyone else about Mr. Downing," she said when she had finished. "I promised. He has an alibi for the murder, and he swore he would repay what he borrowed."

Jake studied his knees. "Fine. But I can't believe you did all that. And by yourself." He tapped his fingers against his thigh. "So, where does that leave us? That information about the stiletto is interesting, and disturbing, but it doesn't really give us a new direction to explore. I can't picture who around here would even know how to wield such a—What was that?" Jake leapt to his feet. "Something just moved in that brush over there."

"I haven't seen anyone come in here other than you. Must have been a squirrel."

"Maybe." Jake lowered back down.

"I'm still trying to figure out why Peanut would have collected all of this information. Was he merely interested in the history of the neighborhood? I remember Flora telling me his wife's family were heirs of the Yellow Bluff Plantation, so used to own a lot of the property around there. And Peanut's property came from them."

"Yes. They owned everything between Broome Street and the marsh from Eighth all the way over to the river, including the Broome Street Wharf. Actually..." He turned a few more pages of the book. "Yes. That's essentially the area covered in Peanut's book. But for Peanut to take an interest, there had to be more than nostalgia involved. And what on earth is 'Golden Bluff'? Say, you know who—There it is again. The rustling."

Leaving Cassie by the fountain, Jake crept toward a cluster of banana trees. He listened once more. Then pounced.

"What the—?" He straightened up, with Paddy dangling from one hand and Metta from the other.

"Paddy," he said. "Didn't anyone ever teach you not to eavesdrop? Metta, this better not have been your idea. And where are your shoes? People already think I don't mind you well enough."

"We weren't ease-dropping." Paddy swung his feet awkwardly. "Not on purpose."

Jake put the children down.

Metta tugged at her dress. "We were looking for lizards, but then we heard you talking. So, we listened."

"That's exactly what eavesdropping is," Jake said. "And it's not a polite habit. The next time something like that happens, announce yourself."

Cassie bit her tongue. Eavesdropping might not be polite, but sometimes it was useful.

Jake turned back to Cassie. "What I was going to say was Mrs. Keene's son-in-law, Charles Hiller, might have a thought about the ledger."

"The insurance agent?"

"He also deals in real estate. And toys. And something else, I think."

"If you think he can help, then, by all means, let's speak with him." Cassie forced herself to her feet.

"Great. But let's go by way of Ambrose Smalls's house. You know, the man whose cart of goods overturned because of that ditch Peanut dug in the road. He wasn't home when I went by last night."

"Can we come?" Metta asked. Paddy nodded enthusiastically.

"Of course not," said Jake.

"But we want to help. We're good at things."

"No, it's too dangerous. Now go on and play."

"There's a light on." Jake strode toward a heavyset house with brown siding and green trim. "That's promising." The house was in need of care, and the battered shed next to it was leaning at a disquieting angle, but flower beds filled every inch of the yard not needed for passage, and they were breathtaking. Every color was represented, every size and shape of petal and bud. Pansies, violets, snapdragons, petunias, sweet alyssum. In one bed alone, Cassie counted three varieties of roses.

Jake rapped on the door. "Mr. Smalls, it's Jake Gordon. I have some questions for you." There was no answer. "Smalls? Are you in there?"

Cassie grabbed his arm. "I heard a door. In the back."

Jake jumped down the steps and ran around the side of the house, and Cassie was about to follow when she heard someone scurrying along the opposite side, by the shed. A man appeared around the corner.

"Jake!" Cassie yelled. "Front!"

The man's eyes widened, and he turned to run. But, in his haste, he failed to notice the open barrel next him and flipped headfirst into it.

Jake arrived a moment later, puffing. After a brief consideration of the legs jerking in the air, he tipped the barrel and hauled the man out by his boots.

"He tried to run but fell into that barrel of mud instead," Cassie explained.

The man started to wipe off his face but seemed to think better of it when he saw his hands. "Not mud. Dung compost."

Jake sniffed his own hands, and Cassie took a step back.

"Why were you running away?" Jake asked.

Mr. Smalls stole a glance toward the shed. "Oh, uh, I wasn't running away. Didn't even hear you knock. I just remembered I had to be somewhere and went out."

"Through the back door? With all your lights on?"

"Closest one to me. And I hate to come home to a dark house." He shuffled over to the water pump and began to wash.

"Fine," Jake said. "Where were you Tuesday night?"

Mr. Smalls snorted. "Where was I Tuesday night? I can hardly remember what I ate for breakfast today."

As an experiment, Cassie took a step toward the shed, and Mr. Smalls straightened up, sending water streaming down his beard in frantic rivulets. He watched her as he picked up a rag and dried his face.

Over his shoulder, Cassie spotted a woman crouched by a yellow-leaved pecan tree in the next yard, watching them. She had on an absurdly large orange hat with what appeared to be an entire stuffed bird sewn into it, so it was unclear why she was bothering with the surreptitious stance.

"Come on, Smalls. It was only a couple of nights ago," Jake said. "Were you here? Somewhere else?"

"Tuesday night?"

"Yes, for pity's sake. Tuesday night."

"Hm. Lemme think, lemme think. Oh, I was in Hart's Road, trying to sell some tea sets. Yes, I went out Tuesday morning and came home late yesterday."

"Do you have any proof? Train tickets, accommodations, purchase receipts?"

"Proof? No. I drove my cart and slept in the back to keep an eye on my stock. Since when do I need to account for my every movement?"

"Liar!" The woman in the orange hat sprang up and charged toward them, her index finger waggling in the air. "Liar! Liar! Liar!"

"What are you doing, Mrs. Whitehead?" Mr. Smalls cast about for cover.

The woman leveled her finger at Mr. Smalls. "I'm telling you, this man is a liar, Officer Gordon. And you're lucky I'm even getting involved, since I reported my prize geraniums missing almost two days ago and, as of yet, no one from the sheriff's office has deigned to come by."

"My apologies, ma'am. We've been preoccupied—"

"That's why I'm here. If I help you with this, maybe you'll have time to see to my matter. What I was going to say was, if it's true this waste of breath has been hours away, driving around Hart's Road since Tuesday, why did I have to push his cart out of my marigolds Wednesday morning, as usual? And right after I'd discovered my precious geraniums had been pilfered, no less? Honestly, Smalls, use a chock. We're on a slope."

Mr. Smalls peered out from behind Jake.

"I was driving a different cart."

"You don't have another cart."

"Yes, I do. I, uh—"

"Where do you keep this mysterious second cart, then? In this eyesore of a shed you've been skulking about?" Mrs. Whitehead charged around the side of the house.

"No! Don't open—"

Mrs. Whitehead screamed.

Cassie and Jake rushed past Mr. Smalls over to the shed, where they found Mrs. Whitehead staring inside, her face twisted in anguish.

"My babies!" she wailed. "What have you done to my precious geraniums?"

Cassie slid the door open wider. Inside, the shed was packed from wall to wall with pots of brilliantly colored flowers.

"Um," Mr. Smalls said. "How did those get in there?"

Mrs. Whitehead lunged.

"All right! I admit it!" Mr. Smalls's words came out in jerks as Jake tried to pull Mrs. Whitehead off his back. "I wasn't in Hart's Road Tuesday night!"

Jake heaved one more time and finally Mrs. Whitehead let go, sending Mr. Smalls tumbling into a patch of orange bougainvillea.

"I was here," Mr. Smalls said, "digging Mrs. Whitehead's geraniums out of her flower bed and repotting them in my shed. I was careful, though! If you'll examine them, you'll see they're unharmed. That's why it took all night. You have to understand, Officer. She always wins the state-fair premium for those uninspired shrubs, when my Jacqueminots are *transcendent*! They deserve a chance."

Jake stared at him. "That's why you lied? Because you stole Mrs. Whitehead's flowers?"

"Isn't that why you're here?"

"No. Peanut was killed Tuesday night."

"I know that. But why… Oh, no, hey. I may have despised the man—he cost me a great deal of money and could have cost me my life—"

"So we heard," Cassie said. "We also heard you had quite the confrontation with him about it."

"Confrontation? I would have welcomed a confrontation. But that requires the participation of at least two people. The gutless toad wouldn't even come out of his house to face me. When he saw me at the door, he ran away up the stairs like a scared little girl."

Cassie resisted the urge to tell the man what he had looked like when *he* was running away only minutes before (a three-letter word also referring to a hooved pack animal with long, furry ears).

"You saw Peanut inside his house?" Jake asked. "I thought he'd already left for work by that time."

"Why else do you think I resisted so much when Starkey tried to make me leave? Granted, it was through the window, and a bit shadowy, but I saw a man inside the house dressed in a classic harbor pilot suit and Panama hat. Who else could it have been?"

"Okay, but you threatened him after that anyway. Said he would pay for the damage 'or else.'"

Mr. Smalls tossed his rag over the pump handle. "I didn't mean I was going to *kill* him. That would be barbaric. I've devoted my life to fine goods and flowers, for Heaven's sake. I meant I was going to sue him. Ask the lawyer, Mr. Baker. He was drawing up the papers for me. He said Peanut had more than enough money to pay for my losses, but my chances of seeing any of that now are pretty much like Peanut. Dead."

CHAPTER SIXTEEN

After setting Mr. Smalls to replanting Mrs. Whitehead's geraniums—that and a day aerating Mrs. Whitehead's lawn with a kitchen fork being the agreed-upon punishment—Jake and Cassie continued on toward Mr. Hiller's office.

"Here we are." Jake came to a stop beneath the awning of a storefront at Fourth and Centre. Wind chimes made from white-and-blue shells tinkled overhead.

Cassie squinted at the sign in the window. "But this says 'Captain Keene's Collectibles and Curiosities Store.'"

Jake pulled her to the side as a mule, who had evidently slipped its rope, pranced merrily past them down the wooden sidewalk, causing several women in elaborate promenade dresses to stumble into the street.

He nodded toward a professorial-looking man who was scribbling angrily in a notepad. "Come Saturday, I suspect Mr. Banks is going to favor us with another scathing *Mirror* editorial about letting livestock roam the streets."

"Jake Gordon, are you going to come in or simply block the door so no one else can?"

Mrs. Keene frowned at them through a sheet of mosquito netting hanging over the doorway.

"Uh, the first one. Good afternoon, Mrs. Keene." Jake whistled a little tune and ducked under her stare into the shadowy interior.

Giving Mrs. Keene an awkward bob of her own, Cassie stepped inside. And was promptly greeted by the gaping jaws of a full-sized stuffed alligator. She jumped sideways, right into a display of dreamcatchers covered with feathers and beads.

"It died of natural causes," Mrs. Keene monotoned as she resumed sorting what appeared to be a pile of animal teeth. She was wearing a different vest today, one patterned like the skin of the creature they were talking about.

Cassie spat out a feather. "That's a relief."

"Fine. I don't know whether it did or not. I just tell people that because it makes the customers feel better. And if I didn't, Flora'd probably never set foot in here."

"Ah." Cassie noted a bin of dried oranges made up like shrunken heads. "Your store is... impressive. But, Jake, weren't we supposed to be going to Mr. Hiller's office?"

"We are." Jake extracted his foot from a box of souvenir beach sand. "Mrs. Keene, we're here to see Charles."

"Good for you."

"I meant, if you could remind me—"

"Right at the penny postcards, left at the flamingos."

Following Mrs. Keene's directions, they found an inner door near the back painted with the words, "C. Hiller, dealer in insurance and real estate, and licensed lumber inspector." A smaller sign next to it read, "Inquire within for children's rocking horses, toy birds, and fanciful animal bells."

Before they had even knocked, however, the door swung open, and they were greeted by a man about Jake's age with spectacles and curly hair.

"Jake Gordon! I thought I heard you come in. And Miss Gwynne, I presume. Good to see you, good to see you, yes, yes." The man ushered them into the windowless room and, after a brief disappearance, emerged from the closet with two chairs. He kicked an empty box aside and placed the chairs in front of his desk, which was piled alarmingly high with books, papers, and rolls of oversized maps.

"Sit, sit, please." He set three mugs on a makeshift sideboard of crates and plywood. "Make yourself at home, as they say. Is it too dark in here?" He put down the teapot he'd just picked up and bustled across the room to light another lamp, then crossed back behind the desk and plopped into his chair. "That's better. Now, can I get you anything to—Oh, blast." He bustled back over to the sideboard and scurried back and forth between there, his desk, and two different cabinets before finally setting a cup in front of each of them, filled to the brim with slightly creamed and very sugared tea. It was like watching a squirrel trying to remember where it had buried its nuts.

"You should move into that stockroom near the front, Charles," Jake said. "It has its own door directly to the outside, and a window, too."

"I'd like to, but Mrs. Keene, I mean Mother, says she won't let me until I give her a grandchild. Say, while we're on the topic of children, I've created a new toy Metta might like. It's a very realistic wooden duck with wheels on the bottom, and when you pull it along by the string, it moves its legs like it's walking. It's even got an actual duck call inside the beak. All you have to do is blow into an opening under the tail to make it quack."

Cassie spat out her tea.

"I'm so sorry." She dabbed at the papers in front of her with her sleeve. "Wrong pipe." When she heard what she'd said, she convulsed again and had to launch into an emergency coughing spell.

"I'll certainly think about it," Jake said, his face pinched.

Cassie gave one last heave and composed herself. "Mr. Hiller, I understand you deal in real estate around here?"

"Yes, indeed. I work with properties all over Nassau County. Are you interested in purchasing something?" He jumped up and began rummaging through the papers on his desk, causing Jake to grab his teacup as it slid toward his lap.

"Actually, I—"

"A summer cottage on the beach, perhaps, perfect for catching those healthful sea breezes." He squeezed himself between Cassie's chair and the wall to reach a pigeonhole file on the other side. "Very popular right now. The Drurys built one last year, private bathhouse and everything, and the Bakers and the Swanns are planning to do the same this spring. Now, if I could just find that confounded pamphlet... Aha!"

Anchoring his foot against the cabinet, he yanked a packet out of one of the overstuffed compartments, and a spray of loose papers flew into the air.

"Aw, now I've done it."

Cassie picked up his spectacles, which had landed in her lap, and handed them back to him as he dropped to his knees and tried to scoop the papers into a pile.

He sighed. "Thank you, my friend. I do apologize. After the month I've had, with all these fire claims, I can't seem to keep my head on straight."

He looked so defeated Cassie felt sorry for having laughed at him before.

"Jake mentioned you were involved in insurance as well," she said. "You sold my aunt the policy for the equipment and things she had at Mr. Adler's store, right?"

"Indeed." He slumped back over to his chair. "Along with, as luck would have it, nearly every other policy impacted by the fire. You know, I used to like that word, 'fire.' It used to make me think of being cozy at home, waiting for food to cook. Now, all I see is ash and ruin. Here." He pulled a newspaper off the bookshelf and slapped it on the desk, making Jake dive for his teacup again. "This is the *Mirror*'s feature about it. All the glorious details."

Cassie leaned forward. It was the same issue Paddy had tried to sell her, which was still tucked in the pocket of her satchel.

A Ruinous Conflagration
ONE OF THE BEST BUSINESS BLOCKS
IN THE CITY CONSUMED BY FIRE
<u>Florida Mirror</u> *Special of Monday, October 15th.*

Yesterday morning our fair Island City was devastated by a calamitous conflagration that destroyed the whole business part of the block south of Centre Street, resulting in a total loss of $—

Cassie whistled. That was no insignificant amount.

"If you look at the third column, where it says 'Insurance Companies Paying the Losses,'" said Mr. Hiller, "you'll see who's listed as the agent for nearly all of them. Yours truly."

"But aren't the insurance agencies the ones paying for the damage?" asked Jake. "How does that put you out?"

"Who do you think pays *me*? If the insurers aren't happy, they're going to make sure I'm not happy, either. And right now, to them, I'm the man who sold the policies on a bunch of buildings that went up in flames. I'll tell you what they haven't said: 'Bully for you, Charles. Why don't we raise your commission rate? How about a bonus?'"

Mr. Hiller pressed his hands on the desk and inhaled. "Forgive me. It's a bit of a sore spot. Especially after paying out on that infernal Brooks policy, which I got only the initial premium payment for before the fire broke out. And it was a big policy, with all the options engaged. So big, in fact, it took all month to get the insurer to produce the check. They only just sent it through last Friday. Now I get to wait and see what kind of punishment there'll be for me... At least I caught a small break here and there. Would you believe, two-thirds of the coverage for the Rhodes Brothers store expired a mere *twelve hours* before the fire?"

"Mr. Hiller," said Cassie. "The Brooks policy you mentioned, that's Atherton Brooks, right? For a gentleman's clothing store?"

"That's correct. The store was near Centre on South Second, between Mr. Bard's restaurant and Mr. Adler's general store."

"Aunt Flora's annex space was in Mr. Adler's store. I didn't realize it was so close to Mr. Brooks's."

"They shared an internal door, actually," Jake said. "Mr. Brooks used to wander in from time to time and annoy Flora and Esme with his dimples while they were trying to work. Usually on his way to or from Weil's barroom, which was on the other side of Adler's."

"To be fair, I should acknowledge that the fire threw off Mr. Brooks's plans as well." One of Mr. Hiller's eyes turned inward as a fly landed on his nose. "Business hadn't been going well, so he'd invested a lot of money in a new idea for the store that was going to turn it all around." He groped along his desk toward a fly swatter. "Which was why the estimated value he gave me for his property and goods was so much higher than I expected at first."

To Cassie's relief, the fly moved on just as Mr. Hiller got the swatter into position in front of his face.

"It truly was an interesting idea, though," Mr. Hiller went on. "Instead of focusing on the everyday shopper, he was going to focus on the wealthy tourists. 'These people have expensive and peculiar tastes,' he told me, 'and they need somewhere in town where they can go to satisfy them.' He said he'd already bought all the materials to renovate and more than tripled his inventory of luxury items. And when I peeked through the window of his receiving warehouse, as I like to do a little due diligence check of my own sometimes, I could tell the shipments were from somewhere fashionable and expensive. The labeling on the crates was all very foreign, maybe even French.

"So I wrote the contract the very next day, and we signed it the day after that, once he brought in the premium. And it was right lucky for Mr. Brooks he got that policy when he did. The fire broke out only a week later. Unlucky for me, of course, but that's the nature of it, isn't it."

Cassie whispered to Jake, "A substantial insurance payout could explain what I heard about Mr. Brooks coming into some money."

"And I suppose," Mr. Hiller went on, "I should be grateful some of that money will actually be coming back around to me. Mr. Brooks stopped in on Wednesday to inquire about one of those beach cottages I mentioned. For his fiancée."

"Good news," Jake said.

"It's something. No, more than something. Given the price of the parcels he was looking at, I'm guessing he's given up on his grand idea for the store and convinced his partner they should keep the cash rather than use it to rebuild."

Jake put down his teacup. "Partner? I thought Mr. Brooks owned the business himself."

"Strictly speaking, a corporate entity owns the business. Meaning, even though Mr. Brooks acted as the agent with respect to the insurance contract, that corporate entity, which is owned by Mr. Brooks and his partner together, was the beneficiary of the policy." Mr. Hiller pulled a packet from a box next to his desk, flipped a few pages, and pointed. "Here's the beneficiaries page."

"'*Aurum*,'" Cassie read. The Latin word for gold. "Who's the partner?"

"I don't know. I only dealt with Mr. Brooks."

As Mr. Hiller restacked the packet, an envelope slipped onto the floor. "*Premium Payment, Aurum*" was written in small, neat capitals across the front. Below that, in a different hand, was the word "*CASH*," along with an amount and the date of deposit.

Cassie picked it up and handed it back to Mr. Hiller.

"Thanks again," he said. "I should paste this in or something. It falls out every time I pick up the file."

"Corporate entity?" said Jake, evidently still catching up.

Cassie tucked her hair behind her ear. "Sometimes people form a separate entity, on paper, to run their business through for tax or liability reasons, or maybe, as in this case, because they have a partner or investor. Then they write up an agreement detailing how rights, responsibilities, and assets, including insurance policies, and so forth are to be allocated, and setting out rules such as one partner can't make certain decisions without the other. Speaking of which, that's how we could figure out who this mysterious partner is. Mr. Hiller, you wouldn't happen to know where we could find a copy of the Aurum partnership agreement, would you?"

"I might. But why so interested in Mr. Brooks?"

"Mr. Brooks's prospective fiancée is a friend of mine, and her brother has some questions about Mr. Brooks's... circumstances. I think this information would help clear some things up."

"I see. The problem is that would take quite a lot of—"

"Charles, you get this girl whatever she wants, understand?" Mrs. Keene had appeared soundlessly in the doorway.

Mr. Hiller snapped to. "Uh, yes, Mrs. Keene, er, Mother. I'll ask the lawyer, Mr. Baker, if he knows anything. He owes me a favor, since I saved his hide last Christmas when he sat on his daughter's favorite toy and broke it."

"In that case, would you mind also asking Mr. Baker whether Mr. Smalls asked him to draft a complaint against Peanut regarding an accident with his merchandise cart?" Cassie asked.

"I suppose I—"

"And I should probably borrow that insurance file, too." Cassie tried to adopt Mrs. Keene's authoritativeness. "There are some particulars I want to take a better look at."

"Oh, well, the main office in Jacksonville has asked me to send my fire-claims files on to Records today, and as you know, I'm on thin ice as it is."

Mrs. Keene crossed her arms.

"But I probably I could message them and tell them my 'assistant' missed the mail coach." He adjusted his tie. "That said, I would be exceedingly grateful if you would return it as soon as possible. You could drop it directly at my house. Two blocks west of the Egmont on Beech Street, green shutters."

Cassie accepted the packet. "I promise."

Mr. Hiller rose to show them the door.

"We did actually have something relating to real estate we wanted to ask," Jake said.

"Oh?" Mr. Hiller looked hopeful, then apprehensive. "You do want to buy something?"

Jake shook his head. "No, that's not it. And I might as well be frank with you. Mr. Shaw is mishandling the inquest regarding Peanut's death, either through intentional malice or unintentional incompetence, and I'm worried to death he'll accuse Flora. We have to figure out what really happened before things get any worse."

Both Cassie's and Mr. Hiller's mouths fell open.

"In that case"—Mr. Hiller straightened his spectacles—"ask away."

Jake handed Mr. Hiller the ledger. "We found this hidden in Peanut's study. Best we can tell, it contains mostly real estate documentation, though we're not clear on which property is which. Can you think of why he might have collected all this? Or what 'Golden Bluff' is? Also, there are symbols on some of the pages that we can't make sense of."

Mr. Hiller perched his spectacles on top of his head and sat down to examine the book. For several minutes, he simply turned pages, making small humming sounds to himself.

"Huh," he said finally, and sat back. It wasn't exactly the insight they'd been hoping for, but there did seem to be something behind it.

"What is it?" asked Jake.

"I haven't the faintest idea what 'Golden Bluff' means. And I don't know what those odd notations mean, either. But there does seem to be a sort of pattern to them—The properties they

mark are all clustered around Peanut's house. For example…"
He leaned back over the ledger and jabbed a finger at one of the
drawings. "This one with the hourglass and skull on it depicts
Widow Abernathy's property, on the east side of Peanut's house.
See? Here's that little creek that runs along the back." He flipped
the page. "This one with the dollar sign and percentage symbol
is the Downings', on the west side. And this one with the flame
is the Starkeys', which is across the street and over one, next to
Miss Hale's. You can see the carriage house where Mr. Starkey
keeps his prized phaeton."

"Was that why you said 'huh'?" Cassie asked.

"No. Well, not exactly. That was because a lot of this is information I collected for Peanut myself, from county records and a few
other sources. I transcribed all the copies myself, too—my hand
still hurts thinking about it."

"Really? Why?"

"Peanut came in some months ago asking if I had the official
surveys and deed paperwork and so on for the properties in the
area encompassing his neighborhood. Something about wanting
to know the history of his wife's family's property. I didn't have
much here, as I only keep files relating to recent matters, but I said
I could see what I could get from the county, for a fee. If I had
known how much hassle it was going to be, though, I would have
asked for more money."

"Hassle?"

"A few years back, in seventy-six, there was a fire. Yes, another
one. Since I've been working in insurance, it seems something's
always on fire. Anyway, among the buildings that burned was the
old county courthouse, along with the records inside. The clerk
in charge of the property records ran back inside several times to
rescue what he could, but he couldn't save everything, and much
of what he did save was severely damaged. Over the years, county

employees have tried to reconstruct what they can, but that's always a tricky process, and there're still some big gaps."

"Did you find everything Peanut was looking for?" Jake asked.

"Far from it. Which was why I was confused when I saw this." Mr. Hiller flipped to another page and held the book up. "These pages contain records pertaining to Peanut's lot next to Flora's. And Flora's lot, too."

"Okay."

"I remember these two properties because I searched for them for quite a while before having to give up. It turned out the Deed Record containing the relevant entries had been destroyed by the fire. The Grantor/Grantee index had been saved, but the relevant pages were too damaged to read. And, as luck would have it, the railroad company's archives, which likely would have contained copies of the information, had been lost due to flooding the previous summer. I told Peanut all of that.

"So, as I know no property transfers have happened on this street for ten years or more, the only way Peanut could have these particular records is if he found a chance transcription in someone's private files. Or he made them up."

CHAPTER SEVENTEEN

"Jake, about the fire last month. Did anyone ever investigate the possibility of arson?" Cassie rose on her toes to check the progress of the line they were standing in for the post office telegraph desk. They had been on their way back to Flora's when she remembered she had promised an overly interested neighbor back in New York she would message her to let her know she'd arrived safely, and she didn't want to risk walking in on her own wake when she returned. Even though, knowing the neighbor, the food would probably be pretty good.

"Of course. Standard procedures were followed. But the investigation was inconclusive."

Cassie looked back down at the newspaper feature about the fire, which Mr. Hiller had insisted she take, despite her assurance she already had a copy of that exact publication, and bit into the hand-sized cookie she'd bought from the bakery next door. She usually hated lines, but, right now, armed with reading material and a treat, she wasn't entirely minding the wait. In fact, as she stood there munching and musing, a packet of papers tucked under her arm, she almost felt like her old self.

> As to the origin of the disaster, a variety of theories have been advanced. Some aver that the fire began in the rear of Steeby's tin shop, which, our readers will remember, came to its location on South Second after burning down in the fire of seventy-six. Others proclaim that the fire started in the

rear of Weil's sample rooms next door. Mr. Steeby wishes it known that there was no fire in his shop all day.

It is not known whether the fire was incendiary. A policeman reports that, right before the fire, he saw a figure of "Ichabod Crane-type" proportions wearing a hat and a long coat run full speed up Centre Street from the direction of the fire, with a soldier's haversack slung over his shoulder; however, the darkness prevented his divining any further details. The first alarm was given at half past midnight, when the mentioned buildings were seen ablaze with "smoke and flames shooting straight up from behind Mr. Weil's barroom like the horns of Jesse himself," according to one witness, who saw the commotion from her home on South Ash Street.

Cassie thought that last bit sounded like something she'd heard before, but it was the policeman's report that caught her attention.

"But this says someone was seen running away from the fire right before the alarm was given," she said. "Who, other than a guilty party, would run away from a fire instead of trying to warn anyone or help put it out?"

Jake pressed his fingers to his temples. "Now you're sounding like Hughes. He was the policeman in that account you're reading. He's insisted from the beginning that arson was involved, but he hasn't been able to prove it. Here." He pointed at another column. "Read this part. It's more uplifting."

It was gratifying to see that, while there were a large number of idle watchers, there were also able hands willing to help save the property of their fellow citizens, some of whom stood to lose all their worldly possessions.

In particular, when it was observed that the post office building was in imminent danger, a small troupe of brave souls, under the guiding light of a rare, mystical moonbow, organized a bucket brigade to keep the roof, front, and sides of the building wet, though, at times, it seemed nearly impossible that our heroic volunteers would be able to hold their ground.

Cassie held her breath. It was as dramatic as a novel, but real life.

Again and again, the troupe was driven back by the flames, scorched and showered in ash, but, again and again, they would return to their positions, unrelenting in their selfless mission until the threat had been defeated. We shall not neglect also to mention the particular contributions of Miss Flora Hale, who, despite her own property having been burned beyond recognition, found it within herself to throw her energies into the saving of others'.

This editor, on behalf of the city, cannot extend too much thanks to those individuals who worked for hours without rest in exposed positions, and to those who carried water to them or otherwise assisted, for their selfless exertions, by which they saved our post office and thereby the remaining portion of the city all the way to the river. It is also worthy of mention that members of every race and creed participated in this valiant effort, showing us just what we can accomplish when our community works together as one.

"Jake, you cruel, cruel boy!"

Jake flinched. "Aw, shoot."

An impossibly tiny woman (which was saying something, coming from Cassie's perspective) with a tight white bun and large red boots emerged from behind the mail counter and bowling-balled through the crowd toward them. Her eyes were as big as an owl's through her spectacles, and her ears appeared to have made an effort to grow to match.

"Good afternoon, Mrs. Rydell." Jake placed one foot behind him as if bracing for impact.

"You know I've been dying to hear the latest about the Peanut situation," the woman chided, "and yet you haven't come by once to bring this poor old woman some relief. Nuh-uh." She held up a hand as he tried to respond. "Miss Porter and Mrs. Keene have been irritatingly tight-lipped, too, and no one else seems to have anything but their own foolish mind-dribble to offer. If I have to listen to one more idiotic debate about Flora Hale, I might murder someone myself. Could people *be* more boring? There's far more to this story, and I want details. What are you doing in this line? Come up to the front. You, too, Cassie Gwynne."

She stomped up to the telegraph desk, where a heavyset teenage boy was putting messages through. "Shove over, Roy. You've the efficiency of a sloth. Jake! Up here!"

His head lowered to avoid eye contact with the people still waiting in line, Jake shuffled toward her like a child obeying his great-aunt's demand for a kiss.

"I've found the most scandalous letter in the abandoned mail pile." Mrs. Rydell took Cassie's telegram form and somehow worked the equipment without slowing her flow of speech. "But you won't hear any of it until you tell me everything you know."

Jake smoothed a hand over his hair. "There's not much to tell, Mrs. Rydell. Except that Cassie and I performed a search inside Peanut's house and figured out someone had been in his study the night he was killed, searching for something."

"You don't say! Mr. Shaw let you in?"

"Not exactly. Oh, and we also discovered that Peanut may have had a lady friend. We found a woman's pendant under his bed, and—"

Mrs. Rydell stopped pounding the telegraph keys. "Ooo! I bet I know who it is!"

Someone rang the bell at the mail counter, which Mrs. Rydell had abandoned to talk with them.

"Jake," said Cassie, "it's Mrs. Shaw."

"Exactly," said Mrs. Rydell. "Roy!"

Jake blinked. "What?"

The boy seemed to be engrossed in something he'd found in his teeth, so Mrs. Rydell threw a pencil at him. "Go help Mrs. Shaw at the mail desk. Do I have to tell you everything?"

As Roy lumbered away, Mrs. Rydell leaned in, ignoring the renewed shifting of the people in line behind them. "As Miss Gwynne said, Mrs. Shaw is Peanut's *paramour*. I'd bet my favorite boots on it."

"I didn't—She is?" Cassie watched Mrs. Shaw, her face back to its normal sour expression, unload her basket of parcels onto the counter.

Jake leaned closer. "Yes, do tell. I haven't heard anything about—"

"You might have, if you'd come by as you said you would." Mrs. Rydell gave her spectacles a righteous push with her finger. "It all adds up, though. Especially after Mr. Meeks and the Palmer boy fell out of the Starkeys' tree last week." She finished entering Cassie's message and, waving off her coins, beckoned the next person in line.

Jake frowned. "What?"

"The Palmer boy climbed up the tree in the dark and, upon finding it already occupied by Mr. Meeks, screamed and let go."

"I don't—"

"And so did Mr. Meeks."

Jake shrugged helplessly. "Uh, what were either of them doing up in a tree?"

"That's exactly what Mrs. Starkey wanted to know when she saw two bodies fall past her window. But Mr. Meeks rolled over and ran off as soon as he hit the ground, and the boy was in a daze, so Mrs. Starkey climbed up herself. When she got to the top, she realized she could see not only into young Mrs. Downing's dressing area—"

"That would explain the boy's interest," Jake said. "But you'd think a man of Mr. Meeks's age would be beyond such things."

Mrs. Rydell kicked her tiny boot in exasperation. "That's what I was about to—Just listen. From the tree, one can see not only into Mrs. Downing's dressing area but also clear to the end of Peanut's second-floor hallway. Mr. Meeks was watching Peanut's house because his sister, Mrs. Shaw, had gone in there. Understand?"

"Yes?"

"Haven't you seen him following her all around town in that distinctly odd, sneaky manner? He no doubt suspected the affair."

"But she's his sister. Why would he get involved?"

"You and I both know Mr. Shaw doesn't care for anyone interfering with what is his, and that includes his wife. Mr. Meeks must have worried about her. Also, Mr. Shaw's his business partner. A marital problem there would be bad for the business."

"I noticed him following her, too, once," Cassie said. "And there was that encounter in Peanut's kitchen yesterday."

"What encounter?" Mrs. Rydell rubbed her hands together eagerly.

Cassie glanced back over at Mrs. Shaw. "Jake, give me your watch chain. I have an idea."

"My watch chain?"

"Quickly. Before Mrs. Shaw leaves."

Jake unbuttoned the chain from his vest and slid off his pocket watch while Cassie dug the pendant they'd found at Peanut's house out of her pouch.

Cassie hooked the pendant onto the chain, knotted the ends behind her neck, and, finally, tucked the pendant underneath the button fold of her bodice. "Now, introduce me to Mrs. Shaw."

"But she and I aren't really acquainted in that manner."

Hooking her arm through his, Cassie propelled them toward the mail counter, where Mrs. Shaw was impatiently watching Roy count out her change.

"Greetings, Mrs. Shaw!" Jake tipped forward with a bow worthy of a circus ringmaster. "How are you this fine morning?"

Mrs. Shaw cocked her head. "I'm well, Officer Gordon."

"I'd like to introduce my friend, Miss Cassie Gwynne, who's visiting from New York. She's Flora Hale's niece."

Mrs. Shaw gave Cassie an appraising look. "The rumors are true. You're the spitting image of Emma Hale. But with a touch of your father's wildness."

"Wildness" now?

Cassie tried to keep her mind on the task at hand. "Good afternoon, Mrs. Shaw. It's a terrible tragedy, what happened to Captain Runkles, isn't it? Peanut, I believe he's called?"

Mrs. Shaw's eyes sharpened. "Yes, it is."

"I understand you were close with him."

Mrs. Rydell slapped her hands on the counter to keep from falling off her stool.

"I beg your pardon," said Mrs. Shaw.

"I saw you in his kitchen yesterday, tending to him. And I thought you might have—known him personally."

Mrs. Shaw's fingers tightened on her shawl. "I have some nursing experience, so I merely came by to offer my help with the body." She spoke slowly, as if trying to decide how much Cassie had seen. "But it wasn't needed, so I left."

"Ah," Cassie said. "My mistake."

"That it is. Good day to you." Mrs. Shaw moved to leave, but Roy held up his mitt of a hand. He was still hunched over the coins in front of him, moving his mouth as he counted.

"Really, Roy," said Mrs. Shaw. "Just keep it."

As she turned to leave again, however, Cassie tugged on the chain around her neck so the pendant popped out from behind the button fold.

Mrs. Shaw froze. Her gaze rose to meet Cassie's.

"Excuse me," said a man in line behind them. "Are you almost finished? I'm trying to get this package out on the next coach."

"I—" Mrs. Shaw snapped back to life. "Yes, I'm finished. For pity's sake." Tossing another glance at the pendant, she rushed out the door.

"Hey!" Roy scratched his ear. "She forgot her basket."

As Jake unlatched the gate to Flora's yard, he looked back at Peanut's house. "I wish I knew what the jury was up to in there."

"Me, too." Cassie lifted her eyes toward the sky. The clouds had thickened into an angry purple-gray.

"I went over there on my way to the stables to see if they'd changed their minds about letting me help, but Mr. Meeks all but laughed in my face."

While Jake was speaking, Peanut's front door opened, and Mr. Ambler shuffled out, a box tucked under his arm. When he saw Jake and Cassie, however, he scuttled away as though he'd been caught in a lady's boudoir.

"I'm not sure that was a good sign," Cassie said.

Inside, they found Paddy and Metta, along with Sergeant Denham, caught up in the ongoing efforts at the perfume store. Paddy and Sergeant Denham were on one of the pink settees by the window, smelling vials and placing them into some kind of order on the tea table, and Metta was behind the counter with Flora, pouring scoops of flower petals and twigs into little cloth sacks.

"Papa, look!" said Metta. "Miss Flora showed me how to make trunk sachets. I did all of these." She gestured with an artist's flourish at the straw-colored sachets lined up on the counter in front of her, each tied neatly with a ribbon.

Kleio marched up and down the row with a watchful eye, her yellow crest at full alert.

Jake deposited a letter he'd picked up from the post office for Flora onto a stack of mail by the bookshelf. "Well done, Metta."

"We cut and sewed them out of feed sacks we got from Mrs. Drury, and now we're stuffing them. The special part, though, what makes the fragrance so rich and long-lasting, is before you stuff them, you have to—"

"Metta," Flora said gently, "remember what we talked about. A perfumer must always guard her compositions and techniques with care."

Metta formed her mouth into an "o" and clapped her tiny hand over it. "Yes, Miss Flora. I'm sorry, Papa. I can't tell you how we do it." She looked to Flora for reassurance then inhaled like she was about to recite a pledge. "Secrecy is paramount in the perfume world. If a perfumer's compositions, or methods, are exposed, others can recreate the fragrances and steal the fruits of her labors. Catherine de Medici's personal perfumer, René le Florentin"—she slowed to pronounce the name with the proper French inflection—"even had his laboratory connected to the queen's apartments by a hidden passageway so no secrets could be stolen on the way."

She picked up a sachet with ritualistic solemnity and held it out. "You'll just have to enjoy the final product."

"I will do that." Jake accepted the sachet with equivalent solemnity.

Cassie searched her memory as she dangled a length of discarded ribbon in front of the kitten, who stood on her hind legs and swatted like a drunken boxer.

"René le Florentin. Didn't he also poison—"

Flora shook her head at her, indicating she hadn't shared that part of the story with Metta yet. It was probably for the best.

"You're looking well, Flora," Jake said. "I'm glad to see you up and about."

Flora swept together some ribbon scraps with her fingers. "Thank you. It took me a little while to come around, but, with Esme's encouragement, I decided I needed to continue on with my life. Nothing good comes of lying on one's back all day."

Sergeant Denham coughed at some private joke, and Esme, who was writing in a notebook at the other end of the counter, bit her lip.

"Besides—" Flora moved down the counter to adjust the heat on one of the stills. "I don't want the store to be closed if a customer arrives. I'm sure people will start coming back around any time now."

Through the window, Cassie noticed two of the ladies from Flora's whist club pass by the gate—she remembered that one of them, Mrs. Grayson, had brought Metta home from Old Town the other day. They hardly slowed, though, and when they saw her looking out at them, they bent their heads together, whispering, and hurried off.

She wasn't as confident as Flora.

"Oh!" Flora turned. "Metta, would you please bring in the orange-peel tea from the kitchen? I put a kettle on ages ago and completely forgot about it."

"Yes, Miss Flora." Metta finished tying the bow she was working on and skipped through the doorway to the dining room, with Danger at her heels and Luna at his. After a moment, the kitten decided to follow as well, timing the swinging of the door well enough to dart through but not quite well enough to avoid a bump in the rear.

Esme examined the tip of her pencil. "How was your visit with the Townsends, Cassie? Are those two really as fancy and important as they tell everyone they are?"

"Esme!" Flora said. "Those are Cassie's friends. And Mr. Townsend is her long-lost love."

"Oh, that's very much overstating things, Aunt Flora." Cassie hoped no one could see the warmth seeping into her cheeks. "As I mentioned, while I may have admired him when we were children, I was only thirteen the last time I saw him, so what did I really know?" Then she thought about Sam's expression when he'd seen her at breakfast. "But I believe I've made a favorable impression finally."

"I knew you would," Flora said.

"Unfortunately, Sam and Lily got into an argument while I was there. And I'm afraid Lily became upset with me, too, for getting involved. She left the table before we'd even eaten anything, and I couldn't find her when I followed."

"What was the argument about?" asked Sergeant Denham.

"Lily wants to be married, but Sam doesn't approve of her suitor, Atherton Brooks. And I was foolish enough to attempt to intercede."

Sergeant Denham slid a vial into the rack in front of him. "Good old Mr. Brooks. Say, Miss Hale. He owes quite a bit on his account with you, doesn't he? Perhaps Cassie could ask Miss Townsend to put in a word with him about paying his debts."

"That's not necessary, Sergeant," Flora laughed. "I'd rather let him focus on getting back on his feet for now, especially knowing he has marriage in mind. He hasn't announced any plans to rebuild his store yet, so I assume he's still trying to recover."

"But at Three Stars, Mr. Brooks was buying all the drinks," Paddy said.

Jake bent to read the title of one of the books on the shelf next to him. "That's right. He should be able to settle up with you now,

Flora. Charles Hiller told us Mr. Brooks took out an insurance policy on his store shortly before the fire and the payout was sizable. Mr. Brooks has even inquired about purchasing a beach cottage for Miss Townsend with part of the funds."

"A beach cottage? And here I was feeling sorry for him."

The front door opened, and the dogs bolted back to the foyer to inspect the new arrival. After a few murmurs, a delicate hand appeared on the curtain.

"Lily!" Cassie fought off an irrational fear they'd been overheard.

"Oh, good, Cassie, you're here." Lily patted Luna's head as she stepped inside. Her cheeks were pink, and she seemed to be having trouble standing still. "Good afternoon, everyone. I hope you'll excuse the intrusion, but I wanted to see Miss Gwynne right away."

Flora moved around the counter to greet her. "Come on in, dear. I'm Flora Hale. This is my home and shop, and you are very welcome. This is Sergeant Robert Denham, Officer Jake Gordon, and Miss Esme Cole."

"Lily Townsend. A pleasure."

Jake and Sergeant Denham offered their hands, and Esme nodded briskly then returned to her task.

"You came to see me?" Cassie asked.

"Yes. We wanted to apologize for this morning."

"We?"

Lily pulled back the foyer curtain, and Sam and Mr. Brooks came into the room.

Cassie watched Sam deliberately stop short of the window and remembered what he had said to her about distancing herself from Flora. Was he actually worried about being seen here? He'd also walked in with his eyes fixed on the ground in front of him, not even acknowledging Cassie as he entered. Had she upset him somehow?

"Everyone," Lily said, "I'd like to introduce my brother, Samuel Townsend, and Atherton Brooks." She took a theatrical breath. "My fiancé."

A crash fell at the back of the room.

"Metta!" said Esme. "You must be more careful! Now I'll have to change my dress." She and Metta had evidently collided by the dining room door, sending the tea tray Metta was carrying crashing to the floor.

"I—I'm sorry," Metta stammered as Esme picked up the teapot shards and threw them on the tray.

Jake held out his hand. "It's all right, my girl. Come over here so you don't cut yourself."

"Yes, don't worry, dear." Flora pulled a handful of rags from under the counter and knelt next to Esme to mop up the liquid. "These things happen. You'll just have to be more careful next time."

"But I *was* being careful." Metta's voice was barely audible.

Flora brushed off her hands as Esme picked up the wet rags and carried the tray out of the room. "My apologies for the interruption, Miss Townsend. Congratulations. What wonderful news."

"Yes," Cassie said, "Congratulations, Lily."

As Lily started forward to embrace her, Sam shouted and ducked. Kleio had been swooping toward his head but, surprised by the evasive maneuver, corrected course and landed on Sergeant Denham's instead.

Sam sputtered. "What on earth? Why isn't that thing in a cage?"

"There's no need for alarm," Flora said. "She's perfectly harmless. And it's actually a compliment if she chooses to perch on you."

"Insofar as one enjoys being equated with a tree branch." Sam tugged his hat back on, keeping a wary eye on Kleio, who eyed him right back. "Lily, we should be moving along. You've that appointment with the tailor."

"You're right, brother mine." Lily turned back to Cassie, sweeping her arms blissfully. "I have a few adjustments to make to my gown before the Egmont ball. Please tell me you'll be there. It's the hotel's annual fête to celebrate the opening of the season and always great fun. And the guest list would astound you."

Cassie snuck another glance at Sam, who was busy picking dog hairs off his clothes. How was she supposed to tell him what she'd found about Atherton Brooks if he wouldn't even look at her? Since he'd evidently already agreed to the engagement, perhaps it didn't matter anymore. But she hoped she still did.

"I'll think about it. Though I don't know if I'd feel right attending such an event while things here are—"

"Nonsense," Flora said. "She'll be there, Miss Townsend."

The front door opened again. Or flew open, rather, and slammed into the wall so hard it knocked a small painting onto the ground.

"For the love of all that's Holy!" came Hughes's voice, high and panicked. "Someone call this woman off!"

Hughes burst through the curtain, leapt over Danger's back, and dove behind the far settee, knocking into the bookshelf and spilling the stack of mail in the process.

"She's officially lost her mind," he said, twitching like a prey animal. "Chased me all the way here from Centre Street."

As though on cue, Mrs. Keene charged into the room, with Miss Porter tottering breathlessly behind.

"Where is he?" Her eyes were shooting sparks. "Where's that insufferable man-child?" When she spotted Hughes, she pulled off her leopard-print gloves and spat into her hands.

"Hughes, old boy," Jake said, "didn't you chase a whole pack of squatters out of that warehouse behind Bock's the other night?"

"Yes." Hughes inched along the settee, trying to keep as much of the chair between himself and Mrs. Keene as possible.

"Then why are you running from a single person?"

"Those men were vagrants, not insane."

"Mrs. Keene," Flora said, "what is happening?"

Mrs. Keene pulled off a shoe. "He cornered my son-in-law. Nearly frightened him to death, the way he jumped out and stuck his nose in his face, asking all those questions. Charles has a delicate constitution. And I've had it with people terrorizing my people! Only I get to do that!"

She lunged over the top of the settee, and Hughes scrambled to get away, only to fall over Jake's outstretched foot. Realizing what had happened in midair, he grabbed onto Jake with a retaliatory grunt and took him down with him, just in time for Mrs. Keene to land on top of the both of them, whooping, with her shoe brandished above her head. Danger and Luna barked in circles, and Kleio hopped up and down on her perch, screeching and flapping her wings. The kitten mewled in distress from beneath Cassie's skirts.

Sam, Lily, and Mr. Brooks pressed their backs against the wall, their hands drawn against their chests.

"Enough! All of you!" Flora pried the shoe from Mrs. Keene's hand but fell backward when Mrs. Keene tried to grab it back.

Cassie was trying to think of a way to intervene when one of the pieces of mail Hughes had knocked on the floor caught her eye: an unstamped envelope with a square of cardstock sticking out of it just far enough to reveal the signature. It was from Peanut. She picked it up.

Miss Hale:

Be advised that I have located evidence proving your house is encroaching on my property and will soon be initiating legal action to reclaim what is rightfully mine.

—T.H. Runkles

It was harsh, from the words themselves to the sharp edges of the perfectly formed small capitals filling the card, each carved deeply and deliberately into the paper like a knife into flesh.

Why hadn't Flora mentioned this? What Peanut was suggesting was serious. If he could really prove this kind of encroachment, depending on how much of the building was over the line, Flora's entire house might have to come down. And, even if he couldn't, the legal costs of defending against such an action could be enough ruin a person all on their own.

Someone passed Cassie from behind and poured a pitcher of water over Jake and Hughes, who she had almost forgotten were still grappling in front of her.

Mr. Shaw.

"I hate to interrupt what appears to be a daily ritual for you gentlemen, but I need a word with Miss Hale."

Holding her breath, Cassie shoved the card and envelope down the front of her dress as Mr. Shaw placed the pitcher on the counter and waited for the sputtering men to stand.

"The jury has concluded its deliberations and returned a verdict. Miss Flora Hale, you are under arrest for the murder of Captain Theodore H. Runkles, also known as Peanut. Officer Stevenson—" Mr. Shaw turned to the policeman who was standing behind him, next to a smug Mr. Meeks. "Take her into custody."

CHAPTER EIGHTEEN

Jake stepped in front of Flora. "Don't you touch her, Stevenson."

Paddy fell in next to Jake and assumed the same stance. "Yeah. You'll have to go through us first."

"I'm real sorry," said the policeman. "But Mr. Shaw talked to Sheriff Alderman and he says I've got to follow the coroner's orders."

Jake turned on Mr. Shaw, his fists clenched. "You don't have the evidence to—"

"Actually, we do." Mr. Meeks picked up one of the perfume vials from the tea table and examined it in the light. "There's a witness who can place Miss Hale near the tower the night of the murder. Which means she lied to us about being at home all night."

"A witness? Who?"

"Tommy McDuffy."

"The thief Office Hughes arrested yesterday?" Cassie stepped forward, ready for battle. "Why would you believe anything he has to say?"

Jake gave a derisive snort. "Let me guess. He said he had 'key information' about the murder, which he could provide in exchange for leniency."

"That is correct," said Mr. Shaw. "He told us he encountered Miss Hale at the corner of White and San Fernando the night of the murder, right next to the tower clearing. And he has proof."

"What proof?"

"When he saw her, he intentionally collided with her to see what he could lift off her person, as he is in the habit of doing, and came away with… Miss Hale, I believe this belongs to you?" He held out his hand. In it was the orange blossom brooch Flora had been wearing the day Cassie arrived. The day Peanut was killed.

Cassie's breath caught.

"There's been some mistake," said Jake.

"It's engraved 'For Flora, Love Emma' on the back."

"Who knows when or how he got that? You can't possibly—"

Flora touched his elbow. "Jake, don't."

"What?" He twisted around. "Flora?"

She dipped her head, her long, dark eyelashes wet against her cheeks. "He's right. I was at the clearing that night, and I did cross paths with someone as I was leaving. I had my head down because of the rain and ran right into him. Honestly, though, I hardly noticed, given the state I was in. The state I'm still in, I suppose. I didn't even realize my brooch was missing until now."

"There you have it," said Mr. Meeks. "A confession."

Flora gasped. "Not a confession to *murder*!" She looked around the room. "I didn't have anything to do with Peanut's death. I swear it."

She met Cassie's eye. "I swear it."

"Why did you tell everyone you were home all night?" Cassie could hardly hear herself over the sound of her heart pounding.

Flora stepped toward her. "At first, because I was embarrassed. And then, when I learned what had happened to Peanut, because I was scared of what people would think, given the circumstances. I thought it best not to complicate things.

"After everyone went to bed that night, I was in the kitchen filling the pitcher for my washbasin when I saw Roger's spare ascot. Just hanging there on its hook, like everything was normal. And I couldn't bear it. I felt so sad and angry, and powerless, I couldn't lie down and go to sleep. Then I had this thought. Maybe Peanut was only hiding Roger from me, to torture me. Maybe I'd jumped to a conclusion, and he hadn't… you know." She swallowed and took up Cassie's hands.

"You understand, right? How grief and worry can take a hold of your thinking and twist it until you almost don't recognize yourself? Well, that's what happened to me. So I went out to the pilots' tower, in the dark and rain like a deranged person, set on making Peanut tell me where Roger was, alive or… not. Only, when I finally got there, I'd lost my nerve. I was—afraid. Not afraid Peanut would hurt me or anything. Not really. But afraid of knowing, for sure, what he'd done.

"So, I turned around and went home, telling myself I'd feel stronger and calmer in the light of day, that then I could face it all like a rational human being. And the rain let up right as I reached the house, like a sign from above." Her grip tightened. "Oh, God. Do you think I passed right by his body and didn't even see it?"

Jake moved toward her then stopped, looking helpless.

"Well." Mr. Shaw gave a haughty sniff. "You're just going to have to tell that story to a trial jury and see if they believe you. I've notified the state's attorney, and Sheriff Alderman will be back tomorrow afternoon to escort you to the state prison. Stevenson."

"No, wait!" Her own reason suddenly forsaking her, Cassie tried to hold on as Flora began to pull her hands away. She wouldn't let her go. It wasn't fair. Flora was her aunt, her family, and, after twenty years of not even knowing she should be looking for her, she'd only just found her. She couldn't be losing her already.

Hadn't enough been taken from her?

Flora's voice floated through the chaos in her head. "It's all right, Cassie. Everything will be all right."

Cassie let the police officer take Flora by the shoulders and watched, dull faced, as he tied her wrists together with a length of rope and lead her away.

Mr. Shaw brushed off his hands. "Now that that unpleasantness is concluded—"

"You fiend!" Before he could finish, Metta slipped from her father's grasp and lunged at him, setting off the dogs. Fortunately, Sergeant Denham reached out as they passed him and caught her with one hand and Danger with the other. Then he whistled, bringing Luna scrambling to a halt as well.

Mr. Shaw touched a finger to his nose as though he'd smelled something rotten and turned to Sam, Lily, and Mr. Brooks. "You three are free to go."

They hurried out of the room without a backward glance, and Mr. Shaw moved on to Hughes.

"But Officer Hughes, we'll need your help searching the house. And the rest of you will stay in this room until we're finished."

"I should be helping with the search, too," Jake said.

Mr. Meeks scoffed. "You're too enmeshed with the guilty party for that."

"Accused," Sergeant Denham said. "Not guilty."

"What exactly do you think you're going to find, you twits?" asked Mrs. Keene.

"The murder weapon, of course." Mr. Shaw folded his gloves and tucked them into his coat. "The state's attorney wants a speedy trial."

Metta began to wail.

"Now, now, dear," Sergeant Denham said. "Crying won't make stupid see reason any more than it'll make blind see light." He patted her back as she threw herself onto the settee and sobbed against him.

Jake sank down next to them, and Mrs. Keene, Miss Porter, and Paddy did the same on the opposite settee. Cassie, too spent to seek out a chair, slid down the counter onto the floor.

It was nearly dark by the time Mr. Shaw and his search team, having found nothing of consequence, finally left. But after the door clicked shut behind them, the group inside continued to sit in devastated silence. Even the animals seemed to sense now was not the time for play.

Cassie's mind, however, was anything but still. How could Flora not have told them, not even Jake, that she'd gone to the pilots' tower that night? And there was Peanut's threat to take away her home, too.

Lying. Hiding things. Those were classic signs of guilt.

All those thoughts and doubts from before, which she had so confidently put away, began to push their way back. Even small comments made here and there by others, so insignificant at the time, echoed about in her head.

You've known your aunt for, what is it, two days?

She's clearly dangerous.

Lucky you don't share a name.

You'd be surprised what people are capable of, given the right situation.

That wasn't even including all the whispers she hadn't been able to discern.

Her thoughts returned to a particular one of Flora's letters. It had stood out to her both because it was one of the earliest, written in the summer of 1865, and because, despite discussing little more than a walk Flora had taken to what she referred to as "the old place," it had felt the most intimate. At the moment, though, all Cassie could think about was the closing line, in which Flora had expressed a hope that Cassie and her father would return to Fernandina, "despite all." What was the "all" that had to be "spited"? It had apparently been enough to keep her father away from the island all these years. Away from Flora.

Not that she believed Flora was guilty. She didn't.

And she couldn't. If she did, Flora would be gone from her life, almost as effectively as her father and her mother and everyone else.

She would have come all this way for nothing, and she would go back to New York more alone than before.

Jake's voice sliced through the air like a knife through rancid butter. "Enjoying yourself, Hughes?"

Hughes had stayed behind after the search and was now sitting in a chair by the entrance to the dining room, a fist on each knee. "No."

"Then why are you still here?"

Hughes clenched and unclenched his fists. "Because she's innocent."

"I know."

"But it doesn't look good."

Each lifting his gaze slightly, the two men looked at one another, then looked down again.

Jake's voice was quiet. "I know."

Cassie wiped away a bead of sweat that was threatening to slide into her eye. It was hot in here. The dogs were panting, and the kitten lolling and the bird drooping, and Cassie's drawers, along with a layer or two of petticoat, had become one with the skin of her thighs.

As no one seemed able to muster the motivation to get up and do something about it, they all remained where they were until finally, just as Cassie felt her consciousness start to melt, Sergeant Denham jumped up and pushed a window open, letting in a stream of fresh air cool enough to drink.

"There's only one thing to be done now," he said.

"What's that?" Cassie asked, or at least she thought she had. Her heat-and-stress-addled brain was having trouble distinguishing between her thoughts and her actual voice.

"Find the real murderer." He returned to his place on the settee and folded his hands on top of his mangrove cane. "And to do that, if you'll pardon the military speak, we'll need a ceasefire. First, Officer Hughes needs to apologize to Mrs. Keene."

Hughes sat up. "But I was only trying to get information."

"By backing a harmless little man into the wall," said Mrs. Keene.

"He stepped backward, and there happened to be a wall there."

"*Be that as it may*—" Sergeant Denham spoke with resonance, then eased back into his normal mellow tone. "We have more important matters at hand."

Hughes stared at his shoes. "Sorry."

"Mrs. Keene?"

"But he's the one—" She clenched her jaw. "I'm sorry."

"Good. Officers Hughes and Gordon are next. And before you object, I want to remind you there is far more at stake here than your egos and petty contests. And that each of you may very well have information that could help the other out."

Jake and Hughes glared across the room at each other until, finally, Jake stood and held out his hand. After glancing around, Hughes trudged over and shook it. When he started to let go, however, Jake held on.

"You first."

"Why me?" asked Hughes.

"You helped them search the house."

"You're older."

"You're younger."

"Stop that this instant." Esme appeared in the doorway to the dining room. Her face was even paler than it had been the day before, and the worry lines around her eyes had deepened into grooves, but her mouth was firm. "Just stop it. Now let go of one another."

The men released their hands.

"If you insist on acting like children, that's how you'll be treated. But I really hope you won't because, as Sergeant Denham said, Flora needs our help."

"Where have you been?" Mrs. Keene asked. "We've all been corralled here for hours, with nothing to do but bite our nails and burn one-dollar notes from Hughes's wallet."

Hughes slapped a hand to his coat. "Do what now?"

"I went to the post office and sent out messages to all the best lawyers in Tallahassee." Esme re-tucked the edge of her turban with her thumb, leaving a small black smudge on the fabric. "Flora's going to need as much help as she can get, and there's no time to waste."

Cassie shifted. She should have thought of that.

"Speaking of children," Miss Porter said, "someone should take Metta and Paddy home."

Mrs. Keene stood and shook out her trousers. "Right. If you'll drop Paddy at Mr. Green's, I'll take Metta to the Florida House and wait with her until Jake finishes up here. The Captain can fend for himself for one evening. Though I'm liable to get home and find him frying up his belt, hoping it'll turn into bacon."

"We have to take the animals with us." Metta grabbed the puppy, who'd fallen asleep on Sergeant Denham's lap. "They'll need looking after while their mother is away."

"Oh, you don't have to worry about them," Cassie said, using the counter to pull herself to her feet. "Esme and I can—"

Miss Porter stopped Cassie with a small gesture. "That's a wonderful idea, Metta. The animals will need a great deal of comforting."

When Cassie saw the girl's expression lift, she remembered how Flora had asked her to take care of her horse, Sage, after the scare of seeing Peanut's body, and realized Miss Porter well knew it wasn't the animals who would need comforting.

Miss Porter patted Jake's arm as Metta and Paddy ran off to round up the animals. "Don't worry, dear. I'm going to go to the jail and sit with Flora right after I take Paddy home. She won't be alone long."

Jake nodded and turned away. Exchanging a look, Miss Porter and Mrs. Keene gathered their charges and left.

"So?" Hughes said as the door closed.

Jake, his eyes still fixed on the bookshelf, didn't respond. He barely even seemed to hear him.

"Fine. I'll start. But not because you told me to." Hughes sat down across from Sergeant Denham. "When I heard what Miss Gwynne said to Mr. Shaw, despite having to stand at the back since I was so late to the scene, as no one had felt it necessary to tell me about what had happened—"

"May I suggest you skip the side commentary?" Sergeant Denham said.

Hughes smoothed his fingers over his mustache. "When I heard what Miss Gwynne said to Mr. Shaw, I thought there might be something to it, so I waited for people to clear out and went to examine the area where the body had fallen for myself. That's when I found footprints in the bushes. A man's."

Jake stirred. "There were a good number of men around that morning."

"No, the onlookers' footprints were soft and wet, fresh in the mud from only a few minutes before. These had a crust, which means they'd been made earlier, with the top layer having had time to dry a little. But not that much earlier, because then they would have been washed out by the rain.

"Also, based on the shape of the prints and the heel depression, I'd say they were made by a dress pump, not an everyday boot. There certainly wasn't anyone in that early-morning crowd dressed in evening wear. And finally, the prints were *in* the bushes, not around them, which probably means whoever made them stumbled through in a rush. I would think the average man, if he had his wits about him, would prefer to walk around, not through, thorny brambles."

Jake hmphed. "Maybe there's something rattling around in that skull of yours after all."

To his credit, Hughes didn't respond to that. "I found this in the bushes as well, caught on a branch." He held up a watch key. "I thought it might be a clue. But I guess it could belong to Peanut."

"It's not Peanut's." Cassie recalled the contents of Peanut's coat pocket. "Peanut's watch is a stem-wind. It doesn't take a key."

"Good. That means it could have torn off the attacker's chain."

"Yes, but, again, there were a lot of people around this morning. Could have been one of theirs."

"True." Hughes rapped his knuckles against his knees. "After that, once I overheard you telling Mr. Ambler about what you'd found, I decided to survey the platform myself. Captain Beale was up there, but when I asked him about what you all had been looking at, he kept trying to get me to lean into his arms, saying he wanted to 'show me.' After I threatened to punch him in the face, he finally explained, but I didn't get much else for my trouble other than this nasty cut." He raised his bandaged hand. "Caught it on some broken glass sticking up between the boards while I was examining the drag marks on the floor."

"That's odd. You'd think they wouldn't let the pilots drink up there," Sergeant Denham said. "Being on duty and all."

Hughes smoothed his mustache. "No, it didn't look like that kind of glass. It was sort of delicate, colorful—"

"Here, let me fix that dressing for you." Esme sat next to him.

"I don't need—all right." He let her take his hand. "Anyway, after that, I tried to cover as much ground as possible, looking out for anything out of the ordinary, checking out suspicious characters, interviewing everyone I could think of. But most of the rest of the day was fairly fruitless, until I heard Shaw had finally called an inquest, and it was going to be held at Peanut's house—which meant I could probably get inside more easily and take a look around in there, or so I thought. But when I went over the next morning I found the idiot jury had the house all locked up, even when they were inside, so I had to go in through the bedroom window. And all I got for *those* efforts was a pretty new bruise on my thigh. The rest of the day was consumed by Tommy McDuffy's arrest and a brawl at Three Star. That's why, today, I've been pursuing my investigation with renewed vigor, digging for information and interviewing more people."

"People like Mr. Hiller?" Jake asked.

"Huh?" Hughes paused as Esme reached across him for Cassie's sewing scissors and used them to cut a length of gauze. "Oh. Okay. When I saw Miss Gwynne come out of the Keenes' store with a packet of papers, I figured you'd been to see him and gotten something useful. So when I saw him come out afterward, I asked him about it... and may have been a little overzealous. Your turn."

Cassie and Jake described what they had seen and heard over the previous couple of days.

"Mrs. Shaw, huh?" Hughes said when they were done. "I thought there might be something like that going on, the way Mr. Meeks has been following her everywhere."

Jake clapped his hands to his knees. "Am I the only one who didn't notice that?"

"I didn't figure Peanut as the object of her affections, though. What do you think? Lovers' quarrel? Peanut and Mrs. Shaw have an argument, and Mrs. Shaw retaliates? Or Mr. Meeks disapproves of the relationship and intervenes?"

"Jealous husband is more likely." Sergeant Denham accepted a mug of coffee from Esme, who had brought out a tray of refreshments. "Maybe Mr. Meeks said something to Mr. Shaw about Peanut."

"Both the evidence in Peanut's study and the footprints Hughes found at the tower indicate a man's involvement," said Jake.

Cassie frowned. "But whoever was in Peanut's study was searching for something. What might Mr. Shaw have been searching for, in that case?"

"We still don't rightly know what *anyone* might have been searching for." Unbuttoning his shirt, Jake retrieved the ledger from its hiding spot against his underclothes—apparently, he had picked up a trick or two from Cassie—and examined it with distaste. "Peanut hid this ledger in there, but who would want it? It's really just a creepy old scrapbook."

"To confirm, Miss Gwynne—" Hughes ran a hand through his hair. "That packet Mr. Hiller gave you doesn't have any bearing on this?"

Cassie took the ledger from Jake and spread it open on the counter. "No, that was the fire insurance policy file for Atherton Brooks's store. I only borrowed it because Mr. Brooks has been courting Lily Townsend, who's a childhood friend of mine, and her brother had some concerns about Mr. Brooks's financial status. But as the engagement has been set now, I'm not certain it still matters." She brushed her bangs out of her face. "That's the reason I was 'watching' Mr. Brooks last night, by the way. Because of my friend. That, and he was making such a fool of himself it was hard to look away."

Why did she keep defending herself to this man?

"I see. But I already told you everything you need to know about him. He's a failed businessman, a lousy drunkard, and a shameless womanizer. There's even a joke at Three Star about how there's not a regular there he hasn't borrowed from, not even Peanut the miser." He drummed his fingers on the arm of the settee. "Say, not to distract from what we're doing here, but may I see that Brooks file? It relates to last month's fire, and I have an interest in the topic."

"Obsession, more like," Jake muttered as Cassie stepped out of the room to remove the packet from her skirts, where she'd stuffed it during the search.

Cassie handed the packet to Hughes and turned back to the ledger. When she reached the property survey for Peanut's lot next to Flora, one of the pages Mr. Hiller had mentioned, she noticed something odd. The drawing depicted a water-filled depression she was sure was in Flora's yard—Flora had told her she used it as an ornamental fish pond during the summers—as being within the boundaries of Peanut's property instead. Which, if correct, would mean the better part of Flora's house was within those boundaries as well.

In Peanut's note, he'd said he had "evidence" supporting his claim. Could this be what he was talking about? An alternate set of deed documents for their respective properties? Could Flora have stolen into Peanut's house looking for them, then, failing to find them, gone out to the pilots' tower and—

She slapped the book shut. That was ridiculous.

Time for a new train of thought.

"Officer Hughes," Cassie said, "what you said about Mr. Brooks borrowing money from everyone at Three Star, is that true? Or were people only poking fun?" She took a swig of coffee from the mug Esme had set in front of her.

"I don't know for a fact. But I did overhear Mr. Brooks telling someone at Three Star once that he wanted to buy a sail wagon, and that if he didn't have enough money, he could probably go 'back' to Peanut."

"Since when do you spend so much time at Three Star?" Jake asked.

Hughes fiddled with his badge. "It's part of my, um, surveillance initiative."

"Your what?"

"After the, uh, incident, with the earl, I thought I ought to work on building a more reliable information-gathering network. So, I've taken to spending several hours a week in various barrooms about town, to keep an ear to the ground. Most of what I hear is of little use. Mrs. Dickerson cheats at cards, Major Drury is scared of outhouses because his brothers tipped one with him in it once, that sort of thing. But it does yield occasionally."

"Clever," said Sergeant Denham. "Where did you get an idea like that?"

Hughes became engrossed with a list of numbers on the page in front of him. "I saw how Jake talks regularly with Mrs. Rydell at the post office so he can hear the news or gossip that comes through there. And it seemed like a… good idea."

From the pinch in his face, Cassie could tell it had caused near physical pain for him to admit that. Jake didn't look any more comfortable.

"Going back to Mr. Brooks," Cassie said. "Don't you think it odd that, when Flora told him about Peanut, he made a point of diminishing his acquaintance with him? Even Mrs. Marsden said he often sat on the stool next to Peanut's."

Esme picked up Cassie's empty mug and replaced it with a full one. "Does that mean he should be suspected? Of the murder?"

"I suppose it's possible," said Jake, "if Mr. Brooks in fact owed Peanut money. But with the insurance money he got, was there really a motive? He could have simply paid his debt and been done with it."

"And, truth be told, it wasn't as if he was unused to owing people money." Hughes turned a page in the Brooks file. "Ah, here's a transcription of the fire investigation report. I've read this bit of literature more times than I'd care to admit."

Jake gave an exaggerated shrug. "And yet, every time, the findings remain inconclusive."

"Amusing," said Hughes. "But I don't agree with the findings. Consider this. The investigator found broken lamps near the wood and fuel storage areas behind both Weil's barroom and Steeby's tin shop; in either place a broken lamp could easily have started a conflagration. But according to the people I interviewed who were at Weil's that night, the rear door had been blocked all day by a surplus delivery of beer. So why would a lit lamp have been back there? Also, Steeby maintains he didn't use his shop all day. I'm telling you. It stinks of arson."

"Let me see something." Cassie walked over to them and peered at the page. "Yes, look here. This says people reported seeing great volumes of black smoke issuing 'straight up' from behind Mr. Bard's restaurant. There was something similar in the newspaper account which caught my eye because, in my house, my father always made sure to close the skylight before bed, in case the weather turned during the night."

Jake took the file and squinted at the passage. "I don't follow."

"Fire feeds on oxygen. I learned all about it when my father worked on a case involving a house fire. It means that fire, once ignited, will race toward sources of oxygen, such as open windows. Therefore, if one wished to draw a fire upward, to enhance its spread, one could do so by opening windows near the top of a building."

"Such as skylights," said Sergeant Denham.

"Which would otherwise usually be closed at night, in case of rain," added Jake.

"Causing the appearance of columns of smoke and flames going straight up in the air." Hughes took the file back from Jake. "As much time as I've spent thinking about this fire, that thought had never occurred to me from reading this passage."

"That means the fire started in a building behind Mr. Bard's with skylights," said Sergeant Denham.

"But doesn't the newspaper say people saw the smoke coming up from behind Weil's barroom?" Jake took the file from Hughes again. "Not Mr. Bard's?"

Hughes grabbed the file back. "Those don't necessarily conflict. It's a matter of perspective. The source could be between them. From the north, on Centre Street, your reference point would be Mr. Bard's. From the south, it would be Weil's."

"Steeby's is south of Weil's," said Jake. "Not in between Weil's and Mr. Bard's."

Sergeant Denham stroked his beard. "That's right. The only buildings between are Mr. Adler's and Mr. Brooks's. And there are no skylights in Adler's, which means..."

"The fire started in Brooks's store," Jake and Hughes said at the same time. They looked at each other and moved farther apart.

Cassie drained her mug. "You did describe the person you saw running away from the fire as tall and gaunt in your newspaper interview, Officer Hughes. That could fit Mr. Brooks."

"But he was out of town that night. He had a ticket for the train and everything."

"That doesn't prove he got on the train. And this morning, Lily said he'd told her about seeing a moonbow here earlier this month. That moonbow occurred on the night of the fire."

"What would be worth going through all of that?" asked Jake.

"Wait a minute." Hughes angled a page toward the light. "This is the address of that old warehouse where those vagrants were squatting. Behind Bock's icehouse."

"That place has an address?" said Sergeant Denham.

Jake tried to take the file back from Hughes, but this time Hughes held on.

"But that can't be right." Jake read as he gave the file another tug. "Those are delivery receipts for the goods Mr. Brooks listed as covered property on his insurance application. That's the address of where the shipments were delivered."

Hughes tugged back. "No, the vagrants insisted they'd been living out of there for months. They'd even made themselves beds from shipping crates they had rummaged from a Belgian merchant ship and filled with hay. They were actually upset because apparently someone had come in a few times while they were out and moved things around. In any case, they claimed the warehouse was theirs because of, what was it, 'adverse possession'?"

"Well-informed vagrants," Sergeant Denham commented.

Hughes threw up a shoulder against Jake's reach and flipped through a few more pages. "Okay, yes, these are shipping receipts. But I'm right about the address." Finally relinquishing the file, he paced the length of the room. Then he snapped his fingers. "The receipts have to be fake. Mr. Brooks probably made them up to inflate the value of the business, for the insurance policy."

"Are you saying Mr. Brooks never bought all those goods he claimed were destroyed in the fire?" Esme asked. "And he was planning to set fire to his building the whole time?"

"It makes sense," said Cassie. "That way, the insurance money was almost pure income."

Jake lowered the papers. "Mr. Hiller will be very interested to hear about this. And the sheriff."

"And Sam and Lily."

"I hate to point this out," said Sergeant Denham, "but we still haven't gotten anywhere with the real issue here. The murder, that is."

The group fell quiet.

Cassie tried to think of what her father would have done. "Let's try being systematic about it." She sank into the chair by the dining room vacated by Hughes. "We'll make a list. First, people with motives, however strong. Anyone who may have had an issue with Peanut."

Hughes snorted. "That's easy. Downing, Smalls, Meeks, Mr. Shaw, Mrs. Shaw, all of his neighbors, anyone else who's ever met him."

"Helpful," said Jake.

Hughes adjusted his bandage. "Okay, okay. How about Captain Beale? Peanut was in the midst of organizing a coup against him. I heard some of the harbor pilot oarsman talking about it at Weil's."

"What do you mean, a coup?" asked Cassie.

"Peanut has been levying accusations within the association for months that the steamer wreck that happened here two years ago, *City of Austin*, was Captain Beale's fault. He wanted to launch an official inquiry. Said he had proof."

"I guess I shouldn't be surprised Captain Beale didn't mention that when I asked him if any of the pilots were quarreling with Peanut." Cassie put down her mug. "Wait a minute. Mr. Smalls said he saw someone with a Panama hat in Peanut's house the day his cart overturned. Peanut doesn't wear a Panama hat, but Captain Beale does."

"We're definitely going to have to have another talk with him," Jake said, setting his jaw.

"What about the man with the nostrils Major Drury mentioned?" asked Sergeant Denham. "It sounds like he and Peanut were up to something. Good or bad, who knows. But something."

"I agree." Jake pulled out his little pink notebook and scribbled in it. "We need to find out who he is and what exactly he and Peanut talked about. He traveled here somehow, likely stayed over at one of the guesthouses. Someone has to know more about him."

"And Mr. Brooks?" asked Esme.

Cassie gulped more coffee. The lack of sleep was affecting her more than she thought. Each sip felt as though it were making her sleepier rather than more awake.

"That warehouse, over by the icehouse," she said, "it's on the Broome Street Wharf, right? Jake, didn't you say Peanut's wife's family used to own that area, too?"

"Far as I know."

"Do you think Peanut owns that warehouse, then?"

"I don't know. It's possible. It's been unused for so long, I never thought about it."

"Assuming he does, and given his possessiveness over his property, what are the chances of Mr. Brooks using his warehouse without his knowledge, even if it was just for show? What if he found out and got angry? Threatened Mr. Brooks somehow?"

Jake combed his fingers through his beard. "Well, those vagrants got away with it for quite a while."

"Whichever the case," Hughes said, "we need more evidence to bring this kind of accusation. Being an arsonist and fraudster doesn't make one a murderer."

"I'm still wondering who around here would know how to use a weapon like a stiletto," said Sergeant Denham.

Sighing, Hughes sat back down and put his feet on the tea table.

Jake kicked Hughes's feet onto the ground. "What we need to do is get out there and gather more information. Split up and talk to everyone, follow all the threads. And quickly. They're going to move Flora to state prison tomorrow, and once that happens, it's going to be much more difficult to get her home."

Cassie squeezed a parlor pillow to her chest. *All the threads.* Should she tell them about Peanut's note? The addition of a second motive wouldn't change anything, though. And her gut feeling about Flora, it was still good. Really good. And the unwavering faith Flora's closest friends had in her, despite what so many others were saying and thinking, should count for something, shouldn't it?

The spot where she'd hit her head on the tree the day before pounded with renewed ferocity, and a haze started to gather at the edges of her vision.

"First thing in the morning, we'll go see Mr. Brooks." Jake sounded like he was walking away down a hallway. "What Cassie pointed out about his comment the other day, how he insisted, for no apparent reason, that he hardly knew Peanut, makes me think he knows more than he's letting on. Not to mention the warehouse situation. We'll have to follow up on this arson and insurance business, no matter what."

"Right. Maybe having some charges hanging over his head will make him more cooperative." Hughes's voice sounded tinny as well. "Then we'll divide and conquer on the rest of the things we talked about."

Esme and Sergeant Denham murmured in agreement.

"We'll sort this out," Esme said. "Whatever it takes."

CHAPTER NINETEEN

Hours later, Cassie gasped awake in the empty parlor, reeling from a dream she couldn't quite remember. As though she were standing at the edge of it looking in, as Flora had put it, and all she could see was the outline of Flora sitting in jail, considering the short, final path before her.

She couldn't let this happen. It wasn't right. She knew it. They all knew it.

She hadn't been able to save her father, but maybe she could save Flora.

She tried to stand but yelped in pain instead. Somehow, she had managed to fall asleep draped over the arm of her chair, and now her back was one big knot. Jamming a fist into her spine, she hobbled across the room and picked up a scrap of paper that had missed the trash bin.

She would try a word association experiment. Her father had done that sometimes when he was stuck, to get his thoughts flowing. She unclipped a pencil from her chatelaine.

> Peanut–Mean–Hairy but bald–Grapefruits–Rocks–Angry neighbors–Smalls–Flowers–Lovers–Roses–Guano–Pilots–Beale–Disaster–Fire–Downing–Insurance–Loans–Brooks–

Garbage. Utter garbage. What was she thinking, getting involved? She wasn't smart enough for this.

Her mind spinning like a carriage wheel in mud, she threw both the pencil and the paper in the bin and moved through the shadows to the window. The street was dark and empty, like her brain.

She bent forward, intent on banging her head against the pane until something shook out of it. But as she did so, the light from Mrs. Abernathy's electric streetlamp shifted through the trees and struck her in the face, triggering a violent sneeze. When she tried to open her eyes, she sneezed again, and she thought of the Huddlestons' dog, Oscar, who had displayed a similar affliction. Only his sneezes hadn't been triggered by light, but rather by a smell...

Her brain sparked. Then sparked again. And again and again in rapid succession, like little dog sneezes.

She searched through the Brooks file, but she couldn't find what she was looking for. Then, experiencing another spark, she ran back over to the waste bin. And there it was, right on top of the trash heap where she'd thrown it, but face up, with her own scribblings on the back. The envelope from Aurum's initial premium payment, labeled in that now all-too-familiar hand.

She had a visit to make.

"What? What is it? Is something on fire?"

Mr. Hiller pulled open his front door in his nightclothes, one leg in a pair of trousers and a bucket of water in his hand. The sun was only just coming up, but the pointed rays breaking through the morning gray were enough to make him squint.

"No, Mr. Hiller," Cassie said. "Nothing's burning. But it is an emergency."

"Oh, Miss Gwynne. You've given me a fright." He put down the bucket and felt around his head for his spectacles. "What's happened?"

"They've arrested Aunt Flora. She's to be moved to the state prison tomorrow. I mean, today."

"I heard. I can't believe it."

"Which is why I need to know, did you find that agreement I asked about?"

"You mean the Smalls complaint? Yes, Mr. Baker said he drafted it as requested, but I don't see what that has to do with Miss Hale—"

"No, the agreement. For the entity that owns Atherton Brooks's business."

Mr. Hiller adjusted his nightcap. "Oh, yes, I have it in the other room. But what does that have to do with Miss Hale, either? Can't it wait until a more decent hour?"

"I don't have time to explain now, but it's important I see it right away. And here." Cassie handed him the Brooks insurance file. "I promised to bring this back. But I don't think you're going to want to send it off to Records just yet."

"Why wouldn't—"

"I'll explain afterward. Please."

"All right. Hold on." Tucking the packet under his arm, he shuffled into the parlor and re-emerged a few seconds later with a wet-letter copybook.

"Here's the agreement. I haven't gone through it yet, though." He placed it on the foyer table and lit the candle next to it. "It's a copy, obviously—I'm assuming one of the parties has the original—so we'll have to turn the pages carefully. They're very thin. And you should know it took a couple of lies and more than a couple of whiskeys to convince Mr. Baker to give this to me, by the way. Apparently, lawyers are touchy about confidentiality."

He opened the book and began to page through it.

"Ah, I think this is what you want." He pointed. "'Agreement regarding the business called Aurum, to be defined as inclusive of all sales, stock, real property, insurance—' No, let's see… Here, this section addresses ownership shares… Okay, there's an amendment. Where's the amendment? Oh, here it is. Or they are, I should say, wow. Sorry, the most recent one says… The 'party of the first' is to own twenty percent of the business, and the 'party of the second,' eighty."

Cassie tapped her fingers against her leg. "Okay, go to where it identifies the parties. There should be a part where it identifies the parties. Mr. Brooks and…?"

"Hold your horses, I'll find it. Back, back, back… The party of the first is Atherton Brooks. And party of the second is…" He licked his finger and turned the page. "Theodore Runkles."

Cassie stomped her foot. "It *was* Peanut. I knew it. That handwriting on the envelope for the premium payment was too familiar. But Mr. Brooks really only owned twenty percent of his own business?"

"Looks that way, after the amendments were all said and done. It seems Mr. Brooks kept giving more and more ownership over to Peanut, for some reason."

"Each time he ran low on money, I'll bet. So that means Peanut was entitled to eighty percent of the insurance payout and Mr. Brooks twenty."

"Yes. But there was something else that caught my eye." Mr. Hiller turned a few more pages and put his spectacles on top of his head. "Here. Under the agreement, all the insurance money is to stay in the company account, controlled by the majority owner, unless a distribution is made to all the owners, at the majority owner's sole discretion, or unless the company is dissolved."

"In other words, Mr. Brooks wouldn't have seen any money without Peanut's say-so."

"Exactly. I received the insurance check for Aurum on Friday and gave it to Mr. Brooks right away. I assume he then brought it to Peanut, the majority owner. But unless Peanut deposited the check and authorized a distribution, Mr. Brooks wouldn't have received anything."

"But Mr. Brooks came to you on Wednesday inquiring about that beach cottage. And was buying the town drinks later that evening, and the next one, too."

"Right. Oh, because—"

"Because Mr. Brooks has full control over all the money now that Peanut is deceased." Cassie's breathing quickened. "Under a partnership, in the event of the death of one of the partners, that partner's interests go to the remaining partners. Or partner, in this case." She gathered up her skirts. "And that, Mr. Hiller, is motive."

Cassie plunged down Third Street toward the Florida House Inn, her feet racing to keep up with her mind. It was all becoming clear. Mr. Brooks, under increasing financial pressure from his debts, and from his need to convince Sam he could support Lily in the lifestyle to which she was accustomed, came up with a fire insurance fraud scheme that would allow him to both get rid of his failing business and gain a large sum of money. Peanut, however, who provided the premium payment so likely approved of the scheme, did not cooperate and withheld Mr. Brooks' portion of the money. Or Mr. Brooks simply decided he wanted the entire sum for himself.

Whichever the case, Mr. Brooks searched Peanut's study, perhaps to get the insurance check back, or to destroy other evidence relating to their scheme, then went up to the pilots' tower, stabbed Peanut, and dragged his body over the side. Down at the bottom, he tried to create the appearance of an accidental fall. In his haste, however, he stepped through the bushes, coating his dress shoes in the guano fertilizer Mrs. Beale had so assiduously applied to the beds. So, he brought his shoes to the Egmont to be cleaned on the Townsends' bill, where Oscar the dog, who evidently had a sensitivity to guano, sniffed them and launched into a sneezing fit.

The front doors of the Florida House's green-white-and-red front porch were propped open, so Cassie charged inside and, following the directions of the startled maid she found in the foyer, pounded up the staircase to Jake's room. She banged on the door.

"Jake!" She pushed the hair from her face. The sun hadn't yet burned off the morning dew, so the air was coating her skin like glaze on a doughnut. "It's Cassie. I've figured it out!"

She heard Danger and Luna barking inside, as well as Kleio reciting the alphabet.

Finally, Metta answered the door, the kitten in her arms. She blinked as Kleio landed in her hair and, apparently dissatisfied with the state of things there, began tugging at the tangles around her feet.

"Where's your father?" Cassie asked. "I must speak with him immediately."

"I don't know. The inn owner, Mrs. Liddy, came to get him a while ago. Officer Hughes went, too."

"Did you hear where they—What's the matter?"

The girl was standing with one leg crossed over the other, frowning in concentration.

"They told me not to go outside, but…" She switched legs. "I *really* need to use the necessary."

"Poor girl. Come with me."

After moving the bird onto a chair inside and closing the door, Cassie led Metta down the hall toward the rear porch and pushed open the door. When they emerged, however, they were greeted by the sight of a dozen or more people gathered beneath the spreading branches of an ancient oak tree in the courtyard below.

Not much to Cassie's surprise, Mrs. Keene and Miss Porter were among them. Esme was there as well, standing off to the side with her hands knotted together.

"What's going on?" she asked no one and everyone at once.

"They've caught Peanut's murderer!" Miss Porter crossed herself and whispered an upward prayer of thanks.

"But I've only just—What do you mean?"

"His *actual* murderer, Atherton Brooks. His room is in there."

Cassie followed Miss Porter's finger to a ground-floor door leading into the north wing.

"Jake and Hughes are inside with the coroner's jury making a final determination. Now they'll have to let Flora free!"

Metta whimpered.

"Oh, no, I'm sorry." Cassie took the kitten, who was still in Metta's arms. "Go, go."

Metta ran down the steps toward the outhouse.

"Too bad the over-coiffed worm won't be standing trial," Mrs. Keene said.

"He won't? Why not?"

Mrs. Keene tossed a stone into the fishpond a few feet away, causing a man to yelp at the splash.

"Because he's dead."

CHAPTER TWENTY

Cassie grabbed the rocking chair next to her to steady herself, which wasn't the most effective idea she'd ever had. "Dead? How?"

"They haven't said anything official, but the maid who found him told us it was an overdose," Miss Porter answered. "Chloral hydrate."

Regaining her senses slightly, Cassie put the kitten on her shoulder and descended into the courtyard.

"Nasty stuff, that." Mrs. Rydell, the postmistress Cassie had met the day before, was perched on top of a planter like a mountain goat, trying to see over the others' heads. She called down to the lavender-robed woman by her ankles. "Mrs. Liddy, you'll remember, the same thing happened to that lumber inspector last year, the one who liked to chase after the teachers at the girls' school. And the year before that, there was that poor girl visiting from Brunswick, only eighteen."

"How do they know Mr. Brooks killed Peanut?" asked Cassie.

"He had the knife he used right under his bed, the derned ninny." Major Drury was present, too, somehow smelling worse than the last time she'd seen him. "Just sitting there, plain as day. They're also saying—I heard couple of 'em in there talking—that he started the fire. For insurance money. And that he and Peanut were partners in his clothing store and maybe the insurance scheme, too, and that's why he killed Peanut. To get everything for himself."

Cassie forgot herself and turned to face him.

"Found a haversack full of matches and turpentine tins and everything," Major Drury went on. "Though I'll admit, I was surprised about that part. I was sure it was the ghost who started the fire, myself. They're drawn to destruction, see—"

"Excuse me, ladies and gentlemen." Mr. Shaw had come out onto the deck, along with Dr. Ames, Jake, Hughes, and three droopy-eyed men whose nightclothes were sticking out from under their coats. "If I could have your attention. As you all know, the body of Mr. Atherton Brooks was discovered in his bed here at the Florida House very early this morning. We have conducted an *in situ* inquest over the body, which included a thorough medical examination by Dr. Ames, and it is the verdict of the jury that Mr. Brooks came to his death by suffering an unfortunate accident, caused by yet another tragic overdose of chloral hydrate.

"In addition, we have discovered among Mr. Brooks's effects clear evidence he was responsible not only for the fire which occurred on Centre Street last month, having had an intent and purpose to commit insurance fraud, but also for the murder of Captain Runkles.

"Therefore, the jury's verdict with respect to the death of Captain Runkles will be amended, and Officer Gordon will depart immediately for the county jail to release Miss Hale, who is no longer under suspicion. Thank you for your attention, and I hope you will remember during the upcoming election that it is due to the unrelenting persistence of your coroner, and the esteemed members of our community who have assisted him, that we have distilled the truth about these matters and seen justice served."

Buttoning his coat, he descended from the step and strode across the courtyard toward the lobby.

"It's a wonder he can keep his feet on the ground with all that hot air inside," said Mrs. Keene.

"Miss Gwynne, may I have a word?" Hughes stepped out of the doorway recently vacated by Mr. Shaw. He had taken off his jacket and rolled his sleeves up to his elbows, exposing a pair of strong forearms.

"Why don't you go on ahead with Jake and Esme to the jail," Cassie said to Miss Porter and Mrs. Keene, who were watching them a little too curiously. "I'll meet everyone back at the house."

Checking that the kitten was secure on her shoulder, she climbed onto the porch and followed Hughes down the narrow hallway. About halfway down, he pushed in the door to one of the rooms, extending his arm to hold it open for her. As she turned sideways to pass by, however, she found herself facing him, closer than expected.

She paused, suddenly aware of her breathing.

"What do you think?" He smoothed back a lock of hair that had fallen over one of his eyes.

"What do I think?"

He smelled of sandalwood and bergamot.

"About Mr. Brooks's room. See anything amiss?"

"Oh, uh…" Biting her lip, Cassie slid the rest of the way inside and looked around. Beneath the window there was a large clothing trunk, its lid propped up by an umbrella. Shirts, coats, pants, and ties spilled out of it, giving the impression of a wide-mouthed monster disgorging itself, but she could see from the creasing that the items had probably been neatly folded before the "investigative activities" of the morning's inquest. A half-empty tumbler and an ashtray sat on the table by the fireplace. Bits of gravel and mud tracked in by the many feet that had come and gone that morning covered the floor. And, despite the open window, over which a sheer curtain fluttered and sighed like a tattered flag, the scent of Mr. Brooks's hair oil, mixed with that of stale liquor and grass, hung in the air.

"The maid who found him said she was on her way to pump water for the morning cooking when she saw Mr. Brooks's door open," Hughes said.

The kitten pressed into her neck as the door trembled and creaked behind them, caught in a current of air flowing between the window and the hall.

"She said that, in and of itself, wasn't so unusual. She'd often closed it for him after he stumbled in late from the barrooms. But this time he'd left the lamp burning on his bedside table, so she went in to put it out. When she got close, she caught something with her foot and it went clattering across the room. Curious that Mr. Brooks hadn't stirred at the sound, she called out to him, and when there was still no response, she attempted to rouse him by shaking. That didn't work, so she ran out for Dr. Ames right away, but there was no resuscitating him."

Cassie finally allowed her gaze to drift to where Mr. Brooks still lay in the bed, and dark memories began to crowd into her brain like passengers filling a train car. Her stomach grew cold and heavy, and her head grew hot and light, until suddenly she feared she might be pulled in two. The room went white.

"Whoa!" Hughes caught her in his arms.

The kitten, apparently seeing no better option, flung herself over Hughes's shoulder.

"I thought you could handle dead bodies."

"It's not that." She rested her cheek against his chest a moment before she realized what she was doing. She straightened up, her face burning. "It just reminded me of something from a long time ago. Forget it." She stepped back. "What was it you wanted from me again?"

"Nothing particular, I guess." Hughes watched her warily as she leaned against the wall. "Or, I don't know. I thought maybe you could take one last look around while I waited for the undertaker, to see if we're missing anything. The theory makes sense, I think, but I have an odd feeling I can't seem to shake."

"I take it, then, you're here with Mr. Shaw's blessing?"

"Yes, but likely only because I was already on the grounds with Jake when Mr. Brooks was found—We'd both fallen asleep somehow, right there at Jake's table. Even so, Mr. Shaw probably would have kicked us out right after we arrived on the scene if Jake hadn't noticed that the object the maid had stumbled on was a knife and said it looked like the sort of knife that could have caused Peanut's peculiar wound. When Dr. Ames measured it and compared it to his notes, he agreed."

"Good eye," Cassie said.

"Then I examined the knife and found a bloodied scrap of fabric caught in the junction with the hilt, which matched the kind of shirt Peanut was wearing the day he was killed."

"Even better eye."

Their gazes met. Then fell away when a *thunk* sounded. The kitten, who'd apparently been hanging onto the back of Hughes's shirt since she catapulted over his shoulder, had finally fallen to the floor.

Hughes clasped his hands behind his back and walked over to the window. "When they found him, he had a bottle of chloral hydrate in one hand, most of which had spilled out onto the pillow around his head, and a gauze pad in the other. Dr. Ames thinks he must have opened it for a dose to help him sleep—heavy alcohol users are known to use it to combat the insomnia that comes along with the habit—but succumbed shortly after taking the inhalation and failed to replace the cork."

Cassie tugged at a button that had come loose from her sleeve. "Strange. Mr. Brooks told me he was a deep sleeper. Unusually so. I wouldn't think he'd be taking any insomnia remedies."

"Well, when we found more empty chloral vials in the waste bin, we sent a man to wake Dr. Palmer, since the vials all bore his pharmacy label. And his records showed Mr. Brooks had purchased a large amount of the tincture from his store over the last month.

They keep track of that so they can limit how much a person can buy, precisely because of these kinds of situations. Apparently, many find they have to take higher and higher doses over time in order to get the same effect, and eventually it's too much."

Cassie had a thought. Glancing at Hughes, who still had his back turned, she steeled herself with a sharp exhale then pried Mr. Brooks's lips open and sniffed. Below a layer of whiskey and stomach acid, she detected a faint sweetness, like that of tinned fruit.

Hughes turned around. "What are you doing?" He covered his mouth.

"I, um, remembered something." She paused. She had never told anyone this before. "When I was very young, about Metta's age, I nearly lost my father to an overdose as well. Laudanum. Thankfully, he recovered, of course. And he later told me it was that very incident which made him decide to turn his life around, to leave his job at the docks and start studying the law. But I was the one who found him."

Hughes dropped his hand.

"I only mention it because the first thing the doctor did after he arrived was smell his mouth. He always started with that in these situations, he told me—I think explaining was his way of comforting me, seeing I hadn't simply run off—in order to try to tell what the patient had taken. Laudanum, for example, gives off a wild, spicy sort of smell. Chloral gives off more of a sweet one."

"I see. But we already know he took chloral."

"Yes, but I was thinking... It stands to reason that the breath test would only work if the person took the substance orally. So, if I smelled chloral inside his mouth, which I did, that would mean he both swallowed it and inhaled it. That seems a bit excessive, doesn't it?"

"He probably mixed the chloral with whiskey." Hughes indicated an empty tumbler and liquor bottle on the bedside table. "Sakes alive. That by itself would put me out."

"Exactly my point." Cassie walked back over to the table by the fireplace. "Another question. Why do you suppose he would have poured a drink at his bedside table if he still had half a glass sitting over here?"

Hughes inclined his head. "And since when does Mr. Brooks leave any glass of whiskey unfinished?"

"Also, if you had a murder weapon in your possession, why would you keep it in your room, barely tucked under your bed?"

"He did have strong motive, though. Mr. Shaw took it with him for the evidence file, but behind the wardrobe we found documentation showing that Peanut owned part of Mr. Brooks's clothing business and—"

"I know all about that. Mr. Hiller and I reviewed the information Mr. Hiller obtained from Mr. Baker on Aurum, the entity that held Mr. Brooks's business, and discovered that under their partnership agreement, not only was Mr. Brooks only entitled to a small portion of the company's assets, but he wouldn't see a penny of company money without Peanut's approval. But once Peanut was out of the picture, he controlled all of it."

Hughes studied her. "It seems what we found was a copy of that same agreement. Though our understanding of it was somewhat simpler than yours. There was also a ledger with it, an actual financials ledger, tracking Mr. Brooks's indebtedness to Peanut. And when we considered those papers in connection with the information about the fire and the insurance policy, and the stiletto knife, of course, not to mention the haversack of incendiary materials we found inside Mr. Brooks' clothing trunk… Well, Mr. Shaw was sure satisfied we had found Peanut's killer."

"It's rather perfect," Cassie said. "Everything all lined up like that."

"It is, isn't it."

Hughes batted the fluttering curtain away from him. "So, what do we do about it?"

Cassie pulled at a piece of paint peeling off the wall. Like Hughes, she had an "odd feeling" about things, but she didn't have any idea where to go from here. Places, people, and questions were flying about in her head like a flock of sparrows caught in a giant net. Her father would have known what to do, where to look, what questions to ask. He'd calm those sparrows with a word and get them to fly out one by one and line up sweetly on a branch so he could see which was which. But, of course, he wasn't there. She was supposed to have the answers now.

There was a shuffling in the hall, and Paddy's head appeared in the doorway. Cassie and Hughes instantly fell in shoulder to shoulder, blocking his view of the bed.

"Paddy," Cassie said, "you shouldn't be in here."

"I'm here on business." He puffed out his chest proudly. Though he was still wearing his usual sailor suit, it was freshly pressed, and his hair was neatly combed. "One of the Egmont message boys took sick, so Mr. Littell asked me to fill in. I get twenty cents a message, plus tips!"

"Good for you, boy," said Hughes. "What's the message?"

"Miss Lily Townsend wishes to see Miss Cassie Gwynne in her suite at the Egmont. Right away."

He held out his hand.

When Cassie arrived at the door to Lily's room, a hotel maid jumped up from where she was scrubbing the floor.

"Oh, I wouldn't go in there, Miss!"

"But I was asked to come."

"Right. It's just that—"

The door flew open, and another maid came tumbling out. There was egg and jam smeared on the front of her dress, and when she saw Cassie and the other girl, she burst into tears and ran down the hall.

Cassie closed her mouth.

"That's what I was going to warn you about," said the first maid. "Miss Townsend's in a bit of a state. She isn't especially pleasant most days, if you ask me, but today, what with the news about Mr. Brooks… The staff's resorted to drawing straws when she calls on the annunciator."

"Duly noted." Cassie squared her shoulders and knocked. "Lily? It's Cassie."

A muffled voice responded from within, so, hoping it was an invitation to enter, Cassie opened the door and let herself in.

The curtains were drawn, making the rectangular glow around the edges of the windows the only light in the room, but, fortunately, she could see well enough to pick her way across the floor, which was littered with lavish debris: silk petticoats, kid gloves, jewelry, shoes. So many shoes.

"In here, Cassie."

Through the doorframe to her left, Cassie made out a mound of blankets and sheets that she took to be the bed. She walked toward it as a pirate toward the end of a plank.

"Thank Heavens you're here." Lily sat up as Cassie lit the bedside lamp. Even wrapped in a bedsheet, her eyes puffy and her nose tinged with red, she possessed an inexplicable kind of glamor and polish that Cassie, while herself a pretty girl, had never been able to achieve with her best efforts. "My life is over. The world is collapsing before my very eyes."

"I heard the news," Cassie said. "I'm so sorry."

Lily flopped her arms. "Sorry? My *fiancé* is *dead*."

"Sorry." Cassie cringed. "That is, I know you cared about him—"

"No! I mean… We'd just finally gotten everything worked out."

Through a slit in the curtains behind the bed, Cassie watched a pileated woodpecker hammer at a tree trunk and dig something out of the wood.

"I'm not sure I understand."

Lily twisted her handkerchief in her lap. "Cassie, I'm—" Her eyes flew open, and she fell to the side and retched into a wastebasket. She sat up and wiped her mouth. "Expecting."

The woodpecker banged his face against the tree again, sending Cassie's own thoughts knocking against her skull. "A child?"

"Of course a child."

"Who's the father?"

"Atherton. That's what I've been trying to tell you. I'll be showing soon, and then," she blew her nose, "it'll be all over for me. We're already an embarrassment to the family, thanks to Father. I won't be welcome anywhere decent ever again." She stared in horror at something Cassie couldn't see.

"But how? I don't understand."

"I was naïve. Stupid. Whatever you want to call it. Maybe I wanted to do something for myself for once. Whatever it was, he swept me off my feet, and I fell. Rather the opposite of that saccharine roller-skating story."

"How long has it been?"

"Two and a half months. Two months longer than it took me to realize how worthless Atherton was. Pretty as they come, charming, too, but worthless. No money, no position—he's completely fallen out with his family. And he's an incorrigible drunkard. A *drunkard*, Cassie. Just like Father. And I know for a fact he's had another woman, at least one, the whole time, too.

"All that and he wasn't even that fun. Once, I wanted to drive to that abandoned fort at the north end of the island, Fort Clinch, and walk up on the walls to see the view over the water, but he refused to take me. He said it was because that sort of thing wasn't becoming of a lady, but I knew it was really because he was a coward."

"A coward?"

"Oh, Atherton had a terrible fear of high places. He wouldn't even take a room on the second floor if it had a balcony. Said looking down made his knees alternate between jelly and unbendable steel."

Cassie chewed her lip. If Mr. Brooks couldn't handle being high off the ground, how could he have climbed up the trellis into Peanut's bedroom, much less the lookout tower?

Let it go, Cassie. Flora's safe. Everyone's fine.

Lily picked at the stitching on her bedsheet. "I knew I had to get a husband before it was too late, and Atherton was the quickest and simplest option. Besides, it was his child, after all. I figured, he has his faults, but who doesn't?"

"Lily, in addition to everything you just mentioned, he was an arsonist, a fraudster, and, it seems, a murderer."

"Well, I didn't know about most of that until today, did I."

"Sam wouldn't help you?"

"I was hoping I wouldn't have to tell him."

"Why?"

"I knew he would go off his head. Send me to a convent to have the baby, then pay the Reverend Mother to keep me there. Now he may still."

"Sam wouldn't do anything like that."

"Not to be unkind, Cassie, but you don't know Sam as a man. He may have been daring and fun when we were children, but everything is serious now. Nothing is done without a reason or purpose or angle, particularly when it comes to the business of maintaining the family. Especially since Father died. Sometimes I look at him and all I see is a humorless soldier on a mission to make up for all of Father's mistakes. And mine, I guess."

Cassie sat on the edge of the bed. "It's a lot of pressure. Being the one who's supposed to have all the answers."

Lily fell back against the pillows. "That's what Sam said, when I finally told him."

"So you did tell him, after all."

"Yes. Yesterday, after you came by the hotel."

Cassie smoothed the sheet with her fingers. Maybe that was why Sam had been acting the way he had at Flora's house. He was distracted.

"But only because I was growing so desperate for him to approve the proposal. And was he ever furious." Lily pushed herself back up. "To tell you the truth, Cassie, the way he was going on about Atherton being 'a drain on the family resources' and so forth, I wonder whether there's something Sam isn't telling me about the—state of things. There've been other signs, too. Complaining when I want a new dress, cutting down house staff, telling me I can't have fresh-cut flowers brought in every week anymore…

"At least he agreed the marriage was the best course of action at this point, after Atherton told him about the insurance money he'd gotten for his business and agreed to let Sam invest it. But their relationship was still tenuous. When we returned to the hotel last night, they had another terrible row—about what, I couldn't even say—in Sam's room. Right as I walked in to see what the matter was, Sam threw a chair against the wall! It broke it into a hundred pieces, not one foot from Atherton's head. I was so afraid someone would hear. After that, Sam grabbed his hat and left."

"Where did he go?"

Lily's face twisted. "I don't know. I haven't heard from him since, and neither have any of the staff. But who knows about them. They can't even get a breakfast order correct."

Lily begged Cassie to stay with her until Sam returned, but luncheon came and went, and then supper, and still there was no sign of him. Finally, Lily fell asleep, so Cassie left a note on the bedside table and headed back to Flora's.

The streets were unusually quiet as she walked up Sixth Street, even at Centre. She turned her head when she reached the intersection, but there were no visitors enjoying an evening stroll, or trinket and food vendors rumbling their carts about. There wasn't even the usual crowd of merry-makers and seasoned drunks toddling about in front of the Three Star Saloon. It was as if the entire town, exhausted from the collective frenzy it had worked itself into over the previous several days, had finally given a long sigh and fallen asleep.

The house was unlit when she arrived—Whatever had overtaken the rest of the town must have made it here, too. Giving Danger's nose a light touch as she closed the front door, she tip-toed through the parlor past a snoozing Kleio, into the dining room past a snoring Luna, and into the kitchen, where she found the kitten curled up in the fruit bowl with a bunch of bananas. She opened up the larder and surveyed her options. She had eaten a few bites from Lily's largely untouched breakfast tray (the replacement one, which she'd had to bring in for Lily from the hall since none of the hotel staff would dare come into the room), but she was hoping she could find a treat of some sort that had miraculously escaped Paddy's bottomless stomach.

"Hungry?"

Cassie turned from where she was hunched over a beautifully stinky wedge of Camembert, a hunk of bread in her mouth.

"Ahnh Fueruhh! Haugh."

Flora, who was standing in the doorway of the larder with a lamp, laughed that deep, musical laugh of hers. "Hello to you, too."

Cassie took the bread out of her mouth. "I'm sorry, did I wake you?"

"Not at all. I was actually waiting up for you."

"Oh, I'm sorry. I was—"

Flora put down the lamp. "Stop apologizing! My *dear* girl. I just wanted to thank you."

"Thank me?"

"Jake told me about everything you did the last few days. To help me."

Cassie started to wipe her mouth with her sleeve but decided to dab her lips with her fingers instead. One step at a time.

"Oh, no, I didn't do anything. Jake and Officer Hughes were the ones who—"

"Shh." Flora set the lamp on the kitchen table. "You're just like your mother, always giving credit to everyone else but never taking any for herself. Do you call climbing up the pilots' tower, searching Peanut's house, and chasing after Mr. Smalls… and Mr. Downing, doing nothing? You even went down to Three Star in the middle of the night, all by yourself. And then there was something about sticking a book in your bustle frame to hide it from the coroner?" She laughed, but more softly this time, and sighed. "Yes. Just like your mother. There was a reason your father loved her so much. That they loved each other so much."

Cassie tucked her hair behind her ear. "Well—uh, you're welcome. And thank you."

"I'm just so relieved to have this all behind us. And did you know there were people waiting to greet me when I came out of the jail? Not just Mrs. Keene and Miss Porter, and Sergeant Denham and everyone, but others, too? It seemed half the town had turned up. Even the ladies from the whist club were there."

How kind of them to put forth the effort, now that it's safe.

"I know people went through some… difficulty with the situation, and how it looked and everything, but they came around, didn't they? Just like I said they would. Oh, Cassie, they were hugging me and apologizing and saying they never for a moment doubted my innocence… I can't tell you how happy it made my heart."

Cassie let Danger take the bread out of her hand and considered Flora's happy expression as the coal range crackled and breathed across the room. How could Flora forgive so many people who had turned their back on her, and so quickly? Even those who'd said they supported Flora hadn't come by to shop or visit or let her know they believed in her, or defended her in any way.

Flora took a small sack of flour down from the shelf. "Here, let me make you something."

"Oh, I—" Cassie took a quiet breath. Maybe she should let Flora have this moment and make her "wondering," as Mr. Shaw had put it, wait for just one blessed minute.

"All right. But I don't want you to go to any—" She stopped herself. "That would be lovely."

Flora patted her arm. "Good girl. How about buckwheat shortcakes topped with cinnamon sugar? Ready in ten minutes."

When Cassie finally made it up to her room, she pulled her shoes off by the door and sat on the bed to undress. Now that she was alone again, her head had resumed trying to wrap itself around the day's events. She was infinitely glad Flora had been released, but had the coroner's jury really gotten the right man in Mr. Brooks? Granted, she'd come to the same conclusions they had, but her conversation with Hughes had shaken her conviction.

So had her conversation with Lily, though in a different way. How was it true? Lily pregnant? And by a near stranger? She never would have predicted that happening to prim, proper Lily, who used to fall apart when her shoelaces got dirty or out of place. Or the lengths to which she had been willing to go to hide it. Lily's description of Sam as a hard-nosed pragmatist had also been disquieting, not to mention her recounting of how Sam had thrown a chair and disappeared into the night, leaving his pregnant sister all alone. Cassie had never thought Sam could act like that. She just hadn't seen it in him. Or perhaps she had, but she'd been too blinded by the shine of her childhood memories to notice.

A thump across the room sent her heart flying into her throat. Someone, or something, had knocked into a chair.

"Hello?" Flora had gone to bed before she had, so she hoped it was the kitten, though she doubted the animal's scant three pounds could move much of anything. "Who's there?"

She felt around her chatelaine for her scissors but realized she'd left them downstairs after Esme cut the gauze for Hughes's bandage. She slid her fingers over the other hooks. Tape measure. Fan. Vesta case—light would be a start. Taking out one of the little matches, she struck it on the bedpost.

The flash lasted just long enough for her to see a skeletal figure loom over her.

She inhaled to scream, but a gloved hand pressed against her mouth and pushed her back into the pillows with surprising strength.

So this is how I die.

CHAPTER TWENTY-ONE

"Quiet down, girl. I'm not here to hurt you."

Cassie had brought up a foot to defend herself but paused when she heard the voice.

"Mmphphs Mmphaw?" The glove tasted of lemons and sweat.

"Yes. Mrs. Shaw. Can I take my hand off your mouth now?"

Cassie nodded the best she could, and the pressure eased from her face.

She wiped her tongue on her sleeve. "What are you doing in my room?" She found another match and leaned over to light the bedside lamp. "You're lucky I didn't have a weapon at hand, or I might have injured you."

"A weapon? You mean like this?" Mrs. Shaw held up a fist and squeezed, releasing a spring-loaded blade.

Cassie fell back. "I thought you weren't here to hurt me.'"

"I'm not. I'm here to get… what's mine."

"The pendant? Here. It's right here. Now, put that knife away, okay? There's no need for it."

As soon as Cassie pulled the pendant out of her pouch, Mrs. Shaw snatched it and clutched it to her chest.

"Where did you get this?" She uncurled her fist to look at it.

"I found it in Peanut's bedroom."

"Peanut's bedroom? What were you doing in *there*?"

"What was I—Goodness, no!" said Cassie. "I went in there after my interview with the coroner's jury. To see if I could find anything that would help explain what had happened." She lifted her chin. "What were *you* doing in there?"

"That is none of your business."

"Don't you care about bringing Peanut's killer to justice?"

"No. I mean, of course I do. Anyone would. But they already figured out Atherton Brooks did it. You have to have heard about that."

"I did. But the problem is, I also heard Mr. Brooks was deathly afraid of high places. And Peanut was attacked at the top of the pilots' tower."

Mrs. Shaw's knife quivered. "You don't think Mr. Brooks killed Peanut?"

"I'm not decided on it. And I'm not entirely sure he caused his own death, either."

"Well, it wasn't me. Neither of them."

Cassie sat up taller and smoothed her dress. "You'll have to forgive me if I don't take you at your word. As you haven't been exactly forthcoming so far, particularly regarding your relationship with Peanut."

The lamp flame flickered in duplicate in Mrs. Shaw's eyes. "All right. But know the only reason I'm speaking to you is I don't want your digging around to air my dirty laundry."

Tucking the pendant away, Mrs. Shaw sat in the desk chair and pulled off her hat. A thick silver braid fell down around her shoulders.

"Years ago, right after I married my husband, I kept house for Peanut. And Gilda. That was his wife, who he treated as if she were, in fact, like her name, made of gold. He cared about that woman more than anything else. Or anyone else." She yanked a hair that was sticking out of her braid. "But then she died, and Peanut fell to pieces. Stopped eating, stopped talking. Stopped work on the house, which they had recently built on a parcel Gilda inherited from her parents."

"The bedroom, and the study," Cassie said. "I assume those furnishings were Gilda's handiwork? From before she died?"

"Yes. She was one of those rare women who are actually good at the sorts of things we women are expected to do. Decorating, sewing, choosing soaps and perfumes." Mrs. Shaw threw her braid over her shoulder. "After she was gone, I started spending more time at the house. To keep an eye on Peanut."

Her face tightened. "It's a terrible thing to watch, you know, someone being worn down by grief day after day until nothing's left but a bitter lump." Wrapping her arms around herself, she took a slow inhale and a slower exhale. "But there were times when I could see him. Who he really was. People just don't understand… Anyway, we grew close. Too close. And my husband has never forgiven either of us."

"When was that?"

"Years ago. And I left my post immediately and distanced myself, as much as it hurt, having to watch him suffering from afar. Putting on layer after layer of scar and bristle, waking up every day harder, meaner, and tougher. And acting as though everyone else owed him something. As though when God took his wife, it created a debt that would never be satisfied, payable by the whole world."

Cassie spoke carefully. "But your pendant was in his bedroom. Recently."

Mrs. Shaw's mouth flattened into a hard line. "Don't look at me like that. I'm not proud of myself. But, yes, we reconnected a few months ago. All it took was a chance encounter by the plank walk one night and we were right back where we'd left off. He later gave me the necklace as a gift." She pulled the pendant back out and cradled it in her palm.

Then she closed her fist over it. "But he's gone now. And I value my marriage. My husband's re-election for coroner is coming up, too, and I don't intend to be the reason he fails."

"No one else knows?"

"Of course not. Except my brother, Carlton. I told him a couple of days before Peanut… was found, though I had a slight sense he'd already figured it out. We've never been able to keep much from one another."

"So what happened in Peanut's kitchen the other day—"

"What happened in Peanut's kitchen the other day?"

"Mr. Meeks came in while you were there and was very—He seemed to threaten you."

"Oh. My brother was only being protective. He was worried about what Richard might do if he found out, especially with the election coming up. But, believe me, I'm more than capable of defending myself."

Cassie didn't doubt it.

Mrs. Shaw drifted. "It was the oddest thing, being in there again with Peanut gone. It was the same place but also somewhere else entirely." She swallowed. "Even with his body lying right there on the table, I kept looking up, thinking I'd heard him coming down the hall."

Cassie's chest tightened. While she was almost certainly responsible for one of those moments, she understood. After her father's death, their house had changed, too. The cheerful yellow wallpaper had become dull and lifeless, the wooden floors tired. The furniture seemed to sag under some great weight. And the round-cheeked cherub figures carved into the fireplace mantel… she couldn't tell anymore whether they were laughing or grimacing. Without her father, the soul had gone from the place.

Yet, after nearly a year, she still looked for her father sometimes, too, certain she'd heard the pages of his book turn or smelled his pipe smoke wafting up the stairs, only to suffer fresh pain when confronted, once again, with the resounding reality of his absence.

She realized there was something this woman needed to hear but probably never would, unless she said it to her now.

"I'm sorry for your loss."

Mrs. Shaw tensed. Then, slowly, her face softened. "You really want to find Peanut's killer, don't you."

"Yes, ma'am. If there's anything you can think of that would help."

Mrs. Shaw closed her eyes and dropped her hand into her lap. "I visited him that night he was killed."

"Peanut?"

"Yes. We had an awful argument. For some reason, I had this feeling I was being watched, followed. I knew it was all in my imagination, but I was worried about being caught. So I told him we should end it. But then he said I should leave my husband, that he was going to build a grand estate, like in the 'good old plantation days,' and he wanted me to live there with him. Only, when he told me what he was going to name it, I got angry."

"Why?"

"He wanted to call it Golden Bluff."

Cassie tried not to react. "What was upsetting about that?"

"Gilda means golden." She spoke as though Cassie were slow-witted. "He tried to tell me he'd picked that name because he was going to build it around his existing house, on the rest of the land that used to belong to Gilda's family. Land he said would have been his, because of Gilda, 'if the railroad hadn't fooled her family into selling most of it.' But I knew what he was really building was a shrine. To *her*. I would always be second."

"How was he going to do that? Build that estate? Most of the property around him is owned by other people now."

"He had a plan to get it back, all of it. Something very complicated. He showed me this ledger book full of lines and symbols and talked about how he'd figured out exactly how to squeeze each person to get what he wanted… Not to make him sound any worse than people already think of him."

"Do you remember any of the details?"

"He didn't say any names or anything, but he mentioned something about people owing him money, or being really old. Maybe a house fire? I guess that doesn't make too much sense. Truthfully, I didn't understand most of what he was talking about. But I do remember him saying that he was about to complete a big deal or sale of some kind, one that would 'kill a flock of birds with one stone.' I don't know. Something about the way he spoke about it—I got the feeling it was somehow… illicit. What if something went wrong? What if that's why he got killed?" She clutched her knife to herself like a talisman.

"I really couldn't say." Cassie eyed the blade. "Did he tell you anything else?"

"Not really. We were interrupted by your aunt's… outburst, out front there with the shouting and the shovel, and after that he was mostly still trying to calm me down. Eventually, he had to leave for his shift on watch duty. Afterward, I sat down for a few minutes to collect myself and must have dozed off. Until I was awakened by someone breaking in through the window."

Cassie looked up. "Someone came in while you were there?"

"Yes, but I hid under the bed immediately, which is probably how I broke my necklace. Now, I'm not one to fear your average house burglar—I came through the war all by myself, so, as I said, I can handle myself—but I couldn't risk it getting out that I was in there. Even criminals gossip." She ran a hand down her braid. "Anyway, it turned out to be two people… One came in through the window and went downstairs to let the other in. They knocked around in the study for a while then left."

"Do you know who they were?"

"No. I couldn't see anything from where I was, and they didn't say much. But I did hear something at one point that sounded like—" She sniffed uncomfortably. "Kissing."

Cassie gaped. "Why didn't you tell anyone about this before?"

"Dear girl. If you don't know the answer to that after everything I've told you, there's no hope of us solving this at all."

CHAPTER TWENTY-TWO

The next morning, after waking by the window with her cheek on the sill and the kitten draped over her shoulders like a shawl, Cassie had little time to think on things further. It hadn't even been a full day since her ordeal, but Flora, herself again—not the forced, overly cheerful version Cassie had seen a couple of days before, but rather a confident, positive, and energetic one—had apparently woken determined to complete her duties for the Egmont Hotel's ball that evening. As such, she had enacted a conscription requiring all able-bodied humans who entered the house to assist, and Cassie and Esme were the first recruits. Jake and Metta were drafted soon after, and, by early afternoon, Miss Porter, Mrs. Keene, Sergeant Denham, and Paddy had joined the ranks, as had those women from the whist club Cassie had seen by Flora's gate the other day, Mrs. Grayson and Mrs. Campbell. Their apology casseroles had even earned them a heartfelt embrace from Flora.

When Cassie saw that, she was astounded anew by Flora's capacity to forgive and forget. She wasn't certain she would have been as generous herself. It also felt strange to be bustling about the way they were, doing something as normal as preparing for a ball, so soon, especially since the doubt gnawing at her about Mr. Brooks had only gotten worse after her visit from Mrs. Shaw. But she didn't suppose she had been given much of a choice about that.

"Metta, oh, Metta, do be careful!" Miss Porter cried as Cassie staggered into the parlor, Kleio ensconced on her head and her arms full of bunting. Metta was trying to reach a jar on one of the shelves behind the counter, and Miss Porter had contorted herself below her, caught between steadying the ladder and readying herself for an emergency catch. Danger and Luna were chasing each other around the room, receiving a swat from the kitten each time they passed her post on a chair, and Paddy, Jake, and Sergeant Denham were working on flower garlands with Mrs. Keene and the whist club ladies by the window.

Flora breezed into the room, dressed for the ball. "Okay, everyone. I think we've just about done it." In contrast to the elaborate gowns Cassie had brought with her from New York, Flora's was a simple, flowing garment of sage-green silk that set off her dark hair, which she wore swept back into a twist. At her waist was a wide belt embroidered with a colorful water lily design, a miniature version of which traced her neckline and the edges of her sheer, bell-shaped sleeves. She was also wearing her orange blossom brooch, which Mr. Shaw had returned when she was released.

"I'm going to head over to the Egmont soon to start arranging the auction items, but if you all would join me in the kitchen first, I'd like to thank you for your help today. I've made a batch of my special potatoes, twice baked and stuffed with asparagus, caramelized onion, roasted garlic, and two types of cheese."

Paddy and Metta led the charge, and soon they were all perched on stools around the kitchen table, their cheeks crammed with stuffed potato.

Esme emerged from her room off the kitchen. "Flora, are you leaving already? I'll come help you. Let me get dressed."

"No, no. Take your time. I'll mostly be tinkering and moving things around. You know me." Flora pushed back from the table, almost falling over Danger, who had stationed himself underfoot in case of a food-on-floor emergency.

"Wait a minute. I want to give you something first." Esme ducked back into her room. She had been slow and solemn all day, still drained from the excitement of the previous few days, no doubt, but she seemed to have a spring in her step now. When she re-emerged, she was carrying an elegant pink vial in the shape of a woman's profile. She placed it on the table with satisfaction. "Here you go. Dream's Edge."

Flora started to put down the basket she was holding but stopped when she saw there was a kitten hanging from the bottom of it.

"Dream's Edge?" She reached toward the swinging ball of fur and disengaged its tiny grappling hooks with her finger.

The kitten plopped onto the floor and scampered off toward the larder.

"The composition you designed for the auction. I knew you hadn't had much time to work on it again, so I decided to give it a try myself."

Flora uncorked the bottle and waved a hand toward her nose.

"Esme, it's—I can't believe it." She laughed in astonishment. "It's far closer than any of my efforts to remake it so far. I'm terribly impressed. Here, I know what I'll do." Flora tucked the vial into her pocket and gave it a pat. "I'm going to offer it up in the auction as a companion to the other one I've decided to bring. We'll call it *Eau de Esme.*"

"Thank you. That's… lovely." Esme smoothed her dress. "Now, if y'all will excuse me, I need to finish a few tasks before the ball. I'll see you this evening."

"I really wish she'd take one of the bedrooms upstairs," Flora said as Esme's door clicked shut. "That room is a glorified cupboard. Cold, too. It does have a fireplace, but Esme won't use it. She says it feels frivolous, burning up firewood just for herself. Such a selfless girl." Flora took the vial back out and turned it over in her hands. "This truly is excellent, though. Exactly like the original version I made, in fact, before I tweaked it that day at Mr. Adler's before—"

There was a knock at the front door, and Flora went to answer it. A few moments later, she came back into the kitchen, her eyes twinkling.

"Cassie, you have a visitor."

"But I wasn't expecting anyone," replied Cassie, her mouth full of potatoes.

Flora winked and held open the door.

Cassie was still swallowing as she entered the parlor, and when she saw who was waiting by the mantel, she was so surprised she burped.

"Sam! What are you doing here?" Maybe if she talked quickly enough, he'd forget what had just happened. "I spent all day yesterday with Lily, waiting for you to return to the hotel. She didn't know where you had gone and was very worried." She dabbed her mouth delicately with a napkin.

When she drew closer, though, she doubted he'd noticed. His expensive frock coat was fresh, and his hair carefully oiled, but his face, aside from the dark circles under his eyes, was the color of an under-ripe banana. And was that rouge on his neck?

"My apologies for coming unannounced like this." Noticing Kleio surveilling him from her perch, he put his hat back on. "And for worrying you both. It seems I may have overdone things a bit the other night. I'd only gone out for some air—all right, a steadying drink or two—but one thing led to another, and, well... I assure you, this sort of behavior isn't a habit for me. I'd had a shock, you see."

"Lily told me." Cassie turned her head from the stale odor of whiskey and cigars drifting toward her. So that's what he had been doing all this time. Even knowing what he knew.

"She told you—"

"Everything. Up through your less-than-gracious exit from the hotel."

Sam fidgeted with his gloves. That was something else Cassie didn't remember Sam ever doing before, fidget.

"I don't know what to say, other than I'm ashamed of myself. I realized I had no choice about Atherton becoming a part of our family, but it didn't make me despise him any less. Each time he spoke, each time he breathed, all I could see was him back at university, spending his family's money as quickly as he could on drinking and women, including *other people's* women…"

Cassie softened slightly. Given the way he said that last bit, she sensed he wasn't speaking in the abstract. "You knew Mr. Brooks at university?"

"He was a classmate, though not exactly a friend, at Yale. He was always performing juvenile stunts such as climbing up buildings dressed as a giant spider or leading races across campus *sans* clothing, or hosting parties with his singing-ninny Glee Club friends, trying to impress a secret society. Not to mention that he had an unnatural number of ties for one man."

Cassie took out a piece of gum and chewed it slowly, letting the coolness of the mint slide down her throat. Based on the Yale men Cassie had known, Mr. Brooks's collegiate behavior wasn't all that surprising. But she hadn't realized he had any sort of history with Sam.

"I didn't think you knew each other outside of Lily."

"I wish we hadn't. I thought I was rid of him years ago. His father died during our second year at school, and, though he left nearly everything to his second wife, from whom Atherton has long been estranged, Atherton received a lump sum that was more than enough to pay for the rest of his education and get him set up in a trade. But Atherton, being Atherton, promptly decided to pocket the money and drop out instead.

"And of course, after all that, he had to end up here. Adding Lily to his book of female conquests. I blame myself, really. Our school connection was probably the reason Lily took notice of him in the first place. Not that it matters now."

"You heard, then?"

"I did hear—that coroner is rather impressive, isn't he, figuring out all of that? And, not to sound callous, I'd say Brooks got what was coming to him. To think I almost welcomed him into our family… However, now *my* problem is back, which brings me to—Ugh! Get off me, you slobbery beast!" He backed against the wall and flung his foot out to ward off Luna, who had come running into the room.

"Wait! Don't!" Cassie picked Luna up. "She's only a puppy."

"I don't understand why anyone would collect all these mangy animals in the first place, much less allow them to roam freely about the home."

Cassie held the puppy closer. "They were in distress. Aunt Flora felt she had to help."

"Ah. A sentimentalist. That probably also explains all those… interesting friends she has. But I'm glad she's been exonerated, of course. For your sake." He touched her arm, but this time it felt different.

"I shouldn't have suggested you turn your back on her the other day," he said. "I should have trusted you knew what you were talking about. You've always known what you were talking about. Even when we were small, stupid children."

Cassie lowered her chin slightly. "I appreciate that." She sniffed. "We *were* kind of stupid, weren't we."

Sam grinned. "Remember the time we snuck into that abandoned house, and we thought we saw a ghost?"

"When you let me tag along finally because Henry was too ill to come out and play? Yes, of course. I remember your foot breaking through a rotted section of floor while we were running away and getting stuck."

"I remember your foot getting stuck in the same rotted floor while you were trying to pull me out."

They shared a small laugh, and Cassie felt her shoulders start to relax.

"Good thing for us that man who'd taken up residence on the back porch heard us screaming and helped us," she said.

"Yes, good thing for us." Sam sobered. "Though, what that man really should have been doing was working so he could get his own place to live." He studied his feet. "Life's different when you're grown. If you fall in a hole, there's no one to pull you out but yourself."

"I don't know if I'd say—"

"Which reminds me of why I came here in the first place." Sam reached into his coat and pulled out a rose. "I realized our conversation at the Egmont had been—interrupted, so I wanted see if we could pick up where we left off. I'd still like to take you on the excursion we discussed, but would you first do me the honor of accompanying me to the ball this evening? I won't want to go if I'm not guaranteed a dance with you."

There was another knock at the door, and Cassie, her mouth still working, went to answer it. It was Hughes, looking vaguely as though he'd arrived there by accident. His hair was recently combed, however, and his suit pressed.

"Oh, it's you," she said, before she realized how that sounded. "I mean, not 'oh, it's *you*.' More '*Oh!* It's you.'" She cleared her throat. Her conversation with Sam had certainly jangled her nerves, which had already been stretched thin by everything else that was ricocheting around in her head like errant buckshot.

And the way Hughes's jawline perfectly traced the edge of his collar wasn't exactly helping her focus.

"Let me try that over. Good afternoon, Officer Hughes. You look—respectable."

Hughes staggered as Luna jumped out of Cassie's arms into his and started vigorously licking his chin. "Uh, thanks." He scratched the puppy's head.

"Did you need something?" Cassie asked.

"Right. I wanted to, uh, ask whether... uh—" He smoothed his mustache. "How is Miss Hale doing?"

"She's in good spirits. Thank you. We've spent all day working on preparations for the ball."

"That's good to hear. And Miss Cole?"

"Fine, too."

A few seconds passed.

"I'm glad actually you came," Cassie offered. "I received an interesting visitor in my bedroom last night."

"Uh—"

"Mrs. Shaw."

"Oh!" Hughes scrambled to regain his hold on the puppy. "What?"

"She wanted her pendant back. The one I found in Peanut's bedroom. She admitted she'd been—involved with Peanut and that the pendant was a gift from him. She also told me she was at Peanut's house the evening of the murder and they'd fought."

"A lovers' quarrel, then."

"No, I don't think that's it. She seemed sincerely devastated by his loss. She also said that after Peanut left for the watchtower, she heard someone come in and search the study. Two someones, actually. A couple. She was hiding, so she couldn't see who they were, but she heard them kiss."

Hughes choked. "I see. That's good—information."

After a few more seconds ticked by, Cassie turned to go back inside. "Okay, I'll tell Flora you called."

Hughes placed his hand on the door, still holding the puppy, who was now licking his ear. "Wait, there was something else I wanted to—"

"Good day." Sam came up behind Cassie. "You're Hughes, right? The fellow who was chased into the parlor by that woman."

Hughes shifted his stance. He may have been trying to look intimidating, but it was hard to tell with the puppy in his arms. Also, the kitten had come out to inspect the situation and was now sitting on his foot. "Among other things."

"That's right. You also fit shoes at Preston's Cash Boot and Shoe Store, over at Centre and Second. Say, you'd better check in with your employer. When I went there the other day to see about some new riding boots, he sounded less than pleased with your attendance as of late."

"As you may have heard," Hughes said, "I've been preoccupied with my other duties. As of late." He put his free hand on his waist, pushing back his coat to reveal his badge and holster.

Sam twisted his lips. "Of course. Well, if you'll excuse me, Officer, I have some matters to attend to. Cassie, I'll be here at a quarter after seven to collect you for the ball. A good day to you both."

As Hughes stepped aside to let Sam through, he kept his gaze trained on him like a cocked pistol. Which he then turned on Cassie.

She didn't like the way he was looking at her now.

"I owe you an apology, Miss Gwynne," he said. "Your taste in entitled dandies is more nuanced than I gave you credit for the other evening."

Cassie dropped her hands to her sides. "That's not fair. You don't understand—"

"I understand perfectly. You're going to the ball with that arrogant gold-kisser."

"Yes, but—"

"There's no 'but' to that. You are or you aren't."

Cassie stepped back, annoyed at the tears gathering in her eyes. Why should she care about what he thought of her social life? Or anything else?

"I don't have to explain myself to you—"

"Exactly right. None of my business."

"That's not what I—"

"Well, I should be going. Give my regards to Miss Hale."

Hughes thrust the puppy back into Cassie's arms and trotted down the steps. When he reached the end of the path, he paused to throw something into the bushes then pushed through the gate.

Cassie suddenly found it hard to breathe.

"Pardon us, dear." Mrs. Grayson squeezed past Cassie with a box of Chinese lanterns, forcing her to move all the way out onto the porch.

Flora came out behind her with her basket on her arm, and others began to follow with their own loads.

"Flora," Mrs. Grayson said, "Mrs. Campbell and I are going to drop the lanterns and garlands at the hall then go home and dress."

"Thank you both." Flora shifted the basket onto her other arm. "Jake, will you have room in your cart for a few extra chairs? Mrs. Liddy has set some aside for us on her porch. Paddy, you're holding that upside down. I mean sideways. No—Metta, help him."

"I put your plate in the larder, Cassie," Miss Porter said as she staggered by, trying to balance a stack of cake boxes, "so you can finish it whenever you—Oh dear."

Flora caught the top box as it started to slide off and pushed it back into place. "We didn't mean to run you over like this, Cassie, but we heard the voices subside and figured Mr. Townsend had left." She watched Miss Porter wobble down the steps. "Did he ask you to accompany him to the ball?"

"Who?"

"Mr. Townsend."

"Oh. Yes."

"How wonderful! Are you excited? I hope you don't find me too overly interested. Since I've never had any children of my own, of course, being a part of this, with you, is… It means a great deal to me."

Cassie smiled weakly, unsure what her honest answer to that question was. She should be excited. If one had asked her thirteen-year-old self, she would have said Sam Townsend was everything she ever wanted, and, despite her earlier bumbling, she now appeared to have her chance with him. The problem was, she wasn't her thirteen-year-old self, and her present-day self wasn't sure how much she actually liked Sam Townsend. What had happened? Had he changed that much? Or had she never really known who he was in the first place? Or was she the one who had changed? Did she even know what she wanted?

She thought about Hughes stalking away from her down the garden path.

"Have I said something wrong?" Flora put down her basket.

Cassie let the puppy run off into the house. Perhaps she was making too much of things again. "No, of course not. I—Yes, going to the ball with Sam is… It's what I've dreamed of since I was young, right? Any girl would be excited about that." There was a bit of truth in that. "What about you? I imagine Jake will be your escort?"

"He'll be presenting the auction with me. And we'll dance the ceremonial quadrille together."

"That didn't answer my question."

Flora frowned. "I don't—"

"I meant, will you be attending together?"

"Oh. No, Cassie. Our relationship isn't like that. We're just close because we've known each other for so long. And not to mention the number of years between us."

Cassie pressed her lips together. "I believe Jake feels differently."

"What?" Flora's eyes flicked to where Jake was loading his cart. "No, I don't think so."

"If you'll forgive my frankness, Aunt Flora, Jake all but admitted to me that he cares for you."

"He said that?"

"Yes." Cassie paused. "But he thinks there's something keeping you from returning the sentiment. Someone else."

"Who else? There's no one else." Flora blushed. "I mean, not else. There's no one."

"His words were, 'her heart is otherwise occupied and there's no competing with it.'"

Flora considered that. "The only things that occupy my heart, Cassie, are my friends, my animals, and my family—you, Emma, Tom. My departed parents. And, of course, Burt." She sighed.

"Burt?"

"Yes, your brother."

"My—I have a *brother*?" Cassie's head began to spin.

Flora gasped. "Lord, don't you know about Burt?"

Cassie couldn't even shake her head. Everything was buzzing, her knees, her elbows, her face.

"How could Tom not have told you about him?" Flora murmured, almost speaking to herself.

Yes, how could he not have told me about him?

Cassie worked her mouth. "He—almost never talked about his life, our life, before New York. Hardly a word about the war, about the island, even about my mother…"

Flora held onto the railing with both hands, as though she didn't trust her legs to hold her up. "I know he never responded to my letters—I understand why he maybe… couldn't forgive me for what happened… but—" She choked back tears. "To put him away, to pretend he never existed…"

She stepped back and buried her face in her hands. With all the helpers gone, the house was quiet, and the only sounds were the rustling of the trees and an occasional creak from one of the rocking chairs lining the porch.

"Aunt Flora." It took all the energy Cassie had left to stand up straight and form her words.

Flora lowered her hands slightly. "Yes?"

"What happened to Burt?"

Making a visible effort to collect herself, Flora walked over to one of the rocking chairs by the door and sank into it. When Cassie declined her invitation to take the one next to her, she drew her knees up to her chest and wrapped her arms around them, like a child might.

"First, understand that I was barely nineteen when we left the island during the war, younger than you are now and far more naïve. And we departed in such a terrible hurry, your father, your grandparents, and me, with you children—we had lost your mother to a swift illness shortly after you were born. I don't know whether it was an official evacuation or not, but the colonel, upon receiving news that a U.S. fleet was on its way, had ordered his troops to abandon Fort Clinch and dynamite the railroad bridge, so anyone who didn't want to be trapped in a war zone had to immediately grab what they could carry and get off the island.

"And it wasn't just that. There were also some who had caught a political fever, as my father called it—where emotions grow so hot they lose connection with whatever logical convictions they might have come from—and began laying waste to the town. Wharves, shops, warehouses, anything they thought might be useful to the incoming troops, were hacked to bits and set on fire. So even as we had to decide, in a matter of hours, what was dearest to us and what could be left behind, we had to watch our own neighbors destroy our home. I'll never forget looking out the train window as we raced away across the bridge, hunched down with coats and blankets over our heads to protect us from the gunboat shells falling from the sky, and seeing our way lighted by the flames of burning lumber yards."

Flora tucked her dress around her legs.

"Tom—I'm sorry, your father—had decided we were going to hide away in the woods. He'd seen, well, we'd all seen, so many families whose fathers, brothers, and uncles had all gone into battle and never found their way home, so were left utterly without means… He didn't want that to happen to us if he was conscripted. Oh, he knew we were strong enough to make our way ourselves, but he was always so duty-driven. You understand. Leaving us was tantamount to abandonment in his mind. Especially for a war he already opposed—he opposed any war, as he could not, as he would say, support 'settling disagreements by trading the lives of nameless soldiers as though they were commodities, not humans.'"

She hugged her knees closer. "So, what I'm trying to say is—we were safe, which is more than a lot of people could say then, and together, but, instead of being grateful, I was petulant and resentful. Selfish. Thousands of people were being cut down by guns and explosions out there, and all I could think about was what *I* had lost, what *I* had been forced to leave behind. What was taken from *me*. I was particularly angry about how I was supposed to start women's college that year, but the term was, of course, suspended, and no one knew for how long.

"One of the first days in our new cabin, while Tom was away gathering supplies, I was watching you and Burt because your grandparents weren't feeling well. You were only two—it was early 1862—and a good sleeper, so you were easy that day. Burt, on the other hand, was four and awake, and was in one of those moods where he couldn't entertain himself for two minutes together. I wasn't angry with him, mind. And I loved that little boy so much—"

Flora searched out a handkerchief and held it to her mouth until she could continue.

"But I was caught up in my own disappointments, and at some point I started ignoring him. Not very kindly either." She bit her lip. "And then I fell asleep. I don't know for how long, but I was awakened by the front door banging in the wind. A sudden storm had come in, and water was pouring through the doorway so hard it was a struggle to get the door shut. That's when I saw that Burt's little fishing pole was gone from its hook. He wasn't anywhere in the house, so I ran out into the rain looking for him. I spent hours searching that night. That turned into days and weeks, searching and calling... until one day Tom and I found that missing fishing pole, dashed on the rocks at the edge of the river, along with one of Burt's shoes. But no Burt."

Flora peered at Cassie over her knees. "He'd been asking me to go fishing all day, and you know what I did? I told him to leave me alone. That if he wanted to fish he'd have to go by himself because I wasn't taking him. Can you imagine? What an utterly stupid thing to say to a child. Especially one as precocious as our Burt."

A chill ran down Cassie's back.

"Tom tried to forgive me, I know he did. I said I was sorry, he told me it wasn't my fault, that it could have happened to anyone... We said all the words, but the truth was—is—that it *was* my fault. I was supposed to keep Burt safe. So, as much as we tried to get on with our lives, It, the Thing That Had Happened, hovered at the edge of every conversation, every thought. It even affected our memories, all that was left to us of that precious boy: the good ones became darker, taken over by a shade that made their colors dull, and the bad ones somehow grew clearer and more vivid.

"So, it wasn't a complete surprise when, as soon as we received word that the war was over and we could return home, Tom made arrangements for us with another family that was headed back to the island, then packed you up and headed for New York. And that was it."

The porch wavered before Cassie's eyes. It was officially too much. On top of everything else that had happened to her these past several days, now she finds and loses a brother, all at the same time? And learns that Flora is responsible for it?

How many other secrets had her father kept from her?

She tried not to flinch when Flora grabbed her hand. "But I kept trying, as you know. I never stopped trying. I wrote and wrote and wrote, and though he never answered, I wasn't going to give up. And, last year, when I heard what had happened, how you and your father were attacked by those robbers in the park, it took all I had not to drop everything and run until I reached your door. But the way Tom had gone away, without even a parting word, and how, even after he had left this world, too, I could still feel his pain… I didn't know the right thing to do."

Tears squeezed from her eyes.

"But when you wrote to me and said you wanted to see me, it felt as if I'd been granted a pardon. A pardon from Heaven. From a sentence almost worse than what I was facing in that jail cell the other night. I just wanted—All I wanted was for you to come home. Then, everything happened with Peanut, and you *stayed*? Not only stayed but defended me, when you had no reason to at all. That's when I felt I might finally be forgiven."

Cassie, the floor still undulating beneath her, took her hand back and held onto the railing. "How could I have forgiven you?"

"What?"

"I—I wasn't even aware of *you* until a couple of months ago. I didn't know my mother had a sister at all until I found those letters over the summer…"

Flora dropped her legs to the floor. "Tom never told you about me, either?"

"No."

She sat back. "So he erased me from his life, too. And yours… I was so sure—I thought you'd come because, maybe, you'd read the letters and decided it was time to reconcile the family—"

"I came because I found those letters and wanted to know who you were." Cassie tightened her grip on the rail. "Not for a reconciliation—Because I didn't even know there needed to be one. And now I'm finding that my entire life was different because of you. A life in a totally different place, without my brother to play with, raised by a father who was carrying a mountain of grief on his shoulders that I didn't even know about? And without an aunt who could have been my friend in so many lonely and confusing moments when I had no mother to turn to? I'm sorry, I need to—"

Cassie stumbled down the steps and through the garden until finally she halted at the gate, and then only because she couldn't get her fingers to work the latch.

Flora fluttered down the path after her. "Where are you going?"

Cassie pulled on the latch again, but it just jangled on its hinge. Out of the corner of her eye, she saw what Hughes had thrown in the bushes: a small bouquet of sweet almond flowers.

"The ball. Or New York."

"You're not dressed. Or packed."

Cassie let her hand fall. She knew she was acting illogically, but all her mind seemed to be able to focus on was running away.

Flora unfastened the latch.

"If you want to go and never look back, I'll understand. But I hope you won't. We both need something bright in our lives, something to outshine the dark that's hovered over both of us for so long." She stepped back. "You're all I have left, you know. Everyone else is gone. And I'm all you have left. We're the only family either of us has in the whole world."

The gate, free of its latch, swung lightly back and forth on its hinges, in and out.

"It's up to you, Cassie."

Cassie closed her eyes. That was exactly what the problem was.

CHAPTER TWENTY-THREE

When Cassie entered the Egmont ballroom on Sam's arm later that evening, dressed in a scoop-necked gown of lavender silk—her scar carefully covered with a black Spanish lace choker necklace—along with matching elbow-length gloves and a silver comb set with amethysts, she had never looked more elegant and composed. On the inside, though, doubt and confusion churned like hot water in a kettle, and, as she didn't have a spout, she didn't know what would happen if they reached a boil.

She and Flora had talked some more, and she had said she was fine, that it was a lot to hear but she was glad to know the truth. But in reality, her pulse hadn't slowed since she learned of what had happened to her brother and how it had torn her family apart.

She wasn't angry. Or maybe she was. Even as young as Flora had been, and with everything that was happening around her, how could she have been so careless? So selfish? The lapse may only have been momentary, but it had cost Cassie a lifetime with her sibling, a relationship unlike any other. And then there was her father. He wasn't blameless in this, either. How could he have deprived her of her brother, too, even if all that was left of him was a memory? And he had done it knowingly and deliberately.

All she knew for sure was she was sad. Sad that her brother had died and sad she'd never get to know him. Never get to play childish games with him, to laugh with him, to point an accusatory finger at him when there was a mysterious smell. To argue with him over politics or literature or whether pickles were delicious or disturbing, to cry with him and share the burden in those moments when life piles on a little too much for one heart to bear alone…

She thought of her father's overdose. Had it been accidental, after all? Why hadn't she been enough for him to want to carry on?

She should have left well enough alone when she found those letters. What had she even hoped to accomplish by coming here, to this place where she was born but that she knew nothing about? And involving herself in the life of a woman who was her family but also a stranger? All she'd managed to do was tear open old wounds, including ones she hadn't even known were there.

She looked over at Sam. Now, he seemed strong, sure of himself. He'd suffered blows of his own, but he hadn't let pain or sentiment defeat him. Lily had called him a "humorless soldier," but when life feels like a war zone, who better to have at your side?

"Sam," she said. "I believe I'm ready for that dance."

It didn't take long to find a group to perform the quadrille with, and as Cassie clasped hands with each partner in the formation, turning and promenading in intricate patterns across the dance floor, she tried to lose herself in her surroundings. They were in the larger and grander hall next to the breakfast room she had visited a couple days before. The walls were papered in a rich ocean blue and draped with gold sashes entwined with flowers, and the ceiling, painted with swirls inset with bits of glass, resembled a starry sky. Buffet tables lined with immense Bombay fans groaned under platters of food; a lively string orchestra played with gusto before a roaring fire.

She was surprised at how many of the guests she knew, even after such a short time on the island. The Huddlestons had Mr. Green cornered by the food tables; Captain Beale and the Marsdens were staging an occupation of the drink service counter. Mr. Smalls and Mrs. Whitehead argued nose-to-nose over a floral centerpiece, and Mr. Hiller blissfully sipped champagne next to a pretty young woman with strawberry-colored hair, whom Cassie took to be his wife despite her delicate and pleasant manner, which made any resemblance to her mother, Mrs. Keene, difficult to discern. Even the Shaws and Meekses were there, smiling and shaking hands and asking people if they could count on their vote.

Flora and Esme, along with Jake and several others, were arranging items for the auction on a small temporary stage in a corner of the room. She didn't see Hughes anywhere, though.

The orchestra finished their piece and began shuffling the sheet music on their stands.

"Thank you for agreeing to accompany me this evening, Cassie." Sam bowed formally. "I was wondering if you might enlarge the favor."

"Certainly."

"Excellent. I believe you're acquainted with the gentleman over there by the shrimp?" He gestured toward a hefty man with liver-spotted skin and tufts of white hair sprouting from his ears. It was Edward Church, the owner of a grocery store empire based in New York, whom Cassie's father had represented in a high-profile matter a few years back.

"I am."

"I thought so. Would you be willing to make an introduction?"

"You want me to introduce you?"

"Lily, actually. Mr. Church was widowed recently, and when I saw he was in town, I remembered your connection to him. Very fortuitous, don't you think?"

Cassie's mouth tightened. *Fortuitous for whom?*

"You don't think him too aged?" she asked.

"Not in the way that matters. His late wife had a child only a couple of years ago. Ah, here comes Lily now."

Lily, who was wearing a high-waisted satin dress and more jewelry than Cassie had ever seen on one person, had struck a pose in front of the ballroom doors, not a trace of the previous day's tears about her.

Sam smoothed his lapel. "I'll go prepare her."

*

In a few short minutes, the deed was done. But as Mr. Church pulled out a chair for Lily, his eyes traveling eagerly over her lovely features, Cassie, rather than being pleased, as Sam clearly was, felt the need to cleanse herself. For some reason, she had assumed that, since Mr. Brooks was gone, Sam and Lily would make peace with their situation and find a more reasonable solution. Instead, they'd gone in the opposite direction.

She watched Lily spear an oyster with a tiny fork and feed it to Mr. Church. At least Mr. Brooks had known what he was getting into.

Announcing that she needed some air, she headed to the far end of the room, where a series of glass doors opened onto a terrace glowing with Chinese lanterns.

It was quiet out there, aside from the usual evening sounds of frogs and crickets serenading their friends and small creatures foraging in the bushes, and the sky was clear and dark. A crisp sea breeze was sweeping westward across the island, and when Cassie felt it tousle her hair, she leaned over the balustrade to catch more of it.

"Fine, Paddy!" came Metta's voice from behind a large planter. "Then I don't want to play with you anymore, ever!"

"But I'm working, Metta," Paddy's voice pleaded. "I can't play right now. Don't be mad!"

Cassie turned around in time to see Metta run away down the large, stone stairs. Paddy ran after her for a few steps then stopped and sniffled.

When he saw Cassie, he wiped his nose with his sleeve. "I want my Baba to be proud of me when he gets back. So I have to do a good job."

Feeling a rush of pity for the boy, Cassie walked over and knelt next to him. "Don't worry. She'll come around. You should never be ashamed of doing the right thing. And your father will be so happy to see how hard you're trying." She swallowed as she heard her own words. "Say, think of how impressed he'll be when he hears how you saved everyone from the fire. A real hero."

Paddy burst into tears.

"My word, Paddy, what's wrong?"

"I'm not a hero!" He threw himself into her arms, blubbering. "I'm a frogster! Like Mr. Brooks."

"You mean a fraudster? Why do you say that?"

"I didn't see any smoke like Jesse's horns," he wailed. "I got that from the newspaper!"

"Paddy, I don't know what on earth you're talking about."

Paddle sniffled. "I didn't sound the alarm. Someone else did. And gave me a whole dollar to say I'd done it."

"What? Who?"

"I don't know. They were wearing a big cloak with a hood. And they only said a few words, in a whisper."

"And you just went along with it?"

He hid his face in Cassie's shoulder. "I—I wasn't supposed to be there. I was supposed to be in bed. But I'd snuck out to take all the left-foot socks off Mr. Perry's clothesline and hide them in his tacklebox, as a joke. So I did what the person said and told everyone I'd come outside because I saw the fire. Then people started calling me a hero, and it felt so nice. Like I actually mattered... I'm sorry I lied!" He started bawling again.

"Oh, oh, no." Cassie patted his head. "It's okay. The important thing is you've told the truth now."

He looked at her, his eyes wide and red. "I did something else wrong."

Apparently, Cassie had become his official confessor. "And what's that?"

"I stole a man's wallet."

"What?"

"On Thursday, outside Three Stars. But I only did it because he was mean to me. When I asked him if he wanted to buy a newspaper, he pushed me down. And he called me a… *rat-eater*. Like the boys at home used to. Some grown-ups, too."

Cassie frowned as he struggled against a memory. *People can be so cruel.*

"So I picked his pocket. But I didn't spend any of the money or anything. See? I still have it." He dug around in his breeches and held out a leather fold.

"What that man said to you was horrible, Paddy. I'm so sorry. But you're still going to have to return this." Cassie took the wallet from him and sifted through its contents, looking for something that might identify the owner. "What did the man look like?"

"He was big. With a black hat."

"Anything more specific?" Cassie pulled a folded square of paper out of the bill crease. It contained a list of botanical-sounding items written in elegant, loping script, and next to each one was a number and what appeared to be a unit abbreviation, though there were some she didn't recognize. It was similar to a recipe, but she wasn't certain the items were edible.

"He had really big nose holes," Paddy said. "Big as grapes."

Cassie lowered the paper. "What did you just say?"

"Hey, what are you all doing?" Metta was back.

"I thought you didn't want to play with me anymore," Paddy said.

"I came back to apologize, you ninny." Metta stared at the paper in Cassie's hands. "What are you doing with *that*, Miss Cassie?"

"Why? Do you know what it is?"

"'Course I do. It's a page from Miss Flora's old notebook, the one where she kept all her perfume compositions." She bent closer. "Looks like part of the ingredient list for a rose-based *eau de parfum*."

Cassie grabbed Metta's hand. "Are you sure this is from Miss Flora's *old* notebook? The one that burned in the fire?"

Metta stomped her foot, making the bows in her hair bounce. "Yes, I'm sure. Here, I'll show you." She took the page and ran her little fingers down it. "Miss Flora used to let me write in the measurements sometimes. You know, 'C' for cups. 'Gtt' for drops."

Gtt. That was one of the units Cassie hadn't recognized.

"Like for how much of something to add to the distiller," Metta continued, "or how many drops of each item to mix together. See, this is her handwriting, and this is mine. I haven't written anything in her new notebook, so this has to be from the old one. Where did you get it?"

Paddy stuck his hands in his pockets. "I stole it. From a man with giant nose holes."

Metta was silent for a moment. "So big you could put whole walnuts in them?"

"Yes!"

"Metta," said Cassie, "do you know who that man is?"

"I don't know his name, but he came to Miss Flora's store one day this summer, while Miss Flora was showing Miss Esme and me how to set flowers on glass for enfleurage. He wanted to pay her money so he could make her perfumes in a factory. But she said no way, never, and tore up the paper he wanted her to sign. They were both very mad."

"It sounds as if he wanted her to enter into a licensing agreement."

Metta shrugged and turned the page over. "I drew this flower, too." She squinted at the page. "I don't know who wrote this, though."

She pointed to a note at the top, which said, "Price for the rest," then listed a very large dollar amount.

But Cassie did. She sighed. "Paddy, I have an important message for you to deliver." She took a five-dollar note out of her pouch and pressed it into his palm. "And I need you to follow my instructions very carefully."

CHAPTER TWENTY-FOUR

Cassie slipped into the pitch-dark room and closed the door behind her. It was colder in here than she'd expected, despite there being no windows to let in a draft, and, even though she had extinguished her lantern, she felt conspicuous in her ballgown.

She put her hands out in front of her and took a cautious step. The floor let out a long, loud groan. She took another, and the floor made the same sound but in reverse, like it was sucking back in what it had just exhaled. Bracing herself, she repeated the painful process several more times, gradually gaining speed—until she cracked her shin against something. Hard.

She snapped her jaw shut, catching a curse before it shot out, and groped the darkness in front of her legs. Armchair, small but upholstered. Her fingers traveled upward until they found the antimacassar at the top; she leaned forward and inhaled. Macassar oil. An uncommonly potent vintage.

Wrinkling her nose, she continued around the room. Fireplace, bed, writing desk. And writing desk chair. She rubbed her shin again.

Washstand, bookshelf, side table. Back to the armchair—

She stopped. There were footsteps approaching.

As the doorknob jangled, Cassie dropped behind the armchair next to a basket of spare blankets, her heart hurling itself against her ribs like Frankenstein's monster. The door's hinges creaked, and a figure appeared in the open doorway, blackened by the moonlight shining through the window behind.

Click.

Click.

Click.

In three steps, the silhouette reached the fireplace and knelt down. There was rustling, and a grating sound—a brick being removed from the wall. A scrape, a crumble. The snap of a match.

Then a lamp blazed to life, filling the room with light.

Esme.

Cradling a battered notebook in her arms so tenderly she almost looked like the Countess of Egmont with her son.

"So it was you," Cassie said, rising. She was so disappointed it hurt. She had really hoped she was wrong.

Esme turned toward Cassie's voice, the beads on her dress turban gleaming in the mixture of moonlight and lamplight like a hundred tiny stars. The angle of the shadows accentuated and elongated her features, from her egret-like neck and arched eyebrows to cheekbones as sharp as diamonds, and Cassie could see now that she wasn't as plain and unassuming as she'd first taken her to be. She wasn't anything she'd first taken her to be.

"I don't know what you're talking about, Cassie."

Cassie gripped the back of the chair. "Peanut got his hands on Flora's formula notebook somehow and was going to sell it to one of her competitors. But before he could do that, someone killed him and took it from him. And, as you're holding the notebook right now, that someone appears to be you."

Esme's icy expression wavered, and a tear appeared in her eye. It hesitated at the crease, as though afraid of something, before finally rolling down her cheek. "That was a mean trick, having Paddy announce the notebook had been found. That someone had left an anonymous message at the reception desk claiming it hadn't burned after all, and it'd be delivered to the sheriff in the morning, along with the 'surprising details of its recovery.'"

"I figured whoever really had it would get nervous and want to check on it."

"Yes, I had to be sure. But how did you know I had it? And here in my room?"

"I didn't. Not for certain anyway. Until you came."

Keeping her movements as small as possible, Cassie began to inch toward the fireplace. She guessed the fire poker was about two arm's lengths away.

"Why did you suspect me?"

"Because of the bottle of Dream's Edge you gave Flora. I'm guessing you made it precisely as it was written in Flora's formula notebook." Cassie steadied her voice. "Which is precisely why it wasn't right. That was the original version. Flora changed it again at Mr. Adler's on the day of the fire but was called away before she'd had a chance to write those changes down."

Esme tightened her arms around the notebook. "You mean *composition* notebook."

"Uh, right. Also, there was that black substance on the cuff of your blouse—I saw you trying to clean it off, that morning you and Flora were working on the perfumes. At first I thought it was from some obscure perfume ingredient you'd been working with, but you had it on your hands again the other night, after the house was searched. You got some on your turban when you touched it... It was ash, wasn't it? From taking the notebook in and out of the fireplace, to consult it as you worked with Flora on reconstructing her formu—compositions. And to remove it so the searchers wouldn't find it when they went through the house.

"And there was Officer Hughes's wound from up on the pilots' tower. He said the glass that cut his hand was delicate and colorful, different from the glass you find in drink bottles and other utilitarian applications. I'll bet if I asked him what color exactly, he'd say periwinkle blue."

Esme's hand flew to her chest.

"Your perfume vial broke off up on the platform, didn't it," Cassie said. "While you were struggling with Peanut, trying to take the notebook back from him. That's why you weren't wearing it the other night."

"Yes."

"But if you knew Peanut had the notebook, why didn't you just tell someone?"

"Because I'm the one who gave him the notebook in the first place!" Esme's voice was as sharp as a blade. As sharp as the blade on the knife that was suddenly glinting in her hand. This one wasn't a slim stiletto, though, designed for expediency and stealth, but rather a saw-edged hunting knife, made to gut and rend.

"*You* gave it to him? Why?"

"I didn't have a choice!" Esme leapt up and paced the room, the notebook clutched in one hand and the knife in the other. "I needed money, quickly. I was being blackmailed. About something I thought I had put behind me. Needed to keep behind me.

"When I told Atherton, that snake who called himself my lover and said he wanted to marry me one day, I needed help, he said he didn't have any money but Peanut would lend me some if I came up with adequate collateral."

Lover? So that was who Cassie had heard in Esme's room that night after the Three Star Saloon. That would explain how Esme had been able to carry her home while she was dead asleep. And Esme's surprise when Lily announced the engagement.

Esme sniffed. "Anyway, I didn't have anything of value to offer, so Atherton suggested I put up Flora's notebook and helped me convince Peanut of its worth, which included telling Peanut about Flora's competitors and how much they wanted to get their hands on her secrets."

"But wouldn't Flora have noticed the notebook's absence? Since it would take time to pay Peanut back and return it?" Cassie inched a little farther.

"I'd worked it out. I'd whisk Flora away on an emergency while she was at Mr. Adler's, so she'd leave the notebook there instead of putting it away in her usual safe back at the house. Then we'd make it look as if there'd been a break-in, that the notebook had been swept up by the thieves while they were grabbing whatever they could. Later, when I got the notebook back, I'd tell her it had been found in a refuse pile, tossed aside by thieves who hadn't understood its value."

Cassie frowned. "That emergency was an accident with one of Flora's delivery vehicles. Did you cause it? Cause someone else to be hurt?"

"That couldn't be helped," Esme said. "It needed to be something serious enough that Flora would drop everything. I couldn't simply take the notebook, see. Only Flora and I had access to the safe, or even really knew when she took her notebook with her to Mr. Adler's, so she would have known it was me immediately."

"But something went wrong."

"A lot more than something. Once we were done staging the break-in inside the store, I climbed out on the rooftop so I could escape on the other side of the block. Atherton was to stay behind and make it look as though Mr. Adler's door had been forced open. Then he would go through the adjoining door to his own store next door and wait until he could leave without suspicion.

"But Atherton, as you and the others showed me, had other ideas, a different deal with Peanut. He'd been planning all along to use the opportunity I created to burn down his store and blame it on the 'thieves.'" She scoffed. "Only, he did too good a job of getting the fire to catch. I saw it blast into the air before I'd even made it off the roof. I didn't know exactly what had happened, but I knew it probably involved him, so I created confusion by throwing lit lanterns behind Weil's and Steeby's, close to where they kept their spare fuel. I figured that since Steeby's had been responsible for the last fire, no one would think twice about it. And as for Weil's, the patrons there are always easily confused by that time of night."

"Like Major Drury, who saw you on the roof and mistook you for a ghost," Cassie said.

Esme gritted her teeth. "Apparently, a little smoke and a cloak and you have a visitation."

"That means—after that, you sounded the fire alarm and got Paddy to say he'd done it."

"How did you know about that?"

"Paddy had a crisis of conscience over the story he'd told about sounding the alarm. He confessed that a mysterious cloaked figure had paid him to take the credit."

"Oh," said Esme. "I assumed he would just enjoy being the center of attention."

"It seems our little scamp has more to him than you thought."

"Well, I had to do something. I didn't want the whole town to burn." Esme stared at the floor.

Cassie took another small step toward the fireplace. "What happened after that?"

"Atherton, who I know now was lying—the worm confessed everything when I confronted him Friday night—told me it'd been an accident, that he'd tripped over his lamp and the flame had caught the drapes… Either way, I had to change tactics. All the burglary 'evidence' we'd set up was obliterated by the fire. So, I told Flora the notebook had burned. And you know the rest."

"Couldn't you have invented some way for the notebook to resurface so she could have it back, as before?"

"Probably. But, given the chance to think about it, I realized that if I kept it, I could use it. If I was the one who helped her reconstruct her lost compositions, I would finally earn her respect as a perfumer."

Cassie resisted the urge to glance at the fire poker. "That was really so important to you?"

"I wasn't expecting it," Esme said. "But her good opinion has grown to mean everything to me. As you said the other night, she cares about me. And that's more than I can say about anyone else."

Her hand shook. "Which is another reason why I decided against returning the notebook. I couldn't risk her seeing through the story and figuring out I'd betrayed her trust. And why I was so angry when I found out what Peanut was planning. I'd been working so hard to earn that money back, scrubbing filthy pots at Three Star, night after night. And then I saw him huddled together with Mr. Bouchard."

"The man with the remarkable nostrils," Cassie said.

"Indeed. They have the circumference of a zucchini squash." Esme twitched her nose. "It was at Three Star that I saw them, actually—I was over by the outhouse pouring out some grease, and there they were, giggling like a couple of boys who'd found a dirty postcard. I couldn't place him at first, but, after a few days, I finally realized who he was. Jacques Bouchard, the most aggressive of Flora's rivals. He had come around once over the past summer and tried to convince Flora to license him the rights to her compositions, but she threw him out, of course. He wanted to turn her beautiful, inspired works of art into abominations made in batches by machines, with assembly lines and chemicals. They can do that now, you know, mix things in a glass tube and claim it's as good as what nature can do.

"And Peanut, the greedy little toad, was going to sell the notebook to him. It was unforgivable." She sucked in a furious breath. "I'd heard them mention getting back together sometime this week, so I knew I had to get the notebook back before then. So, Tuesday night, after Peanut left for work, Atherton and I went and searched Peanut's study. But when we couldn't find it, I thought

Peanut might have taken it with him, maybe even planned to give it to Bouchard that very night. That's when we went to the tower. I pleaded with Peanut, told him selling it would ruin Flora. But what did he do? He laughed in my face and said, 'All the better.' He *wanted* to hurt Flora."

Cassie flexed her hand in preparation. She was almost within reach of the poker now.

"And he knew how devastated I would be if Flora found out what I'd done, so he wasn't the least bit worried I'd tell anyone. He waved the notebook under my nose and said he was keeping it. That the only way I was going to get it back was to pry it out of his cold, dead hands."

Esme's lips curled into a cruel smile. "So, that's exactly what I did."

Cassie's stomach flipped, and, desperate to avoid a corresponding flop, Cassie tried to pretend they were discussing something mundane, like how to prevent the dye from running in colored hosiery (she'd read once that a tablespoonful of black pepper in the wash water would do the trick).

"And Mr. Brooks helped you?" she asked. "With Peanut?"

"Atherton?" Esme laughed. "That coward was so petrified of heights he could barely climb a common stairwell. No, he stayed on the ground. Not that he was of any use there, either. As soon as he saw Peanut's body hit the ground, he ran off so fast he went right through the bushes. I have to say, I was impressed when Officer Hughes figured that part out.

"You see, Atherton was all words and no action. Told you whatever you wanted to hear, but when it came down to it, he was like everyone else, only concerned with himself. That's why I had to get rid of him, too. I was beside myself when Flora was arrested. It had never occurred to me that could happen. So when I learned what he'd done, how fully he'd betrayed me, even getting himself engaged to that insufferable Townsend girl after he'd told me *she* was the temporary one…" She gave an angry shudder. "Besides, if I'd let him live, who knows what that spineless creature would have said to save his own skin."

Cassie forced her mind back onto black pepper and hosiery. "The chloral they found in Mr. Brooks's room was yours, wasn't it. You're both heavy drinkers, but you're the insomniac, not him. You gave him an overdose and made it look as if he were addicted. And you put the weapon you'd used to kill Peanut, that stiletto, where you knew it would be found. The papers documenting Mr. Brooks's business arrangements with Peanut, too."

"That's right," said Esme. "The notebook wasn't the only thing I'd been keeping behind my fireplace. Except, I didn't touch Atherton's business papers. When he showed them to me, I knew they were so poorly hidden even Shaw and Meeks would find them if they searched. And staging the overdose was easy. I'd reached my chloral purchase limit at each of the local pharmacies over the last few months, so Atherton had already been buying bottles for me under his own name. All I had to do was get him to drink a special drink then use the gauze to finish him off. And Atherton's never turned down a drink for as long as I've known him."

Esme glanced at her knife. "I should probably kill you now."

"It won't do any good," Cassie blurted out. "I gave Paddy a second message to deliver tonight as well, a private one to Jake explaining everything I'd figured out, including my suspicion of you. So, whether you hurt me or not, it's all over for you."

Pretty good idea, actually. Or it would have been, had I done it.

Esme found her bottle in her skirts and took a pull. "I really do want to get off this stuff. It's starting to age me, and the insomnia has become intolerable. Unfortunately, while the chloral helped in the beginning, eventually, I needed more and more, and, before I knew it, I found myself with two addictions rather than one."

Cassie prepared to make her grab for the poker. "I understand—"

Esme sprang forward and pinned Cassie to the wall. "You don't understand anything. You with your self-indulgent whining and all your talk of how your heart will never heal from losing your beloved father." She spat on the floor. "Take it from someone who's never had anyone in her entire life worthy of that word, 'beloved,' who's never been beloved to anyone else. It's a gift. That aching pain you complain of, it's a God-damned gift!"

Esme sagged, as though the breath had suddenly left her body. But when Cassie tried to move, the knife came back up.

"And my first chance, my first real chance, to have that is gone, ruined, because of you and your picking, picking, picking. Why, Cassie? I really liked you. We could have been friends! How did those terrible men deserve your consideration more than me? *I* was the victim! I've always been the victim. Everyone is always taking from me, hurting me, and the only way I've gotten anywhere is by standing up for myself... That was what I was doing. I was standing up for myself, and for Flora, and you came after me as if I were the monster!

"You insist on involving yourself in everyone else's affairs, you know, but you haven't even cared to examine your own. Speaking of your father, did you ever stop to ask how he knew where to find you that night you were attacked? And you said those men were robbers, but how do you know that? Did they demand any money or jewelry from you? How did you, Cassie Gwynne, get the simple details of a street market so wrong? Who even put that very specific invitation on your doorstep?"

My God, she's right. Is it possible the attack wasn't a random—

Esme's voice rose to a shout. "Did you ask yourself any of those questions? No, you came here and asked questions about things that didn't have anything to do with you. It was all over. I had the notebook back, that bully Peanut was gone, the investigation was closed... I had a life here, Cassie. Finally, a real life. Now I have to leave it all behind because *you just couldn't let go*!"

The knife flashed above her head.

Then something else flashed: a white, furry missile. It shot out of the basket of blankets, claws extended, right onto the bodice drawstrings dangling above Esme's bustle.

For a split-second, Esme froze in surprise, giving Cassie just enough time to throw herself at her. Esme fell against the desk, and the knife clattered to the ground. But as Cassie charged a second time, Esme dodged to the side and brought something heavy down across her back, knocking her out cold.

CHAPTER TWENTY-FIVE

When Cassie came to, the kitten was standing on her face, licking her eyelids and mewing desperately. She sat up, tumbling the kitten into her lap, and a brief pat-down quickly established she was both alive and, aside from a painful lump between her shoulder blades, unharmed. But Esme was gone.

Cassie jumped up and ran out of the house. As she reached the gate, she heard hoof-falls and the rumble of wheels. It was Major Drury in his donkey cart, jabbering what sounded like an underwater rendition of the "Battle Hymn of the Republic."

"Well, put a stalk on my head and call me a carrot," he said. "Here I am, honored with not one but two angelic visions of womanly beauty in one night."

Cassie hurried toward him. "Major Drury, I need to get—Wait, two?"

"Miss Cole passed me and Eugene here in Mr. Starkey's sport carriage not two minutes ago, going the other way down Seventh. She was scowling something awful and nearly ran us off the road, but it didn't take away from her face none."

Cassie spun toward the neighbors' property. The doors of the carriage house were open, and the flashy spider phaeton that Mr. Starkey kept inside was gone, along with the horse that was usually grazing in the yard.

"I need you to unfasten your donkey for me. Quickly." As Cassie spoke, she tore the top skirts off her dress, stripping the layers nearly down to the petticoat so she could ride astride. She needed all the control she could get if she was going to catch Esme.

After another thought, she tore off her choker as well. The lace was ripped now, and she could never breathe right with it on, anyway.

"But—" Major Drury managed to stutter a response, despite his eyes bulging out of his head. "He's got no saddle."

"If you get me underway in under a minute, I'll give you a kiss. On the cheek."

In a miracle recovery, Major Drury fell upon the fittings, and, less than a minute later, Cassie was wiping her mouth as she tore away from Flora's house on Eugene the donkey, her heart pounding in time with the animal's hooves. As she clung to his thick neck with her entire arms, praying for the first time in years (it was clear Eugene had been ridden by a human about as many times as Cassie had ridden a donkey), she tried to decide what to do. Should she go to the Egmont and find Jake? No, Esme would be long gone by then. She had to follow her. But where was she going? She would have to get off the island somehow, but surely she wouldn't try by train or steamer. It would be too easy for them to telegraph ahead and have the authorities apprehend her at the next stop. Would she take a rowboat? She wouldn't get very far that way either.

As they neared Centre, Eugene collected and took a cockeyed leap over something in the street—a loose railroad tie. It had probably fallen off a repair cart for the railroad tracks that ran alongside the harbor… and onto the mainland. That was it. Esme had to be heading for the railroad bridge.

Conjuring up a quick mental image of the city map—she was certainly glad now she had studied that—Cassie leaned back and used a fistful of mane to pull Eugene into a hard turn, almost doubling him over on himself. They would take Centre over to Front Street and follow the tracks down to where they joined the county road. The route was slightly longer and wouldn't be smooth, but there wouldn't be any traffic in the way once they reached the railroad area, and since Esme was hauling the phaeton, they should be able to gain some ground. And hopefully catch up to her before she crossed the bridge and disappeared onto the mainland forever.

"Look out!" She waved a wild arm at a cluster of festively clad pedestrians who, failing to notice her make the turn, had meandered into the street. They scattered like billiard balls off a break, and she and Eugene hurtled through their midst, leaving them choking on a cloud of dust and donkey flatulence.

In a few more strides, they reached the tracks and turned onto the waterfront footpath Cassie had taken with Hughes the morning she arrived, only five days before, though it felt more like five years. Eugene, his long, furry ears pointed ahead, snorted and puffed below her and charged ahead with the fortitude of a steam engine as he put his wide hooves to good use on the uneven surface below. And when Cassie, upon seeing the country road finally swing into view, shouted an apology and kicked her heels into his sides once more, he jettisoned another blast of gas and opened up his stride.

They continued on in this manner for some minutes, blasting and lurching their way along the wide, dark road, until suddenly Eugene slowed. Ahead was Mr. Starkey's sleek, high-perch phaeton, bouncing and swaying violently as it raced through the scraggly shadows cast by the tangled masses of vegetation lining the road. Esme towered over the dash rail, a mass of untamed curls whipping about her as she struck her crop across the back of the frantic horse below.

Cassie pushed herself up and looked ahead over Eugene's pitching shoulders. Two lines of glowing points growing in the distance told her it was only a matter of time before they reached the bridge. The road began to curve.

"Esme!" Her voice broke as she tried to shout over the thundering hooves. "Stop!"

Esme glared over her shoulder. "Why won't you leave me alone? Haven't you done enough?" She hunched as though to spur her horse on but then straightened back up, flinging her hand into the air. Eugene reared with a scream, and a flurry of pinpricks stabbed Cassie's eyes. Sand.

Shutting her eyes against the pain, Cassie apologized to Eugene once again and gave him a desperate, blind kick. She felt him move forward with renewed speed, and when she forced her eyes open, she saw that they had pulled up alongside Esme's carriage. Holding onto Eugene's mane, she drew up her knees, pressed her feet into his heaving side, and hauled herself into a squat. Once she was in position, she counted three strides and pushed off.

She sailed through the air, her arms flailing uselessly, until she slammed against the folded-down top behind the phaeton's driver's bench. She ricocheted backward, but, as she fell, she grabbed onto the edge of the footman's seat. Beating back a daze, she swung around and hunkered down on the footrest. She peered out. They were on the bridge now, racing along a narrow shoulder next to the tracks. Eugene had pulled away just in time.

The heel of Esme's boot sliced the air next to her ear. Raising a small seat cushion as a shield, Cassie struggled over the folded top onto the driver's bench as Esme rained one-handed blows on her, each landing with a powerful *thwack* that nearly knocked her through the open side.

Just as Cassie managed to stand up enough to face her opponent, the carriage wheels jangled onto the tracks and off again, throwing the women in opposite directions. Cassie grabbed onto the bench and turned around. Esme, however, had recovered more quickly than she and was now standing over her, her knife drawn.

As Esme raised her arm, Cassie, unable to think of anything else, closed her eyes and swung her seat cushion shield upward. And, by nothing more than sheer, dumb luck, Cassie would be convinced forever afterward, the cushion connected with Esme's knuckles and sent the knife flying into the darkness. Seeing her hand empty, Esme let loose an unearthly shriek and launched herself across the carriage.

The world slowed. The beating of the horse's hooves faded into a dull, rhythmic thudding. The roar of the river became a murmur. The wind stilled. Then, as Esme's form hurtling toward her began to dissolve into an assemblage of shapes and colors, Cassie remembered a diagram from her Chinese combat text.

Time resumed with a snap, and Esme was upon her, her head lowered like a medieval battering ram. Following the arrows and numbers on the drawing in her mind, Cassie bent her knees and straightened with force, her arms extended above her head—sending Esme over her shoulder, over the edge of the carriage, and off the bridge into the water below.

Resisting the urge to stare after her in horror and amazement, Cassie grabbed the reins, which Esme had dropped on the foot-board, and pulled up with all her might. The horse halted, and Cassie clambered down to take him by the bridle. Only then did she look out over the edge, her heart still raging. To her relief, she spotted Esme floundering in the water below, apparently unharmed.

"I've got her!" called a distant voice. A man dove into the water and stroked toward Esme's sputtering form. As he pulled her to shore, another man ran down the bank and waded in to help.

Still shaking, Cassie released the heaving horse from his fittings and led him off the bridge. Once they were on solid ground, she threw his lead over a branch and ran over to where the men were wrapping Esme in a blanket.

"You there!" she called. "Don't let that woman get away!"

"Certainly not," answered one.

"Wouldn't dream of it," agreed the other.

Cassie recognized Jake's and Hughes's voices, and when she drew close, a lantern on the ground lit up their dripping faces. Relief washed over her.

Hughes's expression grew serious. "You shouldn't have gone after her like that. You could have been—You might have—She's a dangerous criminal."

"I know."

"I didn't mean you specifically." He ran a hand over his wet hair. "Well, yes, you specifically because you were the one—I mean I would have felt responsible if anything had—"

"But nothing did."

They looked at each other for a moment then spoke at the same time.

"What did you mean, 'I know'?"

"How did you know she was a 'dangerous criminal'?"

They tried again.

"You first."

"You first."

Hughes pushed up his sopping shirt sleeves. "She has a tattoo on her wrist. I saw it at Miss Hale's house when she was working on my bandage. I thought it seemed familiar, so tonight, when I went over to the office to find something more useful to do than fritter the evening away dancing, I combed through the box of old wanted bulletins. And found this." He pulled a folded square of paper from his shirt pocket, wincing when he saw how wet it was.

Cassie carefully unfolded the sheet and held it up to the lantern. Fortunately, the ink hadn't run so much as to make it illegible.

A MURDERER WANTED

A generous reward has been offered for the apprehension of Rosina Torrisi, who murdered Mrs. Maria Angela Torrisi, herself a known madame associated with certain active crime syndicates, in New Orleans, La., some weeks ago. Miss Torrisi is about 22 years of age, stands 5 feet 9 inches high, and weighs approximately 130 pounds. Miss Torrisi is fond of drink, plays on the violin very well, and is said to possess a sultry voice. She wears her distinctive red hair long to the waist and unadorned and has a tattoo in the shape of a snake-haired gorgon on the inside of her right wrist.

When last heard of, she was headed toward the train depot. Look out for her but use caution. She is dangerous and is trained in the lethal use of several kinds of knife.

"You know what a gorgon is?" Cassie asked, impressed.

Hughes snorted. "Course I do. It's like a Medusa, the stone-faced monster woman from that old Greek story. What's that fellow's name? Percy?"

Close enough.

"Anyway, I saw her with her hair down once." Hughes wrung the water out of his pant leg. "One night while she was working in the kitchen at Three Star. Her turban had come loose, and she was rewrapping it. And tonight, when I reexamined the clothing Peanut was wearing on the night of the murder, I found several long, red hairs on his vest. Her turban must have fallen off while she was up there, perhaps during the struggle."

Cassie handed back the bulletin. "But this says 'Rosina Torrisi.'"

"It seems 'Esme Cole' is an assumed name. That bulletin came through from the Louisiana governor's office two years ago, shortly after Miss Torrisi arrived here. But she had disguised herself so well, kept her hair all tied up in that turban for the most part, no one recognized her, and eventually we all forgot about it. Once I made the connection though, my doubts and suspicions about Peanut's death, and Mr. Brooks's even, sharpened.

"As for Mr. Brooks, I thought about the tumblers in his room and wondered whether he'd had a guest that night. The window had been open, so someone could have come and gone without being seen by the inn staff. And then there was what you'd said about those people being at Peanut's house the night he was killed, which reminded me of a rumor that had gone around some time ago about Mr. Brooks and Miss Cole… consorting. But why kill him? Did he upset her somehow? Perhaps she was jealous of Mr. Brooks's engagement to Miss Townsend. Or did she simply need someone to take the fall for Peanut's murder?"

"A bit of all of that, actually," Cassie said. "Esme—I mean Miss Torrisi, told me everything before she attacked me and ran. Speaking of which, how did you find us?"

"I went to the Egmont to question Miss Cole about the bulletin, but Jake told me she'd left right after Flora received a message about her perfume notebook being found. I knew something was afoot immediately, of course. Why would good news make her want to leave?"

"I'd had the same thought." Jake had been hovering at Hughes's side, apparently waiting for a chance to chime in.

"While Jake and I were talking, we realized you'd disappeared as well. Then Paddy told us you were the one who had sent the message about the notebook."

"Aw," Jake said. "You said 'we.'"

Hughes threw an elbow in Jake's gut. "But we still didn't know what to do until Mrs. Farnsworth arrived complaining about how she'd been dusted by a woman driving a sport carriage down Seventh in an evening gown, and Mr. Menor responded that he'd been thrown aside by a woman riding a donkey across Centre, also in an evening gown. I made a few deductions from there and here we are."

Cassie nodded, then covered her face with her hands.

"What's, uh, the matter?" Hughes coughed and adjusted his tie, which was still sopping wet.

"I doubted her," Cassie said. "My Aunt Flora. What kind of family does that make me?"

"It's natural to wonder a little."

"I did more than wonder. I had *doubt*. And while it came and went, it was present right up until the end, until Esme actually admitted she was guilty. I'd found this other note Peanut had written to Flora, you see, in a mail pile in the parlor. He said he was going to file a lawsuit and she was going to lose her home—"

"Wait, did you say the note was in the mail pile in the parlor?" asked Jake. "The one by the bookshelf? That's where new mail goes. If something's there, Flora hasn't gone through it yet."

"But it was unsealed."

"Unsealed or not sealed? I picked up a hand-delivered envelope from the doormat on Monday, on my way in with some other mail I'd brought home for Flora, and I'm pretty sure the flap was just loose. I put it in the pile with the rest."

"She never even saw it."

"And, all that aside," Hughes said, "you were there when she was arrested. You heard what she said."

"I don't follow."

"Peanut's clothes were dry when he was found. Even from where I was standing in the back, I could see how crisp his shirt was, aside from the mud splatter. Which means he fell after the rain stopped. And Miss Hale said it was raining the entire time she was out that night, until she arrived home."

Cassie kicked herself. "She was already home when the murder occurred."

"Obviously."

Cassie was trying to decide whether to punch him or throw her arms around his neck when she heard Flora's voice.

"There you are, Cassie. Thank Heavens!" Flora jumped down from a buggy that was pulling up, not bothering to wait for it to stop, and enfolded Cassie in that cloud of orange blossoms, tuberose, and nutmeg. "When Jake and Hughes ran off, saying something about you being in trouble, we certainly couldn't stay behind."

Behind her, Miss Porter and Mrs. Keene, accompanied by Sergeant Denham and a gentleman with the largest muttonchops she had ever seen—Sheriff Alderman, she presumed—climbed out of the buggy.

Flora noticed Esme, who had pulled the blanket up to her chin and was peering out at her with wide eyes.

"Esme?" Flora turned around. "What exactly *is* going on?"

Jake placed the notebook, which Esme had fortunately wrapped in a tight layer of oilskin, into Flora's arms, and Cassie began to tell her what had happened. Hughes and Jake, and occasionally one of the others, contributed what they knew as well, and eventually, like sewing together patches to form a quilt, they had laid out the whole sordid story.

Once they had finished, Flora remained where she was, unmoving, for so long Cassie almost started jumping up and down, purely to break the tension.

Finally, Flora spoke. "Esme, that woman in New Orleans. Why did you—What happened?"

Esme's face hardened. "That woman—called herself my mother, but never once did she act like it. When I was a child, even though she had her own apartment next door, she left me to live at the bordello, looked after by whoever took a momentary interest. And when I was old enough, she put me to work as one of her girls.

"But that was only until she discovered I had other talents, which was when she offered me up as a lackey to Carlo and Antonio, who owned the place." She tipped her head. "And if you think the bordello business is unsavory, you should see what else these men do. I was made to trick people, manipulate them. Hurt them. One day, I decided I didn't want to do it anymore, but she wouldn't let me leave. So, I had no choice but to… part ways with her. Then I had to run."

"The money you borrowed from Peanut was to pay off someone who had threatened to expose you?" Flora's voice was full of pain.

"Yes. I was accosted one night by someone who'd recognized me, maybe from New Orleans, maybe from the wanted bulletins, I don't know. I couldn't see his face. But he was serious about getting paid for his silence, so I had no choice."

"You could have come to me," Flora said. "I would have understood and tried to help you."

"No, I couldn't. Because I knew you'd never look at me the same way after that, knowing the things I'd done. Who I really was. The same goes for what happened with Peanut. When I found out he was going to sell the notebook and try to ruin you, I had to protect you. But I couldn't tell you. If you had known I'd taken the notebook in the first place, violated your trust… I couldn't bear that. And as for Atherton, well, it was the only way I could keep you from the noose. So, you see? I had to do it. All of it. I had no choice—"

"Stop saying that!"

Everyone fell silent as Flora's voice reverberated over the waterway. The trees rustled in agitation overhead.

"I am deeply sad for you, Esme." Flora's voice trembled, but her eyes were steady. "So incredibly sad. And I wish, with all my heart, I could take away the suffering you've endured. But you're wrong. There are consequences to every choice—consequences we have to live with forever—but we *always* have a choice. Always."

CHAPTER TWENTY-SIX

The birds outside of Cassie's window started their customary chatter even earlier than usual the next day, but it didn't bother Cassie this time because she was already awake. Though the night had been a long one—the sheriff had asked Cassie to come in and submit a statement for the arrest paperwork right away, torn-up dress and all—even after she returned to Flora's she had only been able to manage a few minutes of sleep before popping back awake.

While she had been listening to Esme's rants, Cassie, despite having been in mortal fear for most of it, had come to a realization: Esme's past was almost unbearably sad, but almost everything she'd said about it was in terms of what had happened to *her*, what had been done to *her*, how *she* had been hurt—And, whether she was right or wrong to feel that way, the rhetoric had sounded a little too familiar.

It was exactly the way Cassie had been responding to what she had learned about her family, instantly turning every new revelation into a personal affront. It was *her* brother who had been lost, *she* whom her father had kept secrets from, *her* life that had been damaged by what had happened. It was exactly the kind of thinking Flora had fallen victim to all those years ago, too, which Cassie had been quick to judge her for.

She should be appreciating that her father and Flora had lost Burt, too, and that their lives had changed forever as well. Her father had lost his son and spent the rest of his life grieving for him, silently and alone, so she wouldn't have to carry the burden of his pain—pain that, if she were to believe what everyone here said about the way her father used to be, had changed him so much he was nearly a different man. Flora not only had lost her nephew, but had to live with the knowledge that her actions—her choices—had led to that loss. And all that right on the heels of losing Cassie's mother, Emma, and their family home as well.

Besides, hadn't Flora spent every moment since trying to make up for it? Everything she did was about helping others, both people and animals, and making the lives of those around her better however she could.

What Esme had said about Cassie herself had cut deeply as well. She was right—There was a lot about the attack on her and her father that didn't make sense, and in other such situations Cassie had never been shy about involving herself, asking questions and pushing on inconsistencies until she was satisfied she had uncovered the truth. But when the officers who responded to the attack in the park had called it a robbery gone wrong and closed the book, she hadn't even asked them why. She had simply curled up with her back to it because it hurt too much to think about.

She suddenly understood her father better than she ever had.

Well, no more. Pushing off the covers and a disgruntled kitten, she retrieved paper and a pen from her writing desk and brought them over to the windowsill, where the light was starting to come in. She'd begin by writing the New York coroner's office for her father's file and personal effects—hopefully, they still had them—and go from there.

When Cassie went to leave for the post office a little while later, letter in hand, she found Sam waiting for her on the porch.

"Good morning, Cassie," he said, straightening from where he'd been leaning against the railing.

"Good morning."

"You left rather suddenly last night, so I thought I should come by and see you."

Cassie tucked the letter and her parasol under her arm so she could pull on her gloves. "I apologize—Something important came up. Perhaps you heard."

Sam pulled off his hat, staggering back slightly when he noticed Kleio staring at him through the bay window. "I did indeed, and congratulations are in order, of course. But I meant when you left the table. Mr. Church kept asking where you'd gone."

"I believe I announced I needed some air—Perhaps his memory is going in his old age. Which you and Lily would probably prefer."

"Come, now, Cassie." Sam dropped his hat and stooped to pick it up. "You know what kind of position I'm—we're in—"

"But does Mr. Church know what kind of position *he's* in? Because he will, eventually. Regardless of what you seem to think, he's a smart man."

"We're—hoping it won't matter to him by then. Perhaps he'll be glad to have a sibling for his other young child—"

"Well, good luck with that," Cassie said. "I won't be having any further part in it."

Sam studied her. "I suppose that means you wouldn't be interested in joining us for lunch on Mr. Church's yacht later today. Though he's asked for you specifically. And I'd personally quite hoped for some time with you, as Lily and I will be leaving with Mr. Church tomorrow on an excursion to Nassau."

Cassie bit her lip to keep from smiling. It was astounding: Sam Townsend, *the* Sam Townsend, was standing before her, asking for her attentions, and she felt nothing.

"No, thank you, Sam. I'm otherwise engaged today, but I wish you an enjoyable luncheon. And a very safe trip to the Bahamas."

The weather was clear and sunny, with a slight nip in the air—perfect "wandering weather," according to Flora—so after Cassie returned from her errand at the post office, they decided to complete their planned visit to Old Town.

Flora turned to Cassie as they made their way up the shell road, the dogs following along behind them like a wiggly train caboose.

"So, you sent Mr. Townsend on his way, then?"

"I knew it!" Cassie moved the kitten, who had seemed so forlorn as they were preparing to depart Cassie hadn't had the heart to leave her, onto her other shoulder. "You were standing by the door while I was talking to him, weren't you? I thought I heard something."

Flora shrugged innocently. "To be fair, if I'd stood anywhere else, I wouldn't have been able to listen to your conversation."

"Ha." Cassie brushed the kitten's tail out of her face. "But yes, I don't expect I'll be hearing much more from him anytime soon."

"Did the old flame die out?"

"I'm not sure that's exactly it. But one thing I've learned is old flames burn on old fuel."

Flora trailed her hand through a swath of pink wildflowers growing on a fence. "That's true." She plucked one and tucked it behind her ear. "If it's worth it, though, you could always add some new fuel."

"Aha!"

Flora turned as pink as the flower in her hair.

"I knew Jake stayed for a cup of coffee with you after he walked me home from the sheriff's office. Did you say something to him?"

"I wasn't going to, as there had already been quite enough revelations for one day, but—" Flora lifted her dress to step over a branch. "We'd gone far too long without saying anything. And, turns out, it's a good thing I did."

"It was?"

"Would you know, he thought I was in love with Tom all these years? It seems he'd always been, I don't know, a little jealous of him—the way a younger boy sees an older one who's confident and good-looking and never seems to struggle with anything. Tom certainly always had that competent air of a leader about him. Tom and I were also very close friends and used to spend a great deal of time together because of our mutual interest in poetry. Jake assumed that meant I was secretly pining after him. My own sister's husband, could you imagine? I truly don't understand the insistence that the only kind of love that can exist between a man and woman is romantic love.

"Anyway, when Jake saw me writing to Tom all those years, he filled in the gaps with his own suspicions. He wasn't with us during the war, of course, so he didn't... fully understand what had happened between us, I think. And I'll admit I didn't speak of it much, for obvious reasons. So that's why he never could bring himself to say anything to me. Even after we learned about Tom's passing. Maybe especially after. And I, oblivious creature that I am, never even noticed my own feelings."

She touched her hand to her face, which had flushed again.

"I'm glad to hear it," Cassie said. "But, to be honest, I don't know that it will change your relationship all that much. You two already have such a natural, caring way with each other. And with Metta, too."

Flora threaded her arm through Cassie's and squeezed. "You're right. It's good to get everything out in the open, but what we have is pretty special. All of us are lucky to have each other, and I won't forget that."

A few blocks over from the pilots' tower, they finally arrived at their destination.

"After very much ado, there she is." Flora swept her arm toward a house that could have been cut from a children's fairy-tale book. "This is what I wanted to show you before. The Hale family residence, where we all lived before my father built the other house down on Broome. Your parents stayed on here after the rest of us moved."

"It's—remarkable." Cassie gazed upward as she followed Flora and the dogs through the gate.

The house had been built with one of its corners pointed toward the road and a round brick column running up through its center, making it look like a steamboat puffing along a river of trees and flowers. Above the door, a pair of porthole windows peered out at them as though curious about their approach.

Flora turned the lock and pushed the door open. "It needs a bit of work, since no one has lived here for many years, but it still has plenty of life in it."

Cassie stepped into the small foyer. The walls and ceiling were plain and the wooden floors unfinished, but a handful of well-placed details—an ocean wave motif carved into the molding, sconces shaped like flowers blooming under water, a clock face set into the belly of a manatee—gave the place both a restrained elegance and a playful warmth.

Outside the parlor, she was struck by a scent drifting into the hall. It was faint, so faint she almost wondered whether she had imagined it, but unmistakably familiar. She inhaled, and the animals, their noses twitching upward, did the same. Wood, spices, smoke… an orange pomander ball hanging by the fire? Still pondering this, she entered the room—and was struck again.

A black-bricked fireplace. A rocking chair with armrests like fiddlehead ferns. A rug twined with roses.

She set the kitten down, letting her fingertips linger on the rug's soft, colorful surface. It was as if they, too, were trying to remember something. Then she caught sight of the window. Beyond the glass stood a cheerful stand of thick-limbed orange trees.

She turned to Flora, tingling all over. "I remember this place."

"You do? I wouldn't have thought, given how young you were when we left."

"Yes, but those trees… I remember them in bloom. The falling petals swirled like snowflakes." She picked up one of the figurines on the mantel, a sea turtle hugging a starfish. "I remember these, too."

"Your father made a whole series of them for Burt."

"They do remind me of him. My father, that is."

Flora watched her put the figurine back. "I take it you like the cottage, then?"

"Yes. Very much."

"Good. Because it's yours."

Cassie started. "You don't mean—"

"Please. Accept this gift from me." Flora pressed the key into Cassie's hand. "Welcome home, Cassie Gwynne."

As Cassie closed her fingers around the key, something broke inside of her. Like a levee that had finally gotten so full its walls, unable to bend any farther, had burst from the pressure. A flood followed, rushing up through her stomach and her chest and her arms until it reached her head and, suddenly, she was crying.

She cried and cried, wracked by such deep, heaving sobs her muscles ached. And as she cried, she didn't care that someone else could see her tears. Didn't care that the deep, ugly wounds that had marred her, both inside and out, since the day her father was taken from her were now visible all at once. Didn't care that, now there was a witness, there was no denying her feelings were real. That it was all real.

"There, there." Flora held her close and stroked her hair as though she were a child. "I miss him, too. All of them. But we'll be all right. We have each other now."

Cassie had just come up for air when a thud sounded in the next room, followed by a plaintive mew. Choking on an arrested sob, Cassie hurried into the hall with Flora and tracked the cries around the edge of a sewing table, where they discovered what had happened. The kitten had been nosing around in a basket of fabric scraps and flipped it over, sending swatches of satin, faille, and taffeta flying and trapping herself underneath.

Cassie sat on the floor, laughing with relief, and lifted the basket to release the prisoner. The kitten shot into her lap and burrowed her head under her arm.

"You're all right, little one. We all bite off more than we can chew sometimes." Cassie patted the kitten's back. "And once again, you've helped me find a smile, a bit of peace, where I wasn't expecting it... You know what, I believe I finally have a name for you."

She lifted the kitten and kissed each of her ears. The kitten butted her chin in return and gave her a slow, loving blink.

"I hereby dub you Hesychia, Esy for short, after the Greek goddess of peace and tranquility. As one with an extraordinary power to bring those things to my heart."

Flora was about to show Cassie the garden when Jake rushed in, his face stricken. "Flora, Cassie, have you seen Metta? She was gone when I woke up, and I can't find her in any of her usual places."

Flora froze, and Cassie, knowing now what had happened to Burt, could feel the ice that had just shot through her heart.

"No, we haven't," Cassie answered for her. "But she's always coming up with something or other to do. I'm sure she's safe."

"What if something's happened?"

"Now, there's no need for that kind of talk. Have you asked Paddy?"

"He wasn't home, either. Mr. Green said he came into his kitchen fully dressed before dawn, asked for a sliced apple and three cookies, then ran off."

Flora stirred. "Three cookies." She brightened. "Yes, three cookies!"

"Three cookies?" Jake asked.

"Half for Metta and two and a half for Paddy. They're together somewhere. Come on. We'll help you look."

They had hardly gotten past the gate, however, when they heard the marching of little feet up the road.

Metta popped into view.

"Papa! Miss Flora! Miss Cassie!" She squealed with delight and ran toward them. Danger and Luna ran toward her, causing a near collision.

Jake received her with a relieved hug. "Goodness, Metta. What's happened to you?"

The girl's dress was streaked with dirt.

"We found him! He's alive!" Metta hopped and twirled, and the dogs stood on their hind legs, doing the same.

"Who's alive? What are you talking about?"

Metta lifted a small, duck-shaped object to her mouth (gifted by a grateful Mr. Hiller) and blew into it, releasing a long, loud *quack*. Then Paddy appeared, followed by Roger, who grunted rhythmically as he trotted along: *Urmff-urmff-urmff-urmff.*

Flora grabbed Jake's arm as her legs buckled. "Roger, oh my word, Roger!"

When Roger heard Flora's voice, he gave a squeal almost identical to Metta's, and his *urmffs* accelerated as he broke into a run. Flora threw her arms around him, and he nuzzled into her for several seconds before bending down to snuffle her hands.

"I'm sorry, my love." Flora laughed and cried at the same time. "I don't have any treats for you right now."

"Here you go, Miss Flora." Paddy handed her an apple slice from his pocket.

Metta beamed. "We found him in a stall at the Cranstocks' horse barn. By following the evidence."

Paddy pulled out more apple slices. "I heard the stable boys talking about how they'd caught Neily Cranstock writing nasty words on the barn, and when I saw the way he made his p's, with the big loops backwards, I thought it looked like the fish note."

"And I said," Metta added, "remember how mad Neily was when Miss Flora took his dog Luna home? He even threw eggs at her house. And his father's a fishmonger, too. So, first thing this morning, we went over to the Cranstocks', waited for Neily to come out, and followed him to the barn. And there was good old Roger, rolling around in a pile of hay."

Paddy grew serious. "Neily promised he didn't hurt him. And that he gave him lots of treats."

"He told us he only wanted you to know what it felt like to have your pet taken from you," Metta sniffled. "He was going to bring him back, but when he saw you fighting with Peanut about it, he was afraid he'd get in trouble."

Flora stood. "I didn't realize he felt so strongly about Luna. But I'm still going to have to have a talk with his mother."

Metta grabbed Flora's hand. "Don't get him in too much trouble, Miss Flora. When I told him how sad you were about Roger, he got sad. He said he was sorry and that he won't do anything to hurt anyone's feelings like that ever again."

"What a caring heart you have, child. Just like your father." Flora met Jake's gaze and blushed. "I'll see what I can do. Now, you little Dupins go on inside and wash up. Depending on how clean you get, there may be some fresh orange slices waiting for you when you're finished."

Jake held up a finger. "Actually, looking at you, you'd better go directly under the pump in the back."

Clapping their hands with delight, the children ran around the side of house, and Roger and the dogs loped after them.

Flora turned back toward Cassie, a blissful glow about her. "Are you all right?" Her fingers were intertwined with Jake's.

Feeling a tickle at her ankle, Cassie glanced down and found Esy rubbing against her legs, purring so hard the tips of her fur vibrated in the sunshine. Cassie scooped her up, and as she held her to her chest, looking at Flora's and Jake's expectant faces and listening to the children laugh and splash at the pump, she realized she was. Or at least she would be soon.

The next morning, she woke up snug in her bed, right where she'd gone to sleep the night before.

A LETTER FROM GENEVIEVE

Dearest Reader,

Thank you so much for choosing to read *A Deception Most Deadly*. If my story made you smile, gasp, cry, aw, aha, or laugh out loud at least once, I've done my solemn duty as a writer, and hopefully you'll want to keep up to date with my latest releases—which you can do by simply signing up at the following link:

www.bookouture.com/genevieve-essig

Please be assured, your email address will never be shared, and you can unsubscribe anytime.

As you have already begun to discover, 1880s Fernandina on Amelia Island, Florida, was a special, fascinating place, one far less traveled to in literature than the larger Victorian-era American cities that are so often written about—which is why I wanted to set this series there and bring readers by for a visit. Dubbed the "Newport of the South" and "the Island City" by contemporary travel publications, Fernandina enjoyed its own short but significant Golden Age during these years as not only an important rail and shipping crossroads but also a popular retreat for well-heeled tourists, including members of the Carnegie, Du Pont, and Vanderbilt families. At the same time, Florida, which has always been an outsider to the rest of the country and therefore a haven for outsiders as well—including, at various points in history, persecuted monks, British settlers fleeing the Revolutionary War, pirates, escaped slaves, consumptives, and itinerant "cracker cowboys"—still had a touch of the wild about it. And late nineteenth-century Fernandina, a place where the glittering social elite and patrons of rough-and-tumble saloons shared the shade of the same palm trees, was no different.

Therefore, I have invested hundreds of hours into historical research efforts so I could share this place with readers as accurately and authentically as possible. Many characters in the book are inspired by real (nineteenth-century) residents. Certain events in the book, including the fire on Centre Street, are inspired by real events. The Three Star Saloon, the Egmont Hotel, and the Florida House Inn are real places—You can stay in the Florida House Inn to this day (highly recommended), and, while the Egmont Hotel and the Three Star Saloon are no longer, you can still view Three Star's three-star façade on Centre Street (the building now houses a slightly more sober establishment) as well as a series of houses made with woodwork salvaged from the Egmont.

In any case, I hope you loved reading *A Deception Most Deadly* as much as I loved creating it. If so, I'd appreciate your writing a review. It's invaluable for me to hear what you think, and it will help new readers discover the book.

I'd also love to hear directly from you. It is one of my greatest joys in life to discuss nerdy things like my books and research, so feel free to reach out and nerd out with me! You can get in touch on my Facebook page, through Twitter, Instagram, or Goodreads, or via my website. Happy reading, and thank you.

Humbly yours,
Genevieve Essig

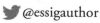 essigauthor

 @essigauthor

 essigauthor

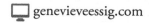 genevieeessig.com

ACKNOWLEDGMENTS

Anyone who has attempted to write a book for the first time knows what I mean when I say this has been one of the hardest things I've ever done. But, it has also been one of the best things I've ever done. Of course, by saying "best," I'm not passing judgment on the book. Rather, I'm referring to how the process by which the book came to be has taught me more about myself than the entirety of my twenties and pushed my limits more than my time in Big Law, and I cannot think of any higher praise for an experience than that. So, while I can't say I've loved every moment of it, I've loved a lot of moments of it and am grateful for the rest—and for everyone whose support and enthusiasm (and even vague worry) carried me through them all.

Particular thanks go to:

My parents, Fred and Yau-Ping Essig, and my brother, Justin Essig, for loving me unconditionally and for supporting me in all my choices and endeavors, even when they fear for me.

My partner, Daniel Alfredson, for being my greatest advocate, in writing and in life, and for always having an inspirational rant at the ready to lasso me out of my occasional slips into existential panic.

My dad again, for reading so many drafts and versions of this story he probably can't even tell you what happens in it by now.

Penelope Campbell, for going above and beyond the call of friendship and agreeing to be my first full-manuscript beta reader who wasn't my dad. Your unwavering, enthusiastic support has meant more than you can know.

Susie Skarford, for also providing an early, hugely helpful beta read of the full manuscript, and Eric Alfredson, Ashley Somogyi, and Sharon and Robert Foley, for reading and commenting on portions of the manuscript.

Author Hank Phillippi Ryan, for, in a shining example of paying it forward, taking time out of her incredibly busy schedule to give me writing advice and encouragement on multiple occasions.

Author Susie Calkins, for introducing me to the Mystery Writers of America group in Chicago and otherwise showing me around the mystery-writer community.

E. Lynn Grayson, my mentor in law and role model in all things, for making it possible for me to pursue my many different dreams.

Jayne Nasrallah at the Amelia Island Museum of History, for being so kind and patient with all my painfully specific historical questions and document requests.

Former Mayor of Fernandina Beach, Johnny Miller, for telling me stories about the island while pouring pints at the Palace Saloon.

The long-suffering residents of a certain neighborhood in South Florida, who shared their plight regarding a local bully in need of fictional retaliation.

Esy the kitten, my missing piece, my missing peace, who is with Cassie and Flora now.

My agent, Dawn Dowdle, for picking me out of the crowd.

And, finally, my brilliant Bookouture editor, Cara Chimirri, for truly getting me. Cassie and I will miss you.